A Dance in Heather

continued . . .

A Dance in Heather

"Lively [and] endearing." —*Publishers Weekly*

"A nice interweaving of medieval British history, pageantry, and love."
—*Library Journal*

"Every scene is beautifully rendered . . . a nonstop read."
—*Romantic Times*

"Vivid and compelling, the 15th century springs to vibrant life . . . From roistering festivals in ancient castles to teeming life in medieval London, she paints an astonishingly vivid picture of the times, and a bold lord, his fair lady and their love . . . a memorable read."
—Edith Layton, author of *The Crimson Crown*

"A glorious love story in every sense—alive and vibrant, enthralling, and intriguing . . . I couldn't put it down until the last page."
—*Rendezvous*

Lady and the Wolf

"Fiery passion . . . [An] outstanding tale of the Middle Ages."

—*Rendezvous*

"*Lady and the Wolf* mixes the plague, primogeniture, the Spanish Inquisition, witchcraft, jousts, grave robbing and some sizzling sex scenes into a brand-new, best-selling, 14th-century romance."

—*Chicago Suburban Times*

"A powerful debut novel that sweeps us into the lives of a medieval family . . . a stunning and poignant climax."

—*Romantic Times*

"Beard is writing tales of love and romance that always have happy endings."

—*Chicago Tribune*

My Fair Lord

Julie Beard

B

BERKLEY BOOKS, NEW YORK

This is a work of fiction. Names, characters, places, and incidents are either the product of the author's imagination or are used fictitiously, and any resemblance to actual persons, living or dead, business establishments, events, or locales is entirely coincidental.

MY FAIR LORD

A Berkley Book / published by arrangement with
the author

PRINTING HISTORY
Berkley edition / June 2000

The Penguin Putnam Inc. World Wide Web site address is
http://www.penguinputnam.com

ISBN: 0-425-17481-6

BERKLEY®
Berkley Books are published by The Berkley Publishing Group,
a division of Penguin Putnam Inc.,
375 Hudson Street, New York, New York 10014.
BERKLEY and the "B" design are trademarks
belonging to Penguin Putnam Inc.

PRINTED IN THE UNITED STATES OF AMERICA

10 9 8 7 6 5 4 3 2 1

To Connor, with infinite love
—Mom

Thanks to the usual suspects: Mary Alice Kruesi (aka Monroe), Pat White, Michelle Hoppe, and Martha Ambrose. Each contributed insightful feedback. Special thanks to my kind editor, Cindy Hwang, for asking all the right questions. And a fond farewell to the late Rusty Luedloff, who was always first in line at my book signings.

Prologue

Alas, these are the last words I shall ever write. Death comes fast upon me. I grow weaker by the moment. Yet I cannot pass away until the truth be known. Read on and thou shalt know a terrible injustice hath been done.

I did not kill Lord Roger Harding, a crime of which I have been accused and for which I am now imprisoned in the Tower. How could I slay the brother of my beloved, Rachel Harding? Nay, I could not, even though he held me in utter contempt and tried to kill me on my wedding day.

Rachel, dear Rachel! To think that she is dead when but two months ago she was alive, a fair maiden—no, not a maiden, for she hath given me her virgin's blood. She was my lover, my life, and would have been my wife if not for her brother's interference. Let me tell thee so that someone might know the truth and remember.

Roger was infuriated to learn that his father had reluctantly given me Rachel's hand. Though I am a viscount, I was once merely a merchant's son, and Roger could never *forget my humble past. He burst into the church in a rage, interrupting the wedding. Later that day he followed me home. When we were alone, he attacked. I tried to reason with him, but in the end drew my own weapon to defend myself. With no witnesses, I stand accused of murder.*

I sought sanctuary in Morton Abbey, where I slept in a monk's cell. Every night Rachel came to me. She would knock six times on the window of my little chamber, and I would crawl through the window to meet her in secret. Arm in arm we would walk to a nearby hill and make love in the heather until dawn. I still remember the feel of her raven hair tumbling down on my cheeks, the scent of her skin mingling with mine.

But our forbidden interludes ended all too quickly. The wretched abbot, fearful that King Henry would soon claim the monastery for his own, was eager to please the king and betrayed me to royal authorities. On the seventh night, when I climbed out the window, I found myself in the arms of the sheriff.

Alas, Rachel saw it all and came running to my side. I used the distraction to free myself, but one of the king's men—blasted coward—drew his weapon and would have killed me with it had Rachel not thrown her arms around me in a protective gesture. I heard the sound of sword piercing flesh, and a moment later her groan of pain. I watched, paralyzed, as her face registered surprise, then horror. She fell to the ground and murmured my name with a pitiful whimper. They would not even let me hold her as she lay dying.

I cannot live without her, and so I now choose to join her in the arms of the Reaper. But my curse hath an eternity to live and to haunt whosoever followeth. I swear by God in heaven and the devil below that the inhabitants of Morton Abbey shall know no peace so long as the sun rises to kiss the stars. I curse the ground upon which it hath been built, and every stone that riseth above.

I shall haunt that place until justice be done in my name. Whoever dwelleth there shall hear my cries of grief evermore. Evermore.

—Lord Barrett Hamilton, 13 September, 1536

One

Miss Caroline Wainwright shut the diary and held it in her trembling hands. The words written in an angry scrawl were almost three hundred years old, but every bit as chilling as if they'd just been whispered over her shoulder.

Fine tendrils of brown hair rose on her nape and she shivered in her nightgown. Outside, a flash of lightning brightened the sky as if a thousand candles had been lit in an instant with a single taper. In that suspended moment of pulsing light, Caroline stared at the portrait of Lord Hamilton, which hung on the wall opposite her bed. He stared ominously back. Eerily illuminated, his dark eyes, tortured yet measuring, seemed to burrow into her soul.

"It is just a painting," she told herself for the thousandth time.

She turned Lord Hamilton's diary over in her hands, gazing at it in the light of her oil lamp. At last she understood the man who'd so long ago captured her imagination. And she understood the reason for his curse. This diary, which she'd only recently discovered, was the beginning of the legend that had nearly ruined her life, and had certainly destroyed her chances of a happy marriage.

In one short week, she would turn twenty-five years of age. If she weren't married by then, she'd lose her home, Fallingate, and her entire income to her brother, George. Unfortunately, not a single gentleman would take her to the altar. Those who were financially desperate enough to marry for her grand income couldn't face the prospect of living in what was rumored to be a hideously haunted estate in a desolate and isolated countryside. Those rich enough to consider Fallingate a second-income property could afford to make a match not shadowed by such ghostly rumors. And since Caroline was so easily overlooked, no one would marry her simply for love, an absurd notion in any event for any gentleman or lady of Quality.

Caroline supposed she had a pleasant enough countenance, but she was no Incomparable. She need only study her own portrait, which hung on the wall near the bedroom window, to confirm that. The portrait had been painted when she was sixteen, but was still by all accounts an accurate likeness. Her face was elegantly heart-shaped, but hardly dramatic. Her eyes were a pleasing robin's-egg blue, but discerning in a way that suggested too much intelligence. The spectacles she now wore did little to emphasize their beauty, in any case. Her brows were graceful, but almost too straight.

As for her hair, it was fashionably piled on top of her head, save for the dark tendrils that would not be tamed. Her neck was thin and long, and her figure had modest, ladylike curves. In short, she was attractive, but not strikingly so. Prone as she was to losing herself in romantic novels and disinclined to commandeer any conversation or situation, Caroline was viewed by others as demure. Or, as her sister-in-law had once unkindly remarked, Caroline had the tendency to fade into the wallpaper.

She loved Love, to be sure, but on the verge of being an old maid, she no longer expected it for herself. Once hoping for a love match, she would now gladly accept a marriage of convenience to secure her future, but even that seemed frustratingly elusive.

"Evening, miss," said Biddie, Caroline's ancient house-keeper and former lady's maid. She entered wearing a dark woolen frock and her usual expression of motherly concern. "Lost in one of your romantic novels, miss?"

"No, Biddie, I've been reading a fascinating diary." Caroline sat up further against her pillow and flipped open the musty pages of the book. "Feathers found it in the attic in a box of forgotten books dating back to the time of Henry VIII. Upon my word, I had no idea they were there. They must have been placed there by Sir Toby."

"Sir Toby?"

"He was the man who built Fallingate shortly after the old abbey was torn down during the Reformation."

"Can't say as I know much about history, miss."

"Sir Toby used the bricks from the abbey to build the foundation of our house. He was every bit as fascinated by the legends of Lord Hamilton as I am. He even purchased that painting after Barrett's death, even though they weren't related."

"Is that so?" Biddie murmured distractedly as she bustled quietly around the room, straightening porcelain figurines and fluffing pillows.

Outside the great house that kept Caroline comfortably ensconced in the style of the upper gentry, winds whirled with cold, biting force, emitting a high-pitched clamor like the wail of banshees.

It was typical autumn weather for desolate Cragmere Moor. And it was the weather that fed voracious rumors that the house at Fallingate was haunted. Suddenly another blinding flash of lightning turned the night into day.

"Oh, damme!" Caroline cried out in surprise as her heart leaped to her throat.

"You should not curse so, miss. Your late parents would not approve."

"Forgive me, Biddie. I am simply anxious for the night to go well. Is Mr. Chrisolme still in his bedchamber?"

"The solicitor? Oh, yes, miss. He has not run away—"

"Good!"

"—yet."

Caroline heaved a sigh. At least a half-dozen suitors from London had come to court Caroline since her come-out eight years before, and every one of them had run screaming from the house before a match could be made, claiming to have seen the ghosts of Lord Hamilton and Lady Rachel Harding. Mr. Chrisolme, it went without saying, offered her very last hope of marriage. "Mr. Chrisolme is still here, and here he shall remain," Caroline pronounced. "I have one week to find a husband, Biddie. And it appears I will succeed at last. I do not care how dull Mr. Chrisolme is. Why—"

Caroline stopped short when she heard a man shriek with throat-choking terror.

"Help! A ghost!" Mr. Chrisolme's voice rang out with an unmanly squeal from one of the guest chambers down the hall. "He is threatening to kill me!"

"Oh, damme!" Caroline cried, throwing back the covers. "Retrieve my robe, Biddie, hurry!"

Caroline flew out of the bed, crossed the room in a flash, and threw open her door while Biddie shuffled behind, helping her into her robe. Caroline had just tightened the sash when she saw a white-faced gentleman flying past her, tugging on his coat and boots as he went, the long strands of hair he had combed from one ear to the other to mute the glare of his bald spot dancing in the air with each jogging step.

"Mr. Chrisolme!" she shouted at his retreating figure. "Don't go in such haste! It's cold and frightfully dark outside. You will lose your way in the bog and never be seen again!"

Caroline paused long enough to see her last best hope of holy matrimony trampling down the wooden stairs, his clappering feet sounding like a herd of wild pigs. "I must go after him!"

"It is no use, miss," Biddie said with a mournful shake of her head. "He's like all the others."

"But it isn't safe! He could wander into the bog. Then I would never forgive myself. Besides, he is my last chance. Without him I will lose Fallingate forever! I must try to reason with him. I will beg if I must!"

Caroline ran after him, her feet scarcely touching the stairs as she rushed toward the front door. Mr. Chrisolme had been so terrified he'd left it wide open, and a fierce wind blew into the entrance hall.

"Mr. Chrisolme," she yelled through one cupped hand as she clung to the door frame with the other, "bear to the left or you will find yourself in Dead Man's Bog!"

She strained to hear his answer, but the only response was the familiar ghostlike shrieks of wind. With any luck he'd find his way to the Silver Stallion, a lonely little inn a mile down the road. Her brother George and his wife, Prudence, who had brought Mr. Chrisolme from London, could take him back on the morrow. If only he could manage to skirt the bog.

"Bear to the left, Mr. Chrisolme!" she cried out again, and started after him, but the wind pushed her back. It felt as if she'd been shoved by an unseen hand. When she stumbled backward, the breeze halted immediately. The door slammed shut with thundering finality, and with it so did all Caroline's hopes of matrimony.

Two

Three men of dubious pedigree trudged their way along a lonely moorland road toward Fallingate. They were cold, exhausted, and utterly out of place among the country squires and gentry of Cragmere. Not that there were many squires about at this hour in this dismal stretch of land.

The ruffians were confident that whatever country houses they'd come upon, though, would make their arduous three-day journey from London worth their while. For before they reached Fallingate, one of their destinations, they would find the Dowager Countess of Germaine's estate, by all accounts one of the most ornate and richest homes in the country.

"What ho!" Lucas Davin, the tallest of the three men, whispered harshly. "Look there!"

He pointed to an approaching figure that looked even more out of place than they. The men crouched down by the side of the road so as not to be seen, and watched dumbfounded as a bald gentleman flew past them, heading toward the inn from which they'd just come. Panting, gasping, wide-eyed, and obviously terrified, the pasty-faced fool ran as if the hounds of hell were nipping at his heels. When he ran out of sight, the men rose and looked at one another with suspicion.

"Lawk! Will yer look at that?" said Lucas, scratching his generous mop of black hair. "Wonder what that chap is running from out here in the middle of nowhere."

"Eh?" replied Robbin Roger, cupping a tattered, finger-less glove to his ear to hear above the howl of the wind. He was the older of Lucas's scruffy companions.

"I don't even want to know wot 'e's runnin' from," said Smiley Figgenbottom. The cunning and little crook rubbed the stubble on his blunt jaw. "I 'ate to think wot kind of beast might be layin' in wait in this bloody-awful place."

"Maybe yer right," Lucas growled as he flipped up the tattered collar of his coat and resumed their trek. His breath plumed out in puffs that looked a bluish gray in the moon-light. "I don't want to know, either. Let's get on with it, mates. It's damned cold here."

"Colder 'an a witch's teat," Smiley replied, hobbling on his stubby legs to keep up. "I'd rather be back at Seven Dials, I would, than out 'ere in this bleedin' moor. The pickin's may be slimmer in Town, but at least in London the wind don't cut through yer like an ice pick."

"Patience, Smiley," Lucas said as they trudged up what he hoped would be the last hill before they reached the Germaine estate. "The real money ain't in London. It's here in the country, where the bleeding lords and ladies keep their goods safe from the likes of us. I'm done with cutting purses and fighting for me territory. I told yer, Smiley, we were destined for bigger things."

"But why in Cragmere of all bleedin' places? Why not sunny Bath?" Smiley struggled to keep up. "This place ain't fit fer a ghost."

Lucas didn't know what had compelled him to journey

here to what certainly had to be the bleakest place in all of southern England. Instinct was as close to a reason as he could contrive. Something had drawn him here. Some . . . desire . . . he scarcely understood. He stopped and looked back down the road, frowning when he didn't see Robbin Roger.

"What, ho! Old man! Are yer with us?" Lucas called, frowning hard when the biting wind made his eyes water.

Smiley pulled up and tugged confidentially on his companion's sleeve. "Let's leave the old bugger. 'E's only slowin' us down. Don't know why the 'ell yer brought 'im. The old cove is past it, mate. Yer should 'ave left 'im to die an old sot's death where 'e was beggin' fer a crust on murderers' row."

In a flash of fury that Lucas could neither understand nor control, he lifted the dwarfish man up by the collar until they were face-to-face. "He's me father, and yer'll treat him with respect, that you will. Understand?"

"So yer say," Smiley said with a surly scowl. "He looks nothin' like yer. 'E's got a face like a rut in the road, and yers the ladies swoon for. Didn't it ever strike yer funny?"

"He gave me his name, which is a sight better than what any other cove has given me. He kept me fed. Taught me to feed meself. I'll not have you showing yer disrespect."

Lucas let go of the petty thief and he fell to the windswept ground, landing with a splash in a puddle.

"Aw, lawk-a-mussy! Easy, Lucas," Smiley cried out, and brushed himself off. "Don't be so touchy! The boys are dependin' on us, is all I mean."

Lucas laughed ironically. "What do yer know about the boys? All yer care about is yerself. Robbin! Hurry up!"

"Robbin" Roger Davin's bent figure appeared in the darkness. He was slowing down with every shuffling step. Lucas knew the old man's feet would be half-frozen by now. He also knew they had to get to Germaine House and Fallingate quickly.

Earlier in the day Smiley Figgenbottom had stolen a horse from the Germaine stables—testing the security he said—and chances are the constable would be called in to investigate. Lucas would have strangled Smiley outright for his carelessness if the little man weren't the best house-breaker in all of Seven Dials.

"Don't know why we couldn't ride the bleedin' 'orse tonight," Smiley said as he rose and dusted himself off. "Went to a lot of trouble to get it, I did."

"Because yer stole it instead of hiring one like I asked yer to," Lucas answered through chattering teeth, blowing on the bare tips of his fingers. "We'll be lucky to get back to Seven Dials without being arrested. But I'm not going back till I see Germaine House. We've got to have a plan before the gang comes out here. After we look over Germaine, we'll go back by way of Fallingate. Two fine jewels in Cragmere's crown for me pocket."

"Why did yer pick these two 'ouses?" Smiley asked.

"I heard a chap in London talk about them right before I cut his purse. He said they were close together and both full of riches. He'd come courting a rich miss out here, but it ended bad like."

"I 'ear about lots of rich 'ouses," Figgenbottem groused, "but I ain't goin' to ride out to every place I 'ear about, now, am I?"

"Shut it, mate. Yer'll have no regrets. I trust me instincts, and that's why yer do what I say and not the other way 'round. Come on, Robbin!"

Lucas hiked back to the old man's side. Robbin gripped Lucas's arm with half-frozen fingers and looked up with an expression of frozen pain.

"There's me boy. Almost there, are we?" he said, running a dirt-caked sleeve under his sniffling nose.

"Aye, Robbin, but we've got to hurry, mate."

"I ain't slowin' yer down, am I, boy?"

"No, Robbin. I'll be trying to keep up with yer for years to come."

Roger Davin's scraggly gray hair shot out wildly from beneath his tattered cap. His nose was a red beak and his fading blue eyes watered fiercely in the cold. When had he gotten so old? Lucas wondered as he stared down at the man. Smiley was right. Lucas shouldn't have brought Robbin along, but the old bugger needed the money and, more important, he needed a sense of purpose. Lucas couldn't believe it when he'd found Robbin, once the most cunning cutpurse of them all, begging for food on the streets.

"Come on, Robbin. I can't do this without yer, mate."

The old man scowled at him doubtfully, then nodded, accepting the charity without calling it such. "Now, house thiefin' ain't me bailiwick, mind yer. But yer got to be careful goin' in. Smart like a fox, boy. Yer got to be smart like a fox."

The old man rambled on, spouting oft-repeated advice as Lucas half dragged him along. When they crested the hill, all three stopped abruptly in unison, stunned by the sight that greeted them.

Smiley whistled low. "Lawk, will yer look at that!"

"Good God," Lucas quietly remarked as his heart began to race. He'd expected the house to be grand. But this was magnificence beyond his wildest imagination.

"What the devil?" Robbin Roger said, his grip on Lucas's arm tightening.

Lucas felt his own body tense as he took in the sight. Seeing the grand tower, the long front marble facade that glowed white in the moonlight, the acres of windows, meticulous gardens and shrubs, and the sprawling stables all conspired to take his breath away. What he felt was not mere envy, or the hatred he normally felt for the rich, but something greater, deeper, something he did not understand. When he at last recognized the feeling, he swallowed hard. It was pure desire. By God and all that was holy, he wanted this place for his own.

"Damme," he cursed in self-reproach.

"Why did yer bring me 'ere?" Robbin shouted, stamping a foot.

Lucas tore his gaze from the magnificent house and squinted at the old man. "What do yer mean, why did I bring yer here? We came to plan a rob—"

"No!" Robbin waved a trembling hand through the air. He thrust out his lower lip and jerked his thumb toward the mansion. "I mean why did yer bring me *here*?"

"Why not? I—" Lucas was cut short when two horses became visible on the road at the bottom of the hill, near the Germaine gatehouse.

"Oh, devil, is that wot I think it is?" Smiley said, turning to run even as he said it.

"Hell!" Lucas cursed. Even in darkness he could recognize the constable's staff. "This is yer fault, Figgenbottom. The constable wouldn't be here if yer hadn't stolen that damned horse from the very place we planned to rob."

As if their harshly whispered voices had carried the distance on the wind, the constable looked their way and pointed. He motioned to his companion, some sort of liveried servant, and both heeled their mounts.

Lucas cursed again, then turned and ran, dragging Robbin along as best he could.

"'urry!" Smiley shouted over his shoulder. "Shove the old bugger aside. Yer'll never make it otherwise!"

As the thunder of horse hooves behind them grew louder, Lucas knew Smiley was right. He'd never escape the constable with Robbin at his side. There was no place to hide on the endless rolling moor. And Robbin couldn't run fast enough. In an instant Lucas knew what he had to do.

"Here!" he turned and called to the approaching riders. Then he gave Robbin a shove. "Go on, old man. Go with Smiley. Let him take yer back to London. Tell the gang to go ahead with our plans. I'll break outta the gaol soon as I can."

"Nay, Luc, I'll give meself up." Robbin's craggy forehead wrinkled with a loving frown as he tried to shove him away. "Run, Luc! Run!"

"No, Robbin." Lucas embraced the old man, then gave him a sound shove that sent him flying down the hill away from the riders. Lucas then veered away from the road and started running through Cragmere Moor, wildly waving his hands above his head. "Come on, yer bloody fools! I'm this way. Can't yer keep up with a common crook like me?"

They could indeed. Soon both riders were upon him, reining in their snorting horses. Lucas bowed with exaggerated elegance. The dour constable raised his staff as if to knock the cheeky grin from Lucas's handsome face, but he didn't earn so much as a flinch for his pains.

Lucas thrust his hands in his pockets and looked around as if he'd been waiting for them. "Took yer long enough."

"Silence, insolent wretch!" the constable barked. "Seize him!"

The burly servant jumped off his horse and wrenched Lucas's arms painfully behind his back.

"Shall I tie him up?" the servant said to the gray-haired constable.

"Yes. We will take him to the countess. It was her horse stolen, after all."

The man who was apparently in her ladyship's employ roughly tied Lucas's wrists and bound his neck in a noose. Then he remounted and dragged Lucas down the hill. Lucas wouldn't give them the satisfaction of falling, and so he ran hard to keep up with the trotting horses.

They passed through the estate's intricate wrought-iron entrance gate and rounded the many-storied mansion until they reached a side entrance so grand it had its own name. The servant called it Soronto Hall. Their arrival must have been anticipated, because shortly after he rapped on the ornately carved door, it opened at the hands of a meticulously dressed butler. He wore knee-length breeches and white stockings and a long-tailed frock coat. His cheeks and nose were gaunt and long and his eyes were as cold and gray as rain. He narrowed his focus on Lucas with a glint of triumph as if he'd finally spotted an elusive rat that had been rampaging through his pantry.

"Is this the one?" he intoned in a sonorous voice.

"Tell her ladyship we've got the horse thief," the constable said as the proud servant tightened the noose around Lucas's neck with a yank. Lucas gripped the chafing rope with both hands, but he made not a sound.

Soon a regal woman with dove-gray hair, imperious blue eyes, and powdery white skin came to the door. She wore the most luxurious purple gown Lucas had ever seen. It glittered with tiny jets and beads sown on the delicate silk. She cast her gaze up and down him with powerful disdain.

"Is this him?" she asked coolly.

"Yes, your ladyship," the constable replied, making a short bow.

"Did you find the horse?" she said, barely moving her tightly knitted lips.

"Yes, your ladyship, at the Silver Stallion."

She smiled thinly. "Place him in the local gaol. He will be abominably treated there until he can be hanged for the crime. That is, unless he shows appropriate remorse."

She turned without another word, rustling off with a

swish-swish of silk. Lucas's nostrils flared as he clenched his jaw. He knew what appropriate remorse would be to someone of her station. He would have to beg and plead for his life, and then he would have to serve her as little more than a slave, ever mindful of her mercy.

The thought choked him more than the rope that rubbed his skin raw. Lucas thought he'd live too long if he ever had to see the likes of such hateful arrogance again. He'd made himself the king of his own underclass so he wouldn't have to grovel to so-called Quality like her. How he despised the rich. One day he'd show them. One day that couldn't come soon enough.

Three

"And so, dear Caroline, yet another suitor has escaped your grasp," Prudence Wainwright said to her sister-in-law the next morning in the drawing room of Fallingate.

George Wainwright's wife—Mrs. Wainwright, as she was universally addressed—had gathered there after breakfast with her two daughters from her first marriage. She commandeered the richly appointed room, with its oak floors, ornate cornices, and Oriental wallpaper, as if she already owned the place. Prudence and her daughters had attached themselves to the Sheraton chairs closest to the fire, leaving Caroline and her former governess, Amanda Plumshaw, to endure the chill toward the center of the room. Banished as they were to the Chippendale sofa, Amanda and Caroline could only look longingly at the flames that flickered beneath the mantel's frieze of classical figures.

Without deference to her hostess, the broad-beamed Mrs. Wainwright had ordered tea and sweetcakes, though she'd just finished breakfast, and busied herself consuming them while her slender daughters occupied themselves with needlework.

It did not take a cynical heart to note the glee glinting in the matron's eyes. Mrs. Wainwright was never quite so friendly to Caroline as she was when one of her suitors had flown the premises. Prudence Wainwright viewed Caroline's failure in this area not with sympathy, but with a sense of triumph born of a mother's greed for her own daughters' successes.

While Prudence herself was not blue-blooded, she'd been accepted by the *ton* because of her marriage to the late Colonel Hallwell, a first cousin of the Baron Chumley. Ever since the untimely death of her husband, she'd spent virtually every waking moment of her life planning marriages that would ensure that her daughters had a more secure entreé into the *beau monde*. And though marrying Caroline's brother George, who was a manufacturer, had been a social step down from her former near glory, Prudence needed the money from George's mill for dowries to secure her daughters' place in Society. She was a matchmaking mama who would be simply mortified if her sister-in-law succeeded where her own chicks might still fail. And she never missed an opportunity to proclaim Caroline's failures to anyone who would listen.

"You do have the worst luck in love, my dear girl," Prudence continued, sipping tea from a delicate china cup. "Of course, I knew this was inevitable. I—oh, Mrs. Plumshaw, would you be so kind as to fetch us some quince jelly? The girls adore quince jelly."

The former governess was nonplussed. Amanda Plumshaw was dignity personified. Her strawberry-blond hair was tucked under a cambric cap without so much as a hair going astray. At forty, her smooth, lightly freckled skin was fair and still attractive. Only the faintest web of lines creased the corners of her green eyes. But for all her maturity, she did not know how to answer such an inappropriate request. She looked to her former charge for rescue.

"Really, Mrs. Wainwright," Caroline said coolly, motioning the footmen toward the kitchen, "we have servants for that. Mrs. Plumshaw, as you know, is my esteemed companion."

"She is a governess," Prudence archly replied.

"A former governess. In any event, she is not a servant."

"But she is not your equal, and that is how you treat her."

Caroline sipped her own tea thoughtfully, then calmly said, "You are most certainly correct. Mrs. Plumshaw is not my equal."

Prudence almost purred with satisfaction at this apparent turnaround.

"She is, in fact, my superior. Her Greek is flawless. Her mathematical skills are to be revered, and her mastery of the harp is sublime. In addition, she is a dear friend. Dearer to me than my own relations."

Caroline stole a glance at Amanda, whose beryl eyes gleamed with triumph.

Prudence harrumphed. "You always did treat your dependents too liberally, Caro. Very quaint, I am sure. You should have let go of George's former valet years ago and saved yourself a pretty penny."

"Neville has served our family his whole life, Mrs. Wainwright. I assure you I keep him busy even though he has no master to dress."

"And do you keep Mrs. Plumshaw busy as well?"

Amanda rose abruptly. She was the soul of patience, but even she had reached her limit. "If you will excuse me, Caro, I will see that Henry hurries with Mrs. Wainwright's quince jelly. A pleasure as always, ma'am." She nodded to Prudence.

"Do not go, Amanda," Caroline said, reaching out and pressing her hand.

"I shall return soon." She smiled with all the genuine grace that Caroline had come to count on and love, and then departed with her dignity intact.

Caroline watched her go with admiration, then turned irritably back to her sister-in-law. She removed her spectacles and placed them on an oval side table, girding herself for battle. In one short week, on Caroline's birthday, Mrs. Wainwright would become mistress of Fallingate. She already acted as if it were a fait accompli. That meant Caroline had little time left to assert the last vestiges of her authority.

"I believe," Caroline said, "we were talking about Mr. Chrisolme, not Mrs. Plumshaw."

"Mr. Chrisolme! Upon my word, I should think you would want to avoid that topic. How many suitors have you chased off, Caroline?"

"I have lost count," she answered truthfully. "But the number is of no consequence. All that matters, at least to you, Mrs. Wainwright, is that you will soon be mistress of Fallingate. Isn't that so? Isn't that why you feel you can insult my companion without fear of retribution?"

Prudence raised both brows. "Why, I have never heard such impertinence from our dear little Caro! It's very unbecoming, I'm sure. Why—"

"Well, well, my favorite girls, all together in the same room," George, Caroline's brother, said, entering through the double doors. The dapperly dressed gentleman went to his wife and kissed the air near her cheek. "Greetings, my dear. Good morning, girls," he added, nodding to his stepdaughters with a dutiful smile.

"Good morning, Papa," they answered in unison, accent on the second syllable.

George then turned to his sister. "Good morning, Mouse."

She smiled wanly. "Good morning, George."

Casting her a patronizing smile, he rocked back on his heels and tucked his thumbs into his waistcoat, which had grown in size since his marriage six years before to Colonel Humphrey Hallwell's widow.

Caroline had never known what George saw in the matronly Prudence, save for her social connections. As a successful mill owner, George might have bought his way more firmly into Society, but he wasn't nearly as clever as Caroline. And though he was strikingly attractive, with keen blue eyes and thick blond lashes, a supple mouth and square chin, George could think of nothing but money and ledgers and business. He couldn't have stumbled his way through a quadrille if he'd been led with a bridle.

And so a half-dozen years ago, when he went to London for the Season and the cunning Widow Hallwell had taken an interest in him, George very agreeably took to trotting around her heels like a loyal pup. He didn't seem to mind that Prudence was five years his senior and more than a little plump. He merely seemed grateful that he'd found someone to organize his life outside the mill, to tell him what cravat to wear with which waistcoat, and whom to play cards with at his men's clubs in London.

Prudence introduced him to all the people who were quite the thing, and though the Wainwrights weren't invited to the most exclusive gatherings, together they plotted her daughters' debut into Society with a determination born of their hunger for acceptance themselves. Their arrangement seemed to suit Caroline's unimaginative brother perfectly.

"I say, Mouse, you will never guess who I saw in London," he said jovially.

The nickname he'd always called her chafed more than

usual this morning, and she had to clear her throat before she could speak civilly. "I haven't the vaguest idea, George. Who was it?"

"Dr. Cavendish."

Caroline's face lit like a candle. "Uncle Teddy? He's in England? So he has returned from his adventures in Africa? It's been so long! What, five years?"

"Yes, and he should be arriving at Fallingate this afternoon. I saw him several days ago during the last trip to Town." Though George and Prudence lived in London during the Season, they spent the rest of the year at Knowlton Park, their country estate, which was a few hours' ride from Fallingate. "He might even arrive while we're still here."

"Oh, no, Papa!" Violet fairly squealed. "He is not bringing any natives with him this time, is he?"

"Why, we must leave at once," Cecilia avowed, flipping open her fan and fluttering it at her neck. "They say he has turned into a cannibal himself!"

"Now, now, girls," George said. "Dr. Cavendish is one of the country's foremost adventurers. Just because he associates with natives does not mean he is any the less a gentleman."

"Yes," Prudence said with a sniff, "but he smokes Cheroots in front of the girls. No gentleman of fine breeding does that."

"At least I know of one person here who will be happy to see the good doctor, eh, Mouse?" He turned to Caroline and raised his brows. George had always disliked their father's best friend and teased her because she was Dr. Cavendish's pet.

"What is it, George?" she said, sipping her tea. "Are you being snide over Uncle's Teddy's return, or are you gloating because last night I lost my last chance of marriage?"

Her brother's smile drooped. "I do not mean to gloat, Caro, I assure you. I feel quite sober and concerned for your future."

"Tea, Papa?" Violet said.

"Yes, please." George tugged on the thigh of his trousers, brushed aside his tails, and sat with ramrod posture in an urn-back chair next to the window. "I sent a footman over to the Silver Stallion, where, it seems, Mr. Chrisolme is still shaking in his boots, practically begging anyone who will listen to fetch him a coach for his journey back to London. I have sent a carriage over to take him back."

"That is very good of you, George," Caroline said. "So even now, in the light of day, he thinks Fallingate is haunted?"

"But of course this house is haunted!" George answered emphatically as he accepted a cup from his stepdaughter. "Thank you, my dear."

Caroline turned to Prudence. "Do *you* believe there is a ghost haunting Fallingate?"

"Well, it is obvious, isn't it?" the matron sputtered.

"If that is so, then why are you anxious for the house? You would bring your girls to live in a place that is haunted?"

"She is not *anxious* for it," George said with a superior sniff. "Mrs. Wainwright is never *anxious* about anything."

"It is clear, my dear girl," his wife said, her fascination with the afterlife overcoming her pique, "that the ghost of Lord Hamilton is jealous of your suitors. That is why they are the only ones who hear anything. Barrett Hamilton clearly wants you to remain a maiden. He wants to keep you for himself, perhaps in anticipation of some sort of otherworldly romantic interlude."

"Oh, this is absurd! No one would think this house was haunted if I had not suggested the very idea myself."

Blinking away her disconcerting thoughts, Caroline put

her spectacles back on and fastidiously straightened the lace edges of her long sleeves. "The matter of the ghost aside, I still do wonder if you are not happy about my plight."

"Now, now, Caro," George said placatingly, "do not ascribe such motives to me. I am exceedingly sorry that our father put such a stipulation into his will. I agree this house should be yours without condition. Mother wanted you to have it. And I have Father's mansion in London, as well as Knowlton Park, and the income from the cotton mill. You have loved Fallingate more than I, God knows. But Father did not trust that you would marry as he saw fit. Not after your mischievous little scheme eight years ago. He—"

Caroline cleared her throat, silencing him just in time. She did not want her smug stepnieces to hear any more details of that humiliating debacle than they already had.

Eight years ago Caroline had utterly botched her come-out in London. After reading so many romantic novels, she had her heart set on a love match. She was all too aware that the only reason any gentlemen of the *ton* would even think of engaging her affections was because of her wealth. Though she was of good gentry stock, she was not blue-blooded. The starched-up lords and ladies of London reminded her of that distinction with condescending smiles and inattentiveness. She didn't care, she'd told herself. None of the young bloods were as handsome as Lord Hamilton, her romantic ideal.

By the time her parents proudly presented her to the honorable third son of an earl, a frail and pimply-faced young man with a limp handshake, Caroline had had her fill of the pretense and refused him, though not overtly of course. She waited until he came down to Fallingate for a house party, and she simply dressed up like the ghost of Rachel Harding and made an appearance one night outside

his chamber, howling with the hideous lamentations of the
dead. The poor spineless lad had run home to Papa, and
word soon spread throughout Society that Fallingate was
haunted.

"I do not think it wise to venture upon such an *old* and
painful subject, do you, George?" Caroline asked firmly.

"No, of course not. I simply want to impress upon you
my true concerns in this matter. We do not wish to live at
Fallingate. We simply would consider the income from the
estate's tin mines a suitable dowry for our girls, who desire
a proper Season in Town. You above all should appreciate
the importance of that."

Caroline simmered.

"Do not worry unduly about your future, Caroline," Prudence said, drawing the subject to a close. "You are a
relation, after all. You are perfectly welcome to stay with
us in London. We're heading into Town early this year."

"I—in London?" Caroline drained of color. Her mouth
went dry. "Why, I thought I would be staying on at Fallingate. Not as mistress, of course, but—"

Mrs. Wainwright's shrill laughter cut her short. "Oh, no,
no, no, my dear! Quite impossible. We will be shutting
the house down for repairs and refurnishing."

Caroline gaped at her. "Whatever for?"

"It is a bit . . . shabby, isn't it?"

"I have never found it wanting." Caroline's voice trem-
bled now.

"Oh, here is the quince jelly!" Prudence said, rubbing
her hands together gleefully as the footman placed a bowl
of it by her side. "Violet? Cecilia?"

"No, thank you, Mama," the girls answered in unison.

"We will find a room for you in London," Prudence
rattled on as she lobbed a spoonful of jelly on the remaining piece of her sweetcake. "Oh, but not as long as the
Harringtons are in from the country. Well, perhaps we can

clean out the governess's old room for you to use until they leave."

"The governess's room! George?" Caroline said imploringly, but her brother turned away and looked out the window while he drank his tea.

"And of course you will be expected to perform certain ... duties," Prudence added, popping the last piece of sweetcake in her mouth.

Caroline turned slowly to regard her sister-in-law with her eyelids narrowed. "What duties?"

"Those befitting any spinster aunt. You will chaperon the girls and tutor them in French."

A chill spread over Caroline's arms as she contemplated that prospect. Violet and Cecilia shrank back in their chairs with equal dread.

"No, Mama!" Cecilia piped in.

"Surely not, dear sister," Caroline protested, sitting at the edge of her chair. "My French is not in the least adequate. And your daughters deserve only the best of—"

"You will be more than adequate," Prudence said with a finality which only a fool would dare question.

Caroline held her breath, too stunned to accept this reversal of fortune.

"Of course," Prudence added with a sugary smile, "if you do not want to chaperon, there are *alternatives*."

This simple statement hung in the air like a sword of Damocles, wanting no interpretation or explanation. There was only one alternative for women who did not marry and had no property of their own. Caroline could become a governess in someone else's house, a lonely assignment for any unfortunate female. So engaged, she would never quite equal the status of the persons who employed her, nor would she be able to relate to her much-younger charges. Socially, she would cease to exist.

"I understand," Caroline managed to whisper at last.

"Well, then, we are all understood," George said quickly, trying as usual to smooth over the awkward silences that marked all interviews between his wife and his sister. "In one week, Caroline, it will be your twenty-fifth birthday. We will ride out from Knowlton Park to have dinner with you to celebrate the occasion."

"Oh, no! No, no, do not bother."

"No bother at all. It is your birthday."

Caroline regarded George with veiled anger and disappointment. The only reason he would come all the way from Knowlton Park for her birthday was to make sure the transition of ownership of the house went smoothly and speedily.

"Are you riding today, George?" Mrs. Wainwright inquired.

"No, my dear. I think we should return home at once. The coach is already waiting."

The girls dutifully rose on their mother's cue and departed without fanfare. But Prudence did not clear the door before delivering a coup de grâce.

"One more item, my dear. You may tell Mrs. Plumshaw that her services will no longer be needed."

"But she has nowhere else to go!"

Prudence smiled. "Yes, it is a pity, isn't it? But unlike you, I do not plan to operate my household as a charity ward. Half your servants are at death's door, because you have been too softhearted to relieve them of their duties. That will all change beginning next week."

She rustled off in her fashionable though unflattering pale yellow muslin morning gown. Just before George disappeared through the doorway, Caroline called out to him in desperation.

"George, you cannot mean to turn out Mrs. Plumshaw!

She has lived here for the past fifteen years. She is part of the family."

George returned to her side and took her hands in his. "My dear sister, I know it will not be easy giving over the reins to my wife, but Mrs. Wainwright must run this house as she sees fit. Surely you agree that servants must know who is in command. You are too sentimental, Mouse."

Caroline squeezed her eyes shut. She had always been too sentimental. Her parents had always said so. She'd been a dreamer, lost in her books, too kindhearted to be a good mistress of Fallingate. Everyone thought so. But now her failings were hurting not only herself, but her dearest friend.

"Amanda is not a servant." She opened her eyes and met George's gaze without blinking. "You cannot turn her out. I will not have it."

"I am sorry, Caro, but you no longer have any say in the matter."

She hated her brother in that moment; hated his weakness and subservience to his wife. She turned stiffly and went to the window, gazing out, unseeing, her hand pressing against a cold pane of glass.

Her brother was correct about one matter. She had been too sentimental. But she could change, and would change in order to keep Fallingate. A pretty, vivacious woman might leave her fate to charm and good fortune. But unassuming women like Caroline could not count on luck.

Her very survival was at stake. It was time to dispense with manners and good breeding and do whatever it took to keep Fallingate from falling into her sister-in-law's clutches. Fortunately, if anyone could help her do it, it was Uncle Teddy. Though not a blood relation, Theodore Cavendish was a kindred spirit. And more important, he was unfettered by the opinions of others. Together they would cook up some sort of scheme to keep her inheritance.

And she already knew the denouement of the petty drama. She would marry before the week was out, even if the only man she could find to marry was a criminal from the worst slums in London.

Four

Two hours later Dr. Cavendish settled with a contented groan in a chair next to the fire that blazed in the library. Rows of musty crimson, brown, green, and gold leather-bound books lined the walls. A rich red carpet covered the floor and tapestries lined the oak-paneled walls. The room had changed little since the seventeenth century and possessed an old-world charm. The doctor gazed at the cozy surroundings and sighed contentedly as the fire warmed his legs.

He'd arrived a half hour earlier in a coach laden with exotic-looking boxes, an Egyptian sarcophagus, and a collection of shrunken heads. They'd all been promptly taken to the old coach house, a renovated structure that Theodore Cavendish used as his permanent English residence. His African manservant and sometime butler, Shabala, was supervising the unpacking while the portly and distinguished-looking doctor thawed himself out before the fire.

He accepted a cup of coffee from Caroline and turned his attention to the women who sat across from him.

"I can't tell you how good it is to be home, my dears, but you must tell me what is troubling you. I sense that all is not well."

Caroline didn't know where to begin and merely bit her lower lip. Only now was she beginning to feel the true desperation of her circumstances.

"I will tell you what is bothering her," Amanda offered. "Caroline is going to lose Fallingate."

"What?" Theodore sat up in attention. "Whatever for?"

In her even-tempered way, Amanda laid out all the facts in as objective a manner as possible.

"And so," she said in sad conclusion, "in one week, if we are all still here, it will be due to the generosity of Mrs. Wainwright, which I doubt exists in much abundance."

Theodore drew in a troubled breath, his chest expanding against his brown waistcoat, and then let it out slowly as he frowned at the fire.

"This is dreadful news. Your father never intended for George to assume possession of this house, Caro. He simply wanted to make sure you were married. He never dreamed it would come to this, I am quite sure. Well, I'd best tell Shabala to stop unpacking. I have no doubt I will no longer be welcome here when Mrs. Wainwright takes over. George never cared much for my occupancy of the carriage house. He could never understand why your father and I were such good friends. Poor George has never been fond of anyone who had more imagination than he."

"Which is everyone," Caroline added wryly.

"Thank God my wife is not alive to see this day!"

"It is all my fault," Caroline lamented. "If I had not started the rumors that this house was haunted, I would have been married long ago. How foolish I was to pass up my only chance!"

Theodore twisted the ends of his mustache between his thumb and forefinger, studying Caroline as if she were part of one of his scientific experiments. The light in his soft brown eyes churned thoughtfully.

"Tell me, my dear," he said at last, "what precisely do you want me to do?"

"I must marry, Uncle Teddy. And I want you to help me find a husband. I have no doubt that my brother has done his best to engage a gentleman—or at least a respectable man—acceptable to Society. But every attempt has failed, and marrying a gentleman is no longer a possibility."

"Then what sort of man do you propose to marry?" Amanda asked with a perplexed frown.

"There is a gaol not far from here," Caroline said with much more calm than she felt. Her eyes, glinting with resolve, locked with Theodore's. "Surely you can find a prisoner there who would risk a few nights in a haunted house in exchange for his freedom."

Theodore's frown melted, turning into a blank look of dismay. "Here, now, Caroline—"

"No!" Amanda cried. Her green eyes shone with dismay. "You cannot even think of marrying a criminal!"

"It will not be forever," Caroline reasoned. "I just need to be married long enough to prove to my brother its veracity and legality. Then I can send my husband off to some far-flung land with a generous income and I will never see him again. We can pretend he died in a boating accident on the Nile."

"Caro!" Amanda whispered reproachfully.

"I would rather be a young widow than an old maid. Widows have all the advantages, you know."

"But if you do not marry a man from among your own order in Society, you will be ruined!"

Caroline frowned petulantly. "You sound almost as arrogant as the nobs in London who favored me only for my wealth."

"I am not arrogant, my dear," Amanda protested. "I am only reminding you that marrying beneath one's station simply isn't done."

"People will not know my husband's a criminal if we do not tell them."

"They will take one look at him and know. He will have no refinement! No breeding! He will speak . . . differently. You will have to keep all the valuables under lock and key the entire time he is under this roof. And that is if you are lucky enough to marry a thief! What if he is a murderer? Oh, Dr. Cavendish, talk some sense into this foolish girl's head!"

The room grew very still as the doctor merely stroked his beard, contemplating the possibilities. The clock struck four.

"Hmmm," Theodore said before the last chime fell silent. "I once debated with my nemesis, Sir Arthur Trumbull, whether it was truly possible to reform an English rogue. In fact, he's placed a bet at the club that he can do it before the year is out. If I could beat him at his own game, I'd have gloating rights for years to come."

"Then you think my plan might work?"

He regarded Caroline with bright eyes. "Do you remember that Aboriginal family my dear wife and I took in after they journeyed here from Australia?"

"Yes?"

"When we first met, they were in the habit of drinking blood and dancing 'round fires waving shrunken skulls. By the time I finished with them, they were smoking cheroots, drinking brandy, and gambling on cockfights."

"Was that an improvement?" Amanda inquired archly.

The doctor shot her a wry smile. "Spoken like a true lady."

"Precisely what are you implying, Uncle Teddy?"

He pointed at Caroline as a confident grin blossomed

amid his well-trimmed salt-and-pepper beard. "If I can civ-ilize an Aborigine, I can surely civilize a common English criminal."

"I own that I cannot believe you're serious," Amanda said, aghast.

"I have never been more serious in my life. In fact, enough of this coffee. Bring me some port. Let us toast to the greatest experiment of my career—turning a rogue into a fair lord!"

Five

"He's a filthy horse thief, but you can have him if you want him. Don't know why a gentleman such as you would, though."

With bloodshot eyes, one of which was askew, the gaoler cast Theodore Cavendish a dubious look over his hunched shoulder.

"What did you say you want with the rogue, Dr. Cavendish?"

Theodore sidestepped a plump rat arrogantly hurtling past them down the dank, dark corridor. "He is going to be part of a scientific experiment. I study human behavior, you see. I examine human beings in relation to their origins and culture. I am going to send him to the wilds of Africa and see how he fares in a new environment. What did you say his name was?"

"He calls himself Robbin Roger and claims he's the most famous cutpurse in all of London. A bleeding braggart, he is. Spit in my face, he did, when he said it. The name's probably an alias, though. They never go by their real names. He'd hang for stealing a horse. No question.

He's a lucky bugger to have you come along and save his worthless neck. When you see his surly puss, you'll have second thoughts, I avow."

"He does not have to be the Prince of Wales. All I want is a chap who is not a hardened criminal."

"Stealing horseflesh ain't no walk in the park."

"No, but it is a far cry from murder, isn't it? I have seen amazing improvements in men once they are exposed to a better way of life."

The grizzly-faced gaoler let out a snort of laughter, revealing a row of rotten teeth. "Yeah, right. Now remember, I'll have to tell the constable he escaped. It'll take some cunning on my part. That don't come cheap, if you take my meaning."

Without looking back or stopping his trek toward the gaol, he held out his palm. Theodore grinned, satisfied that he'd found a gaoler who was so easy to negotiate with. In fact everything about this humbug had been easy. After getting Mrs. Plumshaw to come around—albeit with great reluctance—Theodore had sent for a solicitor in Dorset to draw up a marriage settlement. Then Shabala had made all the arrangements to obtain a wedding license. Now all Theodore had to do was bribe the gaoler and the charade would begin. He pulled a sovereign out of his pocket and put it in the man's grubby palm.

"I understand your needs perfectly, my good man. Now show me the lad. I can scarcely wait to see the sorry sight of him."

"Mind you, the area will be crawling with the constable's men. Once they learn ol' Robbin Roger has escaped, they'll be looking for the crook in every copse of trees, every inn and tavern, every dark alley. So keep him away from here, if you know what's good for you."

But they won't be looking in the drawing room of one

of the most respectable misses in the county, Theodore thought with a quiet chortle.

"Fear not, good man. I will keep him well hidden until I can ferry him out of the country. And the secret will be ours."

Theodore felt his first qualms when the gaoler opened the door of the gaol. The stench of human refuse and sweat that pounded his nose in greeting was overwhelming, even to a doctor who was used to foul odors. He put a monogrammed kerchief to his nostrils and coughed. His gaze darted around the poorly lit barn, where man after man was chained to the walls. In the country, prisons were usually makeshift and crude affairs. Theodore shook his head disapprovingly. In all his travels abroad he'd never seen people treated as inhumanely as they were in English prisons. Of course, he'd seen natives cannibalized, scalped, and sacrificed on burning biers, but never chained like this and left to rot like animals.

Theodore blinked against the darkness, his eyes finally settling on one striking prisoner.

He was not sullen like the others, or bowed, or beaten. Aloof would best describe him. His face was sun-darkened, but not weathered. His hair was a mass of short, unruly black locks. His features were noticeably elegant— high cheeks nearly gaunt below the ridge, long Roman nose, and artfully crafted lips. The very sort of darkly romantic features Caroline would find attractive. The very kind, in fact, that she'd worshiped in that portrait of Lord Hamilton.

"Who is that?" Theodore said, pointing to the handsome man in chains.

The gaoler's eyes widened. "Why, that's him! That's the one I told you about. Robbin Roger."

"He'll do very nicely, thank you."

The gaoler gave him a surly, sidelong glance. "You're

sure of yourself, ain't you? Don't want to talk to the ruffian first?"

Theodore gritted his teeth at the gaoler's persistent doubts.

"My good man," he replied smoothly, arching one imperious brow, "I have dined with kings, queens, tribal chieftains, and cannibals. I have seen natives who talk gibberish learn to speak the king's English better than you ever will, and I have seen noble gentleman turn into savages when backed into a corner. I have no doubt of my abilities to judge human nature. Now release this man at once and I will be off! Or was a sovereign not enough for your pains?"

The gaoler stared at him slack-jawed as he tried to determine whether or not he'd been insulted. Leaving that conundrum for another day, he snorted and rubbed his crusty nose. "Awright, then, you can have him. Good riddance, I say."

He went to the prisoner in question and released his shackles. The man called Robbin Roger rubbed the raw flesh at his wrists and regarded the men suspiciously. The gaoler whipped out a knife and pressed the tip into his throat.

"Now see here, Robbin Roger," he snarled, "or whoever you are, you obey yourself, right? This good doctor here has paid a pretty penny for your freedom. Lud knows why. So don't make him regret it or you'll end up back in here and hanging from a noose quicker than I can say Jack Ketch, understand?"

The keen, black eyes of the prisoner narrowed, then he nodded, but gave no more quarter than that.

"Good then!" Theodore burst out. "Come, my man. Let us quench our considerable thirsts!"

•　•　•

Lucas Davin's first sight of daylight came when the gaoler kicked open the door at the end of a long corridor and poked his back with the tip of his knife.

"Go on, bleedin' bugger. Out with you." The gaoler gave him a boot in the hindquarters.

Lucas staggered out into the open. The light jabbed his eyes and he jolted back with a start. The fresh air pinched his lungs and he coughed. He steadied his breath and creaked open his eyes, but all he could see was mist. It filled and soothed his lungs.

"Bad day for traveling, eh, Dr. Cavendish?" the gaoler remarked.

The distinguished-looking gentleman who had apparently sprung Lucas from prison did not answer. He stepped forward and disappeared into the mist that hugged the land. Then Lucas heard a second voice.

"Ready, sir?"

"Yes," the doctor replied.

A door creaked open, and several horses wickered impatiently. They must be going by carriage, Lucas thought, though he didn't see one. The air was so thick with fog he wouldn't be able to see a castle if one dropped in front of him.

"Come along, lad," the doctor said, then reappeared from the enveloping fog like a kindly apparition. He held out a hand and a welcoming smile softened his deep brown eyes and rosy, round cheeks.

Lucas sneered at him. He hated rich nobs like this who thought they could buy the poor and then feel sorry for them. Before long he'd expect Lucas to grovel before him. This doctor would soon find out, though, that Lucas was his own man. He would escape when they were out of sight of the gaol. Escaping was his specialty.

"Come along, young man."

"Right then," Lucas said, and, walking into the mist,

found himself faced with the finest carriage he'd ever seen. He glimpsed his own scruffy reflection on its polished black surface and hesitated. He frowned at the luxurious green velvet seat and rubbed his dirty hands on the legs of his breeches.

"Go on, lad," the doctor said. "You are most welcome. I am eager to have you as my guest."

Lucas shot him a hard look over his shoulder. Why? he wondered. Why was this stranger being so kind? He couldn't very well escape until he found out that much at least. He glanced at the handsome landau, then an astonishing sight greeted him. A black manservant wearing a meticulous white cravat and long dark tails came around the carriage from the other side. He wore a white wig, which made his shiny black skin seem all the darker. His perceptive eyes took in everything with a quiet calm.

"Good afternoon, sir," he said without so much as a trace of an accent. He sounded like the bloody king.

Lucas couldn't speak for a moment. He'd never seen a black man before.

"This is Shabala, Mr. Davin. I dispensed with the usual footmen and coachman. Shabala is most discreet and perfect for this mission. He's ready to take us away when you are ready to leave."

Lucas tore his gaze away from Shabala and looked away nonchalantly. It wouldn't do to let this chap know he hadn't seen everything in the world. He climbed in and sank down into an unbelievably plush velvet seat. When the doctor sat opposite him, Shabala shut the door and took the reins. He snapped a whip and four horses lurched forward. Urged back by the forward motion, Lucas sank against the banquette and heaved his first sigh of relief.

"So where are we going, mate?"

The doctor's warm eyes twinkled with adventure.

"Where would you like to go? Any favorite taverns where we might quaff a pint or two?"

Lucas sneered. "Don't know much about this godforsaken country."

The doctor chuckled. "If you don't fancy this locale, my good man, you might have a fit of the vapors when you see where we're going. You are not from Cragmere, are you?"

Lucas shook his head, gazing out the window as they drove over a country road.

"You are from London, if I am any judge of your accent."

"The gaoler told you that." Lucas's gaunt cheeks narrowed as he pursed his lips with visible distrust.

The doctor nodded and smiled. "Yes, he did. But I would have recognized your accent even if he hadn't. Are you aware that speech patterns vary according to geography?"

Lucas blinked slowly. So this man thought he was an idiot. It was better that way. Never let the rich know just how smart you are, Robbin Roger had always told him.

"You do not like me very much, do you, Mister . . . Roger, was it?"

"Davin. Lucas Davin."

The doctor nodded with satisfaction. "I thank you for your honesty regarding your identity. We will have to learn to trust each other, Mr. Davin. My name is Theodore Cavendish."

He held out a hand for a shake. When Lucas merely turned his bored gaze out the window again, Theodore tried a different approach.

"You do not like being bought at any price, Mr. Davin. I know that about you already. I saw it in your eyes the very moment I met you. I can tell you have a great deal of pride. That will serve you well in the coming weeks, as long as you do not let it get in the way of progress."

Lucas knew the doctor was being vague just to pique his interest. And it worked. Reluctantly, he turned a hostile eye to the plump man opposite him. "What kind of progress?"

"I am going to conduct a little experiment with you."

Lucas glanced out the window at the passing mist. His brow puckered with a frown and he looked back at Theodore with a hard glint in his eyes. "So yer one of those daft doctors who buy body parts so yer can study the bones? If so, mine ain't for sale. If yer wanted to practice cutting on me, yer should have let me hang and then buy me cadaver from Jack Ketch. That's what happens to all criminals in the end, ain't it? They end up a pincushion for a surgeon's knife."

The doctor grimaced and shook his head. "No, no, dear boy. I am not a surgeon. I would never do such a thing to you. I assure you I have the greatest respect for human life. You see, in addition to being a physician, I am an adventurer. I study foreign cultures and write treatises on the subject. The kind of experiment I had in mind is far more pleasant. We are going to see if we can fool Society for a little while."

Lucas's eyes widened in surprise, and then he grinned.

Theodore smiled. "I thought that might interest you."

"What have yer got planned, mate?"

"I will tell you all about it just as soon as we reach the Maiden's Head. It's the last sign of civilization before we enter Cragmere Moor."

A half hour later they were crammed into a corner table in the crowded tavern, where loose women and lusty men danced closely to the steady rhythm of a fiddle. Laughter nearly drowned out the music, and smoke from several dozen pipes burned Lucas's nostrils in a comforting way. Soon the stench of the gaol was forgotten and his good humor returned.

"Do you think you could imitate a gentleman, Mr. Davin?" Theodore said after the barmaid brought them two glasses of gin. "Do you know anything about the Quality?"

"I know plenty," Lucas said in a low, cocky voice. He sipped from his glass, rolling the springy cheap liquor over his tongue like a gentleman passing judgment on a fine imported wine, then swallowed audibly. "And what I see I don't like, mate, that I don't."

"I suppose envy incapacitates your ability to appreciate your betters."

Anger swirled with the gin in Lucas's belly. He leaned forward in hostile intimacy and jabbed the air with a forefinger. "They ain't better. They're just richer—and fancier. They serve their purpose."

"This is true of most cultures. Well, then, I hope you will not mind toasting to each and his own purpose in life."

Theodore raised his glass, and after a moment of reluctance Lucas raised his with a sardonic smile. Then he tossed back the entire contents in one swallow.

"Well, well," Theodore said, raising his hand to order another round, "a man does work up a thirst in the gaol. Tell me, Davin, what is a rich man's purpose in your estimation? Is it to provide you with ill-gotten money?"

Lucas's dark eyebrows gathered like a storm over his eyes. "I ain't ashamed of what I do. I have me reasons."

Theodore crossed his arms and waited until the barmaid delivered another gin before speaking. Lucas cradled the glass in his dirty hands.

"What are your reasons?"

Lucas looked up at him, then his antagonism eased. Theodore Cavendish seemed different from the other Society gents. Lucas instinctively liked him. And, as the gaoler said, he'd paid a pretty penny to free Lucas from that stinking prison, so perhaps he did owe the good doctor some sort of explanation.

"I steal 'cause people are counting on me."

"Your gang of thieves, no doubt."

"Yer can think what yer like." Lucas squinted through the haze at his benefactor and took another swallow of gin. It was already going to his head. He hadn't eaten in days. But he'd be damned if he'd ask for food.

"Have you ever been foxhunting, Mr. Davin?"

Lucas sat back against his chair, his jaw tightening with mockery. "Oh, bloody right. I just finished a hunt with Earl Lily Liver. But I caught meself a minx instead—his daughter. I'm taking the milk-and-water miss to Gretna Green on the morrow. Just after we have a little game of whist and a roll in the hay."

Theodore blinked thoughtfully at the onslaught of Lucas's sarcasm and swirled a taste of warm gin around on his tongue. He swallowed and stared fully at his companion.

"Perhaps I should rephrase that. Would you *like* to go foxhunting?"

Lucas suddenly pictured Germaine House and remembered his instant and insane desire to have it for his own. To be a part of a life that could never be his. He gripped his glass, strangling it as if it were the fantasy that mocked all he had ever stood for.

"No. I'd rather die than have any part of your bloody Society. And that includes killing little foxes."

"Ah, but then you have never experienced the thrill of the hunt. You've never enjoyed the sensation of smoking a cheroot and drinking brandy after a delicious meal of poached salmon, marrow pâtés, and *fricandeau à l'oseille*. Or have you?"

"What do yer think, covey?" Lucas raised his upper lip in a sneer.

Theodore leaned closer. "I would not condemn a style of living I have not experienced, my good man. And I do believe you are good deep down, Davin. At least you would be if you had enough salmon and venison in your belly to keep you from coveting that of others, and if you were exposed to proper influences. And that is what I am offering you. The right influences. I want you to come with me to a lovely country estate and there we will discuss your future."

"What do I have to do for this . . . *honor?*"

"You have to act the part of a gentleman for a fortnight or so, and then enjoy a lifelong income for your pains."

"And what is this country estate?"

"It is called Fallingate."

"Fallingate!" Lucas nearly choked on his gin. The liquor ripped down his throat and made his eyes water. He'd come all the way from London to view Fallingate from a distance—that and Germaine House—but he'd been arrested first, and here he was about to be escorted through the front door like a country squire. Feeling the effects of his drink, he threw back his head and barked out richly ironic laughter. Ignoring the amused stare of his benefactor, he laughed until his gut ached. At last, he held his aching belly and sighed. He couldn't have planned it better.

"When do we start off?"

Theodore raised his drink in the air. "Let us have a bit more to drink, first. Shall we?"

Lucas grinned and raised his glass. "To your health, Dr. Cavendish. To your beautiful, blessed health."

Six

aroline paced anxiously in her bedroom by the light of a single candle. The room needed every ray the meager flame could spurt, for there was no moon tonight. Waves of rain rolled over the moor and lashed the house like a whip. The inclement weather only added to her concern. Theodore should have returned by now. Had he run off a muddy road along the moor?

Wham! Her window flew open with a burst of wind. Caroline gasped with a start, then rushed to close it, squinting when rain splattered her cheeks. Lord, what weather! She forced the window shut and latched it more carefully, heaving a sigh of relief. But then an uncanny sensation curled down her spine with a shiver. Someone was watching her. She was sure of it. She squinted through the tree branches that troubled her view of the drive down below. There was no one outside. She whirled around. Oh, it was just him, she realized, hugging herself. Barrett Hamilton. No matter where she stood, it always seemed his eyes were trained on her, watching over her like a guardian devil.

She'd noticed it more than ever lately. It was as if he was displeased with her for some reason.

"I ought to take you down!" she snapped at the portrait, wagging a finger at it. "Yes, that is precisely what I will do. As soon as my new husband arrives, I will have you removed to the library, where you hung when my father was alive. Whatever possessed me to put you in my bedroom after his death is beyond me. Why, I—"

"What, ho!" A faint voice rose above the wailing wind.

Caroline halted in her tracks and listened hard. The soft rumble of wheels on gravel rose briefly above the clamor.

"He is here!" she whispered. "Dr. Cavendish is here . . . with my husband!"

She started for the door, then turned back to the painting. The gloating, simmering . . . *sexy* painting. "And not a word from you this time, do you hear? At least not until I am legally wed. In fact, then I will be delighted to have you chase him off, but not until you hear wedding bells!"

She ran down the stairs only to find that the ever-prepared Amanda Plumshaw was calmly waiting in the entrance hall while Feathers the butler and his footmen scurried into place. "You heard?" Caroline asked her.

Amanda's green eyes locked significantly with hers. "Yes, I've been waiting."

"Hurry along. Yes, yes, that's it," Feathers ordered his underlings. "Dr. Cavendish has returned."

When he opened the door, the women took a step back to avoid the slash of horizontal rain. The outline of a carriage on the circular drive was just barely visible in the downpour, and then only when flashes of lightning lit the sky. With her heart pounding in her throat, Caroline watched as two figures emerged from the carriage.

"He is here," came her choked whisper. "Amanda, my husband is here."

"What will we tell the servants?" Amanda whispered

tightly in return. "Where will we say he came from?"

"From Africa. We will say Dr. Cavendish met him abroad."

Dr. Cavendish and the other man ascended the front steps, staggering from one side to the other.

"What is wrong with them? Are they ill?" Amanda asked.

Caroline frowned. "I don't know."

Finally, the rain-drenched men stood in the doorway. Caroline looked from Theodore to the shabbily dressed man next to him. A rather handsome face peeked out from a scraggly mop of black curls. The dirty fellow had flung his arm around the physician's shoulders, apparently for purchase. Both men's cheeks were flushed pink, and suddenly the entrance hall reeked of gin.

"Devil!" Caroline gasped. "They're foxed!"

Theodore wiped the dripping rain from his face, then smiled with tipsy triumph.

"Miss Caroline Wainwright," he announced exuberantly, "meet your new husband. Lucas Davin."

With that, the scruffy stranger smiled at her, eyes ablur, then fell flat on his face with a resounding thud.

A quarter of an hour later, after the footmen carried Lucas off for a thorough bath, and after Theodore had doffed his drenched boots and greatcoat, Caroline dragged him into the drawing room. He took one look at her and Amanda—both white-faced and stiff-backed—and poured two generous glasses of port.

"Here, dear ladies, drink this. You will feel much better if you do. Mind if I join you?"

"I should think you have had enough already, Uncle Teddy." Caroline took her glass with trembling fingers and sipped heartily, welcoming the warmth as the liquor trailed to her belly. She didn't imbibe often, but believed that at the proper moment spirits could work wonders.

"Fear not, my dear," Theodore said. "I am not inebriated. But your husband-to-be is unquestionably apedrunk."

"That much was obvious," Amanda said dryly, and shook her head when he offered her a glass.

"The devil take pragmatism, Mrs. Plumshaw. Drink up. Doctor's orders."

He bent a strong look of concern on her. Startled by his warm attention, she took the glass in spite of her natural reserve.

"What do we do with him now?" Caroline asked.

"First, I plan to smoke. Do you mind?" Theodore said, holding out a case of cheroots. "I know a gentleman never smokes in front of ladies, but under the circumstances . . ."

"Go right ahead," Amanda said, sipping her port. "The ghastly odor will remind me this is real and not the nightmare that it seems."

Hiding a smile from the prim, but still lovely, governess, Theodore took a twig from the fire and lit a cheroot, puffing intently, then exhaled a breath of smoke with satisfaction.

"Well, I did it!" He thumped his chest with satisfaction. "I hope you are happy with my choice, dear girl."

"Of course I am, Uncle Teddy," Caroline replied, then sighed forlornly. "Just because he looks like a chimney sweep who has outgrown his trade does not mean he cannot be . . . reformed . . . as you would put it."

"He looks like a murderer," Amanda declared, swilling down her glass of port with uncharacteristic abandon.

"Well, he is not," Theodore said, leaning an arm elegantly on the mantel. "He is a horse thief."

"A horse thief!" Caroline gasped. "Are horse thieves dangerous?"

"They are if you're a horse." Theodore chuckled. "Have

no fear, my dear, he will look like a neck-or-nothing young blood of the fancy once he's been cleaned. For a poor lad, he has strikingly aristocratic features. You will see what I mean after he has a bath."

"His bath." Caroline blushed at the very idea of him naked. "What on earth will we do with him after his bath?"

"You are certainly not going to let him have carte blanche in the house," Amanda answered decisively. "He will steal the silver."

"But I cannot very well treat him as a prisoner, Amanda. The servants will realize he is not an ordinary guest and begin to gossip."

"I suggest you put him in your rooms." Theodore regarded Caroline seriously through a plume of acrid, white smoke. "Or at least your dressing room. As I recall, the main bedchamber has adjoining dressing rooms on either side, one for the lady and one for the master of the house."

"My rooms? You cannot be serious. He might . . . he might . . . he will try to . . . what if he . . . ?"

Theodore grinned mischievously. "That is a natural part of marriage, dear girl."

"But not *this* marriage. This is a marriage in name only. I thought that was understood."

"Be that as it may, you will want others to think you have consummated your union. Particularly George. If he doubts the legitimacy of this match, he might challenge your claim to Fallingate, even if you have a wedding license."

Caroline sighed, recognizing the truth of his words. "I suppose I did not think this aspect through to its natural conclusion."

"If Lucas Davin sleeps in your chamber tonight," Theodore said, "then the servants will assume he is your lover. George, of course, will hear about it from Feathers."

"He will?" Caroline asked, frowning.

"Of course, my dear! The butler has always given reports of your affairs to your brother. Don't tell me you weren't aware of that."

"I daresay I wasn't," she replied indignantly.

"Once he hears about it, George will *want* to see you married to avoid a scandal. Why not let Lucas Davin in your bed tonight while he is too drunk to even think about trying anything overly familiar. The servants will assume the worst, and if he asks them on the sly about what happened, they'll confirm his lascivious assumptions. If the servants gossip outside the walls of Fallingate, what will it matter as long as you marry promptly? You wouldn't be the first young lady to succumb to her fiancé's blandishments before the ceremony. Others will simply pass off the rumor as the *on-dit* of bored servants."

Caroline mulled this over as she paced, trying to sort fact from fiction. Finally, she halted and smiled in amazement. "By Jove, I think it will work. Uncle Teddy, you are a genius!"

"And what of tomorrow night?" Amanda argued. "And the night after that?"

"I will tell Mr. Davin that our union has already been consummated. He has done his duty and he can jolly well slake his passions elsewhere, like any other fine gentleman. Before he knows it, he will be sailing to India or Africa and I will never see him again."

She ran to Theodore and kissed his cheek. "Thank you, dear man. I knew you would save me!"

"Caroline," he said with a sudden frown, grasping both her arms with his hands. "There is still one last piece of the puzzle to be put in place. I have not quite told him about the marriage."

"What?" Blood drained from her face. "What did you tell him?"

"I told him we want him to play the part of a gentleman.

He doesn't hold a very high opinion of Society, and I was afraid if I mentioned anything as permanent as marriage, he would be off and running. We can tell him about it tomorrow. Once he has a good look at your home, I think he'll agree to the arrangement. A thief would have a hard time resisting the lure of this kind of wealth." He waved a hand at the enormous seventeenth-century paintings that lined the walls in their gilt frames, the elegant furniture, and the objets d'art scattered throughout the room.

"Very well, Uncle Teddy. You know best. Now you are sure he is too inebriated to . . . to try anything tonight?"

Theodore nodded. "I was very careful to make sure that we did not leave the tavern until he was barely able to stand. You are safe . . . at least for tonight."

"I hope you are right."

"And if I am not," he added with a chuckle, "then the ghost of Lord Barrett Hamilton will protect you."

"Oh, dear," Caroline said, picturing Lucas Davin in her bed and Barrett Hamilton hanging on the wall opposite, watching them all night long. "I do hope Lord Hamilton won't be jealous."

"Do not be silly," Amanda reasoned. "We do not believe in ghosts." When there was no immediate response, Amanda looked from one to the other. "Do we?"

"No," Theodore replied distractedly.

"Of course not," Caroline replied, a bit more emphatically than necessary.

The wind howled suddenly. Caroline wondered if she was the only one who noticed how much it sounded like a voice. An angry, jealous voice.

Seven

When Caroline went upstairs, she found Biddie standing in front of her bedroom door, looking befuddled and muttering to herself. The two chambermaids, Mary and Maggie McGruder, were all atwitter down at the far end of the hall. It seemed that her household had turned into chaos from the moment Lucas Davin crossed the threshold.

"There you are!" Biddie said in a rush when she spotted Caroline. "Oh, Miss Wainwright! Oh, dear! Upon my word, I cannot believe my own eyes! There is a *man* in your room. Surely there must be some mistake. Someone from Africa, I hear?"

"That is correct, Biddie," Caroline calmly replied, and reached for the door.

"Oh, no, miss! You mustn't go in. They . . . they undressed him. Bathed him. A stranger! Naked in your room!"

"He may be a stranger, Biddie, but he will not be one for long. Soon he will be my husband."

Biddie sucked in a quivering gasp of air loud enough to

rival the wind outside. Two echoing gasps sounded from the girls, trying to hide in the shadows at the end of the hall.

"There is nothing to worry about," Caroline said loudly enough for all to hear. "Everything is in order."

Caroline could tell from the dead silence that followed that no one in her audience was convinced of this. She sighed. At least Biddie deserved some explanation. Though she was old and had never been privy to her mistress's most private thoughts, Biddie had been a loyal servant and needed to know what was happening in order to calm the rest of the staff.

Caroline gently touched her arm. "Though Mr. Davin is a stranger, Biddie, he comes to me highly recommended by Dr. Cavendish. And that is good enough for me. You know I have to marry by my birthday, dear. If I lose Fallingate, you and all the others will be let go by Mrs. Wainwright. If I remain, your positions are secure. So I must marry Mr. Davin, for your sake if not my own. Do you understand?"

Biddie's eyes widened with understanding. "Oh, yes, miss, when you put it that way I understand completely."

"Good. Now try to make the others understand as well, won't you?"

"Yes, miss."

Caroline sighed and gave the older woman a quick hug. "I knew you would understand."

Just when she'd thought she had the servants under control, Caroline opened her bedroom door and found a crowd of men around her bed. Feathers stood officiously in the center. Beside him stood Neville, the jockey-sized valet she should have let go six years earlier when George married Prudence. Neville looked puffed up and enormously important now that he actually had a gentleman to dress again. Henry, the first footman, looked on dubiously, and beside him stood James and John Blackwood, twin brothers who served as pages under Henry.

She was suddenly anxious about their scrutiny of Mr. Davin. They'd already had a better glimpse of him than she herself. Would they find fault? Would they see his lack of good breeding before he'd even uttered a word? She had her answer when she cleared her throat and they all looked up at her with stunned expressions that seemed to say, "Whatever do you have in mind to do with this rogue?"

At the sight of their betrayed and dumbfounded expressions, irritation flashed through her. Her servants had no right to have any opinions whatsoever on any decision she chose to make. And to the extent that they did have such opinions was simply owing to her allowing them more liberties than she should have. She'd been far too indulgent of a mistress, she could see that now. But such self-reproach wouldn't solve her immediate problem. She had to get rid of them somehow.

"Is he . . . bathed?" Her throat tightened around the word and it came out like a squeak.

"Yes, miss," Feathers said.

Lucas Davin lay peacefully in the center of the bed, his hands folded over his chest, which was swathed in an expensive white ruffled linen shirt. His raven-black hair was splayed across an equally white pillow. Caroline approached the bed briskly so as not to give away her terror, but could not mask her astonishment at the transformation a bath and a shave had wrought.

"He looks as peaceful as a . . . a corpse," she remarked.

"If so, miss," Feathers replied drolly, "then that is an improvement. He did rouse momentarily in the bath, however, before falling asleep again. He has been shaved and bathed from head to toe, and Henry had to do a bit of scrubbing."

"I dressed him in Mr. George's old finery, mish," Neville said importantly, the words lisping through the gap in his front teeth. "Did I do right, mish? Did I?"

"Yes, Neville, he looks splendid."

"Anything else, miss?" Feathers intoned.

"No, that will be all." This implied dismissal did not work as it usually did. The servants made no move to go. It was as if the normally discreet members of her staff were so agog, they could not leave without some sort of explanation. Well, she would shock them into leaving if she had to. She might as well start her Banbury story here and now. There was no going back at this point.

"My . . . *lover* . . ." she said haltingly, "was captured by thieves and held in a place I cannot even bring myself to mention. He is not usually so disheveled. Dirty . . . and . . . drunk . . . and . . . why he . . . he's from Africa, you know, and . . ."

She stopped babbling when she realized Feathers and his four underlings were all gaping at her with slack jaws. Apparently the notion that she might have taken a lover was so shocking that they were unable to recover their usual masks of indifference. At first she blushed, then flushed with indignation.

"Good heavens! Is it so bloody inconceivable that I should have a lover, Mr. Feathers?"

Several of the men gasped, whether because she'd cursed and shown anger or because she'd admitted to a sexual indiscretion, she knew not.

"You may close your mouths, one and all, and go. If I need anything I will ring."

The men all mumbled their acquiescence, then shuffled out the door. She could only wonder what Feathers would tell George. She'd have to tell Davey to make sure there weren't any horses available to the staff. She didn't want

Feathers sending news of Lucas Davin's arrival to Knowlton Park. At least not for a few days.

When the door finally closed, she was alone with her thoughts and the man she was to marry. She could scarcely wait to feast her eyes on what promised at first glance to be a very handsome man.

"Mr. Davin?" she whispered as she crept toward the bed like the mouse her brother always claimed her to be.

The rain had now settled to a dull, steady beat and drowned out her footsteps. There was no real danger of waking him. When she reached the bed, she pulled the lamp closer to his face and drew in a slow breath.

Feathers was right. There had been an astonishing improvement in Mr. Davin's appearance. Dressed in a fresh shirt and clean trousers, he almost looked the part of a gentleman. How sad that he was not, nor ever could be, Uncle Teddy's efforts not withstanding. No matter how much they taught this horse thief, he would never truly rise above his station. She knew that all too well. She was a gentleman's daughter and had had the inviolability of class distinctions very thoroughly drummed into her by parents who'd once had hopes that their money might buy Caroline's way into the nobility.

Why had this lowly but handsome man chosen a life of crime? No doubt there was some flaw in his character.

"Mr. Davin?" she said, wanting to make sure he was truly abed for the night. A little louder she added, "Are you comfortable, Mr. Davin?"

He didn't move a muscle. He was thoroughly unconscious. Uncle Teddy had been correct in his assessment. Lucas Davin would not revive until the morning. She sighed with relief and sat down on the bed for closer examination, pushing her spectacles up to the bridge of her nose with a forefinger.

She scarcely breathed as she surveyed the slender yet

muscular length of him. The first thing that struck her was his absolute masculinity. His well-honed shoulders pressed against the constraints of his shirt. Muscles bulged at his chest like breastplates of steel. A crop of dark hair peeked out from the V-shaped opening of his shirt. His skin was tanned everywhere that she could see. And she blushed to imagine the color of the flesh hidden from her eyes.

She found her gaze drawn to his wild crop of hair. It was unrepentantly black, just like Lord Hamilton's. *Just like Barrett Hamilton.* A chill crept down her arms and she stole a glance over her shoulder at the portrait on the opposite wall. She then realized that both Lord Hamilton and Lucas Davin sported clefts in their chins. She looked back at Lucas, suddenly seeing him in a more intimate light.

"That clever Uncle Teddy," she whispered. "He wanted to make sure I would fall in love with his experiment, so he picked a man who looked remotely like Barrett Hamilton."

But Lucas Davin was more than a pawn in Theodore's chess game. He was a man. A man whom, under different circumstances, she might actually embrace, even kiss. A man who might hold her close, caress her breasts, do all the forbidden things she'd wondered about while reading her romantic novels. Things that she never dared to dream of for herself. She sucked in a long draft of air and noticed the pleasant whiff of soap lingering on his skin.

She allowed her gaze to wander down his chest to the narrow waist and the snug trousers that her servants had managed to pull on him. The taut material only accentuated the masculine bulge above his thighs. A peculiar tingle twisted up from the depths of her body and shook her shoulders with a sudden chill.

"Lord!" she whispered, ashamed at her longing. Then, realizing he was fully dressed, she cried, "Oh, Lord!"

Mr. Davin would never believe they'd consummated a

relationship if he woke on the morrow with all his clothes on.

"I should have told the servants . . ."

What could she have told them? Leave him naked so I can have my way with him? She would have to undress him somehow. She reached out to touch him, but feeling the heat that rose from his skin, she fairly swooned at the prospect. It was one thing to read about strapping, handsome men. Men who were a little wild and dark. It was another thing altogether to think about undressing one in her own bed.

Prickling from embarrassment, she leaped to her feet and raced to the door. Flinging it open, she found herself face-to-face with the very man she'd hoped to find.

"Uncle Teddy! Thank heavens it's you. I need—"

He waved her silent and jerked his head toward the end of the hall. "The servants are listening," he whispered.

Caroline followed his motion and saw Biddie and the McGruder girls, as well as Neville and the twins, all trying to look as if they were doing something other than eavesdropping.

"I was about to knock, dear girl," Theodore said loudly for their benefit, then added softly for her ears alone, "Whisper. What do you need?"

"Mr. Davin is fully clothed," she said *sotto voce*. "Shouldn't he be . . . in a state of dishabille?"

He nodded in agreement, then added loudly, "What is that you say? Mr. Davin wants another drink? Why, that liquorish rogue. He certainly knows how to put the gin away." He opened the bedroom door. "Let me talk to the dear boy. Mr. Davin! You are feeling better, I hear."

When Theodore shut the door behind him, Caroline called out. "Biddie, I am ready to undress. Let's enter the dressing room through the hallway door."

Biddie was at heart a lady's maid. Even after she'd been

promoted to housekeeper, she refused to let any of the maids dress her mistress. She came as she was bidden, shaking her head the entire way.

"You are not going to spend the night with him, are you, miss?" Biddie whispered as they made their way into the dressing room.

Caroline frowned and plucked the bag cap from her head, shaking out her long locks of brown hair. "Why do all my servants think they can make their opinions known in the most impertinent fashion? It is not proper."

"It is because you treat us all as family, miss." Biddie's loving smile faded as she added, "At least that's what Mrs. Wainwright always says."

"Well, if it weren't for Mrs. Wainwright, I would not be sleeping with Mr. Davin at all."

Biddie frowned up at her in complete confusion.

"Never mind. Help me undress."

The feminine dressing chamber, equal in size to her sleeping room, was flounced with pretty laces and peach satins, scattered with elegantly embroidered chairs, and adorned with expensive cabinets filled with delicate china pieces and curios. Caroline removed her jewelry while Biddie opened the wardrobe. As Biddie began to unbutton Caroline's frock, they heard the physician's muffled one-sided conversation through the closed door that separated them.

"No, I will not give you another drink!" Theodore boomed. "You have had plenty." There was a pause. "What? You plan to sleep in Caroline's bed tonight?"

Falling for the doctor's ruse, Biddie let out a little gasp. Her hands began to tremble and she couldn't finish her task.

"You poor dear," Caroline said, unbuttoning the rest for her. "It's all right, Biddie. Just ignore Dr. Cavendish."

"Yes, miss," she answered in a quivering voice as she

helped Caroline out of her gown, corset, and chemise. The housekeeper carefully hung the garments while Caroline slipped into her nightgown.

"I speak for her late father, young man," the doctor's voice continued, penetrating through the adjoining door. "But I am more eccentric than he was. In Africa I saw natives' wives go about bare-breasted."

At this, Biddie whirled to face the door through which the scandalous words had traveled, turning deathly pale. Caroline gripped her elbow. "Steady, my dear Biddie. Gently now."

"So it is not a shock to me if you want to bed Caroline," Theodore continued. "Just so long as you make amends on the morrow. I fully expect you to make your intentions to marry known. Then, of course, a hasty wedding will be necessary."

Biddie began to weep. Caroline gently nudged the old woman down into a chair, furtively glaring at the door. Theodore was certainly overdoing it.

"What?" he continued, grunting now and then, presumably as he struggled to undress the rag-doll figure on Caroline's bed. "You say you have already purchased a license? What forethought, my good man! Now you will not have to go through the embarrassing process of waiting three weeks for the crying of the banns."

Biddie was openly sobbing now. "If your poor mother were alive today—"

"But she isn't, Biddie."

"I should have quit my position long ago. I am too old for this."

"Go to sleep, dear heart. I will let myself in the room. You have had enough. Go on, then."

Biddie nodded and dabbed at her eyes. "Very well, miss, if you insist."

"And tell Feathers he should retire as well. I do not want

to find out on the morrow that any prying ears have been pressed to my door tonight."

Biddie stopped to consider this and, apparently imagining what one might hear if one did eavesdrop in such a manner, broke into a renewed round of sobbing, rushing out the door.

When Caroline entered her bedroom through the adjoining door, she found a perspiring Dr. Cavendish tucking the blankets around a naked Mr. Davin's waist. He dusted his hands and then patted his moist brow with a kerchief.

"Well, that is that. How did I do?"

"I fancy that you were splendid. And should you ever give up your adventures abroad, you might consider a career as an actor at Drury Lane."

"The stage has been set, there is no question," he said with obvious excitement. "Now I leave the rest in your hands. I suggest that in the morning you wake up before Mr. Davin, but remain in the room until he has a good look at you in your nightclothes. Then invite him to breakfast and make a hasty retreat into your dressing room. He will know he was drunk enough not to remember what happened tonight and will doubt his own recollections. If you imply that you did the deed, he should accept your interpretation of the evening with little trouble. I will tell Cook to get busy preparing a feast. The poor boy will need some nourishing food to restore his aching head. He will be so pleased by the repast he will be disinclined to question his hostess. You can do it, Caro! Have faith."

With that he kissed her on the forehead and hastened out of the room. Caroline turned slowly. Oh, so slowly. And considered climbing into bed. But one look at Mr. Davin's unflaggingly masculine chest made her decide otherwise. She curled into a chair by the lamp and began to read.

3 May, 1521

I can hardly believe Providence hath been so kind. Tonight I went to a masque at Harding Castle and met the fairest maid in all of Christendom, the daughter of the Earl of Penwich, Lady Rachel Harding. I saw her dancing a carol from across the great hall. With her grand ruff collar and a sapphire-blue bodice to match her dazzling eyes, she twirled around with uncommon grace, an exotic fairy mask flirtatiously hiding the upper half of her visage.

I watched her through the crowd, and knew in that moment my destiny. For I will have her. I, a mere merchant's son, who contrived my way into the castle behind my harlequin's mask, will one day be worthy of an earl's daughter. I will live but one life, and I will settle for no less than the woman I love. And I know now, at first sight, that Rachel is she.

"May I dance with thee, my lady?" I said, coming between her and her dancing partner a short time later. I immediately recognized the man I had rudely displaced as the Baron Wilmington. His manly pride bristled behind me. But I scarcely heard the murmurs of disapproval. All I cared about was her—her two intense blue eyes studying me through her fairy mask as if she had never seen a creature so bold.

"Will I dance with thee?" she said in her lilting, flirtatious manner. "If thou must ask, then thou must surely know the answer."

"Aye, I do," I said, brave beyond all measure. "I know the answer, and the answer is not what thou might think."

Just then the minstrels struck up a tune for La Volta. I scooped my strong arm around her waist and moved her about the floor as if our every motion had thus been planned by God Himself. In all my seven and ten years on earth, nothing hath ever felt so perfect. When the time came, I put my hands upon her waist and lifted her high in the air with all the other dancers. When the dance was over, I led her to an alcove, alone at last.

"Take off thy mask, my lady," I implored her.

When she refused, I kissed her, finding her sweet lips beneath our halfmasks, tasting more sweet than the ripest berry in high summer. My mind whirled. We swooned. And we then both knew what we would mean to each other—everything. Life itself.

"Take off thy mask," I repeated.

"Nay," she said, sadly this time, for methinks she dost fear the disparity between our stations in life.

"Do not be melancholy, my lady. For one day I will be worthy of thee. I shall win honor in battle, and then I will return triumphant in the king's court. Till then, dear maiden, show me only one glimpse of thy face. I will burn the image into my mind, and like the North Star, it shall be my guide. There canst be no masks, no deception, with true love."

She snatched a little breath at the word love. *Then, shyly, she withdrew her mask. And the sapphires I had seen glittering through the eyes of her mask shone brilliant upon me with love eternal.*

Eight

The first bloody, blasted, cursed thing Lucas saw was daylight. Merciless, eye-stabbing, head-pounding daylight.

"Shut the curtains!" he roared, not knowing or caring where he was or who followed his command so long as someone stopped the blinding light from pummeling his gin-laden head.

He heard the whoosh of material and sensed a darkening in the room. Fancy that, he thought, a bit of pleasure peeking through his pain. Someone had actually done his bidding. Mollified, he creaked open one eye and recognized . . . absolutely nothing. Not the ornate four-poster canopy bed swagged with voluminous blue print draperies, or the majestic portrait on the wall opposite, or the obnoxiously pleasant odor of dried lilacs that permeated the air, or the softness of the goose-down mattress. Hell, he'd never even owned a bed.

Overwhelmed, he shut his eye. "Where am I?"

"You are at Fallingate, Mr. Davin."

The voice was soft and feminine, rich with nuance that

signaled uncommon intelligence. Nothing at all like the merry voice of the peculiar benefactor who had bought him one too many rounds of gin last night.

"Tell me why I'm here," he demanded.

"You are going to marry me."

He sat upright like a shot, then the lingering effects of gin clobbered his head and he winced. "Ow! Oh! What the bloody hell do yer mean I'm here to marry yer?"

He blinked rapidly until at last a feminine form took shape in the fog that was his brain. She approached him like an angel welcoming him into heaven. She had hair that was drawn back in a prim knot, a delicate heart-shaped face, and pale spots of blue behind studious-looking spectacles.

A faint odor of violets hit his senses again a moment later. So she was a lady. A sweet-smelling, delicate, useless thing. Oh, bloody hell, what had he gotten himself into now?

"Pardon me, ma'am," he mumbled. "I'll be gone before yer know it."

He started to throw back the covers, but realized he was naked. With uncharacteristic modesty, he yanked the sheet back over his hips. He looked up slowly, trying to make sense of things. She was actually smiling at him. And she was wearing her nightclothes! Then she leaned forward and kissed his forehead—a gesture at once bold and timid. Her lips were as soft as the petals of a damned daisy. The kiss was so sweet it almost hurt. He clamped his eyes shut and fell back onto the pillow.

Gad, he'd never drink that much again. He pried his eyes open. It was less painful this time. He gazed at her in shock. Nothing was making sense. Nothing at all.

"Y-you were wonderful, my dear," she said, her hands fidgeting at her waist. "You made my first . . . time . . . a pleasure and not the fright I feared. I hope you were . . .

satisfied . . . as well, and now I will get dressed and see
you downstairs for breakfast and I will send the valet in
to help you dress and do not forget to comb your hair
because the servants will gape and so . . ."

She was speaking in a jumbled rush, making her way
with increasing speed to what was apparently her dressing
room. Lucas sat up and opened his mouth to call her back,
but no words would come. His mouth was thick with cotton, his head pounded, and what in hell would he say anyway? He raised a hand in the air to punctuate a point, but
could not remember what it was.

When the door shut behind her, he gripped his head with
his hands. "Oh, hell! Did I *tup* the bloody wench? She
acted as if she was afraid I might do it again." He looked
accusingly down at his distinctively male anatomy. "And
I don't even *remember* it? Damme! How drunk was I?"

His head began to pound anew, telling him that he had
imbibed plenty. "That doctor said nothing about marriage,
blast him."

With his head finally clearing, Lucas looked up and
found a portrait of a distinguished-looking gent hanging
on the far wall. A fancy honeycomb ruff collar circled his
neck like a spool of white cheese. His eyes were intense
and vivid and his mouth was red and seemed to ripple with
ironic mirth. Lucas had the distinct and uncanny feeling
that this lord was glaring down at him in mockery and
disapproval.

"What's the matter with yer?" he muttered. "Not good
enough for the likes of yer? Well, I just tupped me a right
fine lady last night, I did. Even if I don't remember the
first bleeding kiss."

While waiting for Lucas to come downstairs, Caroline ate
her baked eggs in mortified silence. She was quite sure
she'd utterly failed to convince him they'd consummated

their marriage-to-be. She was clearly not the passionate type. Surely he could see that. Why had she ever imagined he might think otherwise? While she might be clever enough to fool her loyal and isolated country servants, she'd never convince a man who exuded so much sensuality. In her heart she was passionate, yes, but not in reality. She thought she'd learned that lesson long ago.

She glanced anxiously at Amanda, who sat to her left. Uncle Teddy sipped coffee to her right. All three had been remarkably quiet. They couldn't talk in front of the servants about the subject foremost on their minds—Lucas Davin. So after various futile attempts to discuss the weather, they fell silent and waited for their guest to descend.

When at last Feathers cleared his throat at the dining-room door, Caroline was poking her fork at her eggs and snapped her head up in time to see Lucas Davin make his entrance.

Her skin turned cold, and then hot, as a profound realization washed over her. Now fully dressed, with a confident demeanor and animated features, Lucas Davin was one of the most dashing men she had ever seen.

"Good Lord!" she couldn't help but whisper.

Theodore grinned from ear to ear and whispered, "I told you he would clean up well. You must trust my judgment, my dear."

At the sight of Caroline, Lucas paused. He frowned uncertainly, then flushed red. She could scarcely believe it. Was it possible he was embarrassed as well? She deemed that a very good sign. Any rogue capable of being embarrassed had to have a least some semblance of a conscience or sense of propriety.

The darkening of his complexion made his lavishly unruly jet-black locks seem particularly attractive. Cut moderately short about his head, a wild curl or two brushing the top of his collar, his hair nicely offset his cheeks, which were broad and high. His sloe eyes were unusually large and expressive. His mouth was somewhat thin, tense at the moment, she would say, but held the promise of sensuality, and his jaw was square and strong. All told he was the very picture of a Byronic hero.

The valet had deftly chosen for Lucas one of George's discarded outfits, an exquisite camel-colored riding coat. Cut high in the front, it was double-breasted, with large lapels. The long tails in the back made Lucas's striking figure look even more elegant. A deep brown waistcoat contrasted richly with the coat, and his white shirt and cravat nicely offset his complexion, which by now had settled from red to a manly, ruddy hue. All told, he couldn't have looked the part of a gentleman suitor better if he'd tried. Which he certainly hadn't.

"Well, well," said Dr. Cavendish, rising and dusting his mustache with a napkin. "If it isn't the lord of the manor himself."

Lucas's snapping black eyes fixed on him, then kindled with fire. "Look here, Dr. whatever yer called yourself. If yer think I'm going to—"

"Darling!" Caroline cried out.

At this unexpected endearment, Amanda made a squeak and covered her lips with a hand. She was no more astonished than Lucas. His eyes widened and a smile seemed to twitch at the corners of his luscious lips.

Caroline jumped up and rushed to his side. Despite the hostile and bewildered look her sudden approach inspired, she gathered all her courage and rose to her toes, planting a kiss on his surprisingly soft skin. He smelled of musk and soap, and the pleasant scent filled her with an odd pleasure.

"Darling," she said, "we should not discuss anything of importance in front of the servants, should we?"

Lucas stared at her a long moment as if she'd gone mad, then glanced around and saw the bland faces of the people who waited on these idle rich. He vaguely recognized the pompous-looking man they called Feathers standing discreetly by the door that must lead to the kitchen. There was an ornately dressed footman in an absurd powdered wig and a page or two, all doubtless looking down on him, especially since they all saw him drunk as a sot last night. Even the servants of the wealthy thought themselves better than a London slum rat. No, he didn't suppose what he had to say was any of their business.

"I suppose not," he allowed grudgingly.

"Why not eat, then, darling?" Caroline continued, emboldened by the presence of an audience, "and then we can discuss everything *privately* in the drawing room. You are hungry, aren't you?"

Lucas's traitorous stomach growled in response and he grimaced. Damn them, but they knew he was hungry. This lady and her physician and the other dame at the table all knew he'd keep his tongue if it meant he could fill his belly.

"Aye," he agreed sullenly, then added in a half whisper, "but see here, you can't shut me up at every turn just because yer have too many servants listening at every corner. Why, I—"

Her eyes pleaded over the top of her neat little spectacles, silently begging him to be quiet. He obliged her, realizing he would destroy the illusion she was so intent on creating if he didn't keep his temper. Well, he'd best go along. There was some money in it, though he'd be damned if he'd marry such a frivolous miss for all the tea in China.

"Right, Miss . . . um," he said awkwardly.

"Miss Wainwright," she offered.

"Oh, right!"

She motioned to a marble-topped mahogany sideboard against the wall. Steam rose from dishes of eggs and freshly baked bread. Lucas's mouth watered. His feet followed the direction of his hungry gaze and soon he was shoveling food onto his plate, heedless of what others might think of the portions.

When he sat down, it was all he could do to keep from wolfing down the food. He looked around, studying the others at the table. He placed a napkin in his lap, as they apparently had done, and then picked up his fork and smiled pleasantly.

"Damme, but I'm famished!"

He dug in and fairly inhaled his food, all thoughts of his hosts or propriety fleeing in the glory of this satisfying moment. When he was done, he shoved back his plate and looked up, only to find the others watching him with barely concealed wonder.

"You were quite hungry, darling?" the wide-eyed Miss Wainwright asked faintly.

Lucas ran his tongue over his teeth, leaned back in his chair and belched. "Aye, that I was."

The older woman with the ginger hair took in a tiny breath. When Lucas shot her a suspicious look, she mustered a polite smile.

"Would you like some ham, Mr. Davin?" Caroline offered.

"Would I ever."

"Henry, would you oblige Mr. Davin?" she said to the footman, who bowed and went to the kitchen, walking with arched back. While they waited in silence for Henry to return, Lucas became aware of his three companions' intense stares, and of the clock by the hearth with its loud *tick, tock, tick, tock.* He tugged at his scratchy cravat and, for want of anything else to do, began to study the leaf pattern carved into the silverware. He held it up in the sunlight, turning it over in his palm.

"Lud, this is beautiful," he remarked in his most flattering tone.

"I told you," the ginger-haired woman whispered. "He already has his eye on the silver!"

"Hush," Caroline told her.

Lucas looked from one to the other, hair bristling at his nape. "What? What's wrong? I used it right, didn't I? Held it fancy like. Didn't drop it on the floor, I didn't."

"Don't worry about these cackling hens, dear boy," Theodore reassured him with a wink as Henry returned with a tray of ham. "They are always clucking about something. Eat up! There is plenty more where that came from. Miss Wainwright is rich, my boy, very rich."

Lucas stabbed a thick slab of ham from the tray being offered to him by the servant. "Don't mind as I do, mate, seeing as how I drank too much last night. Me head is killing me."

Lucas waggled an accusing brow at the doctor and reached for his cooling coffee, which he downed in one slurping swill.

After Lucas consumed two more plates of food with formidable speed and gusto, the group made their way to the drawing room.

Caroline followed up the rear, hanging back at the door as the others continued onward. Feeling light-headed, she gripped the door frame for support. Why was she suddenly so disoriented?

She watched with a sense of unreality as Uncle Teddy guided Lucas to the drawing room with a friendly hand on his back, the two men laughing as if nothing was out of order. But in fact everything was in disarray. Her heart beat with impending doom as she realized that everything had changed the moment Lucas Davin had entered her house. Didn't anyone else realize that?

Until now, the idea of a husband had been vague. It was nothing more than a means to an end. But the idea had taken form in the body of a thief from the slums of London—a devilishly handsome one at that. This wasn't the plot of one of the gothic novels she devoured. She wasn't a character in *The Castle of Otranto* by Horace Walpole, for example, and Lucas Davin wasn't the dark and brooding hero of one of Mrs. Radcliffe's novels. He was flesh and blood, with a will of his own. He wouldn't be handled at her discretion. He might not be handled at all!

Watching him in the dining room consume breakfast as if he'd never eaten in his life, she'd been at first amazed, then painfully sympathetic. How awful it must be to be poor, she'd thought for the first time, to never know when your next meal will come. Newly aware of that uncertainty, she at once began to interpret his sullen glares not as a sign of mean character, but rather as an attempt to preserve the last vestiges of his tattered pride.

She shut her eyes tight against the stinging tears of empathy. That such a handsome and seemingly proud man should be relegated to the lowest of classes seemed so unfair!

"Caroline, are you coming?" Amanda asked.

The former governess stood in the shadows of the hall, lit only by a long narrow window at the far end. In the soft, muted daylight, Amanda appeared willowy and pretty as always, despite the passing of youth and the rigid devotion to manners that stiffened her spirit as surely as the busks that gave form to her corset. And there was something new in her expression. An aliveness that had not been there to such a degree before. She had seemed to change overnight with Dr. Cavendish's arrival. Just as Caroline had changed with Lucas's.

"Is something amiss, Caroline?"

"No." She forced a smile, which then became genuine as she felt a sudden well of excitement bubbling inside. Change could be good, couldn't it? She'd been alone and isolated for so long in the country she hardly knew what change looked like. "I am coming, Amanda. Go in and see to our guest. And have Uncle Teddy introduce you—I just realized that we've been remiss with the introductions."

Amanda disappeared around the door, and by the time Caroline had straightened her pale blue morning gown and reached the richly appointed room, Amanda was offering Lucas a delicate china cup decorated with finely painted lilies of the valley. Even from a distance, Caroline could see Lucas frown and rub his palms on his pant legs, hesitating to take the offering. Obviously he was worried about breaking the delicate ware. He felt out of place here, poor man. Perhaps he felt just as awkward with the country gentry as she had felt with the *ton*.

"No, Amanda!" Caroline cried out with such force all three of her companions gave a start. She bit her lip and blinked hard. "I am sorry . . . it is . . . it is just obvious to me that Mr. Davin does not want any more coffee."

"On the contrary," Amanda said. "He just asked for more."

"Nothing like coffee to still the head after a sodden night of gin, eh, my boy?" Theodore said with a hearty laugh, then planted a cheroot in his mouth to chew and roll around.

"But I can see he is not thirsty," Caroline insisted.

"It's all right, *darling*," Lucas said. His black eyes fixed on her as his lips twisted with a dangerous smile. "I ain't going to steal the cup any more than I'd steal your silverware. Ain't that right, Mrs. Plumshaw?"

He took the cup and riveted Amanda with an audacious glare. She blushed furiously. Caroline looked from Lucas to Amanda with dawning dread. Oh, goodness, he was certainly not a slow-top! He'd known exactly what Amanda was worried about when he'd admired the silver. Caroline was in more trouble than she'd thought.

How silly of her to worry about his discomfort. Naturally, anyone who could cut the purse of a gentleman in Piccadilly Square without getting caught would have no trouble holding delicate china. In fact his hands would be deft at many things. Blushing, she took a deep breath and came into the room.

"Shall we deal at last with this vexatious business?" she said a bit breathlessly, taking her place in an embroidered upright chair. She took her fan from an oval table and snapped it open, fluttering it at her chin. The breeze lifted wisps of dark curls from her heated temples.

"Mr. Davin, you are probably wondering what this is all about," the doctor said.

"Right, mate, that I am." Lucas crossed one leg over the other.

As Amanda offered him sweetcakes, Caroline surreptitiously noted the ripple of muscles above his knee-high boots and felt her head grow even lighter.

"No, thank you, dear lady," Lucas said to Amanda with the faintest hint of sarcasm. He took a loud, indelicate slurp of coffee.

Both women stiffened. Theodore cleared his throat and continued. "You see, my boy, our intention was to—"

He faltered when Lucas took another loud slurp. With eyes wide and mouth slightly parted, Lucas looked defensively from one to the other.

"What? What did I do? I said no thanks to Mrs. Plumshaw when she offered the cake. I didn't steal it, yer know? Ain't I supposed to be polite? Isn't that what yer bleeding fancy folk do?"

"Calm down, my boy," Theodore said. "You have done nothing wrong."

"It's nothing, Mr. Davin," Caroline said reassuringly. "It's simply your . . . manner of drinking. We will address that in the coming days."

"Oh, we will, will we?" He balanced his saucer and cup in one hand and propped his chin in the other, regarding her as a cat would watch a hopelessly trapped mouse. "I look forward to that, Miss Wainwright. I do. There's a number of things we'll sort out. Like exactly what did or didn't happen last night between us."

Caroline's throat cinched off all air. Her heart kaboomed in her chest as she was flooded with embarrassment from the toes of her kid slippers to the tips of her flaming ears.

Lucas took another sip, this time with lips perfectly poised at the rim. And he made not a sound. Not a blessed sound.

Caroline's embarrassment turned to fury. He was having a go 'round with them. Teasing them with their own rules and customs, pretending to drink like a raffish buffoon. That bright, devilish rogue!

"So," he said coolly, leaning back in his chair with the ease of a duke. "Yer were saying, Dr. Cavendish? What exactly is the bargain yer want me to strike with the devil?"

"Er, uh. . . ." Theodore pulled the moist tip of his cheroot out of this mouth and blinked at it while he found himself at an uncharacteristic loss for words. He held the cheroot up for approval. The women nodded and he went through the ritual of lighting it with a twig from the fire. The actions seemed to restore his usual equanimity and he smiled at Lucas with the camaraderie that a man could share only with another man. "You will soon find, Davin, that living in the country has its advantages over life in London. Out here we do not keep to quite the same rigid rules. A man isn't boxed on the ear for having the temerity to smoke in front of ladies. At least not in this house."

By now he had the fat bundle of tobacco glowing and smoking and spewing a nauseating smell. He turned to Lucas and squinted at him through a cloud of smoke.

"What we need, my dear boy," Theodore said, "is someone to act as Caroline's husband. To, in fact, *be* her husband. She needs to be married in one week or she will lose Fallingate. Once she is married and has proven to all concerned that she is, you will be free to go about your business. In fact, you will be given a generous lifelong stipend as long as you keep yourself out of the country. No one must know your true background, Davin, for obvious reasons."

Lucas put his half-drunk cup on a table near his chair and steepled his fingers, placing them before his mouth. So that was it. A marriage of *in*convenience. If they only knew how hard he'd worked to avoid the altar, they wouldn't ask such an absurd thing of him.

"Why me? Why not some gent of your own station?"

The doctor exchanged a sober look with Caroline, sucked on his cheroot, and then blew out of his mouth a perfect smoke ring. He squinted at Lucas through the hole as it wafted through the air, then dispersed.

"No man of good breeding wants to live in desolate Cragmere Moor, my boy. Not when they can live in Town."

Lucas stroked his chin, the crook of his thumb smoothing over his distinctive cleft. "I doubt that would trouble some of the gambling gents at the track who'd do anything for a fancy income. They'd take her to the altar, take her to bed, then take themselves to her bank. She'd never see 'em again, either. Get someone like that."

He stood up as if the audience had ended.

Caroline rose and determinedly came to stand before

him. Her unprepossessing eyes fairly glittered with desperation, the pale blue looking more like chips of shiny, colored glass, intensified by her bookish glasses. She wrung her graceful hands together, and her pink cheeks lost their color as she struggled with her courage.

"Mr. Davin, let me be perfectly honest. I have explored every other possibility. You will simply have to accept my word that you are my last hope of saving Fallingate. To own the truth, I *need* to marry you. Please, do not make me debase myself by begging. I would ask only for your modest approbation and discretion. Is that too much to ask in return for a life of leisure?"

She pulled off her spectacles and pinned him with her impassioned gaze. For the first time he saw a glint of steel in her shimmering eyes, and he warmed inside, no longer feeling quite so awkward. Lud, she was honest!

He was the first to look away. He studied the sheen on his ill-fitting borrowed boots. The last time he'd heard anyone beg to marry, the words had spilled bitterly from his own lips, and an old discomfiting feeling of unrequited longing stirred painfully in his chest.

How he'd wanted Izzie. Lovely, reckless Izzie. Izzie of the voluptuous nature, the angelic whore. The girl who'd wanted what she couldn't have—a lord. Therefore she'd never wanted what she could have had—Lucas. Poor Izzie. Poor, dead Izzie.

He turned his gaze from his boots to Theodore, the fight gone from him. "Can I have one of those, mate?"

"A cheroot?" Theodore looked for his case. "Of course, my boy. Forgive me for not offering before."

He pulled a second cheroot from his case and handed it to Lucas, who rose and helped himself to a twig from the fire, aping the doctor's ritual. He puffed and drew and sucked on the malodorous thing, all the while wondering why anyone took pleasure in such oddities. He puffed awhile in silence, then turned back to Caroline and said bluntly, "How much will I get?"

Her eyes widened, then blinked brightly. Her wrung-out hands reached for a steadying chair. "You mean you will consider it? Uncle Teddy has all the details."

Theodore went to a side table, pulled a document from its drawer, and handed it over. Lucas clutched the paper in his deft fingers and scanned the gibberish of black lines and dots and commas. Then he handed it back to the doctor.

"I don't read, mate. Just speak English."

Theodore raised one brow to a significant height. "How does two thousand a year sound, Mr. Davin?"

In spite of his considerable willpower, Lucas choked on a breath of smoke. It burned his lungs and nostrils. "Bugger! Where in blazing hell did yer get that kind of coin?"

"I came by it honestly, I assure you," Caroline said, turning to the window to look out at the land that had been so generous to her. "I inherited it."

He snorted a derisive laugh. "That ain't honest. It's just lucky."

"Everything hinges on Fallingate," she explained, turning to him with a look that obliterated the distance between them.

They were fifteen paces apart, but he felt as if she were close enough to touch his cheek with her dainty fingers. Close enough to give him one of her achingly sweet kisses.

"I have the income from tin mines. They make me very rich, Mr. Davin. But they compose my entire income. If I lose the estate—and hence the income from the mines—I will be penniless. So you see why I am willing to risk everything on this one charade. It is all or nothing."

He rose and joined her at the window. Everything seemed more peaceful at her side. She was no jumped-up conceited miss of a thing, that was certain. Aware of her—

the clean and violet smell of her, the nearness of her muslin-clad shoulder—he stared out the window and shrugged under the weight of his expensive clothes.

"All or nothing, eh?" he mused. "I've lived me whole life playing those odds."

He gazed distractedly at the leaden sky that spewed endless tears on grass so green it made him wonder at the dirt and grime and choking smell of coal he'd put up with for so long in Town. Some time in the country might be nice. Then he thought of the boys. What couldn't he do for them with two thousand a year? Hell, he could build them a bloody mansion.

Of course, he could never see them again. He'd have to take off for India or some other faraway place. That wouldn't be so bad. Not if it helped the boys. He could never again see Miss Wainwright. His vision blurred as he listened to her breathing—short, quick snatches of breath. She hung on his response.

Poor chit. Poor ignorant chit. She deserved more. She really did. She didn't know about him. Not really. She didn't know the worst of it.

He turned slowly to face her, realizing with increasing astonishment what his answer would be. Seeing her in profile, she looked like a cameo he'd stolen long ago, all creamy and feminine and distant. She turned to face him.

"Well, Mr. Davin? What say you?" she whispered.

"Call me Lucas," he said with an engaging smile. "No need to be formal. After all, we will soon be man and wife."

Nine

An hour and a half later they were married in Norkirk Chapel on the edge of Cragmere Moor. Since it took an hour to travel there by coach, the bride and groom had neither the time nor the inclination to dress for the occasion. Nor was there any desire to seal the union with a kiss. The entire affair, which possessed no more sentiment than a business deal, quietly became official when they signed the parish register in the vestry of the church. Caroline jotted her name in an elegant script, and Lucas carefully signed his name as he had rehearsed with Amanda. He painstakingly scrawled each letter, taking great care not to make any mistake that would signify his ignorance.

By the time they returned to Fallingate, Caroline was actually calm and in surprisingly good spirits. Relieved that Lucas hadn't felt obliged to pretend intimacy, she felt as if a great weight had been lifted from her shoulders. Now she could keep Fallingate. She hadn't yet begun to ponder what she would do with the husband who had helped her secure it.

Later in the day, when the rain cleared and the sun managed to make an appearance in the dreary autumn sky, Theodore helpfully suggested that Caroline take Lucas for a ride to show him the estate. After all, he would need to be conversant on such matters when he was introduced to George.

With the help of the valet, Lucas dressed quickly in riding clothes and reached the stables before Caroline. Always be first. Always be prepared. Robbin Roger had taught him well. But Lucas soon learned that the rules of Society were nothing like the rules of robbery, and the skills he'd practiced in Seven Dials didn't help him a whit in the country with the gentle sensibilities of the "squirarchy."

"Greetings, sir," the groom said when Lucas crossed from the house to the cobblestone stable yard. The boy, dressed in breeches gathered at the knees and a smart cap, nodded submissively and gave a half bow.

Lucas stopped in his tracks and looked guardedly over his shoulder. Who the devil was the boy talking to?

"The horses are nearly ready, sir," the lad added, turning back to his work.

Bugger! Lucas thought, the boy was talking to him. With a peculiar feeling that was not altogether unpleasant, Lucas turned and tugged at his cravat.

"Good day." He cleared his throat and thrust out his chin, wishing for the first time he didn't sound like a rat catcher from London.

The lad didn't seem to notice. He continued to saddle two horses. One, the boy informed him, was a white gelding ominously named Lightning. He had massive haunches, a pinkish muzzle, and blue eyes. The other was a shiny black mare named Daisy whose tail and mane were tightly braided. Lucas came forward, awestruck by the mare's beauty.

"Lud, she's a high-stepper!" He smoothed a hand down her glistening, sable neck. Her muscles were thick and warm, as fine as a piece of artwork in a nobleman's home. Her coat was smooth and silky to the touch.

Lucas knew little about horseflesh, but some horses were so well-bred even a complete idiot could recognize their quality. This horse was one of those. He recognized her quality, just as he'd seen the good breeding in Miss Wainwright, though she was not half so dazzling as the ladies who flounced out of their carriages at the opera as if they were the best part of the show. Lucas patted the shiny black flanks of the mare.

"Fine horse yer got here."

"Thank you, sir," the groom replied, his scrubbed and earnest face dimpling at the compliment. "She's the finest. The mistress rides her."

"Oh." Lucas rubbed his chin and turned a dreaded gaze to the white beast. That meant the mighty gelding would be his to ride. How in blazes would he mount that giant without splitting his tight pants from bow to stern? Yes, money had its disadvantages. One of them was being trussed up like mad King George. The few times Lucas had ever ridden a horse, he'd jumped on with a running leap while trying to escape a charley after a fumbled robbery in Town.

"Look, mate—er, dear boy," Lucas said, putting a hand on the lad's back as he'd seen Dr. Cavendish do so often. "How do yer get on one of these blasted beasts? I mean how do yer do it looking like a gent?"

When the smooth-faced lad stared up dumbfounded, Lucas added, "Mind yer—I mean, mind you—I ain't got much a chance in London to ride. I always take a fly, yer see—you see—or my private carriage." He cleared his throat, wishing he sounded more convincing. "In London I'm too busy with . . . business . . . to ride idly in Hyde Park."

The boy smiled sympathetically, apparently swallowing this explanation whole, much to Lucas's amazement.

"Right, sir. This is how you do it, see?" He entwined his fingers into a cradle. "I'll just let you climb in the crook of me hands with one foot. I'll hoist you up and you swing the other leg over. It'll be easy enough."

Lucas nodded. "Of course." He'd seen that done a hundred times. Why did the prospect seem so daunting now?

Because I don't want to fail.

"Good afternoon."

He whirled around sharply at the sound of her voice, his riding boots grinding on the cobblestones. Caroline marched toward him as merrily as if she were going on a picnic, though he doubted there was much of that done on this desolate moor.

"You found your way," she said sweetly.

He responded to her warm smile with one of his own, though his was a bit more guarded. He wanted not to like her, but he couldn't help it. She was so damned disarming. Her insides weren't all trussed up in laces like most fine ladies. Neither was she a wild bird batting her wings against her cage like Izzie had been.

How ironic that Caroline, though far above Izzie's station in life, was actually more simple and humble. Caroline Wainwright wanted little for herself, it would seem. And for her lack of ambition she'd gotten a crook for a husband.

"You deserve more," he blurted out when she joined him.

His words struck her bluntly, as if he'd insulted a new dress she'd particularly fancied, and her smile faded. Then her blue eyes churned with logic and she shot back, "So do you, Mr. Davin. You deserve more. But sometimes we must settle for what we can get."

Her smile returned, albeit a bit more resignedly, and she

cocked her hat forward, which had gone askew. She looked somehow overdone. She wore a tall black beaver hat that looked like a man's top hat. A royal-blue silk cravat was tied in a bow at her neck. Her V-necked, high-waisted gown was a matching blue that perfectly offset her eyes.

He knew the gentry dressed for every occasion, but he furtively wondered if there were any chance that she'd done so for him. The thought gave him that same curious feeling he'd had when he realized the groom had bowed to him.

"Yer going riding in that, then?" he said, nodding dubiously at her fine gown.

She nodded, and her uncommonly clear blue eyes blinked with doubt. "Is something amiss?"

"What if your horse throws yer? Yer'll dirty your fine frippery."

She smiled fetchingly. "I am an excellent rider, Mr. Davin."

"Lucas."

She accepted a riding crop from the groom, then waited until the lad returned to saddling the horses before speaking again to Lucas.

"Actually," she whispered, taking a step closer so that only he might hear, " 'Mr. Davin' is a more appropriate form of address in front of the servants. Marriage is no impediment to good manners. Only in private should we use our Christian names. And then only if we feel terribly—how should I say?—intimate."

Her cheeks flushed pink and he had the sudden urge to kiss her, to put his hands firmly on her slight waist and pull her close.

"How do yer live with all these rules?" he whispered in amazement.

She began to tug on her blue kid gloves. "How could I live without them?"

When he said nothing, she raised her sparkling eyes to meet his in a challenge. "Is the freedom you have worth the deprivation you endure in exchange for it?"

"I've always thought so." But now he wasn't sure. She spoke to him as no other lady had before. She was the only woman he had ever met who seemed to be without prejudice or guile.

Suddenly he wanted her to know his worth, his dreams of greatness, his certainty that there was more goodness to this world than he had yet seen. And he wanted her to see the value of his life thus far.

"Yer haven't lived until yer've slept under the stars, Miss Wainwright—er, Mrs. Davin," he whispered, shaking his head at the irony of it all. "Yer feel sorry for me, but at least I'm free. Yer can't even leave your bloody house without yer gloves. What kind of life is that?"

She tugged her elbow-length gloves into place, flexing her fingers as she frowned at them. "I have been insulted before, Mr. Davin, but never for being proper. I am not sure you are being fair. You could hardly call my actions conventional under the circumstances."

She smiled wryly, and he was struck in that moment by the subtle charms of a well-bred lady.

"The horses are ready, Miss Wainwright," the groom called out.

"Thank you, Davey. And you may call me Mrs. Davin now. Mr. Davin and I were married this morning. That's why we took the carriage."

"Oh, miss! Uh, ma'am, I should say. Many blessings to you!"

"Thank you, Davey." She started for the horses, and Lucas quickly caught up with her.

"I don't know much about riding," he warned her.

"I will teach you."

He tugged on the cravat that chaffed at his neck and

muttered, "So we play the idiot and the teacher. Fine marriage this will be."

"I must prove to my brother you are who I say you are. And a gentleman of Quality always knows how to ride. Here you are, Mr. Davin, you are to ride Lightning."

"Oh, glorious day," he muttered, reluctantly taking the reins from the groom, who was now, instead of ingratiating, merely irritatingly cheerful. "Don't fail me, Davey."

"Not to worry, sir," the lad said.

Lucas gripped the leather straps dangling from the fine silver bridle and wondered if any of this expensive riding equipment would stop the beast if it took a notion to race off.

"Right, mate, er, lad. Help me up."

Davey locked his hands together and bent down. Lucas stepped into his cradled fingers and hoisted himself up, swinging one leg over the saddle. The young groom did such a fine job heaving him up that Lucas nearly kept going over the other side.

"Whoa!" Lucas hollered, clinging to the saddle.

"Do not dismount yet, Mr. Davin," Caroline said, a wry smile tugging at the corners of her mouth. "We have scarcely begun."

They rode away from the stable at an easy amble. Lucas puffed himself up as he had seen many a fine gentleman do on many a fine steed, but when the groom was out of sight, he heaved a sigh of relief and grabbed hold of his saddle for purchase. The great white beast rocked beneath him with disconcerting motions, and Lucas felt as if he'd pitch to the ground at any moment. When Lightning tossed back his head and snorted out a whicker of air, Lucas's eyes widened.

Caroline covered another smile by coughing into one of her blue gloves. "You look as pale as your horse, Mr.

Davin. Just relax and everything will be fine. You are not riding a fire-breathing dragon, you know."

"So yer say. This beast is thinking about throwing me off."

"Now, now, Mr. Davin—"

"I can tell these things!"

"I thought you didn't know anything at all about horses."

"Aye, but I've got instincts. They never fail me. Why the bloody hell couldn't I ride a graceful mare like yours? She's two hands shorter and walks like Jesus on water."

"Mr. Davin—"

"Lucas," he shot back in return. "Yer can call me by me first name being as how there ain't no servants around. Though it's a wonder yer don't have them waiting in bushes along the road. Yer must have the entire population of Cragmere employed at your house."

"Mr. Davin," she started again, "I do not mind your lack of experience on a horse. But please do not speak so crudely."

"I am what I am. Yer knew that going into this. Yer fairly dragged me to the altar, yer did."

"I do not want to change you utterly. But you cannot say things like bloody hell and use the Lord's name in vain. At least not in front of a lady. You certainly look the part of the gentleman. Now you have to start sounding like one. A few country servants might forgive your lack of social graces, but my brother won't. But not to fear. You're a quick study. See there, you are already riding better. You look as if you were born on a horse."

He gave a snort of derisive laughter, but secretly swelled at her praise. He was relaxing into it, and for some reason riding did seem to be coming naturally to him. Almost instinctively he'd begun to grip the saddle with his knees and slightly arch his back and signal the horse with a light tug on the reins. It was somehow familiar, just as the sight of Germaine House had been.

Perhaps he'd been secretly envious of the wealthy all this time and had falsely convinced himself that what he felt was disdain. He didn't like that notion. Better to spurn what you could not have than long for it futilely.

They rode awhile in silence over Cragmere Moor, Lucas looking like a country squire out to survey his property. Caroline rode sidesaddle, her grace and ease belying the balancing act it took to remain fixed atop her mare. They skirted the marshy bog, where a chill wind whistled through the lonely reeds.

"This is Dead Man's Bog," Caroline said. "Whatever you do, steer clear of it. Else you will not come out alive. A finger of the bog stretches all the way up to the garden behind the house."

Lucas looked at the stalks of marsh grasses and bog cotton that sprouted from the sprawling sopping-wet heath. Now and then a patch of bright green sphagnum moss gleamed through the silver mist that hovered ominously over it. When a raven croaked a warning from the mists, Lucas shivered. "Cheery place, that."

Caroline smiled ruefully. "There's nothing very inviting about this part of Cragmere, save for the house that sits so nobly upon it. My mother inherited Fallingate from a distant cousin, who was a baron in Northern England. This particular piece of property has been in our family for a hundred years. It was purchased from the descendants of Sir Toby Killiam, the man who built the house during the reign of Henry VIII.

"Mother fell in love with the house at first sight. Father fell in love with the income from the tin mines. He kept our London home and preferred to stay there, but I lived in the country whenever possible. My brother George always hated Fallingate. That is why it doesn't seem fair that he should inherit it."

"Yer ever have, what they call, a come-out season? The la-di-da parties and balls and such?"

She smiled at his description of that sacred social rite of passage. "Yes. It must seem like a bunch of nonsense to someone in your position."

"Aye, it does."

"If it's any comfort," she said quite truthfully, "it seemed like so much nonsense to me as well. I rather botched my Season in London. I am a country girl at heart, Mr. Davin. I loathed the ladies and lords who turned their noses up at me during my Season. I am glad that I ruined my chance of making an acceptable match in Society."

She gave him a philosophical smile, gracing him with the quiet defiance that had marked her life in spite of her outwardly meek demeanor. She didn't know why she was being so honest with him. Perhaps it was because he seemed to be the kind of man who would read her heart whether she willingly revealed it or not. She believed what he'd said about his instincts. He was always thinking, taking in bits of information, observing. She'd always admired intelligent men, and they seemed so rare in London, where foppish manners and money were more esteemed than common sense. Now that she'd actually found an intelligent man with whom to converse, she wanted to reveal herself.

"You are a bright man." She frowned in consternation as the lonely moorland road gave way to a small valley dotted with trees. The brisk autumn air rustled through the stalwart leaves that remained on the branches overhead. "Why is it someone with your intelligence ends up a social malfeasant when you might be a productive member of society?"

"Yer mean yer don't know?"

"How should I? I assumed you were a criminal because there was something abominably rotten in your character. Why else would anyone steal? And yet I have seen nothing hateful in your nature."

He barked out a sardonic laugh. "Oh, lawk. Naive, that's what yer are."

She shot him an indignant look and tightened her grip on her thick leather reins. "I should hardly think so."

"No, yer wouldn't, would yer? Trust me, though. Even if I were as innocent as the driven snow, Mrs. Davin, I'd never be able to drag me arse out of the darkest gutters of London. Not for long, anyway. Yer type would shove me back in me hole. Yer see, I've got no connections, no references, no education, no money. But that ain't what led me to stealing."

Her mare tossed back her head three times and whinnied. Caroline brushed a hand soothingly over the beast's neck, steadying the horse as well as herself. Then she righted her shoulders and looked at her riding companion.

"What was it, then? What led you to your life of crime?"

Lucas's eyes twinkled and his lips broke into a wry half smile. "Distribution."

"Distribution of what?"

"Of wealth."

She smiled wryly herself. "I see. You did not care much for the wealth being distributed to others and so you took some for yourself."

"Not for me," he replied quietly.

"For whom, then?" Her heart quickened at the sudden thought that he might actually have altruistic motives for his crimes. That would make everything all right. "Are you telling me you are some kind of Robin Hood? Stealing from the rich to give to the poor?"

His intense gaze sparkled ironically, then focused on the

road ahead. "Nay, let the poor take care of themselves like I did."

"Then for whom do you steal?"

Lucas took in a deep breath. His black riding coat strained against his chest. Then he let out a slow sigh. "Me and mine."

"And what gives you the right to do something that's wrong simply because you feel like it?"

"Let's just say I don't think it's right that some bloody buggers get all the goods 'cause they were born to it."

"Though I cannot say as I agree with your methods of rectifying the problem, Mr. Davin, I agree that the imbalance is unfortunate. I have been accused by more than one of my short-lived suitors of being a dreaded egalitarian."

"Are yer saying yer care about the poor? That yer give any thought to anyone outside the confines of your fancy estate?"

Her heart began to flutter and she cleared her throat. "Upon my word, Mr. Davin, you are being grossly unfair. My servants and tenants will tell you I am a very caring mistress."

"That's easy enough when yer live out here all by yourself in the middle of nowhere. It's easy to feel for the poor and the sick when it's not under yer own nose. When yer don't have to do anything about it."

She frowned and dipped her head to avoid a low tree branch in the leaf-strewn lane. "I take exception to your notion that I am necessarily uncaring because I am wealthy. I have a number of tenants who fall on hard times now and then and I help them in any way I can. It is true I have tea with the Countess of Germaine and consider her a good neighbor. But I am also neighborly with Miss Kinnicott, whose father is but a farmer of modest means. I am no jumped-up miss pretending to nobility.

"In the country, Mr. Davin, we care for one another in

ways not possible in London. The social boundaries are
not quite so rigid. That is why I think there is a ghost of
a chance we will be able to pass you off as my husband.
But it will not work if you persist in hating anyone who
has more money than you. Do not forget, Mr. Davin, that
by virtue of our marriage you are now rich as well. I shud-
der to think how much you must loathe yourself for that."

"I loathe meself plenty."

She reined in with sudden pique. Her horse came to a
reluctant stop, and Lucas pulled his gelding up in response.
The horses bobbed their heads and whickered in protest.

"How dare you!" she cried. "I am offering you the world
on a platter and all you can do is mock it. I grant I have
little to offer a man in terms of womanly virtues. I do not
possess a sparkling demeanor or a dazzling wit. I have
never deluded myself on that score. But upon my word, I
do have money. Why have I chosen to marry the only man
in the world who does not even think my money is good
enough for him? This brings to mind the Scripture about
casting pearls before swine."

His black eyes snapped, then blazed with sudden fury.
"I figured I'd be nothing more than an animal to yer. I
was right. Yer honest. I'll give yer that much."

His anger overcoming his fear of horses, he jerked his
reins and gave a furious kick to his mount with both of
his booted heels. Only Caroline realized what a mistake
that was. She went pale as the horse's eyes turned bright
with a mad look.

"Oh, no," she whispered. Then louder: "Oh, no!"

She caught only a glimpse of Lucas's sorry realization
before the horse bolted forward as if he'd been stung on
the rump by a swarm of wasps. Lucas nearly toppled over
backward, but he grabbed onto the saddle and went racing
off, jostling to and fro atop the horse as he hung on for
dear life.

"Hold fast, Lucas!" Caroline shouted. "Rein him in!"

She heeled her own mount, and despite the awkwardness of her sidesaddle, she managed to gallop after the runaway horse. As she gained in speed, she saw Lightning's reins bouncing down around his churning hooves. Lucas would never be able to pull the horse up, and it would be miles before the powerful animal tired.

Caroline was just beginning to wonder if she'd ever see Lucas Davin again when suddenly fate intervened. Both horses—the first quickly, the second not long after—rounded a bend in the road at top speed and came upon an enormous mud hole encompassing the entire road. Lightning halted immediately, throwing Lucas over his head. He landed facedown with a muddy splash.

Moments later, Caroline reined in with considerably more grace and dismounted.

"Are you well, Mr. Davin? Are you hurt?"

She came to a skittering stop at the edge of the gooey puddle and sighed with relief when he sat up without apparent injury. He wiped a hand over his mud-coated face and glared at her.

Giddy with relief, Caroline couldn't keep from laughing. The sweet sound of her laughter seemed to dance with the jostling russet and orange leaves on the road.

"What are yer tittering at?" he said, surly. "Yer called me a swine. I suppose yer think this is where I belong—in a mud hole."

"No, Mr. Davin, you do not belong there. And I did *not* call you a swine, though I will admit I came close to it."

She burst out with another round of helpless giggling, hugging herself. It felt so good to laugh. She hadn't done so in months, and she'd been afraid she could never do so married to a stranger. But suddenly he seemed like someone she knew.

Lucas grudgingly joined her with self-deprecating

laughter. "So much for pretty frippery." He picked his limp and muddy cravat up off his chest, then let it fall again in utter defeat. "Help me out, if it please yer."

He held up his hand and she sobered. Goose bumps rose on her arms. She wanted to touch his hand, but somehow it seemed improper. She had to remind herself they were married. It hadn't quite sunk in yet. She no longer needed a chaperon.

She met his gaze and saw good-natured humor winking in his dark eyes. Utterly charmed, she reached out to give him a good yank. But before she knew what was happening, he snatched her hand in his and pulled her with all his might.

"No!" she cried out, but it was too late. Caroline lost her balance and fell next to him in the muddy ooze.

"Oof!" The sound exploded from her lungs, though her fall was softened by the mud. Cold, stinking, slimy mud. "Oh, Lord!"

She shoved herself onto her knees, gasping for air, more stunned than she'd ever been in her life. Sputtering incoherently, she wiped her face and blinked at him with scathing intensity.

"How dare you?"

In reply, his cheeks dimpled with the most engaging smile she'd ever encountered. His eyes twinkled with good-natured humor and her anger vanished instantly, though not her dismay.

"My dress is ruined!"

"I told yer not to ride in such frippery. Yer don't have to dress fancylike to please me, Caroline," he said huskily. "I'd sooner see yer naked." He blinked with perplexity. "*Have* I seen yer naked?"

She froze in place, feeling very bare in this particular moment, as if his searing gaze could burn through her muddy gown. She started to shrink back, but before she could reach a safe distance, he rose to his knees and slipped one strong arm around her waist, yanking her to him as easily as if she were a rag doll.

"Good heavens!" she cried at the intimacy, knowing she should push him away but unable to. He was so warm. So hot. She could feel every muscle that wove across his chest. He was holding her! Realizing the danger, she tried to pull away, but he stilled her by putting his hand to the back of her head. His fingers crawled sensuously through her tangled, crimped hair, and she shivered. Her beaver hat had long ago been lost.

"Don't be afraid, Caroline," he murmured.

"No? No, why shouldn't I be?" What was happening? she wondered. Why was he speaking so low? So intently, as if he truly desired her. Of course he would never want her for herself, or even for the slaking of his lust. Money was the only thing any man could want from her, and he didn't seem to want even that.

"Don't be afraid. After all, I'm yer husband."

His hot words prickled along her arms. She started to push at his chest with the flat of her hands, then his words registered. "You mean you . . . you will stay long enough to convince my brother we're married? I thought you would ride off into the horizon and I would never see you again."

He gave a self-deprecating chuckle and brushed a dollop of mud from the tip of her delicate nose. "Hmm. Yer still think I'm a horse thief even after that wild ride? Truth is, luv, it's not usually my fare. Your stables are safe with me."

She almost hugged him in thanks, but felt the palpable tug between them and thought better of it. "You may release me now, Mr. Davin."

"Nay, Mrs. Davin. Not quite yet, luv."

He pulled her close, wrapping his arms carefully around

her, as if she were a rare bird he did not want to lose, but had to be careful not to crush. "Why do yer love it so much?" he murmured as he nuzzled her ear, just barely brushing it with his lips. "Why do yer love Fallingate so much that yer'd risk everything by marrying a man like me to keep it?"

She stilled in his arms. He was embracing her. Genuinely embracing her. Oh, he was so wonderfully soft and firm at the same time. How was this possible? It felt so . . . good. So odd, yet good. She'd never read in her books how warm a man could be.

"Why?" he repeated.

Why did she need Fallingate so desperately? It was her anchor, of course. Her income and her independence. But it was more than that. It was the place where her dreams of romance had thrived in blissful ignorance. Where she'd nurtured the ridiculous hope of marrying for love. Where she'd read romantic novels to her heart's content, and where she'd dreamed of a long-ago lord she could never possess.

"I cannot tell you why I need Fallingate." Her reply struggled through a dam of emotion. "But I do. It is in my blood."

He thought of Germaine House, how intensely and instantly he had wanted it for his own, and he nodded with understanding. Perhaps they weren't so very different after all.

"Shall we return to Fallingate and clean ourselves up?" she asked with a shy grin.

He answered her with a kiss. A long, slow, passionate kiss, full of heat and friction. And, damn her eyes, but she didn't struggle. She tilted her head back in surrender with only an unconvincing whimper of protest. When the whimper turned into a groan of pleasure, he deepened the kiss, his tongue plundering where it should not be. She melted in his arms, having no choice but to admit to herself that if he would have her in that moment, she would give herself, consequences be damned.

He must have let go of her, she realized, when she once again felt a breeze brushing between them. He must have stopped kissing her as well, she realized, when her lips cooled for want of him. She'd been frozen in time, utterly transported. When she heard the distant twittering of a flock of swallows, she opened her eyes. It took a long moment for them to come into focus, and then she gazed at him with something akin to amazement.

"Wh-what did you do that for?"

His rugged, mud-splattered cheeks crinkled with a triumphant grin. "To confirm a hunch."

"What hunch is that?"

"I figured we hadn't consummated, as yer put it. And now I know we haven't."

She frowned, no longer caring what disaster this conclusion might lead to. "How can you tell?"

His eyes lit with devilish amusement. "Because I would have remembered a kiss like that. No matter how stinking drunk I was."

Ten

wo hours later Caroline stood alone in the old Elizabethan gallery. She was freshly bathed and dressed in a high-waisted, long-sleeved green cambric muslin gown. Her hair was knotted on top of her head, with only a few soft tendrils falling around her face.

The walls of this grand room were lined on three sides with floor-to-ceiling windows that stretched upward nearly two stories. The remaining wall was lushly lined with oak paneling. The glass was astronomically expensive to repair and maintain, but the cost was well worth it. In the winter, this was the only place where she could stroll and bask in sunlight.

Presently, however, exercise was the furthest thing from her mind. She stared fixedly out of a pane of glass, focusing on the sundial in the garden. The sun pinned the mounted timepiece in a brilliant ray of light, the kind that gloriously splays through dark clouds as in one of those dramatic paintings of the Ascension of Christ. The sundial's brass gnomon sparked with light as it cast its long shadow on the hour of the day. So often, it seemed, shadows accompanied light.

"Ah me," Caroline whispered to herself. Had she ever felt so full of hope and despair at once?

"Caroline! Are you—oh, there you are!" Amanda said from the far end of the gallery. She made her way at a lively pace along the polished hardwood floor, chatting as she went. "I have been searching endlessly for you. It is time for dinner. Cook has prepared a light repast today so there will be plenty of time to plan the education of Mr. Davin. I am afraid we have quite a lot of work to do. I heard he learned the hard way how *not* to motivate a horse. And I understand you both had to bathe when you returned. The servants were all abuzz today about your wedding. It entirely overshadowed their preoccupation with last night's indiscretion. You know . . ."

Amanda's monologue came to an abrupt stop when she reached Caroline's side. She immediately put the back of her hand to her former charge's forehead.

"Do you have a fever? Did you take a chill during your ride? You were gone so long."

"My constitution is perfectly intact, I assure you, Amanda."

"Well, you look ill. What is it? You look as if you are in a trance."

Caroline finally blinked and inhaled a whiff of Amanda's French perfume. The bracing scent was the governess's one indulgence.

"I am sorry. What did you say?" When Caroline finally looked at her, Amanda was frowning with grave concern.

"Are you positively certain you're well?"

Caroline shook her head, her vague discontent slowly coming into focus. "Yes, I am physically fit. It is my mind that suffers some malaise. And I did not know what it was until this very moment." She looked back out the window at the scenery that was so familiar, yet somehow different.

"Do not go back into your trance, my dear. Tell me what vexes you so."

"I am troubled," Caroline began in a precise, analytical voice, "because for the first time ever I have not even glanced at the portrait of Lord Hamilton. Not once since I awoke this morning. Not once!"

Amanda blinked twice, then smiled. "That's monstrous good news, and entirely understandable. You have been very busy since Mr. Davin's arrival."

"No." Caroline's emphatic reply brooked no argument. She slowly removed her spectacles, gazing at them in her palm, then looked up at her friend with new clarity. It was as if she were just beginning to see life as it really was, not as the romantic fantasy she had created for herself. "I have not looked at the portrait because I . . . I do not want to. It is as if . . . as if a spell has been broken."

Amanda's brows drew together in sympathy. "So you admit you have been obsessed by the legend of Lord Hamilton."

"Of course I was . . . until today."

"That is excellent! Upon my honor, Caro, I'm relieved."

"No, it isn't excellent."

Caroline's lip began to tremble as the memory of Lucas's kiss flooded her memory. She pressed the back of a fist to her still-tingling lips. Oh, Lord, she had enjoyed it! She had warmed to him. He had lit a fire inside her. A blazing and terrifying inferno. And who could possibly put it out? Not her! All she could think about was the next time he would kiss her. This couldn't be happening. She couldn't be vulnerable to the whims of a rogue. This had not been part of the plan.

She began to pace. "Amanda, you have no idea how terrible this is."

Amanda's genteel smile began to fade as understanding slowly dawned. "Caro! You do not mean . . . you cannot have . . . Oh, Lord, you are not attracted to Mr. Davin!" Then she added in a small voice, "Are you?"

Hearing someone else utter her very fears, Caroline shuddered from head to foot. *Yes, I am. I am.*

"No, I cannot be!" She turned to Amanda and gripped her arms. "All my life I have romanticized the notion of marriage. I have consumed volumes of adventures of heroines who fall in love with dark and brooding lords. I fell in love with a man who lived more than two centuries ago because he was the only man who fit my heroic fantasies. And now I find myself married to the very sort of dangerous man I once thought heroic. But he isn't heroic. He is simply dangerous. Amanda, when he kissed me—"

"He *kissed* you!" Amanda's instant and disapproving frown was replaced a moment later by a twinkle in her eye. "What was it like?"

Caroline started to speak, then stopped to consider. When she spoke again, she was calm, her fear turning to fascination. "It was the most remarkable thing I've ever felt in my life. The world spun beneath my feet. Shall I ever regain my balance?"

"Of course you will! Simply remind yourself that he is but a common criminal. You cannot let him affect you this way. A kiss here and there might be acceptable, but keep close guard over your feelings and your virtue. The last thing you need from Lucas Davin is a lifelong memento, if you take my meaning."

Caroline looked up sharply and caught Amanda's significant look. "Oh, yes. Yes, of course, you're absolutely correct. I don't want any lifelong mementos. Oh, but Amanda, he is a good man. I sense it. Doesn't he deserve a chance?"

"Yes, but not from you. He will never fit in with the

gentry. Do not listen to Dr. Cavendish's notions of truly reforming him. No one respects the doctor more than I do, but he's a man! He does not know the ways of the heart. You cannot expect Lucas Davin to become a gentleman for any length of time. Ultimately his true nature will reveal itself. This is a pretense, Caroline, and one that perforce must be short-lived. The longer you play at man and wife, the more you are tempting fate. Eventually, someone will find out your game and you'll be ruined."

"*I* will be ruined! What of Lucas Davin?"

Amanda shook her head in exasperation. "He will only gain by this. He will be a rich man."

"What of his heart? What if I fall in love with him and the feelings are returned?"

"Do you really think a ruthless criminal will give you his heart?"

The question was a delicate knife slicing Caroline's pride. She bit her upper lip and blinked rapidly at the stab. "Is it so absurd to think he might fall in love with me?"

"Oh, Caro, a man like that does not think of falling in love. He will just take what he can and then be gone, even if he is good-natured. This is his profession."

"You are wrong, Amanda," Caroline said, trying control her anger. With great precision she put her glasses back on and slid them up to the bridge of her nose. "He has a heart. I can see it. I did not want to, but I do. I . . . I cannot use him. I just cannot."

She stormed off, and Amanda chased after her. "Caro!" she cried out. "Be reasonable!"

Be reasonable, Caroline thought with a silent laugh. Reason would never again see the light of day in her heart, for she had just tasted the first sweet intoxicating drop of true passion, and she would never be the same.

• • •

Lucas stood naked in the tub. Hot water burned his toes. If felt so good. After his disastrous horse ride, he'd returned with his hostess—Lord, his wife!—then excused himself and walked a couple miles along the moor. He'd wanted to feel something familiar—wind biting his face, pinching his arms. Cold steeling his resolve. Loneliness, his old friend, telling him she wasn't real. Her softness, her virtue. It was all unreal. And even if it were real, it would never be his.

He did not need Caroline Wainwright. His heart, twisting in the wind, did not need another woman. They were frail, troublesome, impractical things. Izzie had been perfectly imperfect. And for that he'd loved her, but she was gone. Best that she was. Old Robbin had taught him good. *You're no one. Do you hear? No one. Never will be. Get it out o' yer mind.*

Lucas reached over his shoulder and rubbed the scars that remained from Robbin's whippings. The skin was mottled and smooth to the touch. He sank down into the steaming bathwater. God, let it cleanse him once and for all. Make him clean.

He squatted until his stones basked in the heat. He was hard still, just thinking about her. Damnation, he ached for her. That prim little nothing of a miss! The grand rich lady above him. That achingly sweet simple woman. Caro. Caroline. Miss Wainwright. Mrs. Davin.

"Oh, bloody hell!" he cursed, and sank onto his buttocks. A wave of water crashed over the edge of the tub. Heat embraced his shoulder and he leaned back with a sigh. He'd never felt this good. This comfortable, and with the memory of a woman tickling his senses, making him want more, want to know more. Making him question all that he had lived for. The boys. Had he been wrong all these years? Had he been living off the mark? Had he really done anything worthwhile? He'd leave a legacy, by

God, he'd sworn it long ago, but was he any closer to that goal?

He took in a long breath and slid down. Down. Until his head was covered with water. In that odd, choked silence, that absence of sound, he remembered.

A muffled voice. From the other room. The room he wasn't allowed in. I'll not have that little whelp here. Not here. Thornton says the child is not yours, Basil. Your father, God rest his soul, thank God he's dead. Remember who you are, Basil. Do not curse at me, young man. What did you say? Yes, I told her to leave. She does not deserve to be your wife! She's a bastard's daughter. What did you say?

And then another voice came, one closer to him. Sweet hands that bathed his little boy's body, stroked his hair. She was crying. We don't belong here, my darling. Never will, luv. Your mama loves you. Don't cry now, child. It will be over soon.

The loving hands pushed him down under the water. He thought it was a game. He began to laugh, but when she held him down, would not let him up for air, his little hands began to flail. Mama! Mama! I cannot breathe! He thrashed, dying for air, wanting another breath more than anything. More, even, than he wanted his mother's love. He would survive. It didn't matter what Nana said about him. He had to live!

Lucas burst up out of the water like a cannonball, sucking in a gasp of air so roughly his voice choked with the effort. Moisture sluiced over the scars on his back. Seething memories sloughed off his shoulders with the dripping water. His lungs burned with lifesaving air. Who was it? Who was his mother? Why had she tried to drown him? And why had he never thought of her before? Never. He hugged himself, suddenly chilled, and his hands touched the scars on his back. Old Robbin Roger's whippings had taught him there was no point in remembering. He was nothing. No one. And if you're no one, you have nothing to remember.

The memories—were they his own?—began to fade. And familiar blankness pushed away his unsettling thoughts. His mind was creating fantasies. This bloody house was disorienting him. Perhaps it was haunted, he thought with an ironic laugh.

Or perhaps it was *her* fault. She, the unremarkable miss—his wife. She was insidiously penetrating his thoughts, his soul. He'd not let her. He had the boys to think of. The boys. The boy.

After dinner, Amanda waited until Theodore had started out for the coach house before going after him. She threw on a light cape and slipped out a side door, hoping to catch him on the pathway. But he walked briskly, and she only saw him just as he entered the coach house door.

She bit her lip in frustration. She dared not call to him, for fear that Caroline would hear her. The only way she could speak with him would be alone, for Shabala had gone to Devon to contact the solicitor who'd drawn up the marriage settlement. She shut her eyes as a wave of vertigo washed over her like a wave on an ocean of distant memories. The wind snapped her cheeks with uncharitable chill, but she scarcely felt it. In any event, the sting was nothing compared with the painful memories that had pushed their way into her thoughts the last few days. She remembered all too well the last time she'd been alone with a man. Were the memories rushing to the fore because of Lucas Davin's arrival, or Dr. Cavendish's?

She hugged herself against the enveloping chill as she debated her options. She had to speak with the doctor, that much was certain. And she was a grown woman. No man could hurt her again as she'd been hurt in younger days.

And she needn't fear for her reputation. Everyone thought her a widow. In any event, it wasn't others' opinions she feared. She was afraid of her affection for him.

She bit her lip until she almost broke the skin, and cursed at the burning tears. She'd thought she'd never weep again. She'd thought God gave women only so many tears, and after they were shed, the well was dry. Oh, why was she being so emotional! Dr. Cavendish was different. Wasn't he?

She wiped away her tears. She had to get hold of herself, otherwise she couldn't help Caroline. She had to keep Caro from making a mistake as foolish as the one Amanda had made so long ago. She drew the hood over her head and marched determinedly to the coach house.

The governess knocked twice, but when there was no answer, she pushed open the door, calling, "Dr. Cavendish? Are you here?"

"Welcome! Welcome!" a high-pitched nasal voice squawked.

Amanda assumed those words gave her leave to enter, but she did so cautiously, for the ineloquent greeting had clearly been made by someone other than the doctor. So they would not be alone after all.

"Is someone here?" she called out, stepping into the doctor's world of enchantment. She searched for the source of the grating voice, untying her cape and laying it on a sofa.

"Welcome! Welcome!"

The sound seemed to be coming from the far wall. Amanda scanned the large two-story room, her eyes sweeping over walls covered with primitive native shields and spears, two chairs by the fireplace, a table covered with bubbling beakers and scientific experiments, and an open staircase that hugged the wall and led up to what was once a loft, but now housed the doctor's large bedroom.

At last she found the source of the strange greeting—a birdcage in the corner.

"I can scarcely believe my eyes!" she said with a laugh. "A parrot!"

She'd seen drawings of such talking animals in books, but had never seen, or heard, a real one. She started toward it when suddenly something pounced on her shoulders. Two arms wrapped around her throat in a stranglehold.

"Oh!" Amanda shrieked. "Help me!"

She spun around to see her attacker, but no one was there. And still the furry arms hugged her neck.

"Mrs. Plumshaw!" Theodore burst out in greeting from the top of the stairs. "What a delightful surprise. I see you have been attacked by Mr. Picklesworth. Let go, you mad beast!"

Theodore trotted down the stairs and her attacker sprang away from her neck. The furry creature pulled himself up into the rafters by clutching an African shield that hung from the ceiling and screeched loudly in greeting. Only then did Amanda get a clear view of what it was.

"A monkey!" she cried out with relief, and then delight. "Mr. Picklesworth is a monkey!"

"A spider monkey, to be precise." Theodore stopped at her side and lifted her hand to his lips in a courtly bow. "Welcome to my humble abode, ma'am."

His lips caressed the top of her hand; his breath warmed her wrist and a shiver shot up her arm. Her hand heated in his in the moment before he let go, in the time it took for him to raise himself up and regard her with unabashed affection.

It had been so long since any man had shown her such courtesy. Such gracious gestures signified little coming from the doctor. He was by nature gallant and extravagant. Every moment was a cause for celebration for him, a chance to explore and live life to the fullest. She dared not think he held her in especial regard. She had misread a man's intentions before, and it had ruined her life. She'd not do it again.

She turned to the parrot, feigning interest. "I have already been warmly welcomed by your parrot, Dr. Cavendish. Do you compensate him for playing the role of butler? And what is his name?"

Theodore's warm brown eyes twinkled with amusement and his lips pursed between his well-trimmed mustache and beard. "That is Professor Snipplewit. And he had best welcome you properly and without compensation. I spent years in Africa training him in the ways of English Society, so if he went squawking about like any other parrot in the jungle, I would pluck his feathers from head to claw!"

Amanda laughed softly and her gaze fell on the laboratory table. The shiny oak surface was cluttered with a fascinating array of amber beakers, apothecary bottles, a mortar and pestle, and boxes of herbs of every color and scent. Her nostrils flared at the scent of mint and thyme, plus the strong odor of herbs she'd never seen before. When her gaze fell on a large open tome that reeked of dust and ancient secrets, her eyes widened.

"What are you preparing? It looks like some native concoction."

"By Jove, that it is. I brought some of these plants back from my trip to Africa. When brewed together in just the right amounts, they have the most profound impact on the mind. They are capable of changing one's entire nature."

Amanda brushed her fingers over the open book, her fingers trailing through a thin layer of dust that covered the yellow parchment. It was written in Latin. "If I did not know better, I would think you were an alchemist, Dr. Cavendish."

When she gave him a teasing grin over her shoulder, he let out a mellow chuckle. "I can see how you might come to such a notion. But I assure you, I have no interest in turning base metals into gold. Improving human nature, however, is another matter."

The very mention of nature reminded Amanda of her mission and she exhaled an unhappy sigh.

"What is it, Mrs. Plumshaw? You are worried about something."

She nodded tensely. "Indeed I am. It seems that Mr. Davin has already . . . kissed Caroline."

He clapped his hands together as an elated smile spread across his bearded face. "Splendid!"

"Splendid?" She looked at him in dismay. "How is that splendid? They've been together but a day and already her defenses are crumbling. She had no intention of consummating this marriage."

"Precisely." He stroked his beard as he began to pace thoughtfully. "This is a very good sign. It must mean there is some natural attraction between them. That will smooth the path for a genuine relationship."

"A genuine relationship! There is to be no relationship. Oh, I know you have high hopes of redeeming the rogue. And that is all well and good for your bet with Sir Arthur. But Lucas must leave as soon as Fallingate is secure. There cannot be any children born of this union, Dr. Cavendish. That simply wouldn't do. It would complicate things terribly. A child is something that can haunt a woman for life."

He drew his bushy brows together over his pudding-soft brown eyes. "Mrs. Plumshaw, I am sorry to hear you say such a sad thing. I'd always thought children a blessing, though my late wife and I weren't fortune enough to know from experience."

His gentle comment made her feel mean-spirited. She blushed and turned quickly away. "I love children as much as any woman. But Caroline cannot be saddled with any lasting memento from this . . . this preposterous marriage. I agreed to help, but only under the assumption that Mr. Davin would leave as soon as Fallingate had been secured for Caro."

"But," he answered, tapping the air with a forefinger as good-natured mischief kindled in his eyes, "what if I can truly reform him, Mrs. Plumshaw? Wouldn't he then be as suitable a husband as anyone else? Then he would not have to break Caro's heart, hmm?"

He'd come up behind her. She could feel the loving warmth that poured from him. It threatened to melt the ice around her heart, and she wanted to weep again. But something about him gave her hope, and her sadness was transformed into a sweet wisdom. She had to trust this man. He knew something very important about life that she had yet to learn. Perhaps he could show her how to mend a shattered heart. She turned slowly and regarded him with a painfully honest expression of tenderness.

She tilted her head as she studied him, trying to see into his soul, to understand how anyone could be so positive. "Are you truly as good-hearted as you seem, Dr. Cavendish?"

His gaze flitted over her features, assessing and caressing, making her feel like a woman to be treasured. "A fine lady always brings out the best in me, Mrs. Plumshaw. Women soothe the savage beast." He placed a hand over his heart.

"How lucky your wife must have been."

"And how fortunate your late husband."

She cast her eyes down and turned away. Even if the doctor did care for her in some significant way, how could she ever tell him that she'd never been married? What would he think of a woman who had lived a lie ever since her arrival at Fallingate so many years ago?

"Back to the matter at hand," she said in a choked voice.

"I fear that if Lucas Davin stays here any length of time, he will ruin Caro. Make no mistake of it."

"My dear Mrs. Plumshaw," he replied in a soft, soothing voice.

He grasped one of her hands and gently tugged until she turned to face him. His very touch made her want something she could never have. He would never understand the truth about her. How could he?

"I had no idea you felt so strongly about Lucas Davin. I have been insensitive, I fear. We cannot go back on our scheme now," he said. "But I will be fair to you and your concerns. Not only will I place a bet with Sir Arthur, I will make a wager with you. I will do everything in my power to make Lucas the ideal husband, and you do everything in your power to keep Caro from falling in love with him."

Her eyes shot up and met his. She laughed in spite of herself. "That's a wager I'll warrant I can win."

"Good." He beamed a broad smile. "I would not want to take advantage of a lady of your estimable character."

She let her fingers relax in his grip, the fear abating. How could she ever have thought he'd harm her? She really did have to let her suspicions go. Still, he didn't understand anything about the hearts of men.

"Why must you strive to make Mr. Davin so appealing?" she said complainingly. "You have no idea the danger such a charming rogue poses to a girl as innocent and romantic as her."

"If Caroline does not find Mr. Davin an acceptable companion, neither will anyone else," he answered. "And we have a world to convince, Mrs. Plumshaw, for Caro's sake. I cannot do it alone. Will you help me?"

She withdrew her hand, which had begun to tingle, and took a few steps to put some safe distance between them. "Well, I suppose we must do everything we can to prepare him to meet George. If Mr. Davin does not speak and act impeccably, Mrs. Wainwright will be the first to notice."

"I daresay that is correct."

"And if we want him to speak very well, we must begin tutoring him straight away."

"I'll start today with a lesson in table manners," Theodore suggested.

She nodded as ideas sprang to mind. "And tomorrow I'll teach him how to dance the quadrille."

"And together we will turn a base gentleman into a true gem."

She smiled at his infectious enthusiasm. He was fifteen years her senior, but his *joie de vivre* made her feel old in comparison. Suddenly she wanted to be young again. She nodded. "Very well, Dr. Cavendish. I will take this as a very serious challenge."

"Good, my dear. We'd best hurry."

He retrieved her cape and draped it over her. She keenly felt the places where his hands accidentally brushed her shoulders. She forced herself to depart as if nothing but the mundane had transpired between them. But before she could exit, he called out to her one last time.

"Mrs. Plumshaw!"

She turned back. "Yes?"

"Did I tell you that you look lovely today?"

Her heart lurched, then resumed with a quick beat. "No, I'm quite certain I would have remembered such a comment."

"Well, you do. Look lovely, that is."

"Thank you."

That was all she said, but when she was far from sight, she hugged herself, and tossed her head up to the cold drizzling rain, feeling warm inside for the first time in years.

Eleven

10 June, 1529

*It hath been eight long years since I held her last.
Dearest Rachel, if thou knewest what I have done for
thee. One day, when we are man and wife, I will tell
thee all my adventures. How I did join the king's
army. How I quickly rose in rank, distinguishing myself through sheer audacity and uncommon bravery
in our majesty's otherwise disastrous campaign in
France. You see, dear Rachel, I knew how far I had
to climb to be worthy of thee, and how little time I
had, and so I took risks no other man would take.*

*I know that a blossom will not bloom forever on
the vine. The prettiest are soonest plucked, and
though they quickly wither in the selfish hand that
takes them, they thrive a time so embraced, more brilliant still. I would be the one to have thee, Rachel, to
cherish thee even after thy beauty fades. From thy
letters, I know thou art waiting for me. But how long
wilt thy father wait? How long before he forces thee*

into marrying another more worthy in his eyes? So many years have passed already.

Good news, fair love. My service abroad hath brought me attention at court. I have enlisted the notice of Thomas Cromwell, Cardinal Wolsey's man. His star is rising. And with his guidance, I will gain favor in the king's government and perhaps even win a title.

Then, dearest Rachel, not even your father will stop us.

Caroline shut the diary and pressed it close, the hard leather corners digging into the soft pillow of her bosom. It was difficult to imagine that the dashing figure in the portrait opposite her bed was once a man who struggled for recognition. Something in the permanence of the paint, in the immortal expression of gentlemanly defiance, so deftly rendered with bold brush strokes, something in the beauty of ancient clothing, made her think that he had never had to strive for acceptance. At least not until the end. He was a lord, after all. But once he had been someone of no earthly consequence. Not entirely unlike Lucas.

She looked up at the painting, at the inscrutable expression, and wondered what Barrett Hamilton would have thought of Lucas Davin. It would appear they had much more in common than a cleft chin.

It was even possible that Lord Hamilton felt then what she was certain Lucas felt now. A hostile disdain for those who were his social betters, combined with an unacknowledged envy for what they possessed. Except that Lord Hamilton had bettered himself for one reason alone—to have the woman he loved. That was such a romantic purpose. That was what had drawn her irresistibly to his legend.

Lucas was driven to succeed, but to what end and for

what purpose she did not know. And her lack of certainty about his nature was very provoking indeed.

Someone knocked on the door.

"Come in," Caroline instructed, and rose from her chair by the fire. Expecting it was Biddie come to turn down the covers, she began to unfasten her necklace. It had been a long day and she was more than ready for sleep.

"I thought I'd say good night."

At the sound of Lucas's voice, Caroline looked up with a start. "I . . . I thought you were already abed in your dressing room. We agreed . . . it was best that way. This is . . . a business arrangement."

Lucas's unusually large eyes turned smoky with an emotion she could not name. Frustration? Irony? Desire?

"Don't get all starched up on me now. I understand me purpose here, and I accept that. I simply wanted to talk."

Then why was he staring at her as if she were already undressed? Her nipples hardened under his intense gaze and she cleared her throat. "Well, then, did you wish to discuss anything in particular?"

He pursed his lips as he considered his answer, looking remarkably uncertain for a man who always seemed to maintain his pride no matter how low he was brought. He was a bit disheveled. He'd discarded his dress coat and his narrow waist was cinched in by his waistcoat. The careful knot of his cravat had been loosened, and his hair, untamed under the best of circumstances, looked downright heathenish.

He raked his strong hands through his locks, pursing his sensual lips as he struggled with his thoughts. "I don't know why I came, except something doesn't feel quite right about this place."

The diary slipped from her hands. She nearly stumbled in her haste to retrieve it. "Oh? What do you mean?"

"It's just that . . . I've been thinking thoughts I've never had before. Memories that don't seem to be me own are coming to mind at the oddest times."

"Oh!" she said with a sigh of relief. "Is that all? You are probably just fagged out. Would you like a bit of brandy before you retire? Feathers brought it up earlier and I have been too busy to have so much as a sip. I rarely drink. I suppose he thought I needed it. And perhaps I do."

"A touch of brandy would be right nice." He closed the door and sauntered in.

She went to the decanter on the table by the far window. Outside, the wind howled with its usual clamor. "You look like you could use a good night's sleep. Has Amanda worn you out with her lessons in etiquette?"

"Mais oui," he said, and flopped down into a high-backed chair in front of the blazing fire.

"I did not know you spoke French." She sat down beside him and handed him a delicate glass, sipping from her own.

"I didn't until tonight. *Je m'appelle Monsieur Davin. Comment vous appelez-vous?"*

Caroline laughed with delight. "That is wonderful! What a quick student you are."

"Mrs. Plumshaw says I ain't supposed to say ain't anymore. I have to say you instead of yer, my instead of me, and Lord instead of lawk." He raised the glass to his sensual lips and took a sip, hissing contentedly as the amber liquid burned down his throat. "And I have to learn quickly. I don't have much time, that I don't."

I do not have much time. Caroline's eyes found the portrait. Hadn't Lord Hamilton said virtually those same words?

Lucas stretched out his long, lean legs. "Mrs. Plumshaw says that every gent needs to know a smattering of French, just to prove he's been educated. Oddly enough, it ain't all that foreign to me. Rather, it *is not* that foreign to me."

"I told you, you are intelligent. See how your diction is already improving?"

He rested his chin on an upraised fist and grimaced. "Aye, but that's not enough, is it?"

She agreed with a melancholy smile. Whatever he learned wouldn't be enough to erase the social distinctions that separated them like iron bars. For though she was not of the nobility, she was firmly established in the gentry. It was simply unacceptable for a lady to marry such a low-born husband.

He rose suddenly, graceful in his movements, and paced aimlessly about. His sharp eyes picked out all the richest items. He looked at her curio cabinet filled with her collection of jade snuffboxes, at her open jewelry box by the bed spilling over with pearls and sapphires, at her ming vase bearing the last rose of the season. It was as if his eyes had been trained to find the most expensive items in whatever environment he found himself in. They caressed each object.

He ran a hand over his face, wiping away the longing that lurked as a shadow in his eyes. How difficult it must be, she thought, for him to realize that he didn't have to steal anymore. Perhaps he already missed the danger of his former profession.

He looked up and found himself face-to-face with the portrait of Lord Hamilton. Lucas's hair seemed to stand taller, like a male dog that suddenly spies another male broaching its territory.

"Who is he?" His voice was demanding and implacable.

When she did not immediately answer, he turned to her. Like a fox that spies a trembling rabbit in the gorse, his lips curled in a smirk. "Yer in love with him. So that's it. Yer have loved before, but yer lost him for some reason, and so yer settling for someone else."

"No!" She tipped up her chin indignantly.

"Don't give me your prim airs, Caroline. Don't be looking down on me like I'm an idiot. I see the love written all over your face."

She rubbed her arms, where goose bumps had risen at the truth. "How dare you be so presumptuous? You know nothing about the contents of my heart."

"I should know something. I'm yer bloody husband!"

"Not in any real sense."

"No, because I'm not good enough for yer, am I? Scratch a rich person, even a nice one, and yer always find the same damned thing under the surface, don't yer? A bloody snob."

"Get out. Now."

Something in him snapped, like a branch on the tree that scrapped her window in the tortured wind. His muscular body tightened and his face flushed red. He marched toward her in a firestorm of fury, looking very much like Lord Hamilton come to life. She cowered back. Was he going to hit her? Had she pushed him too far? He wasn't incredibly tall, but tall enough to loom over her. He gripped her arms, and his fingers dug into her flesh. His hot breath fanned her cheeks in furious, short puffs.

"I'm giving yer me name, damn yer! I'm giving yer me word. Did yer think it came so lightly?"

A stab of guilt hit her full in her belly, and she recoiled, but still he held her fast. While his eyes spewed black venom, his free hands scooped under the back of her head and inched intimately up her scalp.

"I can't be giving it to another after yer, Caroline. Did yer never think that maybe I had hopes of a real marriage, with wee ones and happiness?"

She looked at him then, searching his large, wild eyes and seeing a man. Not a criminal. Not a fantasy. Someone real, and true. Someone who had wanted to kiss her. Someone who had given up his freedom for a reason she could not yet fathom. It wasn't just the money. He wanted so much more than that.

"You . . . you wanted a family?" she stammered.

"Aye, damn yer. Someday. Didn't yer think we street urchins had desires like the likes of the high and mighty?"

"Oh, Lucas, I am so sorry. I didn't know."

A lifelong memento, as Amanda had put it. He wanted a child, bless his soul.

His eyes shuttered, as if he could feel the depth of her sudden understanding, as if her surprise, and instant humility, soothed his raw feelings.

"If that is what you wanted," she whispered, "then why did you agree to this bargain? Was it simply to stay out of the gaol?"

"No." He sneered, recovering his cynicism. "I could have broken out meself in time."

"Then why? Why bind yourself to me if you had hopes for a family?"

"For the boys," he said, his voice shaking with emotion. "Damn those boys."

Did she see tears gather in his eyes? He wiped a shaky backhand over his forehead, as if whatever he'd done for the boys had finally exhausted him unutterably.

"Who are they?" she asked insistently. "Tell me! Is this your gang of thieves?"

Still clutching a fist of his hair, he shook his head.

"So you will not tell me?" she said petulantly, certain that if she could goad him into telling her, she could understand him so much better. "I must know. There is more to you, Mr. Davin, than I had ever imagined. Please, tell me about your life."

"Why should I? Yer don't care," he said sharply, walking away to put some distance between them.

"I feel a bit hard done myself, Mr. Davin. I have confessed to you my life story without glossing over the blemishes. And you will tell me nothing about yourself."

He pinned her with his black eyes. "I'll tell yer about me boys after yer tell me about him."

Good Lord, she thought, was he jealous? Over her affections? She flushed with an exhilarating rush of pride. A man was actually jealous on her account. Her mother would never have believed it. But Caroline could not use this jealousy. That would be cruel. And dangerous. He could not know of Lord Hamilton. She would not risk him fleeing out of fear of a ghost.

"Look at what he is wearing," she said with forced incredulity, pointing to the picture, "a honeycomb ruff collar and a doublet that has not been seen since the time of Henry VIII. Of course he is not my lover. Lord Barrett Hamilton has been dead for almost three hundred years! Can't you see that?"

Lucas's eyes narrowed on the evidence of history, and he seemed dumbfounded to be caught in his own ignorance. Instantly she regretted having pointed out his error. In so many ways his lack of knowledge put him at a disadvantage. But somehow she thought his vaunted intuition would see him through despite this lack. Yes, indeed, if anyone should be quaking now, it was she.

For he had kissed her. And she was grateful. That made her terribly vulnerable.

He turned without saying another word, and as he silently made his way to the door, she heard a rumble of distant thunder. There would be another storm tonight. And only the fearless would be left uncowed before it was over.

Before Biddie came to undress her for the night, Caroline rang for Feathers. When he did not arrive as promptly as usual, she rang again. He knocked on her door a short time later and she bade him enter.

"Yes, miss?" the sagging-cheeked butler said at the door in his usual dry and imperturbable way. Only the dusting of pink in his cheeks betrayed an uncharacteristic fluster.

"Come in, Feathers." She pushed aside her estate agent's ledger books and removed her glasses, rubbing her weary eyes. When the butler stood before her small desk, she folded her hands and said, "I had to ring twice, Feathers."

Coming from such a lenient mistress, this simple statement had the effect of a stinging rebuke. The butler's face reddened, and he cleared his throat, though his mouth remained closed and as shriveled as a prune.

She waited.

He cleared his throat again. "Begging your pardon, ma'am. I was . . . busy."

"You were busy." She steepled her hands and put the tips of her fingers to her chin. "And what was of such importance that you should delay responding to my call? You are not anticipating my brother's possession of Fallingate, are you, Mr. Feathers? If you are, I can assure you I am still mistress of the estate. And with my recent marriage, I shall remain so."

"I was locking up the silver, ma'am," he mumbled.

She frowned and lowered her hands to the desk. "What?"

He raised his head, steeling himself to meet his fate. "I said I was locking up the silver, ma'am."

Caroline blinked, but did not otherwise betray the anger she felt. "You have not put the silver under lock and key for years, Feathers. As you say, we have so few visitors, there is no real danger of it being stolen. Why do it now?"

The butler pursed his lips and squinted his eyes, in more discomfort than Caroline had ever seen.

"Well, you see, ma'am, it's just that . . ."

When his voice petered out, she said, "Is it because of the presence of my . . . my husband? Mr. Davin?"

At this, Feathers coughed. "Well, ma'am, you see, Mr. Davin . . . he . . . speaks in a most . . . peculiar way. And I thought . . ."

"And you thought what?" She struggled to keep her voice down to thwart any eavesdropping servants. "You thought that just because Mr. Davin does not speak the king's English, he is somehow less than I deserve, is that it?"

Her voice rose in pitch as she spoke. It infuriated her to think of the report Feathers would give her brother when he had the chance.

"Well, ma'am, he does seem to notice your finest possessions. It's simply, well I heard conjecture that—"

"You heard what?"

"That he might not be a . . . gentleman, ma'am."

Panic swept through Caroline. If her servants dared to speculate openly among themselves, it wouldn't be long before they started gossiping to the dependents in other households. Granted, the monthly trip to market was weeks away, but such rumors needed to be nipped in the bud before, through sheer repetition, they became presumed facts.

"Mr. Davin has spent many years abroad, Feathers," she said archly, standing so she could meet him eye to eye. "I thought you understood that. Dr. Cavendish met him on one of his adventures. His accent is simply a result of his regular exposure to other languages. I am sure now that Mr. Davin has returned to England his dialect will improve. It already has. I wonder that you have not noticed. Perhaps you're not quite yourself lately, Mr. Feathers."

The old man blinked and nodded, obviously wounded to the quick. She knew that after this set-down, he thoroughly understood her determination to quell such rumors. And she knew he was dedicated enough to his profession to do her bidding, even if he might favor her brother, as

Dr. Cavendish had suggested. Mr. Feathers would ensure that the other servants accepted this explanation whether he believed it or not.

"You may go, Feathers."

"Yes, ma'am."

She watched him depart in silence, then heard a rattling and turned to the window. It had begun to storm, just as she had predicted. She heard a high keening sound and she shivered. It sounded so human. She knew it was simply the wind, that almost lifelike force that rampaged across Cragmere Moor. The question was, would Lucas know that?

Fear of losing him rose up suddenly and nearly buckled her knees. She went to the window, gazing out at the torrent of rain with frustration. If only she could wave a magic wand and make the inclement weather disappear. She couldn't bear it if Lucas ran off now. They were married, true enough. Everything was official. But George would know something was amiss if Lucas ran off before they could meet.

Memories of all the other suitors who'd come and gone reared up in her mind's eye. She'd thought them all brave until they'd fled in terror. Would Lucas do the same?

She remembered his kiss. Oh, Lord, if he left now, tonight, she'd never kiss him again. She'd give half her fortune for one more embrace from him. Of course, she couldn't admit that. And she shouldn't feel that way, but she did.

She heard him enter his dressing room from the hall. She looked with trepidation at the door that joined her room to his. He was going to bed now. Would he hear the howling wind? Would he read too much into it? Would he believe it was a ghost as all the others had?

"Ready now, ma'am?" Biddie said.

Caroline whirled around and saw the housekeeper at her door. "Biddie, I didn't hear you knock."

"Lost in your thoughts, I daresay, ma'am." She added with a soft chuckle, "I shan't ever get used to calling you that, I avow. You'll always be Miss Wainwright to me."

"Yes, Biddie, I'm ready to retire. Do you . . . do you have the keys to these rooms with you?"

"Oh, yes, ma'am." She pulled a ring of keys from the folds of her skirt as she entered. "I keep them close by in case of emergencies at all times. Wouldn't trust anyone else to do it."

"No, of course not. Biddie, leave me the keys to my bedroom and the attached dressing rooms tonight. One of the doors is jamming and I want to see what I can do."

"Oh, no, ma'am. Wouldn't be proper for you to do it. I'll send Henry up."

"No, it's late, Biddie. I'll take care of it myself."

"As you wish."

Caroline was unusually quiet while Biddie helped her undress for the evening. She had to think her plan through very carefully. In the end, she was content that all would work for the best. She would lock Lucas in for the night, securing both the hallway door to the dressing room and the door that opened to her room. She'd unlock it early in the morning and he would never know he'd be temporarily imprisoned.

It would be for his own good, after all. If he thought he heard a ghost in the night, he might run away in fright and end up in Dead Man's Bog.

Twelve

aroline had an unnerving dream in which Rachel Harding was knocking on her window, begging to be let inside. But when she woke to the glare of sunshine, she realized the pounding she heard was all too real. Someone was banging on the door to Lucas's dressing room. She sat up with a jolt.

It was Lucas! He was still locked in his dressing room. Good heavens, she must have overslept!

"Oh, dam—!" Caroline cried out, throwing back her covers. She jumped out of bed, only to realize that someone was banging on her door as well. Her hands fumbled over the desk as she searched for the keys. Finding them, she rushed to open her door.

There stood her distraught housekeeper kneading her hands. "Oh, ma'am, thank heaven you awoke. You've locked in Mr. Davin and he's furious. Where are the keys?"

"Here," Caroline said, thrusting them in Biddie's hands. "Why didn't you retrieve Mr. Feather's keys?"

"He hasn't risen either," Biddie said pointedly.

Caroline's mouth gaped. "Why, I've never risen before Feathers in my life. What is the world coming to?"

"Mr. Davin will want a word with you, I avow, ma'am. You'd better dress quickly. I'll let Neville open the door while I help you ready yourself."

Caroline nodded and dashed off to her dressing room, scrambling to retrieve her simplest gown. Speed was of the essence. She didn't want to meet Lucas's wrath in a state of dishabille.

She heard shouting in the hall and stomping feet on the stairs. Lord, he was going down to the dining room! She'd better hurry before he vented his ire in front of the servants. With deft help from Biddie, she dressed and ran down the stairs, stopping abruptly when she spied the unusual dining room tableau.

Amanda sat in her usual place at the table, dressed in a simple blue morning gown and a soft, flounced cap. Theodore sat opposite her with an outdated copy of the *London Times* spread before him. Lucas paced between them in nothing more than a nightshirt and dressing gown. His hair was a wild mane and his face was drawn in fury.

"How dare you lock me in my own room!" he ranted at the older couple. "My *only* room. Gads, isn't it insult enough that I should be relegated to the dressing room. If I—."

Lucas stopped abruptly when he noticed Caroline standing in the doorway. She swallowed the trepidation that had crept into her throat.

"Good morning, darling," she said brightly, ignoring the glowering stare she received in reply. "Good morning, Uncle Teddy. Reading old news?"

"I have been out of the country so long that even old news is new news to me, my girl."

Lucas ignored the inane banter. He stalked around the table until he faced Caroline.

Lord, he was handsome, she thought. His face was flushed and dramatic and . . . oh, Lord, he was handsome.

"Which one of your sniveling servants did this to me?"

"Did what?"

"Locked me in my room!"

"Oh. That."

At her guilty wince, his eyes widened in sudden understanding. "It was you! You did it. I know what you're about."

She skirted him and his wrath and hurried to her place at the table. "Would you join us for breakfast, darling?" She sat and placed her napkin in her lap. After you dress, that is."

He followed her and gripped the back of her chair with one hand. He leaned close until they were nearly nose to nose. She could do little more than look up in amazement.

"You can't cage me like a bloody animal, Caroline!"

"Your elocution is perfection this morning, Mr. Davin," Amanda remarked dryly. "Perhaps you should become angry more often."

He slashed Amanda a furious glare, and she pursed her lips, but remained silent.

"Mr. D-Davin," Caroline stammered, rising unsteadily. He was so close that she wanted to put her hands on his strikingly intimate nightshirt, but it was so wholly and thoroughly improper she couldn't even believe the thought had entered her head. "Mr. Davin, there has been a misunderstanding."

"Aye, there has been, you arrogant chit!"

"Now, now, good man," Theodore said, tossing down his napkin and rising abruptly. "Enough! You mustn't—"

"At first I thought my door was jammed. Then I realized you'd locked me in. That wasn't part of the bloody deal. I ain't playing no animal for you."

Amanda gasped, not because he'd slipped back into his old way of speaking, but because the fracas had garnered an audience of servants. She waved frantically to Theodore to warn him of the danger.

"Not in front of the servants!" she whispered.

Theodore looked around and saw the crowd that had gathered. There was Biddie at the door, Henry, plus Neville and the MacGregor girls. Even Feathers was making his way toward the spectacle, tugging on his waistcoat and rubbing the sleep from his eyes.

"He's from Africa," Theodore announced to all, waving his hand with forced nonchalance. "Mr. Davin will have to get used to customs here in England. Why, in Africa we would regularly dine in our nightshirts."

Even in his rage, Lucas caught the gist of the doctor's nonsense and turned on him, sauntering recklessly to his side. "Worried what the servants will think, eh, mate? I oughta walk out that door now while I ain't chained, servants be damned."

"Please, Mr. Davin," Caroline implored him, "just get dressed and join us in the drawing room. We can discuss all the intricacies of this particular conundrum there. *In private*."

Lucas turned his blazing black eyes her way and she caught her breath.

He shook his head, approaching her, stalking her so coldly that Theodore took a step toward him. Lucas's hand shot out behind him to stay the doctor, but his eyes never left Caroline's face, never stopped penetrating her flimsy shield. She unconsciously pushed her back against her chair, pushing at the wooden arms, but she could put no distance between them. She turned her head to the side, as if his gaze were the sun burning her fair skin.

"Don't ever cage me again," he whispered, "or I'll hunt you down like the animal you say I am."

She nodded quickly, willing to agree to anything to calm him down. Theodore cleared his throat loudly.

"I say, would you care for breakfast, dear boy?"

Caroline almost laughed out loud. She'd be lucky if Lucas would ever sit at the same table with her again.

Lucas didn't answer; he took a step back, cast a disdainful glance at the table, then snatched a piece of toast from Caroline's plate. He ripped a bite out of it, chewing crudely as he watched her, then strode from the room, taking the stairs in the entrance hall two at a time.

It was Henry, not Feathers, who opened the double doors to the drawing room a half hour later. Caroline made a mental note of it, but then all other thoughts ceased as the door creaked open further, revealing an utterly dashing Lucas Davin behind the footman.

She caught her breath, and heard Amanda do the same.

Lucas's fury, now under control, seemed nevertheless to bubble unseen in his veins, giving his flesh a heightened color. Vitality shimmered off him like a dark halo. His hair had been combed but the unrepentant black locks could not be quelled. They dashed about his face, where life's hard lessons, and only the faintest tempering by maturity, cast his lips in a grimly wry pose. And dressed in a neatly cut midnight-blue coat, gray waistcoat, buff trousers, and an elegantly folded cravat, he looked the very part of a jaded London gentleman. For a stunned moment, Caroline could do nothing but feast her eyes.

"Well?" he said with an arrogant toss of his head. "Where's my coffee?"

Caroline exchanged glances with Uncle Teddy and Amanda. Did they, too, notice that something in Lucas had changed? It was as if any reticence he'd had before was gone. Apparently, he'd decided to play the role of the gentleman husband seriously.

"I assume," he said, tugging down on the cuffs of his crisp white shirt, "that I'm now appropriately dressed for morning coffee?"

"Of course you may have coffee." Caroline distractedly looked to the footman for service, then thought better of it. "That will be all, Henry. I will preside over the tray myself."

The bewigged servant nodded, giving no hint that he'd been flustered by the morning's mayhem. He bowed and closed the doors quietly. He'd make an excellent butler, Caroline thought. He'd been patient, waiting for such a promotion.

Caroline went to the serving table and willed her hands not to shake as she poured the aromatic black brew. "Scones, Mr. Davin?"

"No," he snarled.

She forced a smile and turned, gliding gracefully to him and offering the cup, which he did not immediately accept. She cleared her throat. "I am sorry about . . . your locked door. It is entirely my fault."

"That much, my dear lady, I knew already." He sipped from his cup with great deliberation.

Sensing that the balance of power had somehow shifted, Caroline turned to her other companions with a forced air of calm. "Would you like coffee, Uncle Teddy?"

"Yes, my dear."

"Amanda?"

"Thank you."

The mundane banter gave Caroline a chance to soothe her frayed nerves. After she served her friends, she took a deep breath and addressed the issue forthwith. "I locked you in for your own safety, Mr. Davin." She traipsed breezily to the coffee tray to pour herself a cup, using the activity as an excuse to ignore the sardonic look gleaming in his eyes. "If you wandered off in the night, you might well fall into the bog and never be seen again."

"I said I would be here for you." He spoke each word with seething precision. "You still don't know what my word means, do you?"

She looked up from her ministrations at the coffeepot.

"I'll be here for you," he repeated with angry emphasis.

The declaration seared through the last vestiges of her armor and punched her in the heart. She shut her eyes. No man had ever sworn to be there for her. For her alone. Suddenly her decision to lock him up seemed so far off the mark she was embarrassed by her lack of good judgment. It was fear that had steered her off the path.

She sank down in a chair next to his and stared dolefully at his graceful, strong hands that cradled his saucer and cup. "I know there is no good reason for what I did. But there was a reason. There have been men . . . who left before. They became . . . frightened. They . . . claimed to have seen a ghost."

She swallowed hard and gave him a wincing look, expecting a bark of cynical laughter. When he merely stared at her, she rushed on: "Oh, Mr. Davin, I am sorry! I was afraid you would run away. And I didn't think I could bear that."

A tear spilled over her right cheek and his face lost all its venom. His large black eyes softened, looking like those in a wistful charcoal sketch.

Amanda rose stiffly. "Caro, do not be so sentimental. Of course Mr. Davin would not leave. He has struck a bargain. You seem to be forgetting this is a business transaction."

Ignoring Amanda, unwilling to break eye contact with Lucas, sensing she just might mend the rift if she were indubitably honest at long last, Caroline said, "Do you understand, Mr. Davin? Tell me you do and I will be ever so relieved."

He pursed his lips and stared down at the steam rising from his cup. He frowned, his jaw muscles ticking wildly as he seemed to argue with himself. At last he said on a sigh, "I believe I do, Mrs. Davin. I believe I understand perfectly."

She let out a little soundless laugh of relief. When their eyes locked with a potent emotion that went far beyond lust, or mere attraction, or felicity, she felt queasy and broke the stare. She turned her focus to her coffee and busied herself drinking it, her chest feeling inexplicably constricted.

Theodore began to pace before the fire. "Caro is quite right about all the supposed ghost sightings at Fallingate. Tell me, my good man, did you hear anything last night? Anything out of the ordinary?"

Lucas looked from one to the other as if they'd all gone daft. "Nay. I heard the storm, if that's what you mean. Not much else."

"No shrieking?" Theodore prodded him, waving his hand in the air as he drew imaginative examples. "No voices? No . . . threats?"

"Threats? Lud, no."

"This is very interesting," Theodore said, stroking his beard. "Very interesting. He is the first of Caroline's suitors to sleep the night through undisturbed. That must be because he did not *expect* to hear anything."

"What are you saying, Dr. Cavendish?" Amanda asked.

"All the other men who have come to Fallingate had heard the rumors and therefore expected to hear from Lord Hamilton. They were susceptible to the very suggestion of a ghost."

"Oh, Lud," Lucas muttered. "Try and understand as I might, this is beyond the pale, mate. If you've changed your mind about this farce, then say so. I'll be on the next ship to India."

"No," Caroline said, seeking and finding his attentive gaze. "That is precisely the point. We do not want to scare you off. That was why I went to such extremes last night. I'm afraid we haven't told you the real reason no one would marry me."

She smiled hesitantly, and he wiped a hand over his face as he groaned. "Oh, this is famous. Go on, tell me all of it."

She proceeded to regale him with an abbreviated history of her disastrous brushes with courtship. Lucas listened without interruption, pouring himself another cup of coffee as she spoke with endearing sincerity about her unlucky history with Cupid. By the time she'd finished, he was standing by the fire, his china cup resting on the mantel. He'd been staring at the coals, and when her voice fell silent, he looked up, not without sympathy.

"So these idiotic dandies claim they heard a real ghost?" he said.

She looked so vulnerable, sitting upright in her chair, her cheeks flaming pink, her eyes round like a doe's.

"Yes, they have variously claimed to have heard Barrett's voice, as well as Lady Rachel's."

"Bloody fools."

"It seems their imaginations ran away with them," Theodore concluded. "And you have proven it. You did not hear anything, Davin, because you had never heard the rumors that this house was haunted. Though you lived in London, you did not associate with anyone in Society. Gentlemen in Town propogate the most absurd accounts of the haunting of Fallingate House."

Lucas went to Caroline's side. He tilted her head up with a gentle touch to her chin and stroked her cheek with the back of his hand. "Yer could have told me, luv, about the rumors. I may be a monkey who can ape a gent's fine speech, but I ain't no dandy. Mrs. Plumshaw is right. I made a bargain and I aim to keep it."

Caroline pulled her head from his touch, unable to speak. He had the power to move her unlike any man she had ever known. No man of her station had ever shown this much courage or dependability. How wrong of her ever to have thought Lucas less than herself.

"Yes, I should have told you, Mr. Davin. But I did not know you at all."

He nodded. "So tell me what you will about this ghost. Who is he? I'd like to know in the event I meet him on some cold, dark night."

"Lord Barrett Hamilton," Theodore answered briskly, ticking off the facts. "He died in the Tower during the reign of Henry VIII. He and Lady Rachel Harding were what you might call a pair of star-crossed lovers. They were torn apart during the English Reformation. He had sought sanctuary here when it used to be Morton Abbey. Lord Hamilton did not take too kindly to being betrayed by the abbot and so he put a curse on the place."

Lucas only half heard this explanation. At the very mention of the ghost's name, he turned to stare accusingly at Caroline. "Lord Hamilton? The man in the portrait?"

She nodded.

His hands slowly curled into fists, and he mustered a wry smile. "You said you weren't in love with him. Is that because he's a ghost?"

"No," she whispered emphatically. "It's because of you."

There was a laden pause, which was disturbed only by the ticking of the clock on the mantel.

"Now that that is all settled," the doctor said, rubbing his hands together, "let us get to work. It is clear, Davin, that you are fully committed to our project. Your speech is improved. It is time you learned some manners!"

Thirteen

n hour later, Lucas and Theodore stood before the fireplace in his coach house, puffing on cheroots while behind them Shabala set a small table with china and silverware.

Theodore waved to the finery with his glowing cigar. "What is this, I ask you? This fine china? This silver? It is a symbol of success, my boy. And man alone would not need such simple representations of wealth were it not for women."

"Aye, mate, women are a cartload of trouble," Lucas agreed, drawing hard on his cheroot. He exhaled and white smoke momentarily dimmed his view of the comforting fire.

"If it were up to men, we would live merely for survival and pleasure. Hunting and drinking and smoking to our hearts' content."

Lucas sat down in an odd-looking chair softened with cushions covered with brightly colored African fabric. It looked odd, but it was a damned sight more comfortable than the chairs in any lady's parlor.

"Who needs women?" Lucas said, crossing one leg leisurely over the other.

"We do," Theodore pronounced. He pointed his cheroot at Lucas and grinned knowingly. "My boy, where would we be if we could do as we please twenty-four hours a day? There would be no challenge, no discipline, no culture. Why, even in Africa the men have rituals and ceremonies to make one day more special than the next, to acknowledge one rite of passage or another. To you and me these rituals would seem primitive, but to the natives they lend value to their mundane lives. And I can guarantee that these cultural rites and dances and rules and taboos were all thought up by women! Or at least inspired by them."

"Damned useless females," Lucas growled at the affrontery.

"No, no, my boy. They are very useful. A fine woman is like a fine wine—incomparable, alchemical, and intoxicating."

Lucas had had a taste of both wine and women since his arrival, and he wanted more. An image of sweet Caroline flashed in his mind's eye—her simple and pure face, riveting in moments of despair and hope—and passion.

"Alchemical, yer say?"

"Yes. Alchemy is the art of turning base metals into gold."

Lucas chewed the end of his cheroot and said, "Yer . . . or rather I should say . . . *you* can do that?"

"No." Theodore rose and wandered to the far wall, where his beakers bubbled under candle flames. "I am no alchemist, but I do dabble in native formulas. Men have been striving to create gold for centuries. And they have been trying to understand women for an equal length of time. What I mean to say, my boy, is that a woman is incomprehensible, just like the art of alchemy. And yet a man can feel no higher joy than that he feels when he submits to her magic."

Lucas stroked his chin and regarded the doctor in a new light. "Quite the romantic, eh, mate? You loved your wife?"

Theodore heaved a sigh that filled his portly girth. "More than life itself."

"You didn't have to marry her. You're an adventurer. A wife would be a pack of trouble out in the wilds."

Theodore caught his eye and shook his head with a knowing smile. "You have no idea what a boon she was to me. What a helpmate. A friend. A lover."

"Will you take another wife?"

Theodore shrugged. "She has been gone these five years. I could, I suppose. It has not been on my mind. But here now, we should be talking about you."

Theodore drew up a chair, a formal Chippendale upright that looked out of place with the rest of the African and other exotic artifacts.

"Look here, Davin, I have a proposal to make."

Lucas narrowed his eyes and grinned sardonically. "Not another one."

"The bargain you made with Caro is to stay a fortnight or so and then leave a rich man, never to return."

"Suits me right."

"But I have another idea."

Lucas stared at the fire and breathed deep the heat as he waited for another preposterous scheme.

"What if you were to stay?" Theodore said. "Stay forever. Live your life here as the master of Fallingate, the estimable Mr. Lucas Davin."

When he paused, waiting for reaction, Lucas pictured himself hosting dinner parties and hunting with the gentry, and again that longing he'd felt seeing Germaine House gripped his chest like a vise and squeezed hard. He leaned forward and put his elbows on his knees and dropped his face into his hands. What in God's name was wrong with him? He was having memories and longings he simply could not understand. This was absurd.

"Listen here, Davin, we can do it. I have civilized the most uncivilized natives imaginable. Look at Shabala, here," he said, pointing to the manservant as he put the last piece of silver in place. "When I found him he was hunting in the jungle. Now he is the best butler in England, and I assure you his salary is commensurate with his superior abilities. I can teach you how to hold silver, how to drink, how to hunt. I can even teach you how to fart the proper way."

Lucas began to laugh, then wiped his hands over his face. He threw his cheroot into the fire and leaned back, roaring with laughter.

Theodore grinned broadly, teeth flashing white amid his brown-and-gray beard. "You don't think I can? Just let me have a chance, my boy. I will pass you off before the royalty as one of our most esteemed country squires. All it takes is acting."

Lucas's laughter died away, leaving him alone with the most curious notion he'd ever had: what if? He blinked slowly and studied the fire, seeing in the licking flames the image of Germaine House. How could he ever fit in with a society he'd spent his life abhorring? He shook his head.

"No, I like you, Dr. Cavendish, but I don't mind saying this ain't me style. Why should I stay? As it stands, I'll be a rich man after a mere month's work as the husband of Caroline Wainwright. Why should I hang about and put up with the airs and pretensions of the gentry?"

Theodore's smile faded. His twinkling eyes sobered. He reached out and gripped Lucas's arm. "Because you can have Caro for the rest of your life. And that is no mean possession. Take my word."

Lucas's gut turned a somersault and he broke out in a cold sweat. He'd never be worthy of her. He couldn't even let himself hope to be. She was so damned . . . kind. Lud, he hated kindness. It made him feel older than his years and jaded and utterly without merit. How would he handle a lady of such quality? How would he live his life in her presence? It was all too foreign. And yet he wanted her, he wanted to bathe in her goodness, to know the peace of innocence again.

And he would be the first to admit, he wanted to kiss her again, and a whole lot more.

Suddenly he felt the burden of Theodore's grip and pulled his arm away, rubbing it where the doctor had squeezed too hard. He shot him a hard look. "Why would having a wife be such a boon?"

"Because it is *Caro*." Theodore stared at him through a haze of smoke that filtered up to the rafters littered with shields and banners. "I think you know what I mean."

Lucas closed his eyes briefly. An explosion of colors lit the darkness. A chaos of hope and writhing despair. He opened his eyelids only a sliver. The orange fire filled his vision.

"How would you do this? How would you . . . make me a gent?" he asked hoarsely.

Theodore gestured toward the table, where Shabala was putting the last fork in its place and dusting his hands contentedly.

"First you must study and study hard."

"I can learn, but it'll never feel natural."

"Not at first. But already your speech is improving. That's the easy part, especially with a man as intelligent as you. But to help you change your . . . demeanor . . . I want you to try a little concoction I have made." Theodore pulled a shiny, silver flask from his waistcoat.

Lucas blinked slowly and focused on the object. He had

already put so much faith in this Good Samaritan. Why not trust him with this? "What is it?"

"A tincture I've made from some native African plants. They alter the consciousness. They embolden the spirit and free you from all limitations. They're indigenous to a very small jungle that Shabala pointed out to me."

Lucas leaned forward and took the flask in his hand. The likeness of an African elephant was etched on the front. The thin, cylindrical silver container would fit nicely in his waistcoat, and he slipped it inside, though not agreeing to drink it.

"All I ask, Davin, is that you let me try to create a permanent transformation in your behavior. Now, of course, if you stay I'll have to amend the marriage settlement. Your residency here must depend entirely on Caroline's approval. If ever she withdraws her approbation, you must depart as originally planned. I simply must protect her legally, you understand."

Lucas leaned back, thinking of his ride with Caroline. He'd felt so . . . so right by her side. He'd felt as if he'd found someone he could talk with. She was so much more than any woman he'd ever known. He'd known trulls that would feign interest in him till they could tumble for a pence or two. He'd given Izzie his devotion, but she'd never admit she loved him, even though she did. Caroline was someone who couldn't hide her feelings, someone who listened to him as no one ever had before. As he'd never needed anyone to listen to him until now. Now, when his thoughts were jumbled and foreign to him, when he no longer even knew himself.

"Why, mate? Why do you even want me here? I'm no good. Yer—" He caught himself and blinked with irritation at his poor English. "Hell, listen to me. Will I ever get it right? I mean *you* know that. Why do you want me to stay?"

Theodore burst out with a jovial laugh. "For one thing, my boy, I would like to beat Sir Arthur Trumbull at his own game. We share the notion that good breeding can be taught. But the arrogant coxcomb has placed a bet at Carlton Club that he can turn a trollop into a lady by year's end. I'd like to turn you around first."

"So I am a monkey in a bloody zoo."

At that moment Professor Snipplewit, who'd been dozing in the rafters, let out a prodigious screech.

Lucas looked up at the monkey and said drolly, "Did you teach *him* English, too?"

Theodore leaned forward and placed his hand once more on Lucas's forearm, this time gently. "No, my good man. You deserve more than life has given you, Davin. I recognized that the moment I saw you in the jail. Give yourself a chance. That is all I am asking." He rose and gestured to the dining table. "Shall we begin?"

Lucas rose begrudgingly.

Theodore went to the table and pulled out a chair. "Now a gentleman never sits before a lady . . ."

"Now a lady never asks a gentleman to dance," Amanda said two hours later in the green parlor. It was a cozy, light-filled chamber near the back of the great house and much warmer than the gallery. Henry and another footman were hurriedly pushing the pale green damask furniture against the wall while Shabala placed some music on the pianoforte in the corner. He flipped the pages, looking for dancing music.

"Put the ottoman over there, Henry, very good," Amanda said, pointing to the far wall. When she caught Lucas staring at Shabala, she said, "Dr. Cavendish's manservant has acquired many gentlemanly skills since his arrival in England, not the least of which is proficiency at the pianoforte. And he is the soul of discretion. Even if you make a fool of yourself dancing, no one else will hear of it."

Lucas scratched his head at the increasing improbability of this entire farce of theirs. He would learn to dance with an erstwhile governess to the accompaniment of songs played by an African butler in a haunted house. He shook his head, unable to fathom it.

"Now, Mr. Davin, I think we should begin with the quadrille. It is a precise dance in a square and therefore it should be easy for you to memorize the moves."

Lucas said nothing. He stood in the center of the room, his hands calmly clasped at his waist, dubiously watching the parlor being transformed into a miniature ballroom.

"Take up the carpet, please, Henry." Amanda whirled around the room, giving orders in her competent way. Though Lucas knew she had little regard for him, he couldn't help but admire her dedication to her task.

"There, I think all is in order." She tucked a wayward wisp of reddish-blond hair under her cap and smiled at him. "Do you remember what we learned yesterday, Mr. Davin?"

Lucas grimaced and rubbed his forehead, trying to pull the right lesson from his overloaded brain. "Um . . . I think so. *Je m'appelle Monsieur Davin. Comment vous appellez-vous?*"

"Very good!" She clapped her gloved hands together. "But I was not referring to your French lesson. Do you remember what I said about etiquette? A gentleman never introduces himself to a lady. So if you see a lady you would like to dance with, you must arrange an introduction, which can be done only with her permission through a third party."

Lucas scratched his brow. "Er, aye, I remember that one. But I don't want to dance with any lady other than my wife."

"Of course not, but you must know the rules. If you see another gentleman violating them, you can call him to book. Now, if a gentleman is introduced to someone who strikes his fancy, he may only have three dances with her, and then only if he's very serious about her."

Lucas scowled. "What if he wants a fourth dance?"

Amanda gave him a blank look. "He shan't have it. It simply isn't done."

"Why not?"

"I don't know why not. It just isn't done."

"Oh, Lud." Lucas rolled his eyes.

"And if he persists in thrusting his attention on a woman who does not wish to receive it, I warn you, Mr. Davin, he will put himself at grave risk of being cut."

"Being cut?" He looked at her dubiously. "They allow daggers at these balls?"

"No, no, Mr. Davin," Amanda said, laughing. "Being cut *socially*. By a woman."

"How would she do that?"

"Well, let me recall a good example," Amanda said, tapping a forefinger on her upper lip. "I suppose the best way for a woman to cut a gentleman is to give him an icy stare. If he is so rude as to continue speaking to her when she obviously does not wish to engage in his acquaintance-ship, the lady in question can then give a curt bow. If he fails to heed that dismissal, then he is only asking for the worst possible insult. If she says, 'Sir, I have not had the pleasure of your acquaintanceship,' when she in fact has, then he knows he has gone beyond the pale."

"And to be treated that way is an insult?"

Amanda's eyes widened. "The worst possible! You could scarcely show your face in London after being cut in such a fashion."

Lucas shook his head and heaved a sigh. "Oh, hell. Let's get on with it, then."

Amanda smiled at his reluctant, though obvious, submission. "There just may be hope for you yet, Mr. Davin. Now, the quadrille has a certain logic to it. You begin with four couples. Let me show you. Shabala, you may begin to play."

When Amanda nodded commandingly, the manservant began an elegant and lively tune. "Now picture the four points of a diamond. That is where each couple begins."

Like a young lady half her age, Amanda moved gracefully from point to point, responding to an imaginary partner. As she progressed, she loosened up and tossed back her head with a laugh as if the phantom dancer were flirting with her. Lucas smothered a smile. When she whirled around and caught sight of him, she halted abruptly and tugged down on her skirts.

"I am sorry. I got quite carried away. Well, you now have an idea of what's proper in a quadrille. You must, of course, at all times be graceful. Try it, Mr. Davin. Follow my steps."

He stood behind her and shadowed her movements, with considerably less grace. When he stumbled and nearly fell to the floor, he swallowed his pride and continued with the lesson another quarter of an hour. When they were through with the quadrille, Amanda beamed him an encouraging smile.

"You will be an excellent dancer."

"Oh, hell, don't lie, Mrs. Plumshaw. I'm bloody awful." Lucas waved her off and plopped down on one of the sofas shoved aside for the lesson. "I need a drink."

"No, Mr. Davin, it will only make you clumsier. There are other dances to learn. You must be patient. Remember, Rome wasn't built in a day."

"Rome? Don't tell me we're going to Rome! And where the bloody hell is that anyway?"

"Never mind." The door opened and Caroline appeared,

regarding him with a hopeful smile. "Oh, Caro, your timing is perfect. Will you please play the part of Mr. Davin's dance partner for the quadrille?"

Caroline's smile turned tremulous. "Oh. Well, I am not wearing gloves, I fear."

"Shabala will not say a word to the others about your lack of gloves. He's most discreet. And in any event, Caro, Mr. Davin is your husband. There's nothing improper here."

"Yes, of course," she replied. "I keep forgetting."

"You needn't fear any undue liberties. Mr. Davin will be on his good behavior."

"So you say," Lucas muttered to himself as his eyes locked with his wife. Blood surged in his temples and somewhere much lower. Damnation! What was it about her? She was not outstandingly beautiful. There was nothing remarkable about her physical person. Her eyes weren't particularly brilliant. Her complexion, when she wasn't upset, was rather pale. Her lips were sweetly heart-shaped but not sensual works of art. And yet she gripped him. She utterly gripped him. Watching him through her prim glasses, she seemed to see him and him alone. Perhaps that was it. She possessed a remarkable ability to focus her thoughts, and when she focused on him, he felt important.

"Yes," she said with a soft and genuine smile. "I will dance with Mr. Davin."

She glided forward, her gown rustling in the silence, and placed her right hand in his. He bowed and she curtsied. When he unnecessarily put his lips to the back of her hand in a gallant kiss, he heard her snatch a tiny breath, and smiled to himself. Now he knew without doubt. She felt the same way he did. She wanted him. In truth, he'd known it since the first time he'd kissed her. The question was, when would he be able to do anything about it?

Resisting the urge to crush her to him, he ended the kiss and stood erect, taking his place for the dance.

He caught her blue gaze and winked at her. "Ready?"

"I am ready."

"Very well," Amanda said, and Shabala began to play again.

At first they did not move. Caroline was waiting for Lucas to take the lead, and he was waiting for her. She cleared her throat nervously and glanced up, wondering what he was about, why he hesitated. He gave her a slow, crooked smile. She returned it with a sweet one of her own.

Weary of all the pretense, and so delighted to have her near him, he broke form and turned to her. Shabala stopped playing as Lucas slipped a hand around her waist, yanking her into a close embrace. He could have kissed her cap, she was so close. He could have nuzzled her delicate neck, it was so exposed. But he resisted.

"Have you ever danced a jig, Mrs. Davin?" he said in an intimate whisper.

"No, I haven't," she replied, looking through her glasses with trusting innocence.

Amanda looked on with a perplexed frown, kneading her kerchief. "Is something amiss?"

"Would you like to learn?" he said, cocking her a wry grin. "I might actually teach *you* something."

Her cheeks dimpled with a fetching grin. "Very well."

"Pardon us for a moment, Mrs. Plumshaw." Lucas looked over the top of Caroline's head at Dr. Cavendish's man. "Shabala, a jig, please. Don't fail me, good man."

The sober manservant smiled wide, revealing a stunning row of white teeth. "Yes, sir."

Shabala broke into a jolly tune.

"Shabala!" Amanda admonished him. "That is a most inappropriate song for a quadrille."

With one arm still clenched around her waist, Lucas

grabbed Caroline's hand and launched into a foot-stomping jig. Together they became a whirling dervish vaulting around the room in a free, heart-pumping dance.

"Mr. Davin!" Amanda called out in vain. "That will never do at a Society ball."

"I don't care!" he shouted over his shoulder, laughing as he said it. Caroline, too, broke into laughter, throwing back her head, no longer even trying to keep to any form. She was amazed at how well he danced. He was the most extraordinarily talented man when he was allowed to be himself. And she was astonished at her own coordination. She'd never really known how well she could dance until now, when there weren't any rules to tell her where to put her feet, or which way to position her hips. She had to follow gut instinct to keep up with him, and the knowledge that she could do so was exhilarating.

"Mr. Davin," she shouted through her laughter, "where did you learn to dance like this?"

He didn't answer immediately, instead he spun her in the opposite direction, and she soon was panting for air at the effort to keep her feet going in the right direction.

"You don't learn a dance like this," he answered between steps. "You are born to dance this way."

Amanda, who'd been fuming by the pianoforte, lowered her crossed arms as she began to recognize the grace required to dance to so freely. Soon she was tapping her foot to the beat, and before long she clapped her hands to the rhythm, smiling joyfully.

Much to the disappointment of all, the song came to a sudden finish. It took a moment for the dancers to slow to a stop. Of one accord, they collapsed on the green damask sofa, panting for air, perspiring, laughing.

"Oh, Mr. Davin," Caroline managed to say when at last she caught her breath. "I've never had so much fun in all my days."

"Then you've been deprived." He sat up and looked at her with good-natured irony. "I told you my way of life was more fun."

Still lolling against the sofa, she boldly reached for his hand, and gripping his fingers, she felt the tug of unseen desire. "You were right."

"Well, I daresay there's been enough jollity for one day," Amanda interrupted. "Caroline, you've quite forgotten yourself. You're sitting like a sailor. Might I remind you you're not alone." She looked significantly at Shabala.

Caroline forced herself to sit up. Coils of dark hair clung to the moisture gathered at her temples. She took in one last, long snatch of air, catching her breath at last.

"Oh, Amanda, have some fun! I don't believe Mr. Davin needs any lessons in dancing at all," she pronounced, and rose to her feet.

Lucas stood and took her hand, leading her to the center of the room. "I thank you for your compliment, but I tend to agree with Mrs. Plumshaw," he said diplomatically. "I simply must learn the quadrille or I'll make a cake of myself in public."

Amanda nodded her head with approval. "Just so, Mr. Davin."

"Let us try the quadrille one more time," he said, encompassing the women with a charmingly self-deprecating smile. "I promise to be good this time."

He bowed before Caroline. She was just about to curtsy in return when a sudden creaking groan sounded directly overhead. Plaster began to shower down on their heads. Caroline looked to the ceiling, then screamed. Her eyes shot open wide and she shoved Lucas with all her might.

"Get back!" she shrieked, and the momentum from shoving him hard sent her falling on top of him. Together they stumbled forward and smashed to the floor.

A moment later, another creak split the air and the chandelier fixed to the ceiling crashed to the floor in a chaos of glass and candles.

Instinctively, Lucas covered Caroline in a protective gesture. When he felt her trembling in his arms, he smoothed his hand over her soft hair.

"Do not fear, Caro," he said, even before he knew whether there was anything more to come.

He looked up and saw Amanda staring aghast at the crumpled heap of the lighting fixture. Then he himself focused on the monstrous ball of twisted metal and broke out in a cold sweat.

"You could have been killed!" Amanda cried out, breaking the potent silence.

"Are you hurt, sir?" Shabala said, kneeling beside Lucas.

"No, Shabala, we're fine." Lucas sat up, never letting Caroline go. She looked at the chandelier and clutched his waistcoat.

"Lucas, you were nearly killed," Caroline whispered.

He nodded, then looked up at the ceiling, wondering what on earth—or in heaven—had caused the fixture to fall.

Fourteen

fter dinner, everyone gathered in the library for a glass of port. Caroline paced before the fire, impatiently waiting for Feathers.

"Where is he?" she said, pushing her spectacles to the bridge of her nose. "My instructions were entirely clear."

"Feathers has been somewhat . . . unreliable," Amanda said. She sat next to Theodore on the ottoman. Lucas leaned against the mantel, stroking the cleft in his chin as he watched Caroline pace like a caged animal.

Finally the oak double doors opened.

"You rang, ma'am?"

Caroline was nonplussed to see Henry in the doorway. "Where is the butler?"

"Mr. Feathers . . . well, ma'am, he is . . . indisposed."

"Whatever do you mean?"

"He's not been seen lately. Not since the accident in the green parlor. He left on horseback. He didn't tell anyone where he was going."

Caroline blinked at this, then turned to the others. No one had any comment and she turned back to the footman.

"Very well, Henry. When you see Mr. Feathers again tell him that he has been relieved of his duties until further notice. Meanwhile, you are to assume his position. Bring us port, will you please?"

Henry gave a short bow and withdrew.

"Perhaps my sister-in-law was correct, though I hate to admit it," Caroline said. "It would seem I have kept Feathers on past his time. I cannot tolerate a servant who puts his personal business ahead of his duties."

They discussed Shabala's dependability and his calm during the calamity in the parlor until Henry returned with the port, which he served and then retreated. Caroline took a sip and stared reflectively at the fire.

"It was not an accident. It couldn't have been," she said, and found herself looking to Lucas for confirmation. "Don't you see? The ghost of Lord Hamilton wanted to punish you for dancing with me. He made that chandelier come crashing down."

"Come, Caro, you cannot be serious," Theodore scoffed. "This is an old house. Your sister-in-law, you say, is planning repairs? Perhaps she is right on that score as well. The fixtures probably haven't been looked at in years."

"There was nothing wrong with that chandelier, Uncle Teddy. And even if there had been, why would it have fallen at that precise moment, after I had danced with Mr. Davin? It fell precisely when he was standing beneath it. After we had been . . . close."

"Too close," Amanda commented wryly. "Perhaps your dancing jarred the ceiling. It was a rather raucous affair. In any event, you do not believe in the ghost of Lord Hamilton. Remember?"

"I didn't used to. Perhaps I do now." Caroline went to stand next to Lucas. Heat and comfort wafted from him. She felt better just being near him. "What do you think, Mr. Davin? Is there a ghost in this house wishing you ill?"

He blinked tenderly and touched her chin with a fore-finger. "I've had odd feelings since coming here. But I cannot blame them on a ghost. I feel blessed that you should worry so about me, but don't let your imagination run wild."

"That is the most sensible remark I have heard tonight," Theodore agreed. "We'll have Henry examine the fixture tomorrow. That should tell us whether it fell by accident or design. Meanwhile, drink up, Caro, and get to bed. You need a good night's rest."

She raised her glass to Lucas and smiled ironically. "Here's to your health, Mr. Davin."

"Long may I live," he rejoined, then put his glass to his lips, drinking, his eyes never leaving hers.

He watched through the pouring rain from the stone fence that bordered the garden. Her room was lit by candlelight, and he could make out her slender form. She was a sil-houette, a feminine profile visible through diaphanous curtains.

She paced anxiously, and he knew why. She was wait-ing for *him*. This Lucas Davin. This interloper. He had tried so hard to keep her as she was—a maiden. But then *he* had come, a man he had not expected. A man who did not even fear ghosts.

And so he knew what had to be done. She would pay for this transgression. She would see Lord Hamilton at last.

There! She had snuffed out the light. She would be asleep soon. And then it would be time. She would feel the terror of Lord Hamilton's curse.

Caroline had scarcely fallen asleep when she awoke to the most chilling sound she had ever heard. She held per-fectly still. Had it been the wind?

Rachel.

No! It was a voice. Her heart began to beat wildly. Was she imagining things? She had clearly heard someone calling the name Rachel.

Tap, tap, tap. Tap, tap, tap.

She looked in horror at the window. Someone was knocking, trying to get in.

Tap, tap, tap. Tap, tap, tap.

Caroline's skin crawled with dread. There had been six distinct knocks. That was the exact number Lord Hamilton had mentioned in his diary. Lady Rachel Harding would come each night to the abbey and rap on his window six times.

Rachel.

"Damme!" Caroline whispered with a choked sob. "This cannot be happening."

But she'd wanted it to happen. She'd longed to see the ghost that so many others had claimed to see. But why was he making himself known now, when it was too late? *Or almost too late.*

Gooseflesh rippled over her arms as she realized why he'd come. Barrett knew how close she was to giving herself physically to Lucas. He knew without being told, for his presence permeated this house. Barrett Hamilton was everywhere. The chandelier incident had proven that. There was nothing he didn't see. Now she was sure of her niggling suspicion: the ghost of Lord Hamilton had tried to kill Lucas today. And now he had come for her.

In an instant outrage replaced her fear.

"How dare you!" she cried out, throwing back her covers and hopping out of bed. She put on her spectacles, for she didn't want to miss a thing. "You have already destroyed my chances of a proper marriage. You will not take away my last chance at salvaging my inheritance! Go away!"

She stormed toward the window, where rain lashed and pelted the glass in hard spurts.

"You will not kill the only man I have ever kissed! Do you hear me, Barrett?"

Not knowing from where she drew her courage, she unlatched the window and flung it open. She flinched when wind burst into her face, spraying her with rain. Startled, she squinted and gasped at the cold, and when she wiped her eyes, she saw something that hadn't been there before. A rain-drenched face.

"Oh . . . my . . . God!" Air caught in her throat and shriveled in her lungs.

"Rachel." A moaning voice emanated from the ghostly, tortured face. "Is it you?"

"B-Barrett?" Caroline could scarcely speak. The face started to move toward her, as if disembodied. And of course it was. For it was a ghost. At this realization, Caroline screamed at the top of her lungs. "Aaaaaiiieee!"

Too terrified to flee, she flung her hands to her face and screamed again. Moments later, the door to Lucas's dressing room burst open behind her.

"What is it?" Lucas ran to her side and gripped her, enveloping her in his comforting strength. "Caroline! What is it?"

"Lucas?" She tried to speak, but the image of Barrett Hamilton terrorized her. She looked into his face. "Lucas, is it you?"

"Yes, I'm here. What happened, luv?" He twirled her around and gripped her upper arms with unusual strength. "Tell me!"

She pressed her hands to his chest. He wore only a nightshirt. His muscles filled her palms. She dug her fingers into the linen shirt. He was real. He was real and the man behind her was a ghost.

"I saw . . . I saw Barrett Hamilton. Look, look behind me, Lucas. He is there. I swear he is there!"

Lucas gently pushed her aside and lunged for the window. Outside, a shutter banged back and forth in the wind, squeaking with each motion. A branch scraped at the window. Rain pelted Lucas's face. A shadow lurched below, and Lucas stared intently, trying to make out a figure. But there was no one there. His heart sank. Poor Caroline had been done in by everyone else's absurd fears. He reached out and broke the branch that had been making the noise, then pulled it shut and latched it.

"There. It's all taken care of." Swiping the rain from his cheeks, he turned to her and realized just how pale she was. "You poor thing. It was nothing. A branch was banging on the window."

She exhaled in disbelief. "But the face! I swear I saw a face. A man who looked just like . . . him!" She pointed accusingly at the painting.

"No, Mrs. Davin," he said soothingly, and drew her trembling body into his arms. "There was nothing."

She began to cry in frustration. "You do not believe me. And it's what I deserve after all the years I refused to believe the others."

He gripped her hand in his. "You're ice-cold. I'll stoke the fire." He went to the hearth and worked at the smoldering peat, then threw on a lighter, loosely packed brick of it cut from the bogs. The fire flamed to life.

There was a knock on the door. "Mrs. Davin?" said Biddie. "Are you all right? I thought I heard a scream."

"Yes, Biddie. It was just a nightmare. Go back to bed."

"Very well, ma'am."

Caroline turned back to Lucas. In the firelight he could more clearly see the terror etched on her face.

"He is going to kill you, Lucas. I know he is."

"Lord Hamilton?" Lucas smirked. "Let him try."

"No, don't say that. He'll hear you. He's everywhere. I used to think that his soul dwelled in that painting." She nodded toward the portrait over the fireplace. "But now I realized that ghosts are omnipresent."

She reached up with one hand and touched her husband's face with her fingers. He was so beautiful. So masculine, so dark and brooding and hurt.

"Oh, Lucas," she said, swallowing thickly. "Lucas."

"I like when you call me that. The hell with formalities." Then he added, mocking his old way of speaking, "It ain't me style, ma'am."

Her gaze lowered over his Roman nose, his angular cheeks, and fixed on his lips, the mouth that held so many secrets in its sensuous creases and folds. She leaned in closer, wishing so desperately that he would kiss her again. If he would just do that, she could forget everything else. She tilted her head back and inhaled his masculine scent, felt his moist breath warming her cheeks.

"Caroline," he said huskily.

"Yes, Caroline," she whispered vehemently, opening her eyes just enough to regard him through a row of thick, dark, velvety lashes. His beauty filled her vision. "Don't ever call me Mrs. Davin again."

"Caroline," he repeated, wrapping his arms around her. He brushed his lips across her forehead, then nuzzled his mouth against her ear. "Don't do this to me."

"Do what?" she whispered as she wrapped her arms around his narrow waist, leaning into him.

"Don't tempt me. I can't have you. Don't you see?"

"No," she replied, nestling her ear to his lips. "No, I do not see. I want—"

She stopped mid-sentence as a profound realization struck her. She frowned at him wonderingly. "Are you saying that I tempt you? So much so that you . . . you might not be able to resist me?"

He barked out an incredulous laugh. "How could you even wonder?" He pulled her closer and pressed her hips to his, letting her feel the hard evidence of temptation between his legs.

Her eyes widened as understanding dawned. She'd heard all about this phenomenon from a childhood chum.

"Lucas. Oh, Lucas, I never thought a man would ever want me like that."

"Gads!" He placed his warm hands on her exposed shoulders and growled, "Take off your damned spectacles and let me have a good look at you."

She did as she was told and blinked him into focus. She had little trouble seeing, except when she was reading. Her mother used to say she read so much she would go blind.

He gazed into the startling depths of her glittering blue eyes and saw leaping glimmers of firelight. His own vision, his very soul, seemed to coalesce in their depths. It was in this moment that he finally realized what made Caroline so extraordinary, even more so than London's famous belles. And he understood why he'd never recognized it before. She'd hidden her depths, her ultimate beauty, behind glass.

Until now he could see only glimpses of reflective color through her spectacles; a flash of intelligent perception here, a wink of wisdom there. He had never quite seen the full extent and the utter clarity of her understanding. Until now. It settled him. Made him feel significant and connected to her. It made him want to stay, and not escape, which was his specialty. After all, she was the only woman who had perceived his goodness beneath his tough exterior. The only one who had not denied it, even though she had more reason than all the others to spurn him.

She gazed at him now with touching trust, with womanly hunger sizzling in her eyes, and she would never think to pretend it was anything but that. He understood now why she'd been out of sorts her whole life, unappreciated by her set. Honesty was not a highly prized commodity in Society. And she would never be at ease with the kind of facile lies expected by Society. Was it any wonder that she'd quickly learned to keep quiet rather than say what was wholly honest and entirely unacceptable? Now he knew why she was attracted to him: he was honest, to a fault.

"Why do you wear these damned spectacles?" he asked, pulling them from her fingers and placing them on a table. Then he held her face in his hands while he kissed each eyelid. He came away with the taste of salt, and he realized he'd moved her. Lord, she made him feel powerful.

She gripped his wrists while he held her face like the first rose of spring. "I wear them because they protect me."

"They're a barrier, hiding your light, luv."

"Yes, but I want to see."

"What?"

"Everything. I want to see others more clearly than they see me."

He blinked as emotion stung his own eyes. "Why don't others see you clearly, Caro?"

Her brows puckered with sadness. "Because I am not beautiful. People only see the beauty in life. Love comes easily to the fair of face."

"Perhaps," he said, skimming a thumb over her tender lips. "But they can't keep love long if they don't have beauty inside as well."

"Then I feel sorry for them. For it must be terrible to have love and lose it."

"Have you ever loved, Caro?"

Her blue eyes filled. "No. I've wanted it too much. I've cursed my feelings, for they've caused so much trouble, but they won't go away. I have too much love in my heart, Lucas."

"No," he crooned, and stroked her cheek, "not too much, luv. Just the right amount."

He kissed her heart-shaped lips, and she responded with the yearning that had been bottled up in her heart so long. Heat flowed from her in a wave, shocking him with its intensity. This woman was made for love. She didn't know it, but she was an embodiment of passion in a society that tolerated nothing more than the superficial. Oh, how he would like to teach her how much love a man could take.

With a tilt of his head, a gentle brush of chins, of whiskers grazing rose-petal skin, the caress of noses, the exchange of warm, sweet breath, he pushed her lips open and deepened the kiss. When their tongues met, she went still, her entire being focused on that one intimate and wet exchange. His skilled satin tongue caressed softly at first, and when he'd gotten a good taste of her, he used it to lash her into frantic desire, chilling her skin, awakening her depths. She moaned and threw her arms around his neck, hugging him close, pressing the muscles of his chest against her hardened nipples.

In that singular moment she learned just how deeply a man could kiss a woman and how deeply she could return the kiss.

When he broke away, she shivered and let out a breath of wonder, looking at him as if he were a creature never before seen by human eyes. A mythical beast sent down from Olympus to awaken sleeping maidens.

"Oh, Lucas," she whispered. "That was good. That was very good."

He smiled and stroked her hair, which had tumbled from its braid. "Oh, Caro, I wish I could show you everything I know of love. I could teach you so much."

"I believe you could. I don't believe anyone else in the world could but you." Troubled by his melancholy tone, she put her hands on his chest. Not knowing how to ask for what she didn't even know how to name, she tried to please him with caresses.

When her fingertips brushed over his brown nipples, he sucked in a breath and arched his head back, as if she'd branded his skin. He frowned and laughed and spoke his pleasure in so many groans. Just when she was beginning to think she'd pleased him, he gripped both her wrists and pulled her hands away.

He looked down at her and said, "I can't do it."

"You can't? Or you won't?"

His gaze cooled. "Both."

She pressed her hands to the hollow feeling in her belly. "I see."

"No, you don't. I can't, Caro. For your sake."

She struck him with an angry gaze. "So those were fancy words you just spoke about beauty inside. You were lying?"

He shook his head. "No, luv, I meant every word. Oh, Caro, I wish you could see yourself through my eyes."

"Then tell me. What do you see? Please, Lucas, tell me something good."

He brushed a forefinger along her forehead, where soft flesh met the smooth, downy line of her brows. "I see a simple beauty that comes from goodness so deep in your soul no one could possibly ever take it from you." His finger trailed down her cheek. "I see a pureness that a man like me should never sully."

She felt for his other hand, squeezing when she'd found it, anything to hold him close when he was so determined to move away.

"I see sweet lips that speak the truth, that make me wild with hunger." He dragged his finger over her mouth, skimming the moisture there. Impulsively, he kissed her, his tongue delving into the honey pot that was there for the tasting.

With his free hand he found a nipple protruding from her nightgown. He pinched lightly, and a moist heat bubbled between her legs. She squeezed his hand hard, her head rotating with his fierce kiss.

At length, he pulled back and looked at her with hard, hungry eyes. "I want you. Don't ever doubt it."

"Then satisfy me, Lucas. Don't leave me wanting for something I don't even know how to ask for."

"No." He turned away and went to the window, gripping the frame with rigid fingers. "I'm going away soon, Caro. And I can't leave you with a babe in your belly. Not the child of a bastard whelp dragged from the streets by a Good Samaritan. I may be poor, but I know enough to know that a lady should marry from among her own."

Hope sparked in the darkness, a tiny yellow flame, and a wind of determination from deep in her soul blew it to life. So that was it! He doubted himself. She knew whence that emotion came. That was something she could understand and cope with; she could reassure him as she'd longed to be reassured in her solitude. She'd not let him go merely for self-doubt, oh no. If he didn't want her, if he didn't love her—Lord, how could she even think of such permanence?—then she would let him go. But if it were merely self-doubt, then no, she could not accept that.

"Lucas," she said firmly, coming up behind him. She didn't reach for him, for she had to touch him first with her thoughts to penetrate the wall between them. "I never thought I would meet anyone who could see me. But you have."

He turned sideways, and gazed at her in the safety of darkness.

"I feel so whole," she continued. "I feel as if I understand the world at last. And now I want to feel its warmth.

I want to feel love, Lucas, whether you love me or not. I want to be held by the only man who cared enough to look into my eyes.

"I do not care where you come from. I do not even care where you will go from here. I simply want to hold you. Now. While I may. Please, Lucas, hold me. Make me warm. Touch me deep inside once and I will never forget it. I swear I will be grateful always."

Tears trailed down her cheeks. She could feel him struggling with himself.

"Caro, it is too dangerous. You would get my child. It is not right."

"Only if God is willing. And then I would consider myself the most fortunate of women in all the world. Then I would have some bit of you forever. Only better, for it would be the best of both us."

He went to her in one fell swoop and put his arms around her, burying his face in her neck, surrendering to the love unnamed, unspoken, and eternal that carried him in its maelstrom.

Holding her was the balm he'd been searching for all his life. How could he turn her away?

"I can't . . . resist you," he whispered against her throat, and feeling the twist of desire in his groin, he knew they were done with words. "You give me no choice."

His tongue delved into her ear, dipping and laving her into a passionate frenzy. She laughed contentedly to know that love, even unadmitted love, could conquer the most reluctant heart.

He scooped her up in his arms and carried her to the bed, laying her in the middle. He climbed in and knelt over her, straddling her hips. Her splayed hair was a dark swirl of softness in a bed of down.

He dropped his hands to the bed and lowered his head to hers, stealing another kiss like the thief he was. He breathed her in, knowing that if he left, he would carry her inside of him, just as he would soon give inside of her.

As the kiss heated, she dragged her nails down his muscular arms. He sat up and pulled his shirt off, exposing his dusky skin, which glistened with sweat in the firelight. She ran her hands over his back, marveling at his strength. She wanted it all for her own, to hold his strength and love it.

He unlaced the top of her nightgown, then startled her by ripping it in two down to her waist, casually throwing it open to expose her breasts. They seemed to swell and ache under his touch. He kissed her in the cleft between her breast, and laid his ear there, smiling when he heard the rapid beat of her heart. He leaned over and laved a nipple with his tongue, nipping and tugging gently until she hissed with desire.

He pulled down his drawers, kicking them off the ends of his feet, and nestled up against her side. She felt the hardness pressing into her, pulsing against the remains of her gown. She wanted to know what it felt like, and so she reached out, jumping a little when he jolted at her touch. Butter silk. Velvet steel. The contrast of hard and soft amazed her.

But all thoughts ceased when he ripped her gown completely asunder and nudged her thighs apart, feeling for her most secret place. Finding it, he parted tender skin with magic fingers, nudging softly, insistently, seeking wetness, burrowing in with hard-soft thrusts. When at the same time he rubbed a place she did not even know she possessed, creating a burning feeling she did not even know humans could feel, she flew above herself, shaking and surrendering and exulting in an ecstasy of pleasure. The mythical beast had awakened the maiden.

"Oh, damme!" she cried out as she shook her way back to earth and sank heavily into the soothing down.

He chuckled low, and mercifully ceased his transporting

caresses. He kissed her neck and whispered, "Such a curse from a lady. You sound like a ruffian from Seven Dials."

Her smoky eyes found him, and he knew she only half heard his words. She was already in another world, lashed on by lust. Of course it would take such an innocent to respond that purely to his touch, so much without guile, to make him as hard as a rock and aching to fill her. He longed to make her feel like the woman he knew she was inside.

"Wh-what happened to me, Lucas?" she said, dazed. "Was that right? Was that how it is done?"

He smiled sweetly. "Did it feel right?"

"It felt . . . absolutely, famously wonderful. I felt as if I'd lost control."

"Aye, luv, then that is how it is done. But that ain't the half of it."

He slid over her, their sweat commingling and rendering all friction null. Her hips pressed against his. He nudged her legs farther apart with his knees, and before she even knew what he was doing, he entered, hard and firm, breathless and stunned by her heat and her sweetness and the love he felt, damn him. Yes, it was love. He shouldn't feel this, but he did, and he rocked into her with increasing urgency, knowing with each thrust that he was sealing their bond, whether he remained or not, whether they could ever be happy together or not, that they would be tied together by a rapture he thought he'd never feel again. Only this time the love was returned, and that made it real. Complete. He pushed aside the knowledge that he was selfish, that he shouldn't be making love to her. Knowing it was wrong only made it sweeter, only made him thrust harder.

She met him with each driving motion, looking up at h.m as no woman had before. Their eyes locked, and blurred together, and she groaned and cried out more freely than a bawd. Damme, but she was guileless. Guileless and free.

He rocked hard into her, his bedeviling demons letting go inside, letting him purge himself into this vast pool of goodness. He wanted to touch the deepest part of her, the essence of her purity. He wanted to bathe in it, to wash himself clean. And before he knew what else he wanted, he lurched with his release, throwing his head back in shock, losing himself in the unconsciousness of blinding pleasure.

He sank onto her, and when he could breathe again, he kissed her, over and over, silently thanking her, for he had never made love like that before. And he knew he never would again.

Fifteen

An hour later they made love again, longer and softer, and collapsed a final time in each other's arms. That was when she noticed them. The ugly, mottled scars. She stroked his back, smoothing her hand from his waist over the ridges of muscles that swelled on either side of his spine. Her hand stilled when she felt the strips of skin across his shoulder blades, which had been cut and left to heal badly.

The slow realization of what this meant dispersed the groggy fog of pleasure that she'd been immersed in. He'd been badly beaten long ago. She tightened her arms around him, feeling even more for him than she had just moments before. Now compassion swam with desire, making him more than a man who had just satisfied her most carnal cravings. He was her friend. And he had suffered. And she wanted to know why.

"Lucas?" she whispered in his ear as she stroked his damp hair. He smelled musky and manly and sweet all at once. She inhaled him, loving him.

He rolled over and stretched on his back with a contented grin. "Not again, luv, you've worn me out."

She glanced down at his chest and saw another scar, a short white one that rose in the crook of his shoulder.

"Where did you get that?" she asked, rubbing a finger over the caterpillar-shaped scar.

His smile faded. "Oh, that. That one I owe to Izzie."

"Izzie? Who was she?" Caroline realized she knew absolutely nothing about this man to whom she'd given her virtue and her life. Did he even have a family?

Lucas didn't answer for a long moment. He frowned hard at the ceiling. Then he turned on his side to face her. He bent his arm and propped his head on it and studied her with his uncommon intensity. "Are you sure you want to know?"

Her heart skipped a beat with foreboding, but she nodded nonetheless. "I want to know everything about you."

"Nay." One of his cheeks dimpled in a half smile. "No, you don't. But I'll tell you about Izzie. She was a milliner's daughter. A right pretty filly."

He stroked along the crevice between Caroline's breasts as he spoke, turning his story into an act of intimacy. She felt and listened with equal care.

"She was red-haired and headstrong and I loved her, innocent that I was. It was a long time ago." He bit his lower lip a moment and eyed her closely. "Want me to continue?"

She nodded, already engrossed.

"Without much reason, her mother had high hopes that her daughter would marry a baronet, or at least a country squire. Of course, Izzie, being bold and reckless, wanted to marry an earl's son. I told her it would never happen, and that I loved her and wanted to marry her, but she'd laugh in my face. I wasn't high-and-mighty enough for her, you see. And one night, when I seduced her, out of love for her, she got so mad she stabbed me with my own knife when it was over."

His eyes had a far-off look that shone with admiration. "Quite a woman, she was. Mind you, I wasn't the first, so I didn't take her virtue. She just got mad that someone beneath her had the power to make her feel anything, to threaten all her ambitious plans. She got jumped-up ideas in her head and fancied some lord's son who lived on the Strand. He took her to his bed and she had wild notions that he'd make her respectable. But she got with child and had the poor bleeding thing in squalor. She caught a fever not long after and died. Poor Izzie. She wanted so much from life. Too much."

He blinked away the memories, then leaned forward and gave Caroline a reassuring kiss. "Did I say too much?"

She shook her head against the pillow, and shut her eyes against a surge of warm tears. "Poor girl." She dabbed the corners of her eyes. "What about the other scars? The ones on your back."

He gave a rueful chuckle. "Those came from Robbin Roger. My father. He taught me a lesson or two when I was young."

"But did he have to beat you?"

"I don't blame him. He kept me alive. On the streets, sometimes you have to beat good sense into a lad for his own good."

Caroline sighed sadly. It didn't make sense to her. Poor little Lucas. And poor Izzie. "What happened to the baby?"

"Izzie's boy?" Lucas blinked rapidly, then his face became blank. "I don't know."

"Poor child."

"Right. Don't be sad, now. I speak of Izzie because there's a lesson in her story. She wanted too much, Caro, but you want too little. This shouldn't have happened to-night."

"Yes!" She sat up and took his cheeks in her hands, suddenly desperate at the judgment in his voice. "Yes, it should have happened. It was the best thing that ever happened to me."

"Nay, luv. You deserve more."

"I deserve you, Lucas. You have shown me what it means to be a woman. No other man could have done that. No other man wanted to."

"But there's a difference between us. You're a lady and I'm a rogue. And no amount of lovemaking will ever change that. I may be quick to learn right speaking, but that don't change my insides." He sat up and stroked her cheek, tucking a few damp tendrils of hair behind her ear like a loving father, then kissed her lips softly. "Just remember, Caro, that I told you it was wrong."

"No, Lucas, no, I—"

"Go to sleep, Caroline." He gently pushed her down onto the pillow. Then he smiled so sweetly that she knew everything would be all right. Tomorrow she would make him realize that this night was meant to be. She deserved the passion she'd only read about before. There was a place for such things in a marriage. She just knew it.

She blinked dreamily and sighed. "Thank you, Lucas. Thank you for this night."

He kissed her forehead and waited until her eyelids drooped and closed for the night. Then he drew back, painting a picture of her in his mind. He wanted to remember her like this, for he would never see her this way again. She was too naive to know what was right and what was wrong. But he knew. And he was man enough to do the right thing.

An hour later, Lucas sat alone in the Silver Stallion inn nursing a glass of gin. He paid for it with the coins Dr. Cavendish had given him. Pin money, the doctor had called it with a touch of irony. Lucas had ridden over after everyone else at Fallingate had gone to sleep. He actually had the groom saddle Lightning for him, and the ride from the great house to the lonely little wayside inn had been quick and refreshing. How quickly he'd learned to ride and speak like a gentleman! So quickly it raised even more questions he couldn't answer.

He already had enough questions niggling at his mind. At the wrought-iron gates to Fallingate, he'd hesitated before leaving, certain he'd seen someone running behind a row of hedges. Had it been a ghost? he'd wondered for the briefest moment. But the cold rain had discouraged long contemplation, and Lucas rode on.

Presently he sat alone with his thoughts, staring at the glow of the peat fire, listening to the tapster tell jokes to an old farmer. And as he enjoyed the pastoral scene with a sense a bittersweet longing, the sense that one has when one realizes all will soon be lost, he wondered where would he go. How could he extricate himself from an impossible situation without breaking the heart of a good woman?

He leaned back against the hardwood booth and breathed deeply. The intoxicating scent of Caroline wafted from his skin. He squeezed his eyes tight, remembering the precious feel of her beneath him. She'd taken him so completely, so purely, so full of unexpected heat. He took a stiff swallow of gin.

He could not make love to her again. He'd been weak giving in to her in that way. He'd been full of himself enough to think he could make a woman of her and give her an experience she'd never forget. But he had risked making a mother of her in the process.

He thought of the boys, the dear sweet lads. He'd sworn he'd never bring an unwanted child into the world. He especially had no right to foist one on Caroline. She thought she loved him. Hell, maybe she did. But she was lost in her passion and not thinking right. She didn't know what a burden it would be to have a lifelong reminder of Lucas Davin after he'd gone—the baby of a bastard-orphan-thief. No, he couldn't stay. He'd never fit in. Not really. Mrs. Plumshaw knew that. She was the only straight-thinking one among them. She'd learned her lessons the hard way, just like Lucas, and he wondered what brutal lesson life had given her to enable her to see through Lucas when the others couldn't.

"Mind if I take a seat, mate?" A nasal voice jarred his reveries.

Lucas looked up from his glass to find none other than Smiley Figgenbottom grinning at him.

"Figgenbottom!" Lucas said incredulously. He looked furtively at the tapster, then back at his cohort, and whispered, "What in bloody hell are yer doing here in Cragmere at this bleeding hour?"

"Lookin' for Lucas Davin, mate," the beak-nosed man said with a snarling laugh of victory. "Yer seen 'im?"

He shook off his rain-sodden cloak and sat down beside Lucas, rubbing his hands together. "I knew I'd find yer 'ere. I stopped by the gaol, and they said yer'd escaped already, that yer were far away in another country already. But I knew better."

"Is Robbin all right?"

Smiley waved a hand dismissively. "Oh, right, mate, don't worry about that old bugger. 'e'll outlive the rest of us." Smiley's thirsty gaze fell on Lucas's glass of gin and he licked his lips with a smack.

Lucas shook his head and waved to the tapster for two more glasses. Smiley was nothing if not obvious.

"So look at yer, will yer?" the cunning crook said, touching Lucas's garrick. The sleeved coat had five layers of capes hanging over the shoulders to the middle of the back. "A fancy greatcoat, I see. Wot the bloody 'ell yer been doin'? Tuppin' the Dowager Countess of Germaine herself?"

Lucas flushed with anger. He didn't want Smiley to know just how fond of his new clothes he'd grown. He waited until the tapster had delivered the drinks, carelessly slopping some on the rough-hewn table. Smiley looked as if he might lap it up with his tongue, but he held tight until Lucas slid a glass to him across the table.

"Pay no attention to what I'm wearing, Smiley. Just part of the setup. Is everything in order in London?"

"Runnin' right on course, mate. The gang is finishin' business, as it were, in Seven Dials. Then the plan goes into effect bang up to the mark, as your 'oity-toity friends might say. I wanted to make sure yer were still runnin' it before we brought our arses out to this blisterin', godforsaken countryside. It all 'appens in a fortnight, yer see. We hit Fallingate and Germaine House the same night, just like yer said. Yer still in, ain't yer, Lucas?"

When Lucas merely stared at his smudged glass, Smiley leaned over and squeezed his arm. "I'm in Queer Street right now, mate, and I could use some earnin' off me profession. Yer still in?"

Was he still in? His old life collided in this moment with the new. He'd blended so well into Caroline's home that he'd nearly forgotten who he really was. When she'd touched his scars tonight, she hadn't realize that she'd reminded him of the indelibility of the past.

Lucas felt as if the peat fire had sucked up the last of the air in the stuffy taproom. Sweat drenched his underarms. He tugged at his collar and took another gulp of gin, then wiped the perspiration on his upper lip with the back of a wrist, smudging his fine white cuff.

"Right, mate, I'm in." He coughed and stared at the

liquor in his hands. "Yer know the best way to rid yourself of a woman, Smiley?"

The dwarfish man cocked his head sideways, then shook it. "Nay, can't say as I do. Ain't 'ad no need to be riddin' meself of the skirts like Lucas Davin."

Lucas smiled sardonically. He'd had plenty of practice. Ever since Izzie had died, he'd sent them away. Never saw one worth keeping, until now.

"The best way," he said heavily, "is to make them hate yer. Then they do the riddin' themselves and think it was their idea. Hurts them less that way. Yer know the best way to make a woman hate yer, Smiley?"

"Can't say as I do, mate."

"Yer betray 'em." Lucas blinked slowly, feeling the blessed effects of the liquor. It was numbing him inside. Though not fast enough. Never fast enough. "Yer betray 'em. It works every time."

Sixteen

The next morning, Lucas endured another lesson in elocution and French from Amanda. While he practiced behaving like a gentleman, Caroline and Theodore began to plot his debut as one. They agreed that the most sympathetic audience for Lucas's first performance would be Miss Kinnicott and her father.

Ishmail Kinnicott was an old farmer who lived in the valley just beyond the moor. He cared little for manners or the number of carriages a man possessed. And his daughter Emily was a soft-spoken, sweet-natured twenty-two-year-old who saw only the good in everyone she met.

Caroline asked Henry to send one of the twins to the Kinnicott farm with an invitation to a picnic that afternoon at Bilberry Cottage. Fallingate's land agent, Mr. Dorris, lived at the cottage and was having a picnic supper for the miners who worked for Caroline.

At eleven o'clock, the Fallingate household made its way toward Bilberry Cottage. The servants traveled the two-mile distance in a horse-drawn cart, while Caroline, Theodore, Amanda, and Lucas rode. It was a remarkably dry autumn day and the sun shone down with vigor.

Caroline had never felt more alive. The languor that had succeeded the previous night's ecstasy overflowed her senses, and every glimpse of sunshine made her heady with exhilaration. She only hoped no one would notice the chafing on her cheeks from Lucas's whiskers. If anyone guessed that she was no longer a maiden, though, she would not be embarrassed. She gloried too much in the knowledge that she was at last a woman in every sense of the word. For that reason, she did not even seem to mind that Lucas had been avoiding her gaze. She merely assumed that he took their night of lovemaking for granted, as men were wont to do.

Emily and her father walked into the cottage yard just as the Fallingate party arrived. Emily wore a faded green chintz gown with a dainty white bag cap. Her father dressed as if for a day of work, looking a bit scruffier and older than usual.

"Miss Kinnicott!" Caroline called out, and turned to Lucas as they reined in. "Don't be nervous, Lucas. Emily will like you very much."

He drew in Lightning's reins with the ease of a man who'd been riding all his life, and the horse came to a snorting stop by the wooden fence that bordered the long cottage yard.

"That's a boy," Lucas said, patting the gelding's flanks.

"Upon my word, I do believe you have tamed Lightning utterly," Caroline said with a glowing smile. "Are you quite certain you have never ridden before coming to Fallingate?"

"At this point, Caro, I am not certain of anything at all."

He cast her a look of gentle mockery as he dismounted and handed the reins over to the groom. "It seems I am taming everything in my sight these days."

Caroline blinked in momentary dismay. Was he referring to her? she wondered as she dismounted with the groom's assistance.

"Thank you, Davey. Oh, Miss Kinnicott!" Caroline waved again and straightened her riding habit. Then she hurried to the young lady's side and bussed her cheek. "I am so glad you could come. Good afternoon, Mr. Kinnicott."

"Eh-yup," the wizened farmer said, eyeing her with his hard, slate-colored eyes. "We've work to do at the farm. I told Emily this is nonsense."

"Oh, Father, you'll enjoy yourself as much as I will. Why don't you speak with Dr. Cavendish? He's recently returned from Africa, you know."

"Waste of time, foreign travel is," Ishmail Kinnicott groused, but nevertheless headed for the physician.

"Father will enjoy chatting with Dr. Cavendish." Emily's breathy voice could scarcely be heard above the laughter and shouts of the miners and their families as they played games on the lawn.

Bilberry was a charming two-story wattle-and-daub thatched cottage half-covered in climbing ivy and spilling over with late-blooming roses and shocks of heather. The flowers were lovingly tended by Mrs. Dorris, a kind woman who always busied herself in the kitchen on days like this. Mr. Dorris was a stocky man equipped with worn boots, a low-riding hat, a fat nose, sharp eyes, and a ready and infectious laugh. Caroline heard it rise above the merriment in the yard.

Miners who couldn't quite scrub all the grit from their faces looked happy dancing to a fiddler's bow with their wives, while others rode dangerously and sloppily on two workhorses rushing at a quintain, a replica of a practice target used long ago by medieval knights. Presently, it gave the men a chance to laugh at their own buffoonery. A miner would mount a reluctant horse and charge at the quintain with a lance. If the lance missed the target—a straw dummy—a sack of sand hanging from the horizontal pole from which the dummy hung would swing around and knock the man from the horse, much to the merriment of all.

Caroline smiled to see her dependents so happy. She tucked Emily's hand in her arm and guided her to the garden chairs set up for them near the house.

"Miss Kinnicott, I want you to meet someone very special," she said as they settled. "His name is Mr. Lucas Davin."

Emily looked timidly over her shoulder at Lucas as he spoke with her father and the dapperly dressed Dr. Cavendish, then she turned her rapt gaze to Caroline. "Is that him?"

"Yes."

When Emily's eyes widened and glowed with approval and a little awe, Caroline laughed.

"He is handsome, isn't he? He is from Africa, a friend of Dr. Cavendish's. So he does not yet know all the manners to which we are accustomed. But I think you will find him very nice. He is, in fact, my husband."

"Oh!" Emily looked astonished, then a flash of sadness filled her pale brown eyes for the briefest moment. That was followed by a sweet and generous smile. Caroline knew in an instant what she was thinking: I will never be married, but at least you are, dear friend. Living with her curmudgeonly father, Emily had few social contacts and no dowry. Therefore, she had little hope of ever marrying.

"How delighted I shall be to call you Mrs. Davin."

Caroline hugged her. "I knew you would be happy for me. Would you like to meet him?"

Emily nodded and straightened her shawl. She coughed into a gloved hand.

"Miss Kinnicott, you should have worn a spencer. You will freeze out here in that shawl."

"No, Mrs. Davin, the sun is warm today." She pressed her hands to her chest and gazed at the sun with obvious appreciation. "I cannot remember when it has last been this blessedly warm."

"I think Mr. Dorris had a serious discussion with God about the weather," Caroline said with a laugh as she led her to Lucas.

By now he was talking with the land agent near the quintain. Caroline noted how easily he chuckled and talked, how even Mr. Dorris seemed susceptible to Lucas's charm, his raffish smile and engaging eyes. She tried to hear bits of their conversation, but the horses thundered past them as the men aimed their lances at the quintain. Dirt and grass flew up beneath churning hooves, raising the smell of rich earth.

"Mr. Dorris, I see you have met my new husband, Mr. Davin," Caroline said when she was in earshot.

"Good day, ma'am." The land agent gave a short bow in his no-nonsense manner. "You took me by surprise. I had no idea a wedding was in the offing. But I'm delighted and I welcome Mr. Davin's advice on the mines. We were just discussing your brother's cotton mill."

"Mr. Davin is learning so much about England so quickly, I do wonder that he's not overwhelmed," Caroline said. "I daresay I would be."

"Would you excuse me, ma'am? I see my wife waving to me from the cottage."

"Certainly, Mr. Dorris. This will give Mr. Davin a chance to meet Miss Kinnicott."

Caroline could sense his interest in Miss Kinnicott the moment he spied her. She made the introductions and Lucas bowed low before the frail, blond young woman.

"Miss Kinnicott," Lucas said, and took her hand in his as he stood, "it is a pleasure to meet you."

He eyed her gently, holding her hand longer than necessary. He focused on her wrist, just long enough to make Caroline wonder if he was searching for jewels. She shoved the uncharitable notion from her mind.

"I believe, Miss Kinnicott, that Mr. Davin is learning manners more quickly than I had realized. He is quite the gentleman, as you can see."

He finally let go of Emily's hand, though he still held her gaze captive with his mesmerizing black eyes. "Mrs. Plumshaw is a fine teacher. You'd have nothing but sympathy for me, Miss Kinnicott, if you knew the lessons I've endured."

"Poor Mr. Davin has been inundated with advice on our culture, I fear."

Caroline waited for Emily to jump into the conversation, but she couldn't seem to tear her gaze from Lucas's face. She was obviously besotted.

"Mr. Davin," Caroline said, "perhaps you would let Miss Kinnicott show you around Bilberry Cottage. I must be the judge in a footrace among the lads."

"I'd be delighted." Lucas elegantly offered his arm and Emily laid her pale fingers on top of it.

Caroline watched them go with a curious mixture of pride and an odd new feeling—jealousy. It wasn't that she begrudged Emily time spent with her husband; rather she was happy she had managed to marry a man she cared about enough to want to hoard for herself.

The sunlight peaked around three and then surrendered to a cover of ominous clouds. Caroline couldn't remember a day when she'd had more fun and was sad when the respite from tortured weather ended.

There was something extraordinary about speaking to

people she'd known all her life knowing she had someone special to talk about it all with later. Someone who cared for her in a way no one else ever had.

She was always conscious of Lucas—where he was, whom he was talking with, what expression he wore, whether he was happy or grave. And when she reminded herself that though he was her husband and lover, he was also a criminal who had no intention of remaining in her life, her heart simply wouldn't accept it. This was the man who had made her feel like a woman. She couldn't bear the thought of never seeing him again. She didn't accept the notion in any way.

At the end of the picnic, the servants hurried home ahead of the impending rainstorm. Amanda and Theodore, who'd spent much of the day together, rode back in tandem. Caroline and Lucas followed up the rear, neither in any hurry to return to Fallingate, in spite of the threat of violent rain.

They rode awhile in silence. Caroline held her spencer close to her throat to protect herself against the plummeting temperature. Though she sensed that Lucas truly cared for her, she also realized he was holding back from her. Something was troubling him.

"I daresay tonight's storm may be the worst you have seen yet, Lucas."

A raindrop fell on her hand. "The rain is already beginning."

"Perhaps I'll finally see the ghost of Lord Hamilton," he said wryly. "He usually appears during bad weather, doesn't he?"

"Yes, but we always have inclement weather."

"Not today."

"No, it was delightful, wasn't it?" They rode farther in silence. "You're very serious today, Lucas. Is something amiss?"

"I've been thinking about what happened last night."

A big, fat drop of rain splattered her cheek, then another and another.

"The descent has begun," she said, pulling up her collar. "I hope Emily makes it home before the onslaught. She wore such a flimsy shawl."

"We have to talk about last night."

A few more drops pelted her cheeks before she answered. "What is there to discuss? Some things, I should imagine, are beyond words."

He reached out and impatiently grabbed the reins beneath the throat of her sleek mare and yanked on his own. The horses came to an uneasy stop, bumping into each other as they jockeyed for balance. Caroline gripped her saddle for purchase.

"It can't happen again, Caro."

She frowned at him as if he were a stranger. "What can't happen again?"

He grimaced and muttered an expletive. "You know what I mean. We can't make love again."

"Why not?" She would rather have heard him say he hated her than that he would not make love to her again. She lived for another chance to wrestle in his embrace.

He glowered at her from beneath his firmly set black brows. "I will not risk getting you with child. I told you last night it was not right, but you made me forget myself."

She cocked her head sideways. "So it was my fault."

"No! It was mine."

"You didn't seem to mind last night."

The rain now poured down on them, matting their hair about their ears, chilling them to the bone. Still holding her reins, he led them under a giant oak tree and their horses stopped on a bed of gold-and-red leaves. He dismounted and tied the reins to a low branch. Then he lifted her down from her saddle, resisting the urge to pull her close, to warm her, to deny with his actions all that he had just said. Instead, he let go and walked to the gnarled trunk, leaning against it, heavy with sadness.

"I saw an old friend last night, Caro. After you fell asleep, I met up with him. And I remembered who I was and who you are. You don't know me at all."

She frowned at him. "Has anyone ever known you as I did last night?"

He shook his head and cast his eyes down. "No. Only you, Caro. But love doesn't matter in this world. I learned that long ago. So did Mrs. Plumshaw. And you'll learn it soon enough."

"You're being cruel."

"Yes." He tipped up his chin, his eyes blazing at her. "But not as cruel as I would be if I took you night after night, making you love me. Love isn't enough. I'm sorry, but that's the truth. Love is never enough."

She wearily pushed her bedraggled hair away from her face. "I can scarcely believe the depth of your cynicism. How can you say love doesn't matter?"

"There is a difference, Caro, between feelings and facts."

"What do you mean?"

He rubbed the back of his neck, recollecting, then looked up pointedly. "You say you care for Miss Kinnicott?"

"Dearly."

"Uh-huh. So dearly that you've completely overlooked her needs."

"Her needs are met."

"Not bloody likely. She's poor, Caro. Poor and sick and you don't even know it."

"She is not! Emily is not rich by my standards, but she has never wanted for her needs."

"She's in need of a doctor's care right now."

"We'll be in need of a doctor's care if we stay out in the cold rain any longer." She started for her horse.

"Caro!" he shouted after her. "Just ask Miss Kinnicott and she'll tell you how desperate she is. You're too blind to see it. You live in your mansion dreaming about ghosts and crooks who suddenly turn into gentlemen while all around you there's pain and suffering and you're just too naive to see it!"

"Stop it!" she shouted. "You are trying to hurt me because you regret our intimacy. You are wrong. Emily is not sick."

"She doesn't have long to live, Caroline. I saw the rings under her eyes even if you didn't. I saw the frayed sleeves on her cuffs. She needs help, but because she wants to impress you, because she looks up to you, she won't ask for it."

Caroline stopped when she reached her mare. She gazed at the wet ground, staring at twigs and decaying leaves but seeing Emily in her mind's eye. Was it possible Lucas was right?

"She coughed," Caroline said to herself. "I noticed a cough. But that is not uncommon this time of year. Sometimes she is out of breath."

"Think back and I'll warrant you she's been out of breath for months. Maybe years."

She turned to him, her mind racing through memories. She did remember a coughing fit Emily had had in the early summer. And once when they were walking, Emily had had to return to the house to rest. Lord, was Lucas right? Had she been ignoring signs of need in one of her dearest friends?

"What makes you so sure?" She frowned. "How do you recognize the symptoms?"

"Because I've seen illness before," he said wearily. "Too often. Trust me, Caroline. Miss Kinnicott is very ill."

Her skin crawled with remorse to think he might be right.

He returned to her side, both detachment and concern wafting from him in a cool wave. He chucked her chin with a forefinger. "Life ain't a bed of roses, Caroline. If you didn't know that before, you will know it after knowing me. I told yer last night. It was wrong, what we did. You'll regret it. I was selfish to take you so."

"I think you are being selfish now. Selfish and cruel."

"No; I'm finally being kind."

She felt cold all over. She was drenched to the bone. Why did he have to see the worst in every situation? Why couldn't he find goodness in anything? She didn't like him very much in this moment. And she'd prove to him he was wrong about Emily. Caroline would have noticed if her friend was seriously ill.

"You're wrong, Lucas. And I'll prove it to you." When he cupped his hands for her, she reluctantly accepted his help, stepping into them and hoisting herself into her saddle. "Tomorrow we'll visit Kinnicott farm and you'll see that you're wrong."

He looked up at her with infinite sadness. "I hope you're right, luv. For your sake."

Seventeen

The next morning, Caroline made faces in front of the mirror in her dressing room as Biddie combed her hair. She puckered her lips and quirked her brows seductively, then grimaced at the resulting picture. She pulled back her unpainted lips in a confident smile, then wilted in defeat when the effort made her cheeks ache.

"Are you ill, miss?" Biddie said in her cracking and quavery voice. "You look like your breakfast did not agree with you."

"No, Biddie," Caroline said on a sigh, "I am just imagining what I look like to the opposite gender."

"Lovely, I would say."

"Not with these spectacles."

"Oh, not to worry, Miss Wainwright. You have got to see."

"Only when I read. I do not really need them otherwise. I am just used to them. They make me feel less . . . exposed. But I realize now they've done nothing for me. I've always thought I saw people as they were, but perhaps I've been blind, even with these."

Caroline glanced at the spectacles that lay on her dressing table. Then she watched as Biddie deftly plaited her hair, twisting hand over hand. Lulled by the familiar rhythm, Caroline wondered if she would have noticed Emily's frayed sleeve yesterday if she'd been wearing her glasses.

"Poor Mr. Feathers is moping about, I hear," Biddie said. "Cannot imagine what he did to deserve losing his post."

"He is fortunate that I have retained him at all. He's been given easier duties, and I've given him quarters in the west wing."

Caroline bristled at her housekeeper's implied criticism, and she allowed herself to remember the anger she'd felt over the butler's mistakes. "Feathers has been reluctant to accept Mr. Davin as master here and he has been remiss in his normal duties. He is past seventy, and I daresay it is time he spent his doddering years in peace and quiet."

Biddie blinked in dismay. "Why, I am nearly seventy, miss."

"Yes, Biddie, but you will survive us all and will be running Fallingate fifty years hence."

Biddie beamed at this and gave a soft cackle of laughter.

The door creaked open and Amanda entered. "Are you going driving, Caro?"

"Yes. I am taking Lucas to the Kinnicott farm." Caroline straightened the lace that pressed against the swell of her bosom along her low-cut collar. "Amanda, do you think I was wrong to relieve Feathers of his duties?"

Amanda sat down on a chair next to hers and folded her hands. "He is a bit past his prime, I am afraid. It is very disagreeable to admit it, but Prudence Wainwright might be right where Mr. Feathers is concerned. And Henry is doing such a wonderful job in his post. His elevation was a long time coming. I daresay you did the right thing, and you needn't feel remorse over it. Besides, Dr. Cavendish has decided that Mr. Davin is progressing well enough to meet people of substance. We are inviting the Countess of Germaine to supper, as well as a few others. Henry will be much more capable of handling such delicate social duties."

Caroline frowned. She did not want Lucas to meet Lady Germaine when they were on bad terms. Why did everything suddenly seem so complicated? Apparently, that is what lovemaking did to one's life. She looked in the mirror and pinched her sallow cheeks, then noticed Amanda's penetrating look reflected in the mirror. Did Amanda know why she was taking such unusual care of her appearance? Doubtless. It was surely obvious that everything Caroline did of late was meant to please Lucas.

"There you are, miss." Biddie's wrinkled cheeks rounded in a satisfied smile. "You are pretty as can be. I will tell Henry to call the carriage. Your spencer is on your bed. You'll need it, for it's chilly today."

"Thank you, Biddie." Caroline placed her glasses in the reticule hanging at her waist. Then she led Amanda into her bedroom. "Cook has made an apple pie for Emily and Mr. Kinnicott. Would you please tell Henry to make sure it finds its way into the carriage?"

"Yes, of course. Caro, I—"

"And if Mr. Dorris stops by to discuss the mines with Mr. Davin, tell him to come back next week. Thank him for the picnic, and—"

"Caroline—"

"I wish I could stay, but it is getting late and—"

Amanda stepped in front of her, blocking her path to the door. "Please, Caro, we must talk."

Caroline braced herself. "If you are going to criticize me, Amanda . . ."

"No, my dear." The soft-spoken lady gently gripped

Caroline's forearms. "I realize that I cannot tell you how to live your life. And though reluctant, I have gone along with this charade. Therefore, I account myself to blame for any risk you now face. But I would be remiss if I did not at least warn you."

"Warn me of what?" Caroline pulled back her shoulders, disengaging her arm.

"I saw how you looked at Mr. Davin yesterday at the picnic. I know what that means."

Caroline blushed. "What does it mean?"

"It means you are in love. You are hopelessly in love."

Caroline sighed. "I thought you were going to say it meant that I had . . . had become intimate with Lucas."

Amanda smiled compassionately. "I fully expected that. I just do not want you to be hurt by giving away your heart to a man who may not be here a week from now."

A rumble of thunder sounded in the distance. Caroline glanced up. "Devil, but it's going to rain."

Out of habit, her gaze wandered to the portrait. Lord Hamilton seemed to glare down at her with as much reproach as Amanda surely felt. With all the things that were going wrong, at least the ghost hadn't reappeared. One day she would have to tell Amanda about Lord Hamilton's unwelcome appearance. At present, she suspected her friend might think she was ready for Bedlam if she told her.

"You cannot help your feelings, Caro. But you can protect yourself."

Caroline began to tug on her gloves. "What makes you think I need protecting?"

"Every woman needs protection from the desires of men. Whatever you feel, Caro, you must not give Lucas your heart."

"Why not?" she demanded. "Is love so undignified in a woman?"

"No; heavens, no! But a woman suffers consequences that no man ever need fear. A woman is vulnerable, whereas a man proceeds to his next conquest unscathed."

"Not if he is my husband."

"Your titular husband. What future can you have with a man who will be spurned by Society once his true identity is learned, as surely it will be?"

Caroline could take no more. It was too much to bear. She couldn't help the way she felt. She always felt too much. She started for the door.

"Caroline!" Amanda called after her, but to no avail. As Caroline disappeared through the door, the older woman covered her face and took a steadying breath as memories of her own temptations, and her own downfall, came back in a painful rush. Then she turned slowly and looked up at the portrait. The black eyes gazing down at her held a hint of mockery. How ironic, Amanda thought, that she'd now give anything if only Caroline would once again harmlessly daydream about this portrait of a lord.

Lucas and Caroline barely spoke on the journey to Kinnicott Farm. She held the apple pie in a traveling basket on her lap and listened to the rumble of the carriage wheels, trying to set her features in a mask she had unfortunately neglected to practice before the mirror. She wanted to look aloof. He was taking advantage of her vulnerability, and it hurt.

But in her attempt to appear dispassionate, Caroline merely looked miserable. She blinked hard and tried to focus on the fields of harvested wheat. But no matter how much she tried to ignore Lucas, his presence seemed to fill the carriage. When at last the thatched roof of the farmhouse appeared among the emerald hills, she let out an audible sigh of relief.

"Here we are. You shall see, Lucas, that I was right.

Emily and her father are doing well. I have not been here in two years, but she comes to visit often, and I would be perceptive enough to know from our conversations if she was truly ill."

Looking amazingly dapper with his hands poised on the walking stick Theodore had given him, Lucas eyed her doubtfully. "We shall see."

"Yes, we shall."

By the time the footman had jumped down from the dicky and lowered the carriage step, Caroline was ready to prove her point. Desperately ready. She waited until Lucas stepped out from behind her and offered his arm.

"You shall see that Miss Kinnicott has a most agreeable maid of all work," she whispered as they approached the small wattle-and-daub cottage. "Annie is her name, and she is charming."

Caroline knocked on the door and adjusted her gloves, tucking them tighter against the joints between her fingers.

"Maybe they ain't home," Lucas said.

"Maybe they *are not* home."

"That's what I said."

"No, it is not. Apparently running into your old friend has had an even greater effect than I'd already perceived. You're reverting to your old ways."

"I didn't force you to marry me, Caro."

She took a deep breath. "I am not going to argue with you, Lucas. Perhaps they are outside."

She sidestepped a pile of rotting logs and rusty tools and circled around to the garden, a square patch of earth with rows that once overflowed with vegetables. There she found Emily's father rooting around in the dirt.

"Mr. Kinnicott! Good morning!" As she drew nearer to him, her smile of greeting faded. He was kneeling in the dirt, digging, apparently for roots, with his bare hands, a look of frustration creasing his furrowed brow. A pitifully small pile of roots lay in the grass nearby. "Mr. Kinnicott, I hope you do not mind that we came on a lark. I have a pie for you in the carriage. I will send Annie out for it."

"She don't work here no more," the farmer said, rising painfully to his feet.

"You have a new maid?"

His tanned forehead furrowed with deep wrinkles. "Nay, no maid at all. We do fine on our own. Emily's inside, if you want to see her. Thank you, ma'am, for the picnic. Did the girl some good. I tell her she should get out more often. Get some sun."

"Is she ill?" Lucas's penetrating voice gave Caroline a start. She'd not heard his approach.

"Nay," the old farmer replied, wiping his brow with a forearm, "just lazy. She gets these notions of being a lady. Sits around all day. Lazy filly."

"That does not sound like the Miss Kinnicott I know," Caroline gently argued.

He kicked the earth as if to knock another root from its stingy grasp. "She reads them romantic novels. Gets them from you, I believe, ma'am."

Under his accusing gaze, Caroline turned red. "Yes, they are . . . illuminating."

"May we visit Miss Kinnicott?" Lucas said.

"Aye. When you leave, tell her to get out here and get to work."

Lucas steered Caroline toward the house with a stern grip on her elbow. "Don't say a word, Caro," he warned her. "Angering Mr. Kinnicott won't help Emily."

Caroline cast Lucas an indignant glare over her shoulder, but lost her bluster when she saw the deep concern pressing his mouth into grim lines. She made a perfunctory effort to knock on the door, but when no response came, she pushed it open.

"Miss Kinnicott?"

"In here," came a faint reply.

Lucas stepped in first, then motioned Caroline inside. The chill of the cottage seeped through her spencer in an instant. It seemed all the more bone-chilling as there was no sun in the dank house to warm her shoulders.

They walked through the narrow entrance hall to the cottage's small parlor. Emily sat propped up on a cot by the square window. Soft light filtered through the dirty glass, painting her pale cheeks a soft gray. When Emily heard the shuffle of their feet nearby, she turned her head, tucking a limp strand of hair behind her ear and smiling wanly. The room reeked of cheap tallow candles. Thank heaven she at least had light at night, if not heat.

"Good day, Mr. and Mrs. Davin. What a surprise to see you." Emily began to cough and put a fist to her mouth, trying to stop the racking sound that rattled her lungs.

Caroline frowned in dismay. In that moment she knew that Lucas had been right. And she had been wrong. Horribly wrong. Lucas reached for her shoulder and gave it a reassuring squeeze. Pride demanded that she pull away, but she felt his earnest compassion and she welcomed his support.

"Miss Kinnicott . . . Emily . . ." She started forward and dropped her knees onto the dirty wooden floor. She combed Emily's damp and cold forehead with her soothing, warm palm. In the gray light the circles under her eyes looked like half-moons in an eclipse. "Why didn't you tell me you were ill?"

Emily's sad brown eyes found Caroline's distraught ones. "I did not . . . want to worry you. You have been so kind to invite me to Fallingate. I was afraid if you knew I was ill, you might not want me to come anymore. I so enjoyed our visits."

"But I could have helped you." Caroline's gaze darted around the drab parlor. What little furniture remained was worn and dusty. The fireplace was cold. "You should have a fire to warm you. And a hot bowl of soup. Lucas, will you please make a fire?"

Emily shook her head and gripped Caroline's sleeve. "No. Father is too weary to cut peat and there is no coal or wood left."

Caroline glanced around the parlor with a sinking feeling. Had they burned the furniture in desperation last winter?

"You can take logs from Deer Grove. It is just across the road."

"That is your property."

"I do not care!" Caroline answered, her eyes wide with incredulity. "Besides, Mr. Dorris told your father that he could take timber in exchange for his work at Bilberry Cottage, did he not?"

"Mr. Dorris does not want my father to work for him anymore."

Caroline frowned. "Why ever not?"

"Father is becoming . . . difficult. He argues with everyone. He has grown worse since Mother died. I was encouraged by the invitation to Bilberry Cottage, but then I realized it came from you, and not Mr. Dorris."

"Well, your father has my permission to take as much wood as he pleases from Deer Grove. Lucas, it is across the lane. Would you please fetch something to burn?"

"Of course."

She waited until he exited the cottage. Then she stroked Emily's forehead, blinking back tears of remorse. She gazed down at the young lady's frayed sleeves and shuddered. "Emily, will you ever forgive me?"

"No, Mrs. Davin, you mustn't blame your—"

"I must ask your forgiveness. Somehow I have been blind to your plight. It has been too long since I have been to visit. And when you came to Fallingate, you always had on your finest. But I realize now the signs were there. I was simply blind to them. I am so frightened for you . . ."

She pulled Emily into her arms and hugged her tight. Caroline's shoulders shook as she silently wept into Emily's hair and squeezed her, trying to hold what felt like a bag of bones. Emily let out a weak sigh of relief.

"You are so kind," she said. "Do not cry, ma'am. I will be better soon."

Caroline wiped her eyes, pulling away and forcing a smile. "Of course you will be. Please come back to Fallingate with me and let me take care of you."

· Emily struggled for a breath and coughed. "No, Father would not allow it. I will be better tomorrow. I do quite well when the sun is out, like it was at the picnic. Today is just one of my bad days."

Caroline squeezed her hands. "Then I will have some food sent over. And I will ask Dr. Cavendish to visit and give you some medicine."

Emily said nothing.

"I have worn you out. I will go now. But I will be back soon."

"Do not trouble yourself."

"It will be no trouble at all."

"Very well. Thank you." Emily shut her eyes, and a second later she was asleep.

When Lucas returned with a bundle of firewood in his arms, the women were silent. Caroline seemed to be lost in thought, and Emily was asleep. He quietly started a fire, retrieved the pie from the carriage, and put it in the kitchen, then returned to the cot.

"Caro," he said softly, and touched his fingers to her shoulder. "Caro, we should go."

She looked up with a start. "Oh, Lucas, I did not hear you return."

He bent down and gently lifted her by the shoulders and guided her out the door, holding her weight against him. Outside, it was beginning to drizzle.

"Do you want to say farewell to Mr. Kinnicott?" he asked when they reached the door to the carriage.

"No."

On the return trip, they were silent again. Lucas distractedly twirled his polished oak walking stick between his palms to the rhythm of the carriage's squeaky wheels. Now and then he looked at Caroline, but she never met his gaze. She stared out the window with puffy, red eyes, her right elbow resting on the window ledge, the back of her hand pressed to her thinned lips. Poor chit, he thought. She'd had the wind knocked out of her.

"Caroline—"

"Do not say a word." Her eyes remained fixed on the passing scenery. "You were right. I have been selfish and blind. I will never forgive myself."

"Caro—"

"I do not want to discuss it. I know what I am now, a selfish, self-centered frivolous miss, lost in my fantasy world of romance. I will spend the rest of my days regretting it. And I will thank you not to mention it again. I see now why you could never truly love me, Lucas."

"I did not say that."

"All I ask is that you stay long enough to finish the charade."

He sank back against his seat with a hundredweight of sadness pressing against his heart. It was best that she thought he did not love her. That way she would not seek his bed. But it hurt—oh, how it hurt—to deny love. To let it pass when it was begging to live.

"I will fulfill my end of the bargain, Caro. I told you that at the beginning."

"Yes, you've been more than honest all along."

He shrank back into his seat, feeling smaller for having shown her her own sullied reflection. He thought he'd feel better about it, perhaps even savor a sense of victory, but now all he wished he could do was wipe the mirror clean for her.

Eighteen

hortly before six, Caroline flew down the grand staircase and hurtled into the drawing room, stopping abruptly when she caught sight of Theodore sipping brandy before the blazing fire.

"Uncle Teddy! You have returned. How is Emily? Did you see her?"

Theodore frowned into the burgundy swirl of liquor and sniffed the pungent odor. "Yes, I did."

Caroline's heart beat quicker beneath the fashionably low-cut neckline of her diaphanous evening gown. "And . . . ? Is she doing any better?"

Theodore tossed back his head and finished off the last of his brandy in one gulp. He exhaled with a sorrowful groan. "Caro, Miss Kinnicott is very ill. She has a weak heart."

Caroline's hands dropped to her sides and her shoulders slumped forward. "Yes. Lucas suspected as much. I was hoping against hope that he was wrong."

"Lucas Davin knows a lot about life," Theodore said, arching one brow. "You should heed him more often."

She went to a Chippendale chair and collapsed into it. "I hate being wrong. He warned me. Lucas told me she was not well. How could he see it, a stranger, when I, her lifelong friend, did not?"

Theodore sat down beside her and took one of her hands in his, stroking it. "Now, now, my dear, sometimes it takes an outsider to see the most obvious signs that we ourselves ignore."

"But I am so embarrassed!" She looked to his bear of a face for reassurance. "He thinks I am an idiot."

"Lucas thinks nothing of the sort, I guarantee it. You cannot possibly know what he feels about you, and you should not even try."

"Why not?"

"Because he is your husband. It would not do for a woman to understand her husband."

Caroline frowned. "Why not?"

"Then she would grow bored with him. Love is a mystery, and should remain one."

"Caroline! A carriage is coming!" Amanda burst into the room. "Oh, Dr. Cavendish. I am glad you are back. The guests are about to arrive."

"Oh, Lord!" Caroline shot to her feet. "This really will be the test, won't it? Is Lucas . . . ?"

"Neville is dressing him." Amanda came forward and twirled a finger in the air. "Turn around and let me have a good look at you."

Caroline turned a full circle. Her pink silk petticoat and sleeveless robe whirled behind her. Her hair was drawn up in a profusion of curls that spilled around a wide pink bandeau that swathed her head like a silk bandage.

"Upon my word, you are lovely!"

Caroline blushed and smiled. "Thank you. Did you tell Lucas that he was about to meet the most important person in Cragmere?"

Amanda tapped her fan in the palm of her hand and shrugged. "I am afraid I did not. I didn't want him to become unduly nervous."

"I hope you hens know what you are doing," Theodore said on a note of warning. "I personally would have prepared the boy. It is not every day one meets a countess."

"No, but he is making such good progress," Amanda replied. "And as you yourself have pointed out, Caroline's birthday is fast approaching. Lucas must learn to handle himself in Society. Then and only then will he be ready to meet George and Prudence Wainwright. Hurry along, now, both of you."

Amanda glided out of the room, and Theodore offered Caroline his arm.

"Uncle Teddy, can you send some medicine to Kinnicott Farm?"

"I can try to make her feel better, but I cannot improve her living conditions."

"But I can," she said resolutely, and started toward the entrance hall, feeling older than she did yesterday and not nearly as wise as she had considered herself. "I will bring Emily here. And I do not care what her father says about it. You see, I understand a great deal more about life than I ever have before."

Theodore's chest vibrated with a low rumble of laughter. "Love will do that to you, and a great deal more."

Just as Henry opened the door to an arriving carriage, Lucas trotted lightly down the stairway and tugged on his sleeves. He stopped mid-step when he saw Caroline waiting to greet the guests. Hearing the commotion, she glanced distractedly at him, then looked up again as recognition set in. The pale blue gems of her eyes fixed on him with vulnerable intensity.

For the first time he noticed how truly elegant she was,

with her figure erect, her hands poised, her gown falling like a waterfall from her most feminine attributes. Her nature was as transparent and delicate as her gown. The beauty of such a woman lay not in the uniqueness of her features or the striking contrast of facial lines and curves, but in the very simplicity and honesty of her soul. A soul that would never conceive of, much less attempt, deception regarding matters of the heart. And that utter lack of guile brought out in a man the ferocious desire to protect and cherish. How he would have liked to have protected her.

Suddenly he wished they were alone. Her supposition that he did not love her freed him a bit to admire her more openly. Caro would never try to seduce a man who did not love her. But he heard voices coming out of the carriage, and he dashed down the remaining stairs while he could.

"Come with me," he ordered her, and tugged her by a hand into an alcove beneath the stairs.

"What? What is it, Lucas?"

He gripped her arms and searched her eyes, his gaze darting between hers. "Are you sure?"

"Am I sure of what?"

"Are you sure you want to introduce me to your guests? It is not too late, Caroline. We can call off this charade now and no one would be the wiser."

The flames in her eyes extinguished with a silent hiss. "Is that what you want? To call off what we are so close to achieving? Is being with me so unpalatable that you cannot stay another week?"

The voices were growing louder. Laughter floated into the doorway. He looked up sharply. Damn the world. If only it would go away. But he would not be here, playing the part of her husband, if she didn't need to impress the world outside her haven. That was his only purpose for being here.

"I'm willing to see the humbug through to the end if that's truly what you want," he said. "But when the charade is over, I must go."

A lost look fluttered over her face like the shadow of a wounded bird. She closed her eyes for a very long time, then rallied with a resigned smile and took his hands in hers.

"All right, then, Lucas. Go if you must. But let us show them up first. Let us keep Fallingate and show the world what a farce it is."

He chuckled and smoothed a hand over her cheek. "All right, luv. I'll do my best."

"Good evening, Lady Roth-Parker," Henry said at the door.

"We had best go and greet our guests," Caroline whispered.

"Good evening, Henry. Where is Feathers?"

"Otherwise engaged, my lady."

"Come along, Roger."

"Good evening, Sir Roger," Henry intoned with sublime respect.

Caroline came round the staircase and found her friend Julia Roth-Parker tugging off her gloves and surrendering her rain-splattered cloak to the butler. Julia was in her fifties and wore her silver-and-black hair in a profusion of curls *à la Titus*. She was attractive and quick to smile, which made her hooded eyes sparkle with sensual merriment.

"Good evening, Caroline, my dear." She reached out for a kiss on the cheek. "And who is this scrumptious-looking man at your side?"

Lucas gave her a dashing grin and kissed her hand with a flourish. "I am Lucas Davin, my lady."

"No, call me Julia. Any friend of Caroline's . . ."

"He is more than a friend, Julia. He is my husband."

"What! Well, upon my honor, my dear, you do like your surprises."

"Greetings, Sir Roger, so nice of you to come," Caroline said, kissing his cheek.

Sir Roger Roth-Parker was a portly man of moderate height whose only remaining hair circled the back side of his head like a puny fur stole. His jowls were multiple and his beaked nose gave him a snobbish air, but his words were always gentle, if uninspired.

"Halloo, dear girl," he mumbled. "Where is the brandy?"

"In the drawing room. You will find Dr. Cavendish there."

"Caroline," Julia said, drawing her toward the door, which Henry opened again for the last guest. A priest shrugged off his greatcoat and brushed the rain from his slicked-back hair. "I simply cannot wait to hear all about your wedding, but first let me introduce you to a special guest I brought myself. Father Gregory Anton is visiting from the Continent. I told him he would be welcome. I hope I was not being presumptuous."

"Of course not," Caroline said, and smiled when the deep wave-shaped lines furrowing the priest's brow wrinkled with a good-natured grin. "Of course we are not Roman Catholics, Father, but I have always been fascinated by Lady Roth-Parker's religion."

"I fear I have brought terrible weather with me from France, Miss Wainwright," the priest said with a warm smile. He looked to be around forty years old. He had rugged good looks and a certain gravitas. "Can you ever forgive me?"

"I can hardly blame you, Father," Caroline replied good-naturedly. "Perhaps you could pray for a reprieve."

Julia emitted a throaty laugh and patted Caroline's shoulder. "He just might be able to intercede where your good vicar has failed. Father Anton is known the world over as an expert on spiritualism. His specialty is the rite of exorcism."

"Oh, my!" Caroline's eyes widened and she pressed a hand to her bosom. "Then he has come to the right place. Fallingate is famous for its ghost. Father, you will enjoy discussing it with Dr. Cavendish, I am sure. Lucas, would you show them into the drawing room?"

Lucas led the way with dashing strides and nimble conversation, acting as if he'd been master of Fallingate all his life. Caroline's heart warmed with gratitude. He said he'd do his best, and he wasn't disappointing her. No sooner had the group meandered off than Caroline heard the sound of an approaching carriage. Her nerves began to tingle, for the most important personage in the entire countryside was about to enter Fallingate and, in effect, render her verdict on Caroline's match—Lydia, the Dowager Countess of Germaine.

Lucas was beginning to feel good about the humbug, with a touch of brandy warming his belly and boosting his confidence. He'd even told a few chaste jokes to the delight of Lady Roth-Parker . . . when Doom walked in.

Henry opened the door of the drawing room and Caroline entered with an old dame that Lucas had seen somewhere before.

"I fear they have begun the party without us," Caroline said, leading the new guest toward the others.

Though Lucas still did not recognize the imperious guest, something about her countenance made his blood turn cold. She walked unevenly with a cane, but made her every movement one of significance. She was important, and knew it. She reeked of substance. She wore an exquisite, shiny silver evening gown adorned with pearls that softly molded her slightly plump figure. Her right brow seemed to be permanently arched, and her ocean-blue eyes slowly assessed every detail with calm intensity.

"Julia, you have not seen Lady Germaine since your trip to the Continent," Caroline said.

"No, I have not." Julia dropped a curtsy. "How very good to see you again, Lady Germaine."

The women chattered on, but Lucas barely heard them. Lady Germaine. The Countess of Germaine. The very woman who had seen him the night he was arrested on the moor. Bloody hell! He should have known it seemed too easy. He should have known fate would not give Caroline her chance at freedom and happiness. He should have known he'd fail her in the end. Had he forgotten what Robbin had taught him? *Yer're no one. Never will be, boy. Get it in your hard skull, lad.*

His throat closed and he couldn't draw in any air. His head grew light. Beads of sweat sprang out upon his brow. She was coming his way. She would recognize him. Thief! she would cry. A horse thief in our midst!

"Lady Germaine," Caroline said with touching deference to the woman who so casually wielded such grand authority, "I would like you to meet my husband, Mr. Lucas Davin."

She led the richly garbed woman toward Lucas. He tried to take a step backward, but was frozen in place.

"He is from Africa," he vaguely heard Caroline prattling. "Went there as a child . . . just returned . . . funny accent . . . new to the ways of England . . ."

He could smell the countess before she drew close enough for him to see the whites of her eyes. Her French waters gave her an unnaturally youthful odor. She smelled like a springtime bouquet of sordidly aromatic flowers. She offered him two gloved fingers. He clasped them and bent low over her hand.

"Your ladyship," he murmured. When he rose he looked into her eyes. Her pupils narrowed to pinpoints.

"Mr. Davin," said Lady Germaine, "I believe we have met."

Nineteen

"Yes, I am quite sure we have met," the countess said with an uncomfortable smile.

"I am sure I have not had the pleasure, your ladyship." Lucas felt the tension in the room thicken. The clock ticking in the corner sounded like a cannon, reminding him that he was about to blast apart Caroline's very future. It was just a matter of time before the countess recognized him and then all would be lost.

"How very interesting, Mr. Davin, that you grew up in Africa. You must tell me all about it, for I would find it vastly fascinating. But not before I remember where we have met! I forget these things, you see. Was it at the Ladies' Ball at Fennigan Park?"

Lucas swallowed thickly. "No, my lady. I was not there. I am quite sure I have not had the honor." She would not look away. He cleared his throat, willing the sweat poised at his temples to keep from falling down his cheeks.

"Greetings, your ladyship," said Sir Roger, unwittingly breaking the impasse. He joined them and chatted with the countess, recollecting her to Dr. Cavendish. Then he turned with manly camaraderie to Lucas. "What do you say, Davin? Are you in for a game of billiards? Lady Julia won't ring a fine peal over me for just one game. Nor will her ladyship, I daresay. I used to play with the earl regularly."

"I'd be delighted, Sir Roger," Lucas said, trying not to sound relieved. He made a leg and begged his pardon of the countess, then followed Sir Roger and Theodore. Caroline caught him at the door.

"What is it? What is wrong? I saw your reaction to the countess."

"I cannot do this, Caro," he whispered.

"Yes, you can."

"No, trust me. I cannot."

"Well, my boy," Sir Roger said from the hall. "Are you with us?"

"Yes, I'm coming." Lucas tore himself away from Caroline's bewildered presence. Damn it to hell, if only he could have done right by her.

He turned and departed with an elegant flourish. Caroline's tremulous eyes followed his progress. When the doors closed with a loud click, she swallowed the great lump in her throat and turned back to her guests.

"So, Father Anton," she said warmly, though she could hardly bring her eyes into focus on the man, "tell me more about your exorcisms. I am fascinated."

Shortly after midnight, the light in Caroline's bedroom went out at long last. Lucas had been waiting for that moment all night, but now that it had happened, he had a hollow feeling in his gut, and he wasn't sure that he would be able to leave her without saying good-bye after all.

He frowned down at the pocket watch Dr. Cavendish had given him, feeling an unaccountable rush of sentiment over the object. A second later, a flash of lightning lit the sky, enabling him to see both hands on the timepiece, which pointed portentously to midnight, the witching hour, the time when destinies were decided by unseen fates.

From the dry haven beneath the overhanging roof of the old dovecote, he squinted through the pouring rain, wishing he could see her again. One last time. He hadn't expected this. When he'd first arrived, he never thought leaving would be hard. But the idea of returning to London without Caroline left him cold inside. He wanted to hold her. Just hold her, forever. But he couldn't. For her sake, he had to leave without leaving her with a fatherless child.

He pulled up the collar on his riding coat, tucked his head down, and stepped into the thudding rain. He trotted toward the stable, when suddenly he collided with another figure who was also hunkering down to avoid the rain and barely looking where he was going.

"Oof!" the man grunted, and wobbled out of balance. "Watch where you are going!"

Lucas reached out to steady him, then realized who it was. "Feathers! What are you doing out at this hour? You'll catch your death out here."

"You'd like that, wouldn't you?" The old man worked his wrinkled mouth as venom shot from his eyes. "And that is *Mr. Feathers* to you, lad. You may have fooled Miss Wainwright, but you have not fooled me. I know what you are about."

Lucas smiled sardonically. "Do you? Have I been a bad boy, Mr. Feathers? Am I going to be locked in my room again?"

"You should be. What are you doing out so late? Stealing the silver, are you?"

If it weren't a distinct possibility, Lucas would have been angry at him for even suggesting it. "Don't worry, Mr. Feathers. I'm leaving tonight. I won't harm your mistress any more than I have already."

"I lost my position because of you," the old man said with a trembling lower lip. "Good riddance I say, Mr. Davin. Good riddance."

The old butler cinched his collar tighter around his throat, then leaned forward and pushed his way through the sheets of rain, leading with the hump of his nose. Something about his rocking movement gave Lucas the sense that he'd seen him this way before. But where? Then it came to him. Could Feathers have been lurking about the gardens the night Caroline had seen her ghost?

After turning out the lamp, Caroline moved across her room to the settee at the end of her bed. Still dressed, though it was very late, she sat erect, watching with melancholy as flashes of lightning exposed the haunting features of Lord Hamilton in the darkness.

She sensed his disappointment in her, his desire to regain the power he had once had over her. She felt an odd pang of guilt, as if she'd betrayed him for having allowed Lucas to take the ghostly legend's place in her heart. But it was a very small pang, a mere twinge when compared with the other feelings that nearly wrenched her heart from her chest.

After Lucas had left the drawing room to play billiards, he never returned. Sir Roger rejoined them and said Lucas had suddenly taken ill. Caroline had been humiliated by his absence. She'd felt the silent questions and unspoken judgments of her friends and neighbors.

But even more than that, she'd felt a fear that plunged through her body like an enormous icicle, a premonition of loss that nearly buckled her knees. She was losing Lucas, if he was not already lost. She'd lost him the night she'd made love to him. She should have known better than to give in to her passion. She should have known that once he'd truly known how much love she had to give, he would be frightened off. She simply felt things too deeply.

She didn't want Lucas to go, damn his eyes! She clutched her aching insides, holding back a nearly overwhelming urge to run after him, and waited, praying he would at least say good-bye. And all the while the man in the portrait seemed to be smirking, as if to say: "You don't deserve a good-bye. Not after betraying me." She should have been content with her fantasies about Lord Hamilton. Some women weren't destined to be loved here on earth.

She heard the door creak open, and hope kindled like a tiny flame that licks to life at the edges of a rushlight just before it either crackles into being or gutters out. She knew it was Lucas. She could feel his presence; it caressed her stiff back.

He stood in the doorway a long moment, breathing softly, then said, "I came to say good-bye."

Her shoulders curled over her hands, which still clutched her waist. Then she forced herself to straighten, though she did not turn to look at him. She didn't want him to see the trail of tears on her cheeks in the firelight.

"Why did you bother?" she said in a monotone. "Why not take my best horse and leave while you could? Take the silver while you are at it. My jewels are over there. I will not send for the constable. It would ruin my reputation more than it will have been ruined by your early leavetaking. No one will accept the legitimacy of this marriage if you leave now. But I see that this friend you met has a stronger claim on you than I."

"In truth, Miss Wainwright," came his biting reply at last, "I've saddled up your most bowlegged nag. You'll suffer little loss when I'm gone."

"How can you say that?" she shot back, rising and whirling around, searching for his damnably handsome figure in the shadows of the room. "You have no idea what I will lose when you walk out that door."

"Oh, I think I have a fair idea." He shoved his hands in his pocket and sauntered forward, kicking the door shut behind him with a deft twist of his ankle. "You'll lose Fallingate, and the servants will whisper about your fallen virtue, but you won't be cast out utterly by Society. No one will know for sure what happened during that odd week when the mysterious Mr. Lucas Davin from Africa came and went. Your reputation will recover with a little skillful artifice. That's much better than having it ruined beyond repair. And that's what would happen if I stayed."

"That is not true! You have come so far. You have picked up manners like someone born to the *ton*. You are clever, a quick study. We could still pull off this faradiddle."

He shook his head. His curly black locks danced in silhouette. "It's already over, Caro. Lady Germaine recognized me tonight."

"What?" The breath went out of her. "How could she have? She has never met you. She just thought you seemed familiar. Perhaps you have one of those kinds of faces that people think they recognize."

He moved closer still. He stopped a foot away. Close enough for her to smell his distinctively enticing scent, but too far away to accidentally touch.

"She saw me the night I was arrested outside her estate. One of my . . . cohorts . . . stole a horse from her. She recognized me. I know it."

Caroline pressed her fingers against her eyes and took a steadying breath. "What were doing outside her estate?"

He paused, then ambled to the mantel, beneath which a brazier hissed and glowed in the fireplace. "I was planning a robbery. You see—"

"I do not want to know any more."

"You must know. Caroline, I—"

"No!" she said. "Do not tell me. All I need to know is that I want you to stay."

With his left hand perched on his waist and his right elbow propped on the mantel, he pinched the bridge of his nose and heaved a sigh.

"Do not behave in that manner!" she shouted. "Do not act as if it would take the patience of Job to hear my heart's deepest secrets! I want you to stay. Please, Lucas. I have asked you before and I will ask you again: do not make me beg. Just stay. I need you."

"Damnation, be quiet!" he said, slamming his hand on the mantel. "I do not *want* you, Caroline."

The words hurtled across the distance and pierced her chest.

"Oh," she groaned, and shrank back, pressing a hand to her collarbone. "Don't."

"I don't want you. Can't you figure that out? What would I want with you? A silly, dried-up spinster who falls for someone like me?"

She gasped and staggered back, bumping into the settee. She stumbled sideways and nearly knocked into a small Chippendale table adorned with a decanter of brandy before she caught her balance.

"Do you really think I could respect a woman who would bed a crook?"

She could gasp no more. Her twisting chest could take in no air. As she struggled for breath, shock turned to outrage. Blind with fury, she reached for the heavy glass decanter, and in a fit of rage the likes of which she'd never felt before, she threw it straight toward his head.

"No, Caro!" Lucas yelled, then ducked down just in time to miss the flying object. It shattered above him, smashing into the portrait of Lord Hamilton. Glass flew; sticky port splattered the painting. Alcoholic fumes choked the air. A split second later, the enormous portrait came crashing down. A wickedly unforgiving corner of the heavy gilded frame struck Lucas soundly on top of his head. He, and the picture, collapsed to the floor.

"Lucas!" Caroline cried out. She nearly stumbled over the canvas in her attempt to reach Lucas's side. "Lucas, are you all right? Oh, Lord! You are hurt. What have I done?"

He did not move. He lay on his belly, his head turned to one side. She knelt at his shoulder, wishing a lamp were lit, and when she felt her gown grow soggy at the knees she realized with horror that he was bleeding copiously.

"Lucas! Do not die. You mustn't die."

She touched his head and felt the warmth of blood. She touched his shoulders and chest, feeling for any other injuries. There was something hard and flat in his coat pocket. A flask. It must be brandy, she thought. She yanked it out and unfastened the lid. When a throb of lightning pulsed in the sky, she saw that an elephant was etched into the flask's polished silver surface.

"Drink this, Lucas. It will revive you." She rolled him over and lifted his head, forcing the mouth of the flask to his lips. He swallowed, groaned, then choked. Then the full weight of his head dropped in her hands and he went utterly still. He'd lost consciousness completely.

Of course he had. He was losing too much blood. She'd never again underestimate the signs of illness or impending death. He was dying. And all because of her. The man who had held her dear, who had made love to her, who had taken pleasure from her, though he would not admit it, was dying.

"Oh, Lucas," she said, and began to weep. She laid her cheek next to his and sobbed into his ear. "Please do not die. I love you."

Twenty

aroline scarcely slept at all that night. After crying but a moment at Lucas's side, she'd gathered her wits and sought help from Dr. Cavendish. Theodore rushed to her aid, and she thanked heaven that there had been a doctor so close at hand. He examined Lucas and, finding the source of the blood, made a few stitches in the back of the scalp. With that, the danger passed.

The servants undressed Lucas, careful not to dislodge the white bandage wrapped across his forehead and around the back of his head, then put him in Caroline's bed. After changing out of her bloody clothes into a pale white morning gown, she kept vigil all night long, like a vestal virgin. She sat in a chair and anxiously watched Lucas's breathing in the light of a bedside lamp.

Her head nodded and finally sleep overtook her. Sometime around dawn, when the birds began to celebrate victory over yet another night, she awoke to the sound Lucas's voice.

"Caroline. Caroline?"

Her head bobbed up and she found him watching her. "Lucas? How long have you been awake?"

"For some time. I've been watching you and thinking." He reached for her, holding out his open palm.

She went to the bed and slipped her fingers into his, sitting down beside him. Thick blue veins spread from his wrist down into the pale skin of his palm. She squeezed his hand and shut her eyes in a silent prayer of gratitude.

"Lucas, I was ever so worried. And it was entirely my fault. I—"

"Shhh. It is all right, my darling."

She opened her eyes and stared at him. My darling? She studied his face for signs of confusion or fever, but he'd never been clearer. Her chest swelled with hope at the thought that he might have had a change of heart. There was definitely something different about him, but she could not quite identify what.

"Lucas, are you sure you are well? I—"

He silenced her again. This time with an unexpected kiss. With some effort, he hoisted himself up on his elbow and gripped her neck, pulling her down to meet him. His mouth hungrily consumed hers, parting her lips effortlessly, inoculating her with his very special brand of sensuality. When she groaned, he took the opportunity to deepen his kiss. He sat up fully and pulled her down into his arms.

At long last, after he'd lit a burning torch inside her, making her forget his injury and insults, he sat back against the pillow with an utterly charming and devoted look on his face.

"I love you, Caroline," he said. "Can you ever forgive me for what I said last night? I cherish the ground you walk on and I want you to know it before another moment passes."

She stared in astonishment. He spoke so oddly. It wasn't merely the effusiveness of the sentiments but his tone, his accent. He sounded like a peer of the realm, a born and bred member of the upper crust. She shook her head and shut her eyes, trying to make sense of it all.

"You *love* me?" She opened her eyes and stared incredulously. "You're admitting it?"

He gave her a cocky half smile. "I'll admit it to the world. Nothing is going to stand in the way of our marriage. Do you understand that, my dear girl?"

My dear girl?

"I . . . believe so."

"You doubt me?"

Her hands fidgeted in her lap while she sought the right words. "No, it's simply that . . . you sound so different. Not like yourself at all. You're not usually so formal and forthright and . . . well, confident of your worthiness."

He sat up and pierced her with his soulful black eyes. "That's because I did not even remember who I was until last night. I am most worthy of you, dear lady."

"Last night?" She frowned, utterly confused. "What happened last night? You mean when the painting hit your head?"

He nodded, then astonished her even further by laughing. It began slowly, then crescendoed. He fell back against the pillow, holding his belly, laughing helplessly, as if he'd just heard the most sensational joke of the Season. And just as he stopped and gasped for breath, his face crumbled and he squeezed the bridge of his nose, fighting off a wave of tears. His face turned red and water seeped at the corners of his eyes.

Caroline was frozen with horror. "Lucas, good Lord, you're hysterical. What is wrong? You're not yourself at all."

"No," he said, recovering his composure and regarding

her significantly. "I am both my selves. I just don't know which one.

"*Both* yourselves. Whatever do you mean?"

He gave her a sympathetic smile. "You don't understand at all, do you?"

She shook her head emphatically. "Not in the least."

"I scarcely understand it myself, my love. But when I get it all sorted out, I'll explain everything. Just know that everything will work out." He threw back the covers and leaped out of bed, apparently entirely recovered from the blow. "The sun is shining, Caro. By God, I have never seen such a welcome sight."

"Lucas, you should not be walking around. You could lose your balance and knock your head again."

"Do not worry, darling. I have never felt better." He pushed aside the curtain and bent down, squinting at the sunlight. "An excellent day for company. What say you, my love, to another dinner party? Invite your guests again since I ruined yesterday's affair."

When he turned to her expectantly, she rose and treaded toward him with hesitant steps. "A dinner party? You said last night that you feared Lady Germaine would recognize you."

He turned to Caro with a look of mischief, and something much sadder, lurking in his handsome face. "I am not afraid of her. Let her accuse me as she will. In fact, I welcome the chance to confront her. There is nothing we cannot overcome together, love. Not anymore."

"Lucas, what has happened to you? I hardly recognize you. Perhaps you need a touch of brandy to still your nerves."

She cast about, looking for a decanter, then remembered the flask that had been in his pocket. She found it on the bedside table. "Here, drink this."

"Where did you get that?" he said, frowning at her offering.

"I found it in your coat last night. It revived you."

His features grew very still, very sober. "Ah," he said with resignation, sinking down into the window seat. "So that explains it. I did not remember drinking it, but now I understand."

She stared at him as if he were bound for Bedlam. "You understand what? Lucas, you're frightening me."

"Caro, you worry too much. Give me the flask. I'll gladly guzzle the lot of it. I—"

A determined knock sounded on the door. "Caroline, may I come in?"

"It's Theodore." Caroline put the flask on the table. "Thank goodness. Come in, Uncle Teddy!"

He bustled in with a grave frown wrinkling his high brow. "I have bad news, Caro. Your brother and his wife are due to arrive tomorrow. For some reason they have decided to come a day or two *before* your birthday." He went to Lucas and squeezed his shoulder with affection. "So, Davin, are you well enough to play the game with as much finesse as will be required?"

"He will have plenty of finesse," Caroline said dubiously, "based on his behavior thus far this morning."

So the moment had finally arrived. Lucas was still here, apparently willing and able, in fact eager, to conclude the last act of their charade. He had even said he loved her, though she couldn't quite believe it. She'd always thought he loved her, but the sudden turnabout discomfited her. A chill shimmied up her arms and she shook it off.

Lucas noticed right away, as if every ounce of his being were now focused on her alone. He rose from the window seat and came forward.

"What is it, Caro?" He pulled her into an embrace, one too familiar for company. She tingled all over, so happy to hold him again, but she also felt self-conscious because he shouldn't be holding her like this in front of the doctor.

"Caro, you must trust me that everything will be fine."

"Of course, Lucas, I simply—"

He silenced her with another soul-wrenching kiss. At first she froze and refused to respond, embarrassed by the audacious show of affection, but he quickly worked his magic and she soon even forgot that there was anyone else in the room.

When he drew back, she sagged in his arms, incredulous. She didn't think it was possible, but he was even more passionate than before. He was a different man. No question of that. But whom had he become? And what had made him change?

She cast a furtive glance at the portrait that was now propped up against the far wall on the floor. Lord Hamilton's expression seemed oddly devoid of emotion. The vibrant, almost chillingly alive painting now seemed dead, lacking the spirit that had made it so captivating before. It was as if the spirit of Lord Hamilton had moved on, or into, something . . . or someone . . . else.

She calmly disengaged from Lucas's arms and turned to Theodore.

"Uncle Teddy, may I speak with you a moment out in the corridor?"

The erudite and eloquent physician was speechless. His mouth, which had parted in surprise as he witnessed the kiss, still hung open. He merely nodded and followed her out of the room. When the door was safely shut, Caroline whirled on him.

"Did you see that? Did you hear him? Lucas is a changed man. He has been utterly transformed," she whispered harshly. "Something terrible happened to him when he was struck by that painting."

"You didn't appear to think it was so terrible when he was kissing you."

"I had little choice!"

"We have been training him every day to act like a London buck," Theodore argued *sotto voce*. "Our lessons have finally taken hold, that is all."

"But his speech is perfect, without so much as a slip. It's not even the words, it's his tone, his manner. He reeks of nobility. You can't train someone to act that perfectly. I tell you, Uncle Teddy, he changed. Overnight! Do you know what I think? I think he has been possessed by the ghost of Lord Hamilton!"

"Oh, my dear, you have nearly come undone. No, no, Caro, Lucas has not been possessed by a ghost. Tell me, have you ever seen him drinking from a silver flask that has an elephant carved on its surface?"

She blinked. "Why, yes. Just last night. After he was knocked down and injured, I made him drink from it. I thought some liquor would rouse his flagging consciousness."

Theodore crossed his arms and pursed his lips. "I see. Well, that probably has more to do with his personality change than the portrait."

"He seemed to think the same thing. What does this signify? Are you saying he is prone to liquorishness? I've only seen him foxed once."

"No, my dear. Let him drink from the flask as often as he desires. I will explain what I mean another time. Right now we must quickly prepare for the arrival of your brother. Caro, you are trembling." He put a reassuring arm around her shoulder. "There, there, everything will work out in the end."

"I suppose it must." She leaned into her guardian angel. "I just never thought I would regret the day that we would have so thoroughly tamed the irascible Lucas Davin."

• • •

They spent the day preparing for the Wainwrights' arrival, though in truth everything but their humors were in a perfect state of order. Lucas met with Mr. Dorris and suddenly was fascinated with the details of running the estate. He seemed to be falling naturally into the role of authority. Caroline was amazed. Something had definitely changed, if nothing more than his outlook.

That night she dressed for bed not knowing what to expect. How odd to think that just twenty-four hours earlier she was convinced that she would never see Lucas again. Tonight she fully expected him to come to her bed. She shivered with longing every time she thought about it, though she did feel some trepidation. After all, if he were possessed, it would almost be like making love to a stranger.

"Caroline?" Lucas's voice penetrated through the bedroom door.

She sat at the window seat, looking at the full moon and the mist that floated by her window, now and then obscuring her view. There was no rain tonight, only a whistling wind that caused the tree branch outside to bob and creak.

"Caroline, may I come in?"

She was ready for him. She stood and turned to face the door. "Of course. Come in."

He opened the door and took a long look at her in her flowing white nightgown with her hair tumbling down her back and grinned his approval. "Good Lord, Mrs. Davin, you look resplendent tonight."

The corners of her mouth curled in a guarded smile. "Thank you."

He nudged aside his coat and slid a hand into the side pocket of his close-fitting breeches, sauntering to the fireplace. With a tan waistcoat hugging his cambric shirt, his narrow hips were provocatively visible. His lean legs were poised casually, and she wondered if he tried to be seductive, or if it just came naturally to him.

"Resplendent is a fine word," she said, walking aimlessly to her jewelry box. She unclasped her necklace and dropped it in. "Where did you learn it?"

"It just came to mind. I suppose I learned it when I was young."

She looked up at him with a troubled frown. He had discarded his bandage earlier in the day and looked his old self again, at least in body. "It is not the sort of word young lads learn when they are studying the proper techniques for cutting purses in Seven Dials."

He pulled the flask from his pocket and took a swig, wiping his mouth with a backhand. "Then perhaps I learned it from Mrs. Plumshaw. You are worrying again, Caro. And for naught. We are married. That is all that matters now."

Putting the flask back in his pocket, he sprang away from the mantel and came toward her. He slipped one arm around her waist and pulled her so close she could feel his chest expanding against her breasts with each breath that warmed her cheeks. With his other hand he tilted her head back, then he bent his knees and lowered himself until his mouth could reach her thin neck. He kissed the place where her shoulder curved upward, and soon his lips were swirling erotically over her sensitive, porcelain skin.

She whimpered a tiny moan and arched against him.

"Oh, Caro," he murmured, roving higher and higher until he stood tall enough to kiss the corner of her mouth. "Caro, you are so beautiful. So utterly enchanting."

The words knelled like a distant alarm bell, wrenching her from the moment. She stiffened, then pushed herself away with both hands. When he looked at her in surprise, she frowned. "Do not say things you do not mean, Lucas."

He shook his head wonderingly. "I do mean them."

"How can you? I am not beautiful. Even when we first made love, you would admit to no attraction save for the alleged beauty that lies within me."

He shook his head. "You misunderstood my meaning. You are beautiful to my eyes because of who you are. Caro, the body is simply a reflection of the soul. I make love to your body, but it is your soul I cherish. The body is finite. The spirit is infinite."

She whirled around, putting some distance between them. This talk of eternity made her think of Lord Hamilton. She looked around for his portrait, then remembered she'd asked Henry to hang it in the library.

"You're nervous about your brother's impending arrival," he said soothingly. "Perhaps you could use something to relax you."

He poured her a glass of port from a decanter by the fire and handed her the glass, which she accepted with a welcoming nod. "Perhaps you're right. I am nervous. Everything seems . . . different. And I don't understand why."

"Yes, Caroline, things have changed. I am suddenly remembering so much more." Lucas pinched the bridge of his nose and grimaced.

She saw him waver and took a step forward. "Are you ill? Perhaps you should sit."

"No, this blasted headache comes and goes. Memories keep flooding my head until it aches unbearably."

She blinked sympathetically. "What kind of memories?"

"Just now I was remembering when I was a boy." His face lit with some distant memory, making him look youthful. He went to the window and gazed at the moon while he spoke. "For some reason, I suddenly remembered how my father used to correct my speech. A man is judged not by what he says, Father would say, but by how he says it."

"Your father?" She frowned. "You mean Robbin Roger?"

Lucas turned to her and his eyes narrowed as a glimpse of the past revealed itself with tantalizing detail. "No, not Robbin. Someone else. I remember he presented me to the king. I had never seen Father speak with such formality. He was nervous. When I forgot to bow, he pinched my shoulder. When I recovered, and answered the king's questions and was rewarded with his majesty's delight and laughter, Father rewarded me afterward with a proud clap on the back and a sugared sculpture." Lucas laughed. "That was the best part of the whole day."

He sobered and looked at her with more confusion than she'd ever seen in him. "How can that be, Caro? How can I remember a father I never had?"

Caroline approached him softly so as not to dispel his memories. "You talked to the king? What king was it? Was it Henry?" She was scarcely breathing now. Barrett Hamilton had lived during the reign of King Henry VIII. "Was that the king you remember meeting, Lucas?"

His sober frown melted and mirth twinkled in his black eyes. "Do not be a silly goose. Henry VIII died centuries ago."

She blushed. "Yes, that was a silly suggestion. Of course you never met Henry VIII." Still, she wanted to know. It seemed odd that Lucas would ever have the chance to meet any king. "Was it King George?"

He shrugged. "I suppose it would have to have been. Truth is, I do not really remember. Memories are not my strong suit. And I have a terrible headache. I believe I have not quite recovered from the blow to my head."

When he sank onto the window seat and rubbed his forehead, looking suddenly weary and older than he was, she put down her glass and came to his side. She wrapped her arms around his shoulder and kissed his gaunt cheek. He had lost weight since she'd first met him. How was that possible when he'd had far more to eat here than he'd doubtless had in the gaol?

"Poor Lucas. You have been through so much, thanks to me."

He pulled her close and pressed his cheek to her breasts. "So much that is good. Let memories come as they may. All that I care about, all that is real, is you."

She stroked his hair, careful not to touch his stitches. Touching him made her feel they were close again. Perhaps if they stopped talking and started touching, they could return to that place of extraordinary intimacy they'd shared that one precious night.

"Let us go to bed," she murmured. "Tomorrow we face my brother and his wife, the greatest challenge yet."

He tilted his head up with a cocky smirk. "They do not frighten me."

She laughed huskily. "I do not imagine you are frightened of anything."

His black eyes glittered at her with sudden insight. "Not anymore." He stood and gripped the back of her neck and pulled her close, kissing her cheek roughly, her eyes, her eyebrows, her nose—anything he could explore, murmuring all the while, "I love you. I will never stop loving you. I love you. Always, always, always."

She shuddered, wanting to believe him. He kissed her deeply on the mouth, and his hands dragged over her skin, down her neck, tugging on the ties of her sleeping gown until it fell open and her breasts emerged. His hot hands found them, enveloped them, and she dug her fingers in his neck as a spasm of pleasure tore through her, rendering her inner resistance a heap of cinders.

He knelt before her and kissed her flat stomach, his

tongue whirling over white skin that rarely saw the light of day. His hungry lips found her nipples and laved over their hardened buds. Caroline gripped his strong shoulders.

"You are so beautiful," he murmured low in his chest, looking up at her as if she were a goddess on Olympus. She tensed at his praise, then forced herself to accept it. She forced herself to see herself through his eyes. Perhaps he was right. Perhaps she was beautiful after all. In his arms, she certainly felt like a goddess. She'd never been more powerful. A man was groveling before her, and his reward would be the deepest, most secret part of her.

"Will you make love to me?" she whispered, and as she said it, her words became superfluous, for his right hand crawled up her bare thigh, circling the skin that was softer than silk. He didn't stop there. They stood entwined in the middle of the room for a long while, he exploring secret territories, she surrendering all doubts, all dignity, all control. When at last she let out a tortured groan, he stood and carried her to the bed.

Her carried her limp and woozy body to the bed and laid her down. The very moment her head touched the pillow, the window burst open. A cold wind whirled around the room, rustling papers on her writing table, knocking over glass.

"Barrett!" came a doleful moan.

Caroline gasped and sat up, half expecting to see someone in the window. "Did you hear that?"

"The wind?"

"No, a voice." She felt a deep chill settle on her.

"I heard nothing." He stroked her cheek. "You're shivering."

He rose from the bed and shut the window.

By the time he returned, she'd forgotten the voice. She no longer felt any anxieties. She needed to make love to Lucas with an urgency that seemed to have been building for centuries. She would do anything to make love to him now. Sacrifice anything, simply to have him.

Utterly naked, without shame, wanton and wanting, Caroline watched as Lucas disrobed. Each peeled layer of clothing revealed what she had memorized from the last time they'd made love—wrought muscles, hard planes, gleaming skin, and undeniable desire.

He climbed in next to her and slid over her. They melded together perfectly, each nook and corner of their bodies fitting snugly, their skin touching like two textures of silk. They joined together effortless, his aching need filling her fully, heatedly. He pumped into her with an urgency he'd never known. She clung to him with an aching sweetness that seemed unearthly.

And in that moment when he thrust his last, he cried out, "Rachel! Oh, God's wounds, Rachel!"

Twenty-one

The next morning before the visitors arrived, Theodore gathered everyone in the library to meet Jeremy Grenville. He was an amiable, impeccably dressed, and keen-eyed solicitor in his thirties who seemed to revel in the boring and arcane details of his profession. As he chatted about his practice in nearby Devon, it wasn't long before everyone's eyes glazed over.

Theodore had asked Grenville to draw up an addendum to the original marriage settlement. As Grenville took tea and strived to impress everyone present with his grasp of law, Caroline stood in the middle of the library, barely aware of the people around her. She watched Lucas, who stood at the far end of the long room, flipping through a book. He frowned so earnestly at the words, it looked as though he were reading, though she knew that was not possible.

Lord, she loved him. If she lived a thousand years, she was quite certain she would never make love with the intensity she'd experienced last night. Perhaps she felt so close to him simply because she'd nearly lost him, but last night it was almost as if their spirits had become one. Their bodies joined but then seemed to disappear as some more powerful force took over. And it wasn't just him; she'd felt an almost supernatural ecstasy as well.

It was madness to think this way, but how else could she explain their extraordinary closeness? And making it that much more precious were her very real concerns about Lucas. Seeing him now from a distance, she noticed once again how thin he had become. He wasn't eating properly. And then there was that other grave matter, so to speak, which she hardly even wanted to admit to herself.

She was now absolutely convinced that Lucas was possessed by the ghost of Lord Hamilton. Her last doubts on that score had been shattered when he'd called her Rachel. Now she wasn't sure if it was Lucas who loved her or Barrett. In any event, she didn't care, for she loved him and she was determined to help him somehow to regain his former identity.

Presently, as the others chatted in a low drone, she gazed at the portrait and wondered how she could help Lucas. How on earth could she send the ghost who'd overtaken him back into the portrait?

"Caro, are you with us?" Theodore said. "Caro?"

She blinked and turned to find them all gazing at her with concern.

"Is anything wrong?" Amanda gently inquired.

"I'm sorry. I was thinking about . . . something else. What is it you wish to discuss?"

"I have asked Mr. Grenville to draw up some additional papers," Theodore said. "Since Lucas now plans to stay, it is imperative that he sign them. I want this all settled before George arrives. He'll ask to see the marriage settlement, and I plan to refuse. But I can't do it in good conscience unless I think I've truly taken care of your future."

"What is there to be concerned about?" she inquired, joining the others around the great mahogany desk that dominated the room. "I thought everything was in order."

"When I had the original documents drawn up," Theodore explained, "I had assumed that Lucas would be leaving. I made no provisions for a lengthy stay, which now seems inevitable."

The solicitor stood up as straight and nearly as thin as the quill pen he held poised in his hand. "Mrs. Davin, I believe you will find everything in order. All I need is your husband's signature."

"What is the purpose of this document?"

Grenville cleared his throat. "Ma'am, it ensures your control of your property in the event that Mr. Davin chooses to stay at Fallingate. The original document merely specified how much he was to receive upon his departure. If he stays, he will still receive his yearly income; however, he will not assume control of Fallingate. In other words, he cannot dispose of it as he pleases."

That sounded fair enough, but she suspected there was a very large stick hidden in the legal terms written on the document, a stick that would be used to beat Lucas with, with no quarter given, should he decide to disobey the terms of the settlement.

"Mr. Grenville, I appreciate your prompt attention. Before my husband signs this document, I would like to discuss it alone with him and Dr. Cavendish and Mrs. Plumshaw. Will you excuse us a moment?"

"Most assuredly, ma'am." He sketched an officious bow and departed.

"Lucas?" she called tenderly to him.

"Yes, darling?" He looked up, and catching her eye, his features softened from their studious pose. He smiled, dimples cutting his handsome cheeks with crescent moons.

"Uncle Teddy wants to talk about some points of law. Would you join us, please?"

He snapped the book shut and slipped it back onto the shelf. He strolled over with leisurely elegance and stopped next to Theodore, clapping him gently on the shoulder. "Well, my good man, what shall we discuss?"

At the show of affection, Theodore frowned guiltily and turned his focus to a dry cheroot he'd pulled out of his pocket.

"Ahem." Theodore coughed into his fist. "Before we introduce you to Caro's brother, Davin, there is something you need to sign. Do you remember when I encouraged you to think about staying at Fallingate? I said that I hoped you would but that I would have to attend to Caro's legal concerns in such an event."

Lucas listened with careful scrutiny. "Yes."

"Mr. Grenville has been good enough to draw up a document stating the circumstances of your marriage. You will be Caro's husband in name only. You will receive two thousand a year, but you must agree to live abroad in order to receive it. Unless, of course, Caroline decides she wants your company, which we all know she does."

Caroline shot a sideways glance at Lucas. His smile was gone. He regarded the doctor with half-hooded eyes.

"As you know, it is my dearest hope that you remain, but Caroline must agree to it. If she ever changes her mind and you insist on remaining at Fallingate against her wishes, you will lose not only your income but your freedom."

"His freedom?" Caroline said, taking a step forward. "Whatever do you mean?"

There was a long, awkward pause, which finally Lucas himself broke.

"He means, darling, that I will go back into the gaol." He thoughtfully combed one of his gracefully sculpted hands over the cleft in his chin and down his neck to the top of his gray striped cravat. "It is where I thought I would end up all along."

"That is monstrously unfair!" she said.

"Now, now, Caro, it's not quite as coldhearted as all that. If Lucas tries to wrest control of Fallingate from you, divorce proceedings will be undertaken, going all the way to Parliament if necessary. To ensure a divorce, of course, he'll either be declared insane or an adulterer or both. In any event, when his life comes under scrutiny, his past will no doubt come to light."

"Why would I want to do anything so cruel?" Caroline said indignantly.

"To protect your assets, my dear. I know you are sentimental, Caro, but I would be remiss if I did not prepare you for any eventuality. Women have few rights, and that's why any document we draw up must have teeth. If Lucas behaves himself, it won't bite. Fair enough, Davin?"

"Yes, of course," Lucas replied smoothly, no hint of anger or betrayal in his voice. "It is what I would want for my own daughter."

"See?" Theodore said with relief. "Lucas understands. He loves you, Caro, we all do. So let us look after your interests as your father would have expected us to."

"But you are not being fair to Lucas. You are giving him no choices, no control. You are treating him like a caged animal or a child. That is no way for a man to live. You have stripped him of his dignity."

"Caro," Theodore argued, "if an agreement offers no incentive and no threat of reprisals if it is broken, it is a worthless document. And Lucas has an abundance of choices. He can stay or go. Either way he becomes a rich man. I fail to see how this belittles him in the least."

Amanda sat forward in her chair, adding her thoughts. "Lucas will have much more say over his destiny than he did before he met you. To think what I might have done with my life if I had had the freedom to travel abroad with two thousand a year!"

Caroline whirled on her. "But you are a woman, Amanda." She began to pace. "No one expects a female to be free. A man must have his dignity."

"I am sure Mr. Davin does not think we are trying to unman him," Theodore said, his eyes twinkling with compassion. "Is that not so, Davin?"

Lucas thrust his hands in his pockets. "Of course, I do not think you are trying to humiliate me."

He spoke overprecisely. Damn him, Caroline thought, why was he speaking like a bloody earl? She longed for his ragged speech, his charming hostility, his engaging sense of discomfort.

"He is trying to disarm you, Lucas," she said. "And I mean no insult, Uncle Teddy, but you do not have Lucas's well-being in mind. You are thinking only of me, and I am grateful. But I see no lawyer representing his interest."

"He is from Seven Dials, Caro. Most thieves do not have lawyers."

"If they had them, perhaps they would not need to steal to survive," she returned, color pinching her cheeks. "Their lawyers would do it for them.

"Caro," Lucas said, and held out his hands.

It was all she could do to keep from running into his arms. Instead, she walked to him with head held high, eyes locked in his mesmerizing gaze. She reached out and gripped his hands. He squeezed her fingers and the extraordinary heat of his being flowed into her arms, warming her magically.

"Caro," he whispered, "we must do what is right for you. You are what matters most to me."

"But you are already and indubitably my husband. You don't have to sign that paper. It will only weaken your position. I don't want some document dictating the course of our marriage. I will not have you being threatened or bullied by a lawyer for my estate."

"I don't mind if it means you will be well cared for." He stroked her cheek, the back of his titillating fingers trailing down her skin. She pressed the hand to her cheek. "All marriages are about money in the end."

"But not ours!"

"Caro, do not worry. I know who I am now. No one can ever take that away from me again. I will survive regardless of what happens in the future. Do you understand?"

"Lucas, I—"

"Come, then," Theodore said from the distance. "Enough of your sentimental protestations. Time is wasting." He pulled out his pocket watch. "George will be here soon. I refuse to introduce Lucas as your husband unless he signs these papers. You may be angry with me, but it is for your own good."

"I would be delighted to sign, Dr. Cavendish," Lucas answered, ending the acrimonious discussion.

He squeezed her hand one last time and went to the desk. He began to study the document spread out before him.

"There, old chap, I know you can't read, so you'll have to trust me that all is as I say." Theodore went to the door and called the solicitor back in.

Before they had even returned to the desk, Lucas had scanned the document. "This is entirely acceptable, Dr. Cavendish, though Mr. Grenville has misspelled 'esteemed' twice."

Lucas dipped the quill into the ink pot and scrawled his signature with a mighty flourish. The scratch of the quill on paper echoed in the silence with all the force of a cannon.

Theodore frowned as if a snake had just writhed across the page. "Upon my word, you can read!"

"And you miswrote the date," Lucas humbly added.

Mr. Grenville grabbed the document, scouring it to find his errors.

"You can read!" Caroline said. "Then why did you pretend you couldn't when you first arrived? Did you intend to deceive us?"

"No," he said, eyeing her calmly. "I couldn't read before and now I can."

"But Amanda didn't teach you how to—"

"Please, Caro," he said, rubbing his forehead. "My headache has returned. I don't understand this any more than you do. If you don't mind, darling, I will lie down for a moment until the guests arrive. I want to be corky when they arrive."

Caroline watched him go with unaccountable sadness. She had gained the husband of her dreams, but lost the man she loved.

Twenty-two

hortly after noon, George Wainwright's carriage rumbled to a stop in front of the house. Caroline had been pacing in the drawing room, and felt a wave of nausea at the sound of the squeaking wheels. She went to the window and saw the handsome landau poised in the gray mist. Her servants bustled into the entrance hall to greet the guests. She had just managed to seat herself in a chair by the table when Henry opened the double doors and in walked her brother.

"Why, George, what a surprise," she managed to say around the lump in her throat.

He was chatting amiably with Theodore and did not even answer. The two men strolled to the fireplace while Prudence Wainwright followed, her eyes scanning the room possessively.

"Greetings, Caro," she said, tapping her fan against her palm, and continued without pausing for breath, "I was thinking of putting up a floral silk in this room, perhaps yellow. What do you think?"

"It would look lovely, I should imagine," Caroline replied. She took in a steadying breath. "But I would like to discuss it first with my husband."

Prudence's pudgy eyes widened with a start. Her fan dropped to the floor.

George looked over. "What is it, my dear?"

"Your *husband*?" Prudence asked incredulously.

"Yes. I will have to consult my husband before I make any significant changes in the decor. He is the master here now."

George started toward his wife when she began to sway. Prudence took a step to catch her balance. Her foot came down on the fan. The carved ivory snapped under her weight. George gripped her arm to steady her.

"Oh, dear," Prudence said. "Oh, dear. Thank you, Mr. Wainwright, I do not know what came over me. I misheard, I am sure. I thought your sister said something about a husband."

When Prudence laughed giddily, George did his best to wrap an arm around his boxy wife. "I say, Caro, you should not jest so. You nearly gave Mrs. Wainwright a fit of apoplexy."

Caroline took in a deep, satisfied breath, pulled back her shoulders, and regarded them with a sense of freedom the likes of which she'd never felt before. "I am not jesting, I assure you, George. I am surprised Feathers hasn't already informed you. I am married. Ask Dr. Cavendish. He witnessed the nuptials."

The Wainwrights turned to him in unison, horror clearly etched on their gentle, well-bred features. Theodore nodded.

"I am afraid so, Wainwright," the doctor said. "It is all official and perfectly legal. A license was purchased and the ceremony was performed by the Reverend Gerald Wilton."

"That old sot?" George said, screwing up his face in disgust.

"He was sober during the wedding ceremony, and that is all that matters," Theodore replied.

George turned a hurt gaze to his sister. "You might have told me, Caroline. To think you have been courting someone all this time when I have been doing my best to find a husband for you. After the number of times I brought gentlemen from London, this is the thanks I get!"

Caroline folded her hands into a white-knuckled grip. "I have not been courting all along, George. This was . . . rather sudden."

"Who is he?" Prudence said, having finally recovered herself. "I trust he has an acceptable family."

"He is—" Caro stopped when she felt Lucas's presence. He stood in the doorway, sleek in his black coat and gray waistcoat, his face less tan than before—more suitably pale as a gentlemen's complexion should be—his hair as neatly combed as it had ever been, and he was wearing a confident smile.

"Mr. and Mrs. Wainwright, I presume?" He came forward and fixed his uniquely charming gaze on Prudence.

She gasped as if he'd made some improper suggestion, then exhaled a self-righteous breath with a little whimper when he gallantly kissed her hand. Prudence let out a wordless utterance of surrender that could only be described as a girlish giggle. Caroline struggled to hide a triumphant smile.

"Mrs. Wainwright, I am most enchanted to meet a woman of such estimable quality. I am your humble and devoted servant."

Prudence blinked hard, trying to regain her perpetual air of disapproval.

"This is Mr. Lucas Davin," Theodore said, filling in the

silence. "I met him in Africa. His parents were missionaries."

"Missionaries?" Prudence recovered from her momentary enchantment and sniffed as if someone had just brought in a rotten fish. "Missionaries? How unfortunate. No patents of nobility in the family?" When Lucas and Caroline merely stared at her, she shook her head. "Such a pity. Not even a baronetcy?"

"His father," Theodore added extemporaneously, "became an adviser to the local tribal king. Very well-connected people. Very important."

"Oh," Prudence said, raising her brows with a hopeful smile.

"Very well connected in Africa, but what good does that do here?" George snapped, and Prudence's smile dissolved. "I do not care if he is the bloody prime minister of that godforsaken place," George said. "And to think you once had the chance to marry the son of an earl! It is obvious to me, Caro, that you have married this man with little concern about your reputation or future. You have squandered the opportunities offered by your fortune. And you did it just to keep Fallingate!"

As she listened to her brother's blunt words, the corners of Caroline's mouth curled slyly upward. "Many a marriage has been made for the sake of property, George. I should think you would be happy that for once I was using my head, not my heart."

"If you were using your head," Prudence replied, "you would not have married the son of a missionary. That won't get you through the door at Almack's, my dear."

"I have never cared for London Society, ma'am, and you well know it," Caroline replied.

"He is in this for money, my dear." George thrust his hand in his pocket and went to the window, looking out as he ground his teeth. "I thought you had hoped for more than that."

"How do you know what he married me for? And why do you speak about him as if he weren't in the room?" She went to George's side and resisted the urge to box her brother on the ears. "You still do not think any man could possibly find me alluring, do you?"

He surveyed her with eyes that had dulled to a slate color. "I will not insult you by answering that. You must simply accept that I have only your well-being in mind."

"Do you?" she returned hotly. "Or is it your stepdaughters you are concerned about? Without the income from Fallingate's mines, you will not have as much dowry for the girls, though I can't imagine why it should matter. You're rich as Croesus."

"Do you really believe I am only thinking about my own interests?"

"Yes, I do."

"Caro," Lucas said placatingly. His deep, honey-smooth voice soothed like a balm. She turned to see him pleading with his eyes. "Do not argue on my account."

"There is no argument," George said, coming to a stand behind his wife. Together they made a fortress that exuded waves of hostility.

Caroline gathered her courage to face them without cringing.

"If the doctor says you are married," George continued in a soft purr, "I will take his word for it. But I want to see the marriage settlement."

"Caroline is of age, Wainwright," Theodore replied. "You have no right to look at the settlement. I assure you it is entirely legal and entirely in her favor."

"You can rest assured that my solicitor will be looking into the matter, Cavendish. If he finds anything amiss, I will challenge this union. Caro, I think you will find your husband may not be who you think he is."

A flash of foreboding prickled her skin. "Whatever do you mean?"

George tucked his thumbs in the pockets of his waistcoat. "I have a feeling all is not as it would seem. Perhaps I am wrong, but I mean to find out one way or the other."

"You will do no such thing! He is my husband and it is none of your business. You are simply angry that I managed to fulfill the stipulations of Father's will. I am sorry, but I have succeeded, George. And your little Mouse did so without your help. That is really what is bothering you."

"Do not be a fool."

She stepped toward him, emboldened by righteous anger. "You had nearly convinced me I was a fool. You made me feel incompetent and sentimental and silly. You made me feel that because I had imagination I was different, when in truth I was just smarter than you, George. I know myself better than you do. And I know I have taken the appropriate and wisest course of action."

"We will see about that, my dear." Prudence rose and puffed herself up like a sail raised in a storm. "We will find out what disgrace you have wrought on this family. For him to marry so quickly he must be desperate indeed."

"Mind your own affairs, ma'am," Caroline shot back.

"Everything that concerns you is my affair, for your reputation will taint my girls'. Let us leave at once, Mr. Wainwright. I am feeling ill."

"I should imagine it is upsetting to lose the jewel you thought to add to your fortune," Caroline said, and would have said more if Lucas hadn't come up behind her and gently gripped her arms.

"If you call this ghost-ridden, dilapidated home a jewel, my dear," Prudence replied as she waddled toward the door, "then I would say you have been too long in the country."

"At least the house now remains in the possession of people who appreciate it."

George sniffed. "We will see how much Mr. Davin appreciates it after he gets a glimpse of Lord Hamilton's ghost."

Caroline's mood darkened at the mention of the ghost. She straightened the lace on her cuffs. "He has not seen or heard from any ghosts at all."

George's right eye began to tic as it often did when he was distressed. "We will see about that."

"You sound disappointed, George. Did you hope the ghosts would chase away my husband just as they chased away my suitors?"

"I do not bloody well care what happens in this house. But let me be the first to warn you that your husband's life may be in danger."

Caroline's gaze shot up discerningly. "What do you mean?"

"Did it ever occur to you," George said in a hard tone, "that Lord Hamilton's spirit might try to kill Mr. Davin?"

"Now you are being the fool," she replied quickly but without much conviction.

George gloated. "Am I the fool? Dear sister, the ghost went to great lengths to keep you from marrying your other suitors. He must be terribly angry that you have outwitted him."

"Upon my word, I own that I have never heard anything so absurd in all my life," she snapped.

"Perhaps, but if something happens to Mr. Lucas Davin, just remember that I was the first to warn you."

Without another word, George held out his arm. Prudence ceremoniously laid hers on top, as if they were readying themselves for an introduction at court. They marched out of the room with heads held high. When the doors closed behind them at the hands of unseen servants, Caroline exhaled a gusty sigh of relief.

"Oh, Lord! Thank heaven they are gone." She crumbled into a chair and sprawled her legs out in unladylike fashion. "I thought they would never leave us."

"They were only here a matter of minutes." Theodore withdrew his pocket watch and studied its face.

"It seemed an eternity. And you, poor Lucas, how did you endure it?"

He sat down in the chair beside her and took her hand in his, looking as unflappable as a falcon that has weathered a brutal storm.

"Nothing," he said, caressing her with his intelligent eyes, "nothing in this world could shake me from your side, Caroline."

She gripped his hand and admired its strength. Overnight he had become utterly devoted. She was beginning to think she could get used to the change, but even if she did, her mind still would not be at peace. George's warning had sounded a ring of truth: Lucas was in danger. The falling chandelier had just been the first incident. Then came the falling painting, confirming the danger. Now, added to that, was his worrisome appearance. He was definitely losing weight. Nothing about him was as it should be. Whatever could she do to make things right?

An hour later, Lucas rode Lightning in a fast canter along the path that wended through desolate Cragmere Moor. Mist rose up to hide the moorland road from view, but the horse seemed to know its way. Lucas hunkered down over the reins, fending off the blows of raindrops. It was merely a drizzle, but it had the desired effect. It cleared his mind.

He had performed well today. He had fulfilled his promise to his wife. He had put her interests before his own.

Too often he had seen the suffering of dependents who had no recourse under the law. He had not wanted that for Caroline, and so he had pulled off the scheme they'd planned and worked for. They had convinced George Wainwright that she was legitimately married. Now she would be mistress of her own fate. They had fooled Society, pulled off their act, and he smiled with savage triumph.

Still, he was making her miserable, he thought as he listened to the steady pounding of horse hooves on the beaten path, as he felt the pounding reverberate through the saddle. She was worried and frightened. She sensed that she did not know him anymore. Had she ever? Had he, for that matter, ever known himself? He would tell her who he was—who he *really* was. Just as soon as he fully remembered.

He tossed back his head and smiled at the cold rain. He laughed at it; the sound was a ragged tear in his throat, a forceful exultation from deep in his pained gut. Ever since the painting had fallen on him, the memories had come rushing back. Painful glimpses into a past that was shockingly unfamiliar—the smell of polished wood, the blare of a hunter's horn, the sobbing, racking tears that marred an otherwise perfect gilded chamber, the sense of sorrow over a leave-taking that never should have been. These memories came back in colors so bright they hurt his eyes, in the pitching of his stomach as he wrestled with reality, in the taste of bile that rose on his dry tongue.

"God, help me!" he cried out, and reined in hard.

Lightning didn't like it. The beast whinnied angrily and reared back, thrashing the air with its hooves. Lucas, now a solid horseman, leaned into it and clung deftly to the saddle until the horse's hooves fell back to the ground with a muted thwomp.

"Sorry, old boy," Lucas said. "We're not done riding yet."

They would ride until he no longer felt pain, or until he remembered who he was, whichever came first.

The cold bit him to the bone. He was shivering now. With shaking fingers, he reached into his waistcoat and pulled out the elephant flask. He looked at it with bitter longing, then unfastened the stopper. This would help him recall. He was having trouble remembering things that had happened just yesterday, but could remember the littlest details of his childhood. He had to remember everything, then he could make sense of it all.

He put the small metal opening to his lips and tossed back a mouthful. Then another. This was the key to everything. If only the pieces of the puzzle would come together. He would tell her then. He would tell Caro everything, just as soon as he figured it all out himself.

Twenty-three

Smiley Figgenbottom had it all planned out. He would knock on the door to the servants' entrance at Fallingate and claim he was a chimney sweep. Only little men and boys could ply that trade, and so his half-pint size made him look the part well enough, though in truth he was a little stout for the job. He'd stolen some feather dusters to complete the image, and no one could lie as well as Smiley. The servants would fall for his trickery easily enough. Then, when they weren't looking, he'd snoop around until he found Lucas.

As it turned out, his chicanery was unnecessary. Before he could round the house, he saw a windblown and soaking Lucas ride into the stables on a sweating and rain-soaked horse. Smiley glimpsed his fancy figure from afar and blinked twice. Lucas looked even more like a lord than he had the last time they'd met at the Silver Stallion Inn, only this time he wasn't wearing his fancy garrick. More fool he. A man without a coat could catch his death of a chill on a day like this.

Pushing the tattered cap away from his brow, the crook

hobbled to the stable entrance and whistled low.

"Lawk-a-mussy, will yer look at that! A regular lord of the manor, ain't yer?"

Lucas's arrogant face tilted down toward his former cohort with a snapping motion, and his look of idle curiosity darkened with distaste. "What are you doing here?"

At the sound of Lucas's aristocratic accent, Smiley chuckled and lifted his sagging breeches. "Eh, now, yer talk fancy, too, eh? Who is this? Earl Lily Liver or the Lucas Davin I've always known?"

A sardonic grin creased one of Lucas's rugged cheeks and he threw his leg over the saddle and slid down until his boots hit the cobbled stable yard. The groom came for the reins, cast a sweeping, disdainful glance at Smiley, and led the horse behind the stable to cool him down.

"I do believe you are suffering from a misconception," Lucas said at last as he tugged down on the fancy cuffs of his shirt and pulled on the sodden sleeves of his tailored riding coat.

"Wot's that, mate?"

"You have never known me."

Smiley's mocking grin wilted and he took a hobbling step forward.

"Wot do yer mean? I know yer like a brother."

"I have never met you in my life, my good man," Lucas replied patronizingly in a rich and oozing voice, his black eyes ruthlessly hard.

"Like bloody 'ell. Yer don't 'ave to pretend with me, Luc. Don't worry, I won't tell yer wife wot's 'appenin'. I just came out to tell yer the robbery will take place Tuesday week."

Lud, had Lucas changed his mind? Smiley had heard he'd married the dame who'd rescued him from prison. If Lucas had his hands on her coffers as well as her dumplings, then maybe he didn't need to steal anymore.

"Yer still in, ain't yer? This is all an act, ain't it? The gang is countin' on yer. So are the boys."

The smug superiority vanished from the dashing face at the mention of the boys.

Smiley laughed encouragingly. "That's right, Lucas. Yer remember the boys."

Lucas frowned and rubbed the line between his brows with two fingers, massaging it, as if he were trying to rub some recollection from his head. Then his face went uncomfortably blank. "No, I do not remember your boys."

"Not me boys, Luc, yers!"

"I'm sorry. I don't remember anything."

Smiley blurted out a guttural burst of laughter. "Wot's the matter, mate? Yer ain't forgotten about the plan, 'ave yer?"

Lucas finally came back to life, shaking off his silent thoughts. "Look here, you scoundrel. I have never seen you before and I never want to see you here again. Do you understand?"

"Look 'ere now," Smiley said, marching forward and giving him a winking glare. "Enough of this playacting. I didn't come all the way out from London to be treated like a leper. I even brought Monty Trowley to see yer. Thought yer'd be 'appy to see 'im. Met 'im on the way. 'E was 'appy to 'ear yer were so nearby. Said 'e wanted to thank yer for your 'elp. 'E's a fine lad. 'E's a butcher now. Went to talk with the cook. Awe, now, Luc, don't tell me yer don't remember Monty."

Lucas didn't answer. He merely gritted his teeth. His jaw muscles ticked. He turned toward the house and didn't look back, leaving Smiley to wonder if his partner in crime really didn't remember him, or if he was just trying to get out of the robbery scheme.

Well, there was no getting out now. It was just a matter of time. Lucas's wife would find out soon enough whom she married. And when she found out, Lucas would be back in Seven Dials, leading the gang as he always had. Once a crook, always a crook, Smiley thought with a satisfied smile.

Caroline was painting with Amanda in the gallery when Henry announced Monty Trowley. She told the butler to send him in, and while Henry walked the long length of the gallery to the door to retrieve the visitor, Caroline placed her paintbrush on her easel and began to wipe her hands.

"I wonder who this Monty Trowley is?" she said musingly as she looked from her canvas to Amanda's. The former governess had chosen to paint the garden, and as usual did so with precision and skill. Caroline sighed, knowing that her own work would never compare favorably.

Caroline's subject was one near and dear to her heart— Lucas. She found herself sketching the lines of his handsome face, then filling it in with a mixture of white, brown, and pink paint, creating flesh tones that in no way did justice to him. Then she mixed black and gray to create shadows beneath his eyes and cheeks. Lucas had grown so gaunt of late.

"Every time I look at your work, Amanda, I want to give up. Why did I ever suggest we paint today? Clearly my heart is not in it."

"You are nervous. You wanted to do something other than worry about what George will do, or how Lucas is fairing. Really, Caro, you must abandon this notion that he is possessed by a ghost."

"But have you seen how thin he has become?"

"He has no time to eat! This place has been Bedlam ever since his arrival. Dr. Cavendish and I have been absorbing his every spare moment with lessons. Now that

George has been convinced, perhaps life can return to normal."

"But what is normal? I long for the old Lucas, but if he returns, then he will become indignant and leave me. He knows me as no one else does. He sees my faults so clearly. So, you see, I am in a quandary, Amanda. I like the new adoring Lucas, and yet I do not."

They were interrupted by the sound of footsteps echoing in the enormous gallery. Both women looked up, graceful as two deer craning their necks at an odd sound in the deep woods. They saw an earnest-looking young man with a rustic cap in his hands, whose boots, though recently polished, were covered in road dust. He had thick, wavy red hair, freckles that made his skin appear orangish, and green eyes that told anyone who cared that he could never tell a lie.

"Mrs. Davin," Henry said, clearing his throat, "this is Mr. Monty Trowley. He says he is an acquaintance of Mr. Davin."

"Thank you, Henry." Caroline turned her most welcoming smile the visitor's way. "We are happy to have you, Mr. Trowley. This is my friend Mrs. Plumshaw. Forgive us for not receiving you in the drawing room. I had not expected your arrival."

"Pardon, ma'am, for the intrusion." He spoke plainly and sincerely. He looked now and then at the ceiling so high above them, as if he'd never seen so great a gallery before. "I came for the ride with a friend of Lucas's, I mean, Mr. Davin's. Smiley Figgenbottom was on his way and I wanted the chance to thank Mr. Davin myself."

Was Smiley Figgenbottom the friend who had come to see Lucas before the accident? Caroline's eyes narrowed on the young man. He probably knew more about her husband's past than she did. This just might be the chance she'd been waiting for to learn more about him.

"It sounds as if you know my husband well, Mr. Trowley."

"As well as any of the boys. Perhaps better than most, being as how I was the first. He's a great man, Mrs. Davin, your husband. He doesn't like to hear it, but I keep hoping one day he'll accept my thanks."

"You make him sound like a saint," Amanda said dubiously, placing her oil brush down on her easel and wiping her hands clean on a soft rag.

"He is a saint," Monty said, nodding. "At least to me. And to many others like me."

Caroline's heart warmed at the praise. "What did my husband do to earn your gratitude?"

"He kept me off the streets. I would've been an orphan when my mother died. But Lucas, he found my relatives, and gave them a yearly allowance to make sure they'd keep me proper. Few relatives will keep an orphan, you see. I was fed proper, now I'm a butcher with a chance to buy my own shop in London. Wouldn't have happened without Lucas, er, Mr. Davin."

A moment of silence followed this testimony. Caroline looked at Amanda, and found her own stunned expression mirrored back to her.

"You say Mr. Davin supported you?" Amanda asked incredulously. "For how long?"

"Oh, I'd say fifteen years. My ma, she died birthing me."

"And how did he manage it?" Amanda persisted. "How many orphans has he helped?"

"Dozens," Monty answered. "Lucas's boys, we all know how lucky we are."

"Where did he get the money?" Amanda said, then halted when Caroline put a hand on her arm, but already the question had been raised.

Monty looked to his feet and twisted his cap in his

hands, clearly unwilling to reveal the source of Lucas's income. It was unnecessary, in any event, for Amanda and Caroline both knew he'd been a thief.

"So he was a Robin Hood after all," Caroline whispered, her heart beating with gushing compassion. "You see, Monty, he never told us what he did with his . . . money."

Amanda swallowed thickly and blinked away the tears that had pooled in her soft verdant eyes. "I am sure your mother would be grateful if she knew what he had done for you, Mr. Trowley."

"She knew," Monty said, looking up with a bittersweet smile. "Lucas told her before she died he'd look after me. Izzie, he said, your boy will never be hungry, I promise you. That's what Lucas told me he said, anyway. He wasn't my father, but he was there when she had me in an alley. My father . . . I never knew my father."

Tears poured down Caroline's cheeks. This was Izzie's son. The girl Lucas had loved, the one who'd hoped beyond all reason to marry a lord. She'd died birthing her lover's bastard, and Lucas had been there for her, even though Izzie had rejected his affections. He'd been there for her. Just as he'd sworn to be there for Caroline.

"You are a very lucky young man," she said in a quivering voice. "Lucas cares deeply for those whom he loves."

"I had no idea," Amanda said, her usual mask of efficient propriety gone. "I had no idea."

"I'd like to tell him I may be buying a shop in London," Monty said, cheering up. "I think he'd be proud."

Caroline wiped her tears. "I know he would be. Would you join us for coffee in the drawing room, Mr. Trowley?"

"Yes, ma'am. My pleasure."

They went to the drawing room and chatted amiably while the footmen brought in refreshments. Monty cautiously nibbled at a crumpet until Caroline convinced him there was plenty more in the kitchen. By the time Lucas had returned from his ride, the young butcher had consumed nearly a plateful.

"Lucas," Caroline said when he walked in the door. She rose from her chair with an excited smile. "You will never guess who has come for a visit. Mr. Trowley!"

Monty stood and beamed affectionately at his mentor. Amanda watched the scene with glistening eyes. Lucas was the only one who showed no emotion.

"Mr. Trowley?" he said, as if he'd never heard the name before. He halted just inside the door and frowned, then his eyes found Caroline and his indifferent expression brightened. "Darling, how was your painting?"

He came to her and kissed her cheek. Anxious to see his reaction to their guest, she pushed him away. "Lucas, you are being obtuse. You remember Mr. Trowley. He is one of the orphans you have been so kind as to help. You really should have told me about your good deeds."

He looked at Monty, but no recognition lit his black eyes. "I'm sorry, I . . . I don't remember."

Monty's affable smile faded and his eyes were too honest to hide his hurt.

"Lucas! Surely you do. It is Izzie's son," Caroline said with a touch of impatience. "You *do* remember Izzie?"

Lucas, clearly agitated, poured himself a cup of coffee. "If I remembered him, my dear, I would admit it."

"Mr. Davin hasn't been himself," Caroline said in a low voice to Monty.

He whirled on her, his eyes blazing with anger. "I have never been more myself, I can assure you. I did not invite Mr. Trowley here and I don't see why he doesn't leave immediately since I obviously cannot recollect any past association we might have had!"

"Lucas!"

He slashed her a guilty look and let his proud shoulders slump with a sigh. "I apologize." He wiped a hand over his drawn face and regarded Monty guardedly. "Let me speak with Mr. Trowley alone."

Caroline cast a worried look at their guest.

"Don't worry. I won't bite his head off, darling. I just want to talk with him."

"Very well," she said hesitantly. "If that is what you wish. Though I do not mind staying. In fact, I would like to—"

"Please, Caro."

She nodded and put on a happy smile for her guest. "I believe my husband would prefer not to have any servants during your discussion, Mr. Trowley. So please help yourself if you want more crumpets and coffee. I hope you will stay for dinner. Stay as long as you like, in fact. Will you join me, Amanda?"

"Of course." The women exited without further fanfare, leaving Lucas and Monty Trowley to their dubious reunion.

When Lucas joined her a half hour later, Caroline was absorbed once again in her painting. It was only after she dabbed in the thin dark line to distinguish her husband's cleft chin that she realized how much the portrait, even though crudely executed, looked like Barrett Hamilton. The black eyes she'd created seemed to penetrate her soul, just as the original painting's had once done.

Unnerved, she dropped her brush onto the easel and stood abruptly, taking a step back to gain perspective. It *was* Barrett Hamilton. But it was also Lucas Davin. She could not tell the difference between the two.

"You look as if you have seen a ghost."

She heard Lucas's resonant voice and whirled around with a start. "Oh! You scared me half to death. I did not hear your approach."

His piercing, thoughtful black eyes studied her features

as if she were a painting of his creation. "You were absorbed in your work. I see you were painting your favorite subject."

He was frowning. Did he think she'd painted Barrett Hamilton? "But it is you," she hurried to explain.

He quirked his brows and a sardonic smile curled the corners of his mouth. "Of course."

"Is Mr. Trowley staying with us?"

Lucas pursed his lips and put his hands in his pockets, strolling to the nearby window. "No, I sent him on his way."

"Lucas! You should have encouraged him to stay. He clearly thinks the world of you. I wanted to hear stories about your times in London."

"We did not spend time together, Caro."

"But you knew him. More importantly, he knew you. I am envious of him. Do you realize I know nothing about your past?"

"It is best that way," he said, his voice as cold as the wind that whistled through the dead roses planted in a bed outside the window. "At least for now."

"You cannot run from your past, Lucas."

"Can't I?" He pivoted and glared at her. "I have run from my past so artfully that I did not even remember it. At least not until . . ."

His voice trailed away and he put a hand to his brow. His eyelids squeezed together as he grimaced.

"What is wrong?" Caroline went to him and put a hand on his arm. She could feel the heat radiating from his skin in waves, even through his coat. "You are burning up. You must be ill. And you are as pale as a blank canvas."

"I am not ill. I am just . . . angry at you."

"Why? Why, darling?"

"First you want me to forget my past, and now you insist I remember it."

She squeezed the thick muscles of his arms. "That is because I have realized I was wrong. I wanted you to become someone you are not. I wanted to marry a lord, or at least someone as respectable as a lord. And now that you are acting like one, I recognize the error of my plan. I loved you the way you were before. I miss that man, Luc. I scarcely recognize you anymore."

He yanked his arm from her grip. "Stop it. You are talking nonsense." He gasped and groaned as the pain in his head increased.

"You do not even look like yourself anymore. You have lost weight. The picture I just painted looks as much like Lord Hamilton as you. You have become one and the same. Ever since that damned painting fell on your head."

"Stop!" he roared. His face was drenched in sweat. He looked at her with haunted eyes, dark circles underlining them. "Can't you see I am not well?"

He pulled the flask from his waistcoat and took a swig. "I have had enough of your good intentions and concerns about my person. Do not ever talk to me again about Monty Trowley, or about my past. Is that clear?"

"I will tell you what's clear. You are not the man I married. I did not wait all these years to end up marrying someone who was as much without character as all of George's friends in Town. I want the irascible Lucas Davin back. Do you hear?"

"I hear too bloody much!" He marched off toward the far end of the gallery, his boots pounding loudly on the wooden floor.

"Damme!" she cursed, then turned back in frustration to her portrait. She was just about to paint a big black *X* over her creation when she heard a thud and a cry of alarm.

"Mr. Davin! Oh, poor Mr. Davin! Fetch Henry! Hurry!"

Caroline heard Biddie's worried cries and dropped the brush back onto the easel. She ran across the gallery and into the hall, then her feet came to a skittering stop at Lucas's head. He'd fallen flat on his back. Fortunately, there was no blood this time.

"Biddie, what happened?" Caroline knelt and cradled his head in her lap.

"He came out of the door and then just collapsed."

"Get Dr. Cavendish! And hurry."

Twenty-four

fter Theodore examined Lucas, he left him in Biddie's care and brought Caroline to the library for a serious discussion.

"What is the matter with him?" she asked worriedly as soon as she'd closed the door.

Theodore paced to the fire and leaned his arm against the mantel, gazing thoughtfully at the flames. "I shan't lie to you, Caroline. I do not know what is troubling Lucas."

The anxiety that had been coiling inside her twinged with no sign of relief. "He was burning up. Is it a fever?"

"Yes and no." Theodore turned to her and tucked his thumbs behind his lapels. "He does have a fever. He must have taken a chill."

"Yes," she said ruefully, coming to sit at the sofa. "He went riding without protection. Davey mentioned it to me, how cold Lucas was when he returned."

"But the fever didn't make him collapse. I believe that Lucas is still suffering from the blow to his head. It seems to have disrupted his thoughts. He can now remember his distant past, but can't remember his life as it was a month ago. When I was studying medicine, I read about cases of persistent memory loss. The problem can be initiated by a blow to the head, or a painful loss affecting one of the humors. In the case of injuries to the head, the loss of memory can come and go, and even result in seizures."

"I wish I could believe it was that simple, Uncle Teddy. But how can you explain his sudden ability to read?"

"Perhaps he could read as a child then somehow lost the ability when he blocked his memories of that time. Perhaps some terrible event made him want to forget everything about that time in his life."

She shook her head. "He is possessed."

"Come, Caro, you are too free with your imagination."

"Don't forget the falling chandelier! It was no coincidence that it fell nearly on top of Lucas just after he had danced with me."

"No, it wasn't a coincidence. It was a rusty fixture. Henry examined it and said you were fortunate it hadn't fallen long before."

She bit her lip, frustrated by her inability to share with him the most damning proof of all. She could not tell the physician that Lucas had called her Rachel while making love to her. His loss of memory had nothing to do with that. Nor with his loss of weight.

"I believe, Uncle Teddy, that he is not remembering his own past, but the past of Barrett Hamilton. He claims he was presented to the king! He spoke of it most convincingly. That is not a memory that a thief from Seven Dials could possibly recall under any natural circumstance."

Theodore stroked his beard as he mulled this over. "I above all would be most likely to accept your theory, my dear. After all, I have seen native witch doctors put their patients into trances and cause them to suffer convulsions and hallucinations of the most profound order. Though I am reluctant to accept a supernatural explanation for Lucas's problems, I will not close my mind on the subject. Time will tell which of us is correct."

"Indeed."

"But if my theory is correct, then I must warn you that all his memories may come rushing back at a moment's notice. Some word, or action, may trigger them, or they may flood back of their own accord. So be prepared. In the meantime, I do not want to interfere unnecessarily with Lucas. He is presently the greatest experiment of my career."

She narrowed her gaze on him. "I do not like the sound of that, Uncle Teddy. Are you risking his life in the pursuit of a scientific enterprise? Are you plying him with secret medicines of some sort?"

He gave her a mirthless half smile. "You know I would never give anything to Lucas that would harm him."

She crossed her arms. "I suppose I know that."

"Look here, my girl, I'm going to up to Hatherleigh today to consult with Dr. Graham, one of my mentors. He might be able to enlighten me on a few of these conundrums. While I'm gone, make sure Lucas drinks plenty of beef tea and keep him warm. I'm quite certain, my dear, he will be perfectly fine once he's rested a bit and recovered from his fever. He's been through quite a lot, after all."

When the doctor departed, Caroline replaced Biddie at Lucas's bedside and practically force-fed him an enormous bowl of beef tea. When she was through, she tucked him in and sat beside him, stroking his forehead, his cheeks, kissing his temples, and generally making a tender fuss over him. He tilted his head back and studied her with his sleepy, sloe eyes.

She leaned down and pressed her lips to his. As usual, her mouth tingled intoxicatingly, and she felt her heart

pouring into him. She loved him. The knowledge brought
tears to her eyes. Whoever he was, she loved him. She
might not like his current disposition, but love transcended
such transitory feelings. God, let him be well, she silently
prayed.

When she had her emotions under control, she ended
the tender kiss and pulled away. "I am sorry we quarreled,
Lucas. I know you are not well. I should not press you to
talk about difficult things when you are feeling weak."

He squeezed her hand. "Not to worry. Just accept me,
Caro. Accept me and my love. Please. I was a fool to try
to push you away before."

"That's long-ago history, dearest. I—" She stopped
when she realized he'd fallen asleep. Poor darling. He really wasn't in good health. What an ingrate she was. He
had given her everything he had to give, and still she found
him wanting. He had to find it very frustrating.

How she wished they hadn't quarreled. She should have
known he was ill. She felt very self-centered again. Just
as she had when she'd realized that Miss Kinnicott was ill.
Reminded of Emily, Caroline pulled the covers closer to
Lucas's chest and went in search of her friend.

"So Lucas is sleeping now?" Amanda said, a worried
frown marring her faintly freckled complexion.

"Yes. Uncle Teddy has reassured me he will recover.
He has a slight fever. And he's weak. He has not been
eating. I'm very worried," Caroline said as she presided
over the pouring of tea. "Tea, Miss Kinnicott?"

"Yes, if you please," Emily said sweetly from a chaise
longue near the parlor window.

Amanda sat next to her on a sofa, sipping from a cup.
She'd ordered the footmen to carry Emily here for the
afternoon. The green parlor was small and cozy, and
therefore warmer than any other room.

"You should have some more crumpets, Miss Kinnicott," Caroline said, handing her the teacup. "It will help restore your proper weight. Lucas is not the only one who needs to fatten up, I fear."

"I am not hungry," Emily replied with a wan smile. Her limp, mouse-blond hair was pulled back in a halfhearted knot. The circles under her eyes seemed darker than ever, but her voice was stronger than before. And she had been more quick to smile ever since she'd arrived for her extended visit to Fallingate the day before. "You are too good to me, Mrs. Davin. And you have so much to contend with. I think I should return to Kinnicott Farm."

"I shan't hear anything of the kind." Caroline sat on the edge of the chaise and pressed the back of her hand to Emily's forehead. "You are still so cold. I will fetch another blanket."

"No." Emily gripped her hand. "You have done enough. I should not have come."

"You had no choice," Caroline replied with a conspiratorial smile. She wanted Emily to think that she'd been a pawn in Caroline and Amanda's scheme to spirit her away from Kinnicott Farm for a few weeks. If Emily felt maneuvered, she would not feel guilty about leaving her father alone. "I kidnapped you from your farmhouse and then sent a note 'round to your father that he could expect you back in a fortnight. So you see he has no choice in the matter, and neither do you. You have to be warm and well fed. Uncle Teddy says so."

Emily raised the rim of the cup to her thin lips and sipped thoughtfully. She placed it back in its saucer and cast an admiring glance at her benefactress.

"You are so courageous, Mrs. Davin. I do not know how you were able to be so firm with Father."

Caroline smiled triumphantly. "It was frightfully easy. When he came around to find you, I told him this was for your own good. I assured him Cook would send food to him as well. This seemed to soften his temper. It is all a matter of finding the right approach."

"Still, you were courageous," Emily insisted with a note of awe.

"Was I?" Caroline smiled wistfully and lifted her china cup to her lips, sipping, then licking her lips. "I would not have been courageous if not for my husband. He made me realize how selfish and blind I had been. Not intentionally, mind you. But I learned from him that ignorant neglect is just as reprehensible as that which is purposeful. Once I truly recognized your plight, Miss Kinnicott, I had no choice but to be courageous—for your sake."

She looked back at Emily and felt she'd at least done one good thing in her life.

"Your husband is a fine man."

"Yes, he is."

"Is that what marriage is about? Learning to be courageous?"

Tears burned Caroline's eyes, and she waited for them to subside before nodding. "It is when you marry the right person. The right spouse can make one see clearly what is most important in life."

"Then you love him?"

Emily asked these overly initimate questions so innocently that Caroline could scarcely be angry.

"Yes, I do love him." She looked at Amanda, but saw no disapproval in her delicate features. "I think even Mrs. Plumshaw has begun to see Lucas's virtues."

Amanda nodded. "Yes. That is why I cannot understand your present discontent. Not only is Lucas Davin proving to be honorable, he has begun acting like he was born to the *ton*. That is what we were striving for."

"That is what we were striving for before the painting fell."

"Oh, heavens," Amanda returned in exasperation. "You still are going on about that ghost."

"What?" Emily perked up at this, sitting a little straighter against the rolled arm of the chaise.

Caroline answered quickly, meaning to win her houseguest over before Amanda could convince her of her own point of view.

"You see, Miss Kinnicott, I believe that my husband is possessed by the ghost of Lord Hamilton. Mr. Davin has been acting strangely ever since he was struck on the head by Lord Hamilton's portrait. I know it sounds absurd, but why else would a man's behavior change so utterly and so quickly? Instead of leaving as he had planned, he's freely professed his love and is now eager to join Society. How very unlike him, don't you think?"

Caroline had told Emily of Lucas's true history when she'd gone alone to Kinnicott Farm to fetch her. It had taken a confession of courage from Caroline to embolden Emily to leave her father. Caroline knew she could trust Emily implicitly. Emily was eager to help solve some of her friend's problems.

"Perhaps," she said, her cheeks coloring slightly with excitement, "perhaps the painting merely knocked some sense into Mr. Davin. He realized what a remarkable wife you would be and he decided to be on his best behavior in order to keep you from sending him off to India."

"That is something to consider, Caro," Amanda remarked.

Caroline rose impatiently and went back to the tea tray. Pouring herself another cup, she took a slow, steady breath, contemplating just how much she should say. "I can understand your hesitation to believe my theory. After all, you have never seen the ghost. I myself was a cynic until . . . until he appeared outside my window not long ago."

"What? No, it cannot be!" Amanda exclaimed. "You saw a ghost? You never told me!"

Caroline felt a peculiar little smile come over her. She had told Amanda many times she wished to see the ghost. It had been a game with them, wondering what Barrett Hamilton's spirit would look like.

"You saw him?" Amanda squeaked.

"Yes!" Caroline rushed forward and sat next to her on the sofa. "I could scarcely believe it, Amanda. At long last the ghost came to see me. But by then I did not want to see him. It was an intrusion. Lucas was there, and of course he did not see it or believe it. But I swear, I *swear,* Amanda there is a ghost. There is no question in my mind. Do you believe me? Say you do."

Amanda blinked doubtfully, then stared hard at her dear friend. "I have known you so long, Caro. You have been dreamy and romantic, but never superstitious. You never really believed there was a ghost even when others claimed there was, though I know you wished it to be true. So it is not like you to fall for whimsy." She heaved a sigh. "Yes, I suppose I must believe you."

Caroline hugged her. "Thank you. Now I know I have not gone stark-raving mad."

"This is very exciting," Emily said breathlessly. Amanda and Caroline turned to her and both burst out with giddy laughter, neither quite believing she was having this fantastic conversation.

"Just do not have me committed to Bedlam," Caroline said as her laughter died. "It is rather exciting to share it with you. But you now understand why I am so worried about Lucas. He is possessed, Amanda. There can be no other explanation. It is affecting his health. I fear if I do not do something to help him . . ."

Caroline could not finish her dire prediction.

"Perhaps . . . oh, no, that would be silly," Emily said timidly, then fell silent.

"What?" Caroline asked. "Go on, Miss Kinnicott. I cherish your opinions."

Emily licked her lips and looked up with uncertain eyes. "Since there really is a ghost, you should learn as much as you can about him, especially if you think he has control of Mr. Davin. Perhaps you should read more of the diary you told me about. The one written by Lord Hamilton. It may reveal some insight into his character. And it may tell you why Mr. Davin is behaving as he is now."

"Oh, Emily, that is a splendid idea," Caroline replied. "You are such a help to us already. I am so glad you came."

Emily flushed with the first color Caroline had seen in her cheeks in months. "I am glad I can help. I have lots of ideas about lots of things. Father never wanted to hear them, but if you do . . ."

"We have all the time in the world to talk about wondrous things, my dear," Amanda said, and patted the girl's hand reassuringly.

"Meantime, I will read more of the diary this afternoon," Caroline pronounced, latching onto this bit of hope. "It may give me the answers I have been looking for."

Amanda looked out the window and mused over Caroline's predictions. At last Amanda understood why her former charge was so convinced that Lucas had been possessed by Lord Hamilton. Amanda did not doubt for a moment that Caroline had seen a ghost. But she did not think that the ghost had anything to do with Lucas's behavior. And she doubted that the diary would give Caroline the answer she needed.

She watched silently as Caroline hurriedly drank her tea and made her exit. Amanda knew exactly why Lucas was acting so strangely. And she meant to confront him about it this very day. They had much in common, the former governess and Lucas Davin. Too much, in fact. If anyone could help Lucas, it was Amanda Plumshaw.

Twenty-five

After searching the entire house, concern growing with every footstep, Amanda found Lucas in the garden, of all places. He didn't seem to care, or even notice, that drizzling rain had created a silvery sheen on his locks of black hair and on his greatcoat. She'd had the good sense to wear a cape, whose hood protected her from a deepening chill that felt like the ominous breath of old man winter. She strolled toward the sundial. He stood there, simply staring at a bed of roses that had been pruned for the winter.

"You should be in bed," Amanda said. "You would be called to book by your lovely wife if she knew you were out here exposing your person to the elements."

He looked over his shoulder at her and gave her a slow, wry smile. Then he turned a melancholy gaze back to the withered rosebushes. Amanda came to a stop at his side.

"You look as if they have betrayed you somehow," she said empathetically.

"I do feel betrayed. I had hoped to find a remaining blossom."

"So late in the season?"

"I saw some the other day at Bilberry Cottage."

"Oh, but it's warmer in the valley."

He shrugged. "A man cannot be blamed for hoping. Caroline loves roses. I thought to bring her something. She seems . . . displeased with me."

Amanda's heart tugged as she noticed the bewildered tone that thinned his manly voice. "Women are hard to understand, Lucas. You must not worry too much about your wife's moods. She loves you very much."

He looked up eagerly, soaking in her words of reassurance, touched by her use of his Christian name.

"Surely I am not telling you something you do not already know yourself, Lucas. It should be obvious that Caroline adores you."

He blinked several times and gave her a self-mocking smile. "Of course. But I believe I am not the man she fell in love with."

Amanda gently laughed. "I am quite sure that's what every bride realizes the morning after her wedding day."

He didn't laugh. He didn't even seem to have heard her. "What is troubling you, Mr. Davin? I know you are not the man you now appear to be. You are not a gentleman. So you can be honest with me. For I am not a lady."

He frowned darkly and focused on her. "You are rather harsh today, Mrs. Plumshaw."

She hugged herself against the pervasive cold. He didn't seem to be affected by the temperatures at all. "I am just being honest. You see, we have much in common, you and I."

He thrust his hands in his pockets and strolled to a water fountain that was now dry, save for a pool of raindrops that festered with decaying leaves in the stone bowl.

"I did not think I would ever be on your level," he said. "You are a refined and respectable widow."

"That is only what I want the world to think," she replied in a voice so laden with old pain and unwanted knowledge that he looked up sharply. "Does this surprise you, Mr. Davin? Once upon a time, I came to Fallingate in straits more desperate than yours."

"How could that possibly be?"

"I am a woman. And a woman's plight is always worse than a man's."

"I am not your friend, Mrs. Plumshaw." Lucas's voice was hard and distant. "Do not confide in me. You do not even like me."

"That's not quite true. I will admit Caroline's reputation has been foremost on my mind, and you will soon understand why, and that forced me to be wary of you. But I do like you, Lucas. You behave more honorably than any gentleman I have ever known."

"I will take that as a compliment." His large eyes blossomed with genuine interest. He sat on a stone bench by the water fountain, and she knew then he was ready to listen.

"When I was twenty," she began, sitting next to him on the cold stone, "I became a governess for a well-known marquess whose primary residence was in London. He was very dashing and handsome, and I mistook his unusual attention in a governess as something romantic and sincere in nature. He told me, most inappropriately, that the marchioness did not understand him, and that I alone could comprehend the passion of his soul." She stopped as her thoughts turned sickeningly back in time.

"I was flattered by this intimate confession. So much so that I made the biggest mistake of my life. I showed him a glimpse of stocking. And soon the plain cotton that covered my legs was replaced with silk." She hissed the word with hatred.

Lucas said nothing. He merely thought of Izzie. She'd

sold her very life for a pair of silk stockings from her noble lover. How easily good women were bought by bad men, he thought.

"The marquess soon lost interest. I saw him squeezing the marchioness's new abigail in a hall one day, and I knew then the mistake I had made. I was sickened by the realization. He made no attempt to hide his indiscretions with his lustful friends and soon I became fair game. Heartbroken and lost, I did not think enough of myself to say no, as I might have in spite of my compromised situation. Soon I was with child. I was promptly put out, and would have had my child in an alley like your poor Izzie if not for the generosity of a widow lady who took pity on me. I had a boy. She wanted to keep him to help around her house. I gave her every last penny I had, and the promise, which she insisted on, that I would never come see him again. She was going to claim he was a distant relative. I knew she could give him a better life than I ever could. It would keep him out of the workhouse, and so I agreed."

She thought for a moment that Lucas had turned to stone. His nose was flared and still, his eyes as hard as granite. Then he moved, turned his head toward her a fraction, and said, "I am sorry, Mrs. Plumshaw, for the despicable behavior of the lascivious members of my gender. If the marquess were here now, I would kill him with my bare hands."

She shut her eyes and smiled bittersweetly as tears warmed her eyelids. "Thank you." She wiped her eyes and sniffled. "When I learned you had taken care of orphans, Lucas, it made me think about my son. I wondered if I had died on the birthing bed, would my boy have been fortunate enough to meet someone like you?"

"I could try to find him for you." He looked at her, as an equal for the first time.

She shook her head. "No. I do not want him to know he is a by-blow of a despicable affair, and I am sure he is being well cared for. The widow was truly kind and much more respectable. And perhaps she was even a better mother than I would have been in my dire state. After I left London, I nearly took my own life. But I fell into the position of governess at Fallingate. Caroline saved my life. Even at so young an age, she became a friend. Her friendship became my anchor. In many ways, she did not fit into Society any more than I did. She is such an individual. And Society loathes individuality."

She turned on the bench to face him more fully. He was a handsome devil, just as the marquess had been. But Lucas had something her lover had not had—a heart.

"What I really want to say is this, Lucas. I have hidden my past for so long that I nearly gave up any chance to love again at all. I convinced everyone that I was a widow, but also convinced myself that I did not need love. That is a dangerous pretense. You are trying so hard to be what you think she wants you to be that you are leaving no room for the man she fell in love with. Caro has an odd notion that you are possessed by a ghost."

A silent moment passed during which they both smiled at Caroline's romantic notions.

"She thinks there must be some grand explanation for your sudden illness and your change in behavior. I know better, Lucas. You are twisting yourself into someone else when what you should be doing is clinging to your very soul. If you want to remain a part of Society, then so be it. But do not lose your soul. Nothing is worth that."

He blinked his enormous black eyes, and lifted her right hand into both of his. He gently smoothed his palm over her knuckles and then lifted her hand to his lips in a kiss.

"Thank you, Mrs. Plumshaw, for telling me your story. I will consider your advice carefully."

She had said her piece. And she felt more peaceful than she had in the last twenty years. She smiled contentedly and stood. "I hope you will call me Amanda in the future. I think we know each other well enough for that. I must be getting back before Caroline wonders where I have gotten myself to."

She started away, but he called her back.

"Amanda, when are you going to tell Dr. Cavendish what you have just told me?"

"Soon," she replied confidently, and felt joy bubbling through her limbs. "Very soon."

Upon leaving the green parlor, Caroline went straight to her bedroom and fetched the diary. As she reached for her spectacles, her fingers tingled with anticipation. Was Emily right? Was there some clue in the diary that Caroline had overlooked that might tell her something important about Lucas's plight?

She sat at the edge of the bed and picked the diary up from the bedside table. It seemed heavy, portentously so. She carefully opened it and leafed through the fragile pages until she reached the last entry.

Alas, these are the last words I will ever write. Death is almost upon me. I grow weaker by the moment. Yet I cannot pass away until the truth is known. Read thou and knoweth a terrible injustice hath been done.

She'd read that before. She quickly scanned the words, paying more attention this time. Suddenly it occurred to her that she didn't know the exact cause of Lord Hamilton's death. She had assumed he'd been executed, but why then did he speak of growing weaker? Was he ill?

She flipped the page over, knowing it would be blank, but finding it so was nevertheless disappointing. There were no more clues to his death or life. She stared numbly at the last, blank sheaf in the book, thinking of all the questions that still remained after his death.

Unconsciously focusing on the crease between that page and the binding, she began to notice a ripple of paper. That piqued her interest and she ran her finger along the crease. The page had been folded over to create some sort of pocket. Opening the book wider, she probed inside the secret place and felt loose sheafs of paper. Growing excited, she carefully slipped her fingers inside the flat pouch and removed a folded note. It consisted of two pages. The handwriting on the first page was uneven and weak. She moved to the window seat to decipher it in the sunlight.

2 October, 1536

> *My last entry. Good riddance, world. I see the shadow of the Grim Reaper. He hath come at last to call. I have not eaten for more than a fortnight. I cannot keep food in my belly, for some reason. Perhaps grief is the cause. That must be so. Ah, well . . . The sooner I die, the sooner I shall see my beloved Rachel. Soon, dear Rachel, we will be together. Forever.*

> *—Barrett Hamilton*

When Caroline read the last line, she burst into tears. The pain of lost love twisted in her heart like a vise. For some reason, she knew these lovers intimately. She knew how decimated Barrett had been, and she could feel Rachel's love for him as if her spirit were in this very room. If only there was some way to reunite these star-crossed lovers and set them free.

Caroline understood at last the depths of their love, for

she had finally experienced it herself. She knew love's sunshine and its shadows. To imagine having such a love torn away from one was unbearable.

She hugged the open book to her chest as she wept, feeling, of all things, gratitude for having felt love at all. Even if Lucas's love were torn from her now, the pain would be worth it for having felt the pleasure. Then another thought sobered her in an instant.

"Oh, Lord!" she whispered. Her watery eyes darted back and forth wildly as she realized what she'd just read. She sniffled and pulled the book into her lap and lifted up the final loose entry. Her eyes scanned the words and she bit her lip until it hurt. Lord Hamilton had died of starvation! He'd been too grief-stricken to eat.

She pictured Lucas in her mind's eye—thinner, fainting, gaunt, pale. No wonder! He was replicating the last days of Lord Hamilton's life. That meant his life was in danger.

"I must put an end to this at once," she said, and stood abruptly. The notes fell from her hands. They separated, and wafted to the floor. When she bent to pick them up, she realized she hadn't read the second page.

She placed the book on the window seat and unfolded the second note. It was written in elaborate, bold script and was dated twenty-five years after Lord Hamilton's death.

Sir Toby:

I have procured the diary of Lord Hamilton as thou didst request. I am sending it forthwith to Fallingate. The intelligence hath come to mine ears from Queen Elizabeth's secretary that thou hast created a great house worthy of her majesty's scheduled visit. I do hope to visit Fallingate when I journey with the court.

One final word. My inquiries in London did reveal that Lord Hamilton died under the misapprehension

*that Lady Rachel Harding died at the abbey upon
which Fallingate has been built. Verily, Lady Rachel
survived that accident and lived long enough to birth
Lord Hamilton's natural child. She passed away
birthing the bastard, and it hath come to no one's
ears what happened to the child. A sad tale indeed.*

James Donald, Esq.

Caroline stared hard at the words, scarcely believing her
eyes. "A child! Poor Barrett. Poor Rachel."

Barrett Hamilton was taken to the Tower after Rachel
had been wounded by the guard's sword. He'd thought her
injury fatal. But she had survived, and he never knew it.
He never knew that their love had given birth to a child.
That might very well mean that somewhere in this world
a descendant of Lord Barrett Hamilton stood as a living,
breathing testimony to Barrett's great love for Rachel Harding.

"How cruel life can be," Caroline said, and sadly folded
the letter, placing it back in the diary. How cruel and dangerous.

She knew at last why Lucas was growing thin. His life
was being sucked away by the curse of Barrett Hamilton.
This proved that she was right and Theodore was wrong.
Lucas's life was in danger, and there was only one way to
save him. And there was only one person who could do
it—the priest who was staying with Lady Roth-Parker. She
would invite them over immediately. The time had come
for an exorcism.

Twenty-six

That very afternoon Caroline went to visit Lady Roth-Parker. She spoke to Father Anton about her predicament, and after hearing his many arguments against the idea, she managed to convince the priest of the necessity of conducting a rite of exorcism. After all, there were few Roman Catholic clerics in England, and fewer still who had Father Anton's particular experience with spiritual matters. When she spoke movingly about her fears that Lucas might die, the priest relented.

The prospect of exorcising a ghost excited Julia Roth-Parker to no end. Sir Roger had departed for London, so it was agreed that Julia and Father Anton would come to dinner at Fallingate the next day. After the meal, they would tell Lucas of the priest's purpose.

Caroline feared there would be a price to pay for keeping her husband in the dark. But she did not care. She was acting in his best interest. She'd sworn after discovering Emily's illness that she would never blindly ignore another's needs again. Yes, she was doing right. Let the storm of his wrath come as it may.

• • •

The next night they had an early dinner at six, as was the custom in the country. Dr. Cavendish returned shortly before the guests arrived, and though he didn't have time to chat privately with Caroline about his discussions with Dr. Graham, he was able to change out of his riding clothes and dress for dinner.

After dessert was served, Lucas and Theodore remained at the table for port and cheroots while the ladies went to the estate room for coffee. Father Anton excused himself to attend to a private matter to which only Caroline and Lady Roth-Parker were privy.

Caroline quickly diverted the women toward the formal estate room. Located at the far south end of the house, the oblong, gilded room was built over what had once been the monks' quarters—the very place where Lord Hamilton had been betrayed by the abbot of Morton Abbey. During years past, some of the more superstitious servants claimed this was where the ghost of Rachel Harding still came in search of her lover. Of course Caroline had never believed it before, but now she kept an eye on every corner of the room.

Once they arrived and the twin footmen opened the massive double doors, Lady Roth-Parker was the first to voice her approval. "Upon my word, Caroline, this is a splendid room. I have not been in it in years. I remember your parents entertaining many a lord and lady from London here."

"Yes, I remember as well, Julia, and with great fondness." Caroline enjoined the women to sit in the sofas and chairs gathered in the center. Emily and Amanda sat on a gold-trimmed sofa while Julia and Caroline claimed matching chairs.

After the coffee tray arrived, Caroline sent the servants away. "Henry, please tell the gentleman, and Father Anton we are ready for them when it's convenient."

Amanda questioned her with her soft, green eyes, but Caroline refused to meet her gaze. Amanda was perceptive enough to know that Caroline was up to something. But if she tried to explain, even to her best friend, what was about to happen, she was sure she would lose her courage. Lady Roth-Parker, of course, knew what she was about, but said nothing. Once an experienced London Society hostess, Julia was the soul of discretion.

A half hour later, Lucas and Theodore wandered in smelling faintly of smoke and liquor, laughing at some joke.

"Greetings, darling," Lucas said, bending to give Caroline's cheek a brief, but still sensuous kiss.

All his kisses felt that way to her. Her skin hummed where his lips touched, and she felt a terrible wave of guilt for deceiving him.

"I daresay," Theodore said jovially, coming to a stand next to where Amanda sat, "I cannot remember when I have seen so many lovely ladies all in one room at once."

"Watch yourself, old man," Lucas growled, sitting on the arm of Caroline's chair. "I am the one who should be charming these belles."

"I taught you everything you know, you young cub," Theodore returned with a teasing grin. "So do not interfere with my flirtations."

"I own that I fear a duel is coming, Caro," Julia said with a throaty laugh. "And between two such handsome men."

"You flatter them unnecessarily," Caroline returned with a smile. "And should they come to blows, it will serve them both right."

"Hear that? I am being called to book by my own lovely wife," Lucas said, his black eyes gleaming with rakish mirth. "You did not warm me about that prospect, old man."

"That, my boy, is something every man has to learn for himself."

Everyone, save for Caroline, laughed. Anticipating the priest's entrance, her heart had risen too high in her throat, it seemed, and she could scarcely breathe. Father Anton had gone for his vestments and holy water, as planned, and would join them any moment.

The conversation took a jovial turn as Theodore regaled them with his antics in the wilds of Africa. Caroline scarcely heard a word he said, though. She was rehearsing in her mind how she would break the news to them all. There was no easy way to put it, and she realized she might have made a grave mistake not telling everyone her plans beforehand.

In the end, the priest solved her dilemma by making his entrance and clearing his throat loudly. He wore a surplice and a purple stole and carried an ominous-looking black bag. When the conversation fell silent and all eyes turned his way, he said, not without a certain theatricality, "Let the exorcism begin."

What followed was absolute and dumbfounded silence. Slowly, all eyes turned from the priest, who had gone to a table and was now unpacking his bag, to Caroline.

She felt as if her skin had crawled away, leaving her utterly exposed. Suddenly the idea of an exorcism seemed completely preposterous.

"Well . . ." She stopped and cleared her throat. "You see . . . I asked . . . I mean, I implored Father Anton to help me . . . to save Lucas."

Lucas rose from the arm of her chair and stared down at her as if she'd turned into a foreign creature. "You *what?*"

Her heart was now kabooming in her chest. She struggled for air. Now was not the time to lose the strength of her convictions.

"I asked Father Anton to exorcise the ghost of Lord Hamilton from your body," she said simply, as if she were describing the weather. Then she forced herself to look up into Lucas's dark and angry face.

"This is outrageous!" he nearly shouted.

"Caroline," Theodore said reproachfully, "you have gone too far."

"Have I?" she returned hotly. "I am acting as I think best for my husband. You do not love him as I do, so you are not as concerned as you should be. That much became clear when Mr. Grenville was here," she added significantly. She rose and turned on Lucas. "And you should not reproach me, either. I am simply doing what you advised me to do—I am being sensitive to the plight of others."

Caroline began to pace before the fire. "I have just learned that Lord Hamilton grew thinner and thinner, that he wasted away until he died. Does it not strike any of you as odd that Lucas is thinner, that he suffers from headaches, that he fainted?"

"That does not mean he is dying," Amanda returned. "Let Dr. Cavendish examine him again."

Caroline stopped and looked at her with utter gravity. "This problem goes beyond medicine, Amanda. Do you remember when Lucas was nearly killed by the chandelier? Remember when he was then injured by the falling portrait? I think my brother may finally be correct about something. The ghost of Lord Hamilton is trying to kill Lucas. And he is doing it by taking over his very person."

"Caroline," Theodore said, "your brother is merely trying to find a way to keep Fallingate for himself. He will say anything to scare Lucas off. And there is a reason Lucas isn't eating. He—"

"No, Dr. Cavendish," Lucas said, his jaw ticking furiously. "Do not try to talk sense into my wife. She is determined on this course of action. I have tried to reason with her myself, but to no avail."

It took all the courage in Caroline's slender body to meet the snapping anger in her husband's black eyes.

"My wife does not believe that I could possibly be as well mannered as I have been unless there is some supernatural explanation. You see, she still finds me wanting, no matter what I do. Frankly, it's insulting."

He started for the door.

"Lucas!" she cried out, stopping him with the force of her convictions. "Leave if you must, but not before you undergo this rite. If you are not possessed, it will be obvious that I have been a fool. But upon our marriage vows, I beg you please give me this chance. I am only thinking of you, Lucas. I swear!"

He paused at the door, his body rigid, as if two beings were warring inside him, one pushing and one pulling. She knew the ghost wanted him to leave. But Lucas nevertheless turned slowly and regarded her with a sneer that reminded her of the charming thief she'd first met. She never thought she'd be so happy to see a man regard her with utter contempt.

"Very well, Caro," he said saucily, that familiar glint in his eyes. "I will give you your moment of insanity. Just to prove you wrong."

He went to the chair that the priest had placed next to the table lined with his holy accoutrements.

"Get on with it, Father." Lucas flopped down and leisurely crossed one leg over the other. "Get on with the show."

"Clear the area, please," Father Anton ordered in a solemn voice. "The devil is crafty. If a demon has possessed Mr.

Davin, and if he comes out of his body, objects may fly through the air and injure someone."

There was a moment of hesitation, then everyone moved at once to do the priest's bidding. No one spoke, each trying to absorb the momentousness of the occasion. In the silence, the wind howled with its usual clamor. The double glass doors that opened to the terrace outside rattled from the force of it. Caroline had chosen this room because of its association with Lord Hamilton. Now she wondered if that had been wise. The very walls seemed to be taking on a life of their own. Perhaps they should have gathered in the drawing room.

The priest did not seem concerned. He methodically re-arranged his objects on the table—a crucifix, a bottle of holy water, incense, which he lit, and oil. As the cloyingly sweet smell of the incense filled the air, Father Anton explained what he was about to do.

"As I have told Mrs. Davin," he began, "an exorcism does not strictly drive the devil or a demon out of the possessed individual. The process merely binds the demon in a promise to submit to the ultimate authority of God." He handed the crucifix to Lucas. "Hold this and no matter what happens, do not let go."

By now everyone stood in a semicircle behind the priest. He turned to address them solemnly. "Normally, I would do this with another priest or two. I do not have that luxury tonight. Since I, too, have felt the presence of unnatural spirits here, I will proceed anyway for the good of the inhabitants of this house. Therefore, I welcome your prayerful presence. I must warn you, however, that if any-one is guilty of any sin and is not reconciled with God in heaven, he or she should leave the room at once. Demons are crafty. When they are driven from one man's body, they will find the weakness in another. And you will be possessed before you know what has happened. Is there anyone who wishes to leave the room?"

They looked at one another around the semicircle. Lucas smiled at them, enjoying their discomfort.

"What is wrong? No one is as weak in soul as I am? You have no sins as I surely did to attract this evil spirit?"

"You must not mock this procedure, Mr. Davin," the priest calmly advised him. "Your biting tongue only encourages the spirit within you. There are many reasons for a man to become to possessed. Having sins on one's conscience is just one of them. You are not necessarily at fault here."

"Glory be," Lucas replied, and rested his chin in his hand with a bored look.

Caroline looked around. All the smiles and anticipation had vanished. Now everyone was wide-eyed and sober. Emily's cheeks were flushed scarlet.

"Miss Kinnicott," Caroline said, going to her side. "Perhaps you should go to your room. This might be taxing for you."

"I would not miss it for the world, Mrs. Davin. Please do not make me go. I will be fine, I promise. My faith in God is strong. Upon my word, I have not seen this much excitement . . . ever!"

"Pray, do let her stay," Lucas said dourly. "It is much more fun to have an audience. You can serve refreshments afterward."

"Lucas, I am not doing this for our amusement," Caroline snapped.

"Please, Mrs. Davin, no discord," the priest said. "We must be quiet and strong or the devil will find our weaknesses. He's already trying to put a wedge between you and your husband. I can see that happening as we speak."

A flash of lightning brightened the unusually dark night sky. Caroline looked up distractedly. Was it her imagination, or had the room suddenly turned chilly? She shivered and rubbed her arms.

"Does anyone else feel what I feel?" she whispered.

Amanda went to Theodore's side. "It is colder," she replied. "And I smell something odd."

"That is the work of the demon," Father Anton calmly explained. "He is growing nervous. He senses that he might no longer be welcome here, and he would be most correct in that assumption. Now, Mr. Davin, you must be strong of spirit. You must will this ghost from your person. I cannot do it alone. Is that clear?"

Lucas sucked in his cheeks as if he'd just tasted a sour lemon. "Perfectly, mate. Absolutely perfectly clear."

The priest either did not notice or chose to ignore his sarcasm. "Then let us begin with a prayer. The pater noster."

They began to pray the "Our Father" as a group, all except for Lucas, and the louder they prayed, the louder the wind howled, until it seemed they were nearly shouting to be heard. Coals in the fireplace seemed to crumble before their very eyes, and the fire went low. By the time they had repeated the prayer a half-dozen times, the room was much darker, lit only by a single kerosene lamp on a side table and half-dozen beeswax candles scattered about the room in wall sconces.

"Now I will begin," Father Anton said. "Raise your head, my son."

Lucas looked up. In the pulsing, weak light, shadows plunged below his eyes and made his cheeks more gaunt than before.

Julia took in a short gasp. "Good heavens, he looks like a demon."

"Nonsense," Theodore whispered in return.

The priest began in a low, sonorous voice. *"Exorcizo te, omnis spiritus immunde, in nomine Dei Patris omnipo-*

tentis," he said, making the sign of the cross on Lucas's forehead with a thumb dipped in holy water. *"Et in nomine Jesu Christi."*

Lucas grimaced and shut his eyes as Father Anton made the sign of the cross yet again. Suddenly the wind gusted and one of the doors to the terrace flew open with a burst of cold air.

"Oh!" Emily cried out.

"Good Heavens!" Julia said.

Caroline looked up with a start and froze, half expecting the ghost to walk in, or out, of the door.

"It is just the wind," Theodore said with a reassuring chuckle. He rushed to the door and forced it closed. "Another storm is brewing. Please continue, Father."

The priest hadn't even looked up. He and Lucas were locked in each other's gaze. And this time even Caroline had to admit Lucas did look demonic.

"Christi Fili ejus, Domini et Judicis nostri, et in virtute Spiritus Sancti, ut descedas ab hoc plasmate Dei . . ."

The Latin words began to meld together in Caroline's ears as the air grew stuffier. She began to perspire in a most unladylike fashion. There was something wrong. Something terribly wrong, but she couldn't determine what.

She shivered and focused on the priest's motions. He touched Lucas's mouth, his ears, and his nostrils.

"Ephpheta, quod est, Adaperire! Be opened!" he roared with unexpected force, touching Lucas's ears again.

This time both the doors blew open with a bang. All the candles guttered out instantly.

"Oh, dear!" Emily cried out.

"What is happening?" Julia rasped in terror.

"Ignore it!" the priest shouted. "It is the demon. He is trying to distract you."

"He is succeeding," Julia said for all of them.

There was a bellowing crack of thunder. Caroline jumped in spite of her determination to be brave. A moment later a flash of lightning seemed to strike just outside the doors. It lit the room with three pulsing jabs of white light. Suddenly the night had turned to day. In that brief moment of illumination, an amorphous figure could be seen looking in through the terrace doors.

"Oh, good God," Julia gasped with amazement.

"That's him!" Caroline cried out. "The ghost I saw outside my window."

His body was almost formless. His moan could be heard above the pounding rain. *"Rachel. Rachel."*

"It is Barrett Hamilton!" Amanda said. "Dr. Cavendish, do something!"

No one moved. There was another blinding flash of lightning. But this time the figure was gone. The terrace was empty.

"Where did he go?" Amanda asked.

"If he was ever there in the first place," Theodore growled dubiously.

"Oh, he was there," Lucas said in a low, cynical voice. "And by God, I mean to find him."

He jumped up and started for the terrace doors.

"No, Mr. Davin!" Father Anton shouted after him. "This is a critical time. The demon is deceiving you. He is trying to lure you out to danger. You must resist until the exorcism is over. He wants you to follow."

Lucas flashed a wickedly mischievous grin and clapped Theodore on the back. "Then he's getting what he wants, mate. Come on, Teddy. You veer to the left. I'll head right. Let's round the topiary garden and meet in the far center."

"Right, my boy, but be careful not to fall into the bog. It lies just beyond the garden," Theodore said, and the two men jogged out into the vicious storm.

The women looked at one another, then at the priest, who was fuming.

"This is the devil's work, Mrs. Davin. Your husband is in even greater danger than he was before. I fear for his life."

"Can you not do something?" Caroline asked pleadingly.

"It is in God's hands now, my child."

"Oh, devil!" she cried out. "Then I will take care of it myself. Come, Amanda, we have to save these men from themselves before it is too late."

"Wait for me!" Emily said.

"No, I insist you stay inside." Caroline turned to stop her.

"I will not be left behind," Emily said with altogether more verve and energy than Caroline had ever seen in the young lady.

Caroline was so nonplussed she nodded her acquiescence. She grabbed Amanda's hand and led her into the gathering storm. "Come along, then."

"Come along, Miss Kinnicott," Amanda said in turn, grabbing her hand.

The women struggled to close the doors behind them and crossed the rain-slashed terrace. Raindrops now fell only intermittently, but the wind was gusting and buffeting them at every turn.

They negotiated three short steps down to a gravel path, then walked onto the soft, moist grass that carpeted the large topiary garden. It was the last place Caroline wanted to be, especially on a night like this.

As a child, she would wander around the garden by day, looking up at the enormous shrubbery pruned into the shapes of animals. But by night, she avoided the place. She used to imagine that the animals came alive in the darkness and turned into monsters—a dragon, a falcon, a mean-looking rooster, and a griffon frightened her the most.

Now she shivered with the same thought as she tiptoed through the grass past the eerie-looking figures that were twice as tall as she. The wind howled grievously, but when it abated momentarily, she heard Lucas's voice. He was beyond the topiary garden, shouting muffled orders to Dr. Cavendish.

"This way, Amanda. I hear Lucas. Stay close. Do you still have Emily?"

"Miss Kinnicott is clutching my hand. Rather desperately, I fear."

"Do not let her go, Amanda. She—" Caroline stopped short when she saw a figure dashing from one side of the garden to the other some distance away. "Oh! What was that? I saw something."

"What?"

"There!" She stopped and pointed to a far row of hedges. A flowing figure seemed to float from one bank of shrubs across a clearing and disappear behind another tall manicured row. "The ghost!"

Amanda and Emily pulled up beside her, each struggling to keep their balance as the wind buffeted their bodies.

"Perhaps it was just Lucas," Amanda said hopefully.

"Over here, Davin!" they heard Theodore shout.

"It was Dr. Cavendish, not a ghost!" Amanda cried out with relief.

"No," Caroline argued, "his motions were too fluid for a real man. It was not Uncle Teddy."

"But I just heard him. I am going to find the doctor."

Before Caroline could react, Amanda took off and began to trot across the garden grounds. "Dr. Cavendish! Where are you?"

"No, Amanda! Come back! You cannot go alone!"

But she did, nevertheless, and was soon out of sight.

Caroline, already chilled by the weather, began to shake in earnest. They were alone. She and Emily. She turned to her companion, who, in spite of a reddened nose and trembling lips, had eyes that reflected a soul of faith.

"Miss Kinnicott, I am afraid it is now you and I. Alone."

"Do not worry, Mrs. Davin. We will be fine."

"Do you think?"

"Yes."

Caroline swallowed hard, squeezed her eyes shut, and gave several tense nods as she gathered her flagging courage. "Yes, of course. I am not afraid." She forced her eyes open, gripped Emily's hand, and led her toward the giant falcon. "Come this way."

They rounded the big green bird and went to the far end of the wall of shrubs where they'd seen the figure disappear. As soon as they rounded the corner of a manicured row of tall hedges, they saw yet another heart-stopping sight—a figure rising from the soupy, craggy edge of the bog, which lay a stone's throw away.

"Look there!" Caroline whispered in a trembling voice. "There is someone—or something—coming from Dead Man's Bog. Nothing ever comes out of Dead Man's Bog alive."

"Alive or dead, here he comes," Emily remarked.

The women clutched each other as the figure loomed larger. He staggered, like a body come back to life, but without ears or eyes or any sense of balance. Marsh reeds and soggy grasses flowed from his arms.

"Is that the ghost?" Emily asked breathlessly.

Caroline frowned. "No. No, it is not him at all."

She exhaled with relief as it became more evident with each step that the thing coming toward them was indeed a man. A rather ordinary man at that, save for the marsh grasses trailing from his soaked coat.

"Is it . . . ?" Caroline finally recognized the figure. "It is!

It is the orphan Lucas helped. Over here, Mr. Trowley!"

He staggered toward them, and nearly collapsed at their feet before he regained his balance.

"Oh, Mrs. Davin, I thought . . . I thought I'd never find you."

"Heavens, you are soaking wet, and covered in weeds," Caroline said.

The red-haired fellow gave her a weak smile and swiped away the algae clinging to his face. "Thank God, Mrs. Davin, I thought I would never escape that bog alive. It nearly pulled me to my death."

"What were you doing there, Mr. Trowley?"

"Trying to find my way back to Fallingate. I came earlier in the day after I thought of a way to help Lucas remember me. But I got lost and I've been trying to find my way out of the bog ever since."

"Oh, you poor man! You do not know how lucky you are. I think you are the only one who has ever come out alive. Mr. Trowley, this is Miss Emily Kinnicott."

"Evening, Miss Kinnicott," he said, politely sketching a short bow even though he was shivering with cold.

"Good evening, Mr. Trowley," Emily said, her eyes fixed on him with curious intensity.

He looked up at her, and his weariness seemed to fade. He straightened a little.

"Mr. Trowley may soon buy a butcher shop in London," Caroline added.

"London!" Emily's eyes lit. "How very exciting. I've always wanted to live in London."

"Emily, could you show Mr. Trowley into the house? Ask Cook to warm him some brandy and feed him properly. Have Henry arrange a hot bath. And if you see Mr. Davin on your way back, send him this way."

"Of course. Come along, Mr. Trowley. We will find you

a nice, warm fire. I could use one as well. I am always cold, it seems."

Off they went, leaving Caroline alone. It was only after she watched them go, thinking what a nice couple they would make, that Caroline realized that she had engineered her own solitary traipse through the garden she feared most.

The house loomed behind her like a malevolent spirit. The wind cut through her like a giant sickle. All of a sudden she desperately wished Lucas were here to warm her. He had been right. The exorcism was unnecessary. It certainly hadn't gone as she'd planned.

The ghost had made an appearance, but well before the priest might have pulled it out of Lucas. The only good thing to come of it was that Lucas had gotten himself into such a temper he had begun to act like his old self. That meant there was hope for him yet!

Twenty-seven

manda had been following the sounds of Theodore's rustling search through the large garden, but had taken every wrong turn until now.

"Dr. Cavendish! Finally, I found you!"

He stopped abruptly and turned, squinting in the darkness. "Mrs. Plumshaw! What are you doing here?"

"I am looking for you! I was so worried." She rushed forward, longing for the comfort and, frankly, the warmth of his presence.

"Mrs. Plumshaw, you should not have come out here." Theodore started toward her. Just before they met, she tripped on what felt like a rock.

"Oh!" She stumbled forward into his warm chest.

Theodore caught her and pulled her close. "Are you all right?"

"Yes. Yes," she said, welcoming the warmth and cushioning of his girth. She steadied herself, regaining her balance and dignity. "Thank you. I nearly tumbled to the ground."

She waited for him to let her go, but still he held her

tight. Confused, she looked up into his eyes. They bored into hers with emotion she had only dreamed of seeing there.

"Amanda—" He faltered and searched her face, smiling as awkwardly as a schoolboy. "Amanda . . . may I call you that?"

"Of course, Dr. Cavendish."

"Theodore. Call me Theodore."

She allowed her fingers to rest on his waistcoat. They tingled from his warmth. He was so good to her, such a kind man. And handsome, too. Distinguished looking. And wise. So wise!

"Very well, Theodore."

"Amanda, I have been meaning to tell you . . . to ask you. . . ." When words failed him, he leaned down and pressed his lips to hers.

His mustache tickled her nose, but that wasn't the greatest sensation she felt. She felt passion. Passion she thought long dead. Amanda's head swooned. It had been so long. And never had she been kissed by such a good and loving man. Never by someone who truly cared for her. This realization brought tears to her eyes. She surrendered to his kiss, wrapping her arms around his neck, feeling safe and warm in spite of the wind that angrily whirled around them.

He kissed her for the longest time, then withdrew and touched his forehead to hers. "I never thought I would feel this way again, Amanda. How can I ever thank you?"

"No, it is I who should thank you, Theodore. I—I have so much to tell you about myself. About my past."

"I do not care about your past one whit," he said firmly, gazing paternally down his nose. "Do you understand, young lady?"

Young lady. She laughed at this and then, when she realized he was utterly serious, searched his face wonder-

ingly. How it could be? How could he accept her uncon-
ditionally? He kissed her again, and the question faded in
the tumult of her loving feelings for this dear, dear man.

When it was over she smiled with utter contentment. "I
am so glad I tripped."

"Me, too." He chuckled and looked down. "Though you
might have hurt yourself. I wonder what on earth you
tripped—"

He stopped abruptly when he spied the object that had
caused her to stumble. It was not a rock at all, but a foot
attached to a leg sticking out from under the bushes.

"What the devil?"

"Who could it be?" she asked.

"Only one way to find out." Theodore leaned over and
dragged the body out, grunting with the effort.

"Oh, no! It is Mr. Feathers!" Amanda cried. "Is he . . . ?"

Theodore knelt and tried to take the former butler's
pulse.

"He is nearly dead." Theodore pressed his ear to the
man's chest, then put a hand to his forehead. "It appears
he has a very grave case of pneumonia. We'll be lucky to
revive him. We must get help putting him to bed."

Amanda looked at the servant's pasty-white face, which
was now almost blue in the moonlight. "But what was he
doing out here?"

"That's a question to which I mean to find an answer.
That is if I can save him." Theodore gave her a potent
look. "The answer just may enlighten us as to the identity
of our supposed ghost."

Twenty-eight

After Emily and Monty disappeared inside the house, Caroline continued her search for Lucas. She had just reached the row of giant shrubs at the far end of the garden when she heard a moan and rustle on the other side of it. She froze. Was this the ghost? Or an interloper? She had her answer a moment later when a figure plunged through the greenery with a bloody face and a fist poised for a blow.

Caroline started to scream, but stopped immediately when she realized it was Lucas.

"Good heavens! What happened to you?"

He stopped the blow in midair when he recognized her, then he grimaced in pain.

"Caroline! I thought you were . . . Oh!" He grabbed his head and steadied himself.

"Lucas, what happened? Did you find the ghost?"

With a backhand, he wiped at the blood dribbling from his nose. "I found him, indeed. But he was no ghost. I rounded the back of the maze of shrubs yonder and the first thing I encountered was a fist in my nose. A very human one at that. As I went down, I saw a man running away. Your ghost, Caroline, is all too mortal."

Lucas endured the doctor's probing touch with as much dignity as he could muster. By now his nose was swollen and painful. Caroline and Amanda looked on, happy to be in the cozy quarters of the green parlor after their hectic and freezing jaunt out of doors. Mr. Trowley and Miss Kinnicott were in the kitchen warming themselves. Father Anton and Lady Roth-Parker were still in the estate room.

"Your nose is not broken, Davin," Theodore said, wiping the blood from his hands on a towel. "But you took quite a blow. Just try to avoid another brawl for the next few days and you should recover nicely."

"I will be on my good behavior," Lucas said wryly, and smoothed the wrinkles from his bloodied waistcoat and shirt. "At least we now know the ghost who has been haunting Caroline is human."

"But who could it be?" she asked. Theodore poured port and served everyone. "Thank you, Uncle Teddy. I think I am frozen inside as well as out."

He raised his glass and winked at her. "This will thaw you out, then."

"We think we know who is behind the ghost of Lord Hamilton," Amanda said, and when Theodore handed her a glass, she smiled, adding, "Thank you, Theodore."

From the corner of his eye Lucas could see a smile burgeoning on Caroline's windburned cheeks. She was staring excitedly at the older couple.

"Well, well, well." Lucas smiled, too, in spite of his pain. "At least something good has come of this night."

Amanda cleared her throat and assumed a prim expression. "When Theodore . . . when Dr. Cavendish and I—"

"Oh, Amanda, do not stand on formality," Caroline insisted. "Call him Teddy!"

Amanda blushed like a schoolgirl, and not the dowd she once considered herself. Then she sat forward and with wide eyes said, "When Teddy and I were in the garden, I tripped on something. It turned out to be the leg of poor Mr. Feathers."

"What? Mr. Feathers?" Caroline asked with dismay. "Was he . . . ?"

"Nearly dead, I am afraid," Theodore answered. "But not quite. He has a bad case of pneumonia. He's in his bedroom in the west wing, and I've done all I can for him, but I wouldn't be surprised if he never awakens from his unconscious state."

"Oh, no!" Caroline let out a sigh and sank into a chair. "Poor Feathers. It is my fault. I broke his heart. He probably became ill because I demoted him. If I had not replaced him with Henry. . . ."

"Do not blame yourself, my dear," Theodore was quick to reassure her. "It was not as if you turned him out in the cold. He's very old, Caro. The question is, what was he doing in the garden at that hour in such inclement weather? The timing seems a little suspicious following close on the heels of our so-called ghost."

"You saw no sheet or costume near Feathers's body?" Lucas inquired.

"No."

"Hmm," Lucas said, stroking his cleft chin. "I saw Mr. Feathers out late one night in the middle of a downpour. It seemed odd at the time. Now it seems downright suspicious."

"Yes," Theodore agreed.

"But it could not have been Feathers who punched me," Lucas said, grimacing at a twinge of pain in his nose. "The man who hit me had great strength."

"Perhaps," Caroline remarked, "Feathers had an accomplice. But who would it be and what motive would they have?"

"Well, it wasn't Monty," Lucas piped in. "So don't even begin to suspect that dear lad."

"Monty?" Caroline touched his hand and smiled. "You remember him now?"

"I saw him in the garden with Miss Kinnicott." Lucas's mouth canted with an amused grin. "He said he wanted to sing me a nursery rhyme. It was a foolish ditty I'd made up long ago. I could scarcely believe he'd remembered. When he began to sing, my memories came flooding back. I was enormously relieved that I'd finally recollected him."

"So you're sure it couldn't have been Monty Trowley?" Theodore inquired.

"Yes!" Caroline and Lucas said in unison.

"Then do you have any ideas who it might have been, Davin?"

Lucas shrugged, then carefully touched his nose. "Someone with a mean right hook."

Theodore sighed heavily. "I do not think we will find any easy answers tonight. We should interview all the servants on the morrow and see what they may know of the butler's affairs. In the meantime, I suggest we all get a good night's sleep."

"No." Caroline's voice rang out with all the forthrightness and clarity that she'd acquired in the last few tumultuous days. "I do not want to retire until I know what is happening to my dear husband."

She caught Lucas's gaze and tenderly held it. "I'd thought he was possessed, and I was terribly wrong. And for that I beg your forgiveness, Lucas." She looked away. "You must have felt very betrayed. But you must believe I thought I was acting for your own good. It didn't seem to me that you had any answers. I read something in Lord Hamilton's diary that led me to believe you might be literally wasting away. I . . . I loved you too much to let that happen."

He came up behind her and graced her with his forgiveness in the form of a gentle kiss, which he placed on her wind-strewn hair. He squeezed her arms and she reached across her chest with both hands to touch his fingers.

"Thank you, Lucas," she whispered, blinking back tears. "Thank you for understanding."

"My darling, how could I blame you for doing the best you could to understand an incomprehensible situation? I scarcely understand myself."

Caroline turned to Theodore. "Did Dr. Graham suggest any answers?"

"Dr. Graham said that most likely—"

"No, Theodore," Lucas said feelingly. "Let me explain what happened."

"Dear boy, I doubt very much you know what has happened."

"Let me tell Caro what I know. Please."

Dr. Cavendish looked confounded, but then nodded his acquiescence. "If it's important to you, by all means."

"Yes, it is."

Lucas raked his hands through his hair as he gathered his thoughts. "I should have told you this earlier, Caroline, but I feared that if you knew, you would try to stop me. I've been taking a potion."

Caroline went very still. "A potion?" She slanted a suspicious gaze at Dr. Cavendish, who returned it steadily.

Lucas pulled the elephant flask out of his waistcoat. "Do you know what this is?"

She frowned at it. "That is the flask of brandy that I used to revive you the night the painting fell on your head."

He stroked the silver surface of the flat container with

a mixture of longing and loathing. "Yes, you started it all. Unwittingly. This was a potion Dr. Cavendish gave me. He said it would alter my personality. I don't believe it is responsible for the changes in me, but I do believe it triggered memories I'd long ago forgotten. Memories of a time when I lived the life of a gentleman."

"Look, here, Davin—"

"Please, let me finish, Theodore. It is important that Caro hear this from me."

Theodore frowned and bit at his mustache, then settled back next to Amanda. "If you must."

"When the painting hit my head, I was nearly unconscious, but awake enough to hear you profess your love. It made me want to be a better man, for you, Caro. And then you gave me the potion, which I had resisted to that point. I believe the potion somehow caused the memories to return."

"And what happened then?" she asked.

"Suddenly I could read again, and ride like the wind, and I was intensely interested in the running of the estate. Everything about me changed."

"What did you remember?" Caroline asked.

"Memories of . . . of a childhood spent in wealth beyond anything I have ever experienced. I remember being presented to the king, foxhunting, being taught to play whist by a valet, learning French from a tutor, dancing with cousins, hunting with my father. It all came to me so quickly after the painting hit my head."

He looked at their astonished expressions. "And those are the good memories. There were painful ones, too. I cannot remember them now, and I do not want to. At first I thought they were fantasies. But why would I fantasize about bad things, too? When I realized the images were real, it gave me enough confidence to believe that I deserved Caroline, that I was in fact Quality."

"So that explains your sudden affection and optimism about our future," Caroline said.

Amanda sat forward on the sofa. "Lucas, you may have already answered your own question. You say you started to remember these things when you regained consciousness. That was not only after you drank the potion, but after you were struck on the head. When I was a child, my brother fell out of a window and struck his head. He was never quite the same. He could not even remember his own name. Perhaps your head injury had the reverse effect. Perhaps it jarred free memories you had forgotten."

Lucas held her with a steady gaze. Caroline looked from one to the other and said in hushed amazement, "You mean perhaps Lucas really was raised in a mansion with servants? And he really did meet the king and go fox-hunting and learn French?"

"I'd thought it was the potion that triggered the memories," Lucas said to Amanda.

"And I'd thought it was a ghostly possession."

"Look here," Theodore said with finality, "I simply must interrupt all this wild speculation." He stood and tugged down on his waistcoat, deftly rearranging his watch fob as he did so. "That potion, my boy, was nothing more than a placebo. It did nothing to change your personality, nor could it possibly have triggered your memories."

"A what?" Caroline asked, frowning in further bewilderment.

"A placebo." Theodore pulled out a cigar and put it in his mouth, chewing as he sought the words. Then his eyes brightened and he tugged the cigar from between his lips. "The best way for me to explain is to define the word itself. The term *placebo* refers to a medicine that is designed to please a patient more than it is designed to cure him."

"What does this all have to do with Lucas?" Caroline sank into a chair and put her fisted hands on her knees.

"Really, Uncle Teddy, could you please get to the point?"

"I am just trying to explain, my dear. I gave Lucas a potion that was ineffectual. I wanted to see what would happen if he *thought* the medicine would change him into a gentleman. That was the experiment to which I referred the other night. As I suspected, the suggestion of change did a great deal to Lucas. He was under the impression that my potion would alter the way he thought and acted, and so he acted accordingly. And, as I've just learned, his desire to please you probably also played a role. As for the memories, I agree with Amanda. I believe the blow somehow loosened suppressed images."

"Are you saying the potion was a hoax?" Lucas growled.

Theodore pinned him with a firm glare. "Don't get in dudgeon, Davin. I did this because I knew you were capable of learning the social behaviors necessary to keep you in your rightful place as Caro's husband."

"You tricked me!" Lucas shouted.

"Yes, I did. I tricked you into realizing that you already have within you everything you need to be worthy of your wife. Was that such a terrible thing to do?"

Lucas flushed red, then shook his head and began to pace before the fire. "You deceived me."

"I had your best interests in mind, Davin. I had more faith in you than you did. Curse me for that, if you will, but I have no regrets."

Caroline shook her head wonderingly. "So the medicine was harmless?"

"It consisted of little more than sugar, water, and a touch of brandy. I did include a small amount of an African plant that invigorates the body. I wanted Lucas to feel some effect, so he would think it was working. But it had no effect on his mind or temperament. The only thing it might have altered was his appetite. The plant suppresses hunger.

I should probably ingest some myself." Theodore patted his ample girth and chuckled.

"It suppresses appetite?" Caroline looked at Lucas and relief washed over her features. "That is why he lost weight! So he is not dying. Thank heavens!"

"The plant also occasionally causes headaches, but they are nothing to be concerned about."

"That explains his illness completely!" Caroline said, all smiles now. "Oh, Lucas, that is wonderful! Your headaches were troubling you so. If you stop taking the placebo, all will be well again."

"No." He turned to her with regret shadowing his striking face. He'd grown even handsomer since losing weight. "I did not invent the memories. And until I find the home and the family to which they belong, I will never know myself. And neither will you. How can you possibly love a man you do not even know?"

Twenty-nine

The next morning Caroline stood stoically in the gallery, alone in a pool of silvery light that poured in from dozens of windows. She stared unseeing at the pruned rosebushes standing brittle and lonely in the dying garden. She did not need these sorry sentinels to remind her that she could still lose Lucas Davin.

She had never really known him, she now realized. Ironically, he did not even know himself. And it made her love him all the more. He was a lost soul, and she wanted to hold him tight and let him know she would love him no matter who he was, no matter what he had ever done, and no matter what he would ever do. She was capable of that kind of love. The unremarkable Mrs. Lucas Davin sensed she possessed a rare gift, an ability to love without limits or conditions. She only hoped that whoever her husband turned out to be, it would be someone who wanted such a gift.

The door suddenly opened, ending her reverie.

"Mrs. Davin," Henry said. "Mr. and Mrs. Wainwright

are approaching on the drive in their carriage." He paused. "I thought you would like to know."

"Thank you, Henry." Lord, what next? She would have to deal with George and Prudence. They were undoubtedly up to something. She could face them as long as Lucas was at her side.

She lightly knocked on the door of Lucas's dressing room. There was no answer. She knocked again more firmly. After a long pause, she heard a surly, "What is it?"

"I need to talk to you, Lucas."

Pause. "Come in."

She entered, then stopped at the sight of the traveling bag. He stood at the foot of the bed, with his back to her, folding a shirt and placing it neatly inside. When the shirt didn't fit quite as he had planned, he yanked it out with a snap of his wrists and refolded the garment with painstaking concentration.

"You do not have to pack your clothes, Lucas. Neville would be delighted to do that for you."

He gave her an irritable look, then turned back to his work. "I would rather do it myself. It takes my mind off of my current predicament."

"You'll make Neville very unhappy."

He grunted an unintelligible response and went to the armoire. He pulled out a silk cravat and scowled at it with his head tilted sideways. "Is this one of the fashionable ones, or one that's hopelessly out of date?"

A tiny smile creased the corners of her mouth. "It is quite fashionable. Uncle Teddy brought it back from Hatherleigh yesterday." She watched with fascination as he tossed it in his bag. "Where are you going that makes you so mindful of your appearance?"

He snapped his head her way. "Anywhere I go I should be mindful of my appearance. I have you to thank for that.

It seems I have acquired a taste for the finer things in life. As for my destination, I'm going to London to speak to my fathe—" He raised an ironic brow. "To see Robbin Roger. I cannot stay here another day until I find out my true heritage. He is the only one who can tell me who I really am."

She stepped forward and rested a hand on the bedpost. "I understand your eagerness to see this resolved. And though I shall count the minutes until your return, I wish you Godspeed."

His face softened. "I knew you would. I am sorry I must cause you further anxiety, but I must find out who I am, Caro. What has my life been about? How can it mean anything unless I understand where I have come from?"

"Your life has meaning no matter what name you call yourself."

"I'm not at all certain of that. I even begin to question my efforts for the boys. Was I helping them or merely using them to seek revenge against rich people like the ones who apparently abandoned me?"

"Does it matter what motivated you if you helped them in the end?"

"I suppose not, but there has to be a better way to make peace with life's injustices than stealing."

"I agree. But there is another way to look at the discrepancies in your life. You now have the best of both worlds, Lucas. You can enjoy the pleasures of a gentleman while still retaining the courage and honesty of one who is unshackled by Society's rules. Without stealing, you can still use your righteous anger to help the boys. You now have plenty of money to benefit them in any way you see fit."

He stopped his packing and eyed her thoughtfully. "You're right. That's another reason I want to go to London, to set up a trust for the lads. I need someone to look after them when I'm not in Town, to see that their needs are being filled. If I stay here, I can't look after them like I once did."

"Perhaps Monty Trowley could do that for you."

He caught her eye and grinned. "You clever girl. Monty would be just the man. He was an orphan himself. And he's smart. I'm so bloody proud of him." He turned back to his packing. "Talk to him about it while I'm gone, will you, my love?"

She bit her lip, then asked quietly, "How long will you be gone?"

His hands stilled and he tightened his lips, answering, "As long as it takes."

"Don't shut me out now, Lucas. Come back, won't you? Please?"

He turned to her and pulled her in his arms, stroking her hair. "I will do my best to come home to you, Caro. You who have awakened so much in me. But I must be a man to you, a whole man, not a leech, not a lapdog for you to play with. Otherwise you would not love me long. Don't you see?"

No, she didn't see. She merely wanted him to stay. But she'd read about men's foolish pride, and so she nodded. "Of course."

She pulled back and stroked his face, trying to memorize everything about him, just in case fate intervened, and he thought better of the golden shackles the gentility endured and the rules and the boredom of rustic life. She would not feel secure until he had finally returned.

"Before you go, I need you for one final performance. My brother and his wife have just arrived at Fallingate. I need you to stay at least until they leave. It would look very bad if they thought my new husband had abandoned me so soon. Will you stay?"

"Of course," he said distractedly. "We have come this

far in the charade. No sense ruining it now."

She reached up to kiss his cheek in thanks, but he turned his head just as she neared him and their lips collided. They locked together in familiar rapport, and her face heated with instant desire. They did not grope or feel for one another, but merely sent all their feelings through their mouths, those tender portals. When he pulled away at last, he stared at her with blank wonder.

"It never ceases to startle me how much I want you, Caro."

She smiled deeply, finally at peace. He would come back to her. For he would remember a kiss like that. And it would bring him home, to the home where he belonged.

They were standing arm in arm in the drawing room when George and Prudence Wainwright entered.

"Well," George said, his eyes momentarily glazing over, "what an unpleasant surprise, Mr. Davin. I had not thought to see you here today. I thought you might be out conducting . . . business."

"Greetings, George," Caroline said coolly. "Salutations, Mrs. Wainwright."

The plump matron took her battle position next to her husband. "Good afternoon, Caroline," she said archly, refusing to look at Lucas.

Caroline said, "Is there something you are concerned about regarding the execution of Father's will?"

"As a matter of fact, Mouse," George said, "there may be. You see, we have learned some information about Mr. Davin that puts a thorough blight upon this marriage."

She swayed slightly and Lucas squeezed her hand against his side with the crook of his arm. As long as he was with her, she need not fear the world.

"I am not in the least concerned," she said.

"What is it you have found, Mr. Wainwright?" Lucas asked.

"I think the best person to answer that question is the Dowager Countess of Germaine."

This news left both Lucas and Caroline momentarily speechless. Prudence's mouth parted in a vicious grin. "What is the matter, my dear? You have gone pale. Are you ill?"

"Th-the Countess of Germaine is with you?" Caroline stammered.

"She will be here any moment," Prudence replied. "She is following in her own carriage. We spent the night at Germaine House. We knew we would be welcome *there*."

Caroline wasn't bothered by her sister-in-law's sarcasm. She was too worried about what the countess would say. She looked up at Lucas and saw he'd turned pale as well, but his lips were set in grim resolve.

"She remembered where we met," he said calmly.

"Indeed," George replied. "May I sit, Caro? This used to be my house as well."

"Yes, of course."

They all sat with starched spines, and when an uncomfortable silence refused to give way to polite banter, George said, "Where the devil is Feathers?"

"He is gravely ill," Caroline said stiffly. "He has pneumonia and isn't expected to recover. He has been unconscious for some time. You may say your good-byes, but he won't hear you."

George looked momentarily lost at this news, then recovered his haughty frown. "A pity. But he had a good life."

Caroline made no reply and they remained silent until Henry announced the countess. She entered with her usual small, certain steps, each one punctuated by the tap of her cane on the floor. She did not pause to gain her bearings in the new room but wafted toward the others with an air of superiority as natural as the nobility that flowed through her blue-blooded veins.

Everyone rose. Caroline dropped a curtsy and Lucas sketched a bow. Lady Germaine stopped when she saw him and narrowed her icy blue eyes. "You, sir, are not welcome here in my presence."

"Forgive me, Lady Germaine," Caroline shot back without missing a beat, "I do not wish to be rude, but my husband is master of this house. If you cannot speak in front of him, then I must ask you to leave."

The countess took in a sniffling breath of surprise. "What did you say?"

"There is no need to quibble," Lucas said, standing. "I will excuse myself of my own accord. Caroline, the countess has something important to say and you should hear it."

"Whatever she has to say to me can be said to you as well."

"If that is what you want," George said impatiently, "then so be it. Let me be the first to say it: your husband is a horse thief. Lady Germaine remembered where she had seen him. She recognized him from the night the constable arrested a man for stealing one of her horses."

"What of it?" Caroline snapped in return.

Prudence gasped. "You do not deny it?"

"Why should I?"

"Davin could be hanged for that crime, Caro," George said gravely.

"Not if Lady Germaine drops the matter."

"Why should she?" Prudence argued.

"He is not a thief. He made one mistake," Caroline said, her gaze never leaving the countess's. "He didn't even steal that horse. He just took the blame for someone else's crime. Would you condemn a man to death for that?"

"Come, Caro," George said impatiently, "he is the master of a ring of thieves from Seven Dials. He is probably planning to rob Fallingate itself."

George stood and paced around the room, his hands clenched behind his back. "Is that what you were planning, Davin? To rob Fallingate?"

Caroline turned to Lucas, confident he would deny it. But when she saw his guilty frown, her heart fell.

"You see, Caro, you have been taken for a fool. Poor little Mouse, you always were so naive."

Lucas met Caroline's eyes with an intensity that wouldn't be denied. She saw his regret, and took heart. By Jove, here was a thief with a conscience! That was the first thing she'd noted about him. By God, he had a conscience and character. Of course he was planning to rob Fallingate. He'd be a fool not to! And that was before they'd met. How could she take offense at that?

"I do not care if my husband planned to steal the jewels from around my neck. I love him, George, and you will not convince me to put him aside."

"How did you learn about my past?" Lucas asked, squeezing her hand.

"Mr. Figgenbottom told me all about your plans," George said with great satisfaction.

"Smiley told you?" Lucas scowled. "How did you find him?"

"Lady Germaine's servants caught him snooping around the estate. I came at her behest and questioned the little rat myself. He was most talkative when he had his belly full of liquor. He wanted to know if I had another sister of marriageable age. Someone short in stature."

Lucas stifled a snort of ironic laughter. Leave it to Figgenbottom, the arrogant little fool.

"I would think carefully, foolish chit, before you stand by an avowed thief," the countess said, turning to Caroline. Sternness emanated for her aristocratic countenance, seeming to lend her words especial weight. "You have your family to think about. Forget love, child, it does not last. Your family name, however, goes on."

"My family name is Davin," Caroline replied firmly.

"Do not be a fool, Caroline. I hold you with too much fondness to see you cast aside your reputation."

"Have I not already done that, Lady Germaine?" she asked with spirit. "How can I go back now?"

"There are ways to undo disasters such as this. You must think of your father's legacy, child, more than you think of your own heart's desire. Remember your mother's cousin was a peer of the realm. You must sacrifice for the greater good."

"What would you know of sacrifice, Lydia?" Caroline challenged, daring to use the noblewoman's Christian name.

The room fell silent. The old woman shut her wrinkled eyelids and waved the others away. "Leave us. I must speak with this impudent girl alone."

Prudence was the first to start for the door. She pulled herself up, heaving her bosom up with her forearms. "I will wait in the carriage. Nothing on this earth could persuade me to stay in the same house with this . . . this . . . horse thief. Come, Mr. Wainwright."

"We will await you in our carriage, Lady Germaine," George said, "and then we will follow you back to Germaine House."

They quit the room first, then Lucas followed, catching Caroline's gaze to make sure she would be all right. She nodded, and he shut the door behind him.

"I have a story to tell you, Caroline," the countess said. "May I sit?"

"Of course, your ladyship," Caroline said guiltily. "Forgive my rudeness. But you struck a sore spot."

"That much was obvious, my dear." The countess sat imperiously on the sofa. Caroline sat next to her. The older woman rested both her hands on her cane and gazed off into the distance. "Once upon a time, I had two handsome sons. The youngest was a charming child we named Thornton. The oldest, Basil, was to inherit the title as the fourth earl of Germaine. Naturally, we focused all our attention on Basil and raised him with the necessary sense of responsibility required of a first son. And he did not disappoint us, at least until he brought home a woman he claimed was his wife."

The countess flushed red and steadied her trembling lips. "Even now it grieves me. This . . . this trollop . . . was named Elizabeth. She was a baker's daughter," she said with rasping disdain. "She was not at all an appropriate choice for a future countess. She was not Quality, she was not born to the *ton*, and she was completely out of place. I would have thrown her out the first day she arrived at the estate, but she was with child."

"She was going to have your grandchild?"

Lydia nodded. "I tolerated that woman and her child for six years. I begged Basil to put her aside and to divorce her. She was a disgrace. But he would not do it. He claimed he loved her. He lost his head, just as you have."

Caroline blinked solemnly. "What happened to them?" She only vaguely remembered stories about Lady Germaine's eldest son.

"Basil died in his thirties. He drank himself to death two years after his father died. I believe it was because of his marriage. Though Basil loved Elizabeth, she never fit in. She was not happy at Germaine House. She cried all the time. She was . . . unstable. I thought she belonged in Bedlam, but Basil refused to send her away."

"What happened to Elizabeth and the boy after Basil passed away?"

"I put them out." Her voice was cold and flat. "I gave her plenty of money and told her never to return."

"You turned out your own grandchild?" Caroline whispered, aghast. "How could you?"

"Easily. I had the family reputation to think of."

"But he was to be the fifth earl by birthright!"

"My second son, Thornton, produced letters convincing me that the child was a bastard and not a blood relation at all. He convinced me the child was fathered by one of Elizabeth's former lovers. I could not very well let this boy inherit the title under those circumstances. So Thornton became the fifth Earl of Germaine. Tragically, he was killed two years later in a hunting accident. And now I have no one to carry on the family name. The title will revert to the crown upon my death."

"Do you regret turning the child away?"

"I do. But only because, as it turns out, he was a legitimate heir. I learned upon Thornton's death that he'd forged the letters that cast doubt on the boy's legitimacy."

"Oh, how sad."

"Yes." The countess blinked as if suddenly very weary of all her years. "Though Thornton was charming, he had but a tenuous sense of integrity. However, dear girl, if the child had truly been someone else's, I would have had no qualms about my actions."

"Where is your grandson now?"

The countess shut her eyes. "I do not know. I ordered my solicitor to search for him, but after several years I gave up hope of ever finding the child. I have no regrets, however," she added harshly, raising her finger in the air. "And that is my point. Sometimes we must make difficult choices for family honor. Sometimes we make the right choices, and sometimes we make the wrong choices. But

family honor must be paramount, Caro. I cannot, as your
neighbor and friend, stand by and watch you destroy your
reputation and life. End this marriage now, if not for your
own sake, then for Mr. Davin's. He will never fit in and
he will be just as miserable as Elizabeth was. I will help
you make amends in Society. Society will accept any excuse I give for this debacle. Let me help you. With George,
we will restore your reputation while there is still time.
What say you, my dear, will you do what is right?"

Standing outside the doors to the drawing room, Lucas
pulled away and wiped a shaking hand over his numb face.
Perspiration had gathered on his upper lip, and he sluiced
it away with deft fingers. He had heard enough of the
countess's lecture. More than enough.

   Yes, it was time to leave. Only now he knew exactly
what to ask Robbin Roger. That old cove was the only one
who could tell him what he needed to know—his true
identity. Lucas thought he knew at last. And his suspicions
shook him to the marrow.

Thirty

aroline said her farewells to the countess and then, finding that Lucas had left already, went to the green parlor to visit with Monty and Emily. After her emotional interview, she needed to talk to someone just to calm her frazzled nerves.

When she entered the room, Monty and Emily looked up with cheery expressions.

"Mrs. Davin, come play cards with us," Monty said, his freckles coagulating on his cheeks with a broad smile. "I was just teaching Emily to play piquet."

"No, thank you, Mr. Trowley. I've had rather an unnerving day."

Emily regarded her delicately. "Does it have anything to do with Mr. Davin's abrupt departure?"

"So you've heard?"

Emily exchanged a look with Monty. "Mr. Trowley said the servants were all abuzz about the countess's arrival and Mr. Davin's leave-taking."

"Yes," Caroline said, sitting at the card table. "He's going to London on business. He asked me to see if Mr.

Trowley would be interested in running a trust for the orphans. Since you'll be living in London when you purchase your shop, you can be there for the boys. You will be handsomely paid for your efforts on their behalf. Would that interest you, Mr. Trowley?"

"More than I can say, ma'am."

She smiled at him, understanding why Lucas was so proud. He had done so much for Monty and all the others. She wished Lucas could fully accept the goodness he'd done in the world.

"How long will he be in Town?" Emily softly inquired.

Caroline shrugged and put on a false smile. "I do not know. I worry for him. He's . . . he's going back to Seven Dials."

"Whatever for?" Monty said with a frown.

"He wants to sort things out. I worry for him. He's not the man he used to be. I hope he's not robbed or murdered."

"You worry too much, ma'am," Emily said.

"Perhaps not," Monty said, frowning as he shuffled the cards. "I was heading to London in two days. Perhaps I'll go tomorrow and see if I can find him. Help him in any way I can. In any event, he'll have to instruct me on how to care for the lads."

"Would you, Monty? I would be ever so grateful. Lucas would never admit he needed help, but it would be nice if he had a friend nearby in case some difficulty arose. I believe Mr. Dorris is leaving for London by coach tomorrow afternoon. Perhaps you can travel with him."

"I'll go to Bilberry Cottage immediately to ask him." He stood and gazed tenderly at Emily. "May I visit you again, Miss Kinnicott?"

Emily brushed back a stray tendril of hair from her temple with a fluttering gesture. "Of course, Mr. Trowley. I am feeling stronger by the day. Perhaps we might take a walk soon. Perhaps before you leave tomorrow."

He grinned with unabated pleasure, looking the very picture of youthful kindness. "Yes, yes, I hope so. Fare you well, ladies."

"Mr. Trowley," Caroline called out, "if you find Mr. Davin . . . tell him I very much want him home again."

Monty nodded, gave a quick bow, then departed.

Caroline watched him go, then turned a teasing grin to her friend. "I do believe Mr. Trowley is utterly besotted, Miss Kinnicott. Do you always have that effect on men?"

Emily giggled, putting the back of her hand to her thin lips. "Oh, Mrs. Davin, you should not tease me so. He is a dear man, though, is he not? I rather hope Father likes him."

"Just in case he does not, we will keep you here a few more weeks. We will tell your father you need more time to recuperate. By then, you will know Mr. Trowley's intentions. It will be some time before he can purchase his shop, and he will doubtless return with Lucas. If Mr. Trowley's intentions are honorable, I shall prevail upon your father to accept him."

Emily sighed. "I should not hoard Mr. Trowley's affections all to myself. I am not well enough to marry."

"Nonsense," Caroline pronounced. "Dr. Cavendish says that with the right nourishment and long walks, your heart will gain strength. I see improvements in you already."

"Thanks to you." Emily reached out and grasped her hand. "Forgive me for thinking only of myself. You are worried. Can you possibly doubt that Mr. Davin will return as soon as he can?"

Caroline shrugged and tried not to spill the tears that pooled in her eyes like rain in the cusp of a rose petal. "Lucas is very proud. He always has been. I just hope that if his search for his identity is thwarted, he can somehow find a way to love me anyway."

"He will, most assuredly. Mrs. Davin, you must have more faith."

"I know Lucas is an honorable man."

"No, not faith in Mr. Davin. You must have more faith in yourself."

Caroline looked at her, nonplussed.

"You still do not see the woman you have become, do you? Of course, you don't have the advantage of perspective as others do. Yet I assure you, if you could see yourself as I do, as Mrs. Plumshaw does, and Dr. Cavendish, you would not fear Mr. Davin's absence now. You would know that he has no choice but to return to you."

"How can you be so sure?"

"You are a beautiful woman, Mrs. Davin. Your eyes shine with love and hope. Your lips are always delightfully quick with a laugh and a kind, generous word. You are the embodiment of kindness, love, and courage. I saw these qualities in you before, but now they beam from you like a brilliant show of falling stars. Love has made you simply radiant."

"It has?" Caroline asked weakly.

"Yes. And for you to not recognize this is a slight to that love."

Caroline blinked and focused on her friend. "Goodness, Emily, you are even more of a romantic than I am."

"I am a realist, Mrs. Davin, with a romantic bent. If you do not believe me, then I would have you read from the diary you lent to me."

"Lord Hamilton's diary?" Caroline recoiled, leaning back in her chair. "I am not sure I care to read any more from that book. Now that I know there is no ghost, it no longer seems important."

"But you must. It's on the chaise over there. Will you be so kind as to retrieve it for me?"

Caroline did so reluctantly. Emily took the book from

her and flipped through the pages. "In this entry, Lord Hamilton writes about a visit from the man he later killed, Rachel's brother. Barrett writes:

> " 'He speaketh harsh words, saying Rachel loves me not, that she despiseth me and will not see me again. He nearly convinced me, for he spoketh of the disagreement we had two nights ago when Rachel parted in tears. Yet I cannot believe that which my heart sayeth is a lie. I alone have known Rachel as a lover. I alone know her heart's desire before even she can speak of it. I must keep faith in our love. For without that, we are nothing against the world. It is not I that she loves, but a soul, some bit of God within me. For me to lose faith in that is the worst kind of blasphemy. She loves me. I will never doubt that again. For to doubt her love is the death of love itself.' "

Emily shut the diary and looked at Caroline. "You see? You must have faith, Mrs. Davin."

Caroline said nothing. She merely nodded and grabbed Emily's hand, squeezing hard. Her tears, at last, spilled over like a sweet and gentle rain on a thirsty, fallow field.

The coach was to leave that afternoon at three. Mr. Dorris had business in a town not far from Fallingate, so the journey to London would begin in earnest the next day after a night at an inn. Monty came to the library to say his farewells to Caroline alone. He thanked her for her hospitality and reassured her he would find Lucas in Seven Dials.

Caroline looked up from the papers Mr. Dorris had given her to sign and smiled. "I know he will be back safely, Mr. Trowley. And I appreciate your efforts to see it done."

Monty perked up at her certainty. "You have heard something, then?"

"No. But I have faith he will return. Faith is a wonderful thing, Mr. Trowley. I highly recommend it."

Monty hesitated then looked furtively over his shoulder. "There is something I'd like to have faith about."

She grinned. "Yes, I suspected as much."

"You know what I am about, then?"

"I believe I do. You want to marry Miss Kinnicott."

His face registered surprise, then beamed with love. "Oh, yes, ma'am. That would be my dearest wish. But would her father give me her hand? She is such a fine lady and I am . . . well, I am an orphan. No family connections."

"But you are industrious, Mr. Trowley. You will soon own your own shop. And you are good-hearted. I will see to it that Mr. Kinnicott accepts your offer."

"You will? How? How will you make him accept my offer?"

Caroline smiled again, mischievously this time. "I have no idea. But I will find a way. Love demands no less of me."

Suddenly the doors opened. Henry's face was flushed and his eyes were unusually lively. "Ahem. Mrs. Davin, your husband has returned. He brought another Mr. Davin with him. Mr. Robbin Roger Davin, that is."

Henry stepped aside and Lucas swept into the room. If candles had been lit, they would have snuffed themselves out in deference to his brilliance, she was sure. Her heart leaped and she rose slowly, utter happiness washing over her. Monty Trowley faded from her sight as she focused on Lucas alone. Oh, what a wonderment love was. What bliss!

"Lucas, what are you doing here? You couldn't even have reached London by now."

He stopped in front of the desk and locked eyes with her. She'd never seen such excitement in their depths. His angular face was windburned, his hair wildly tossed. He'd ridden hard back from wherever he'd been. His skin smelled of cold and wood smoke.

"Caro, I have something very important to tell you. But you might as well hear it when I tell Lady Germaine. I need to reach her estate before your brother leaves. Is he still there?"

"They had plans to stay until tomorrow," she replied. "Why do you need to see George?"

Without answering, he turned and started for the door.

"Lucas! You can't leave before you explain your sudden return."

He stopped abruptly and smiled with chagrin. "Forgive me, darling, I'm getting ahead of myself." He returned to the desk. "Greetings, Monty."

"Good day, Luc," Monty said exuberantly.

"You see, darling, I was on my way to London when it suddenly occurred to me that a few things weren't adding up where your brother was concerned. How did he learn so quickly about my past? I took a detour to Knowlton Park on my way to Town. Mr. Dorris told me where it was during the picnic at Bilberry Cottage. When I arrived at your brother's country estate, I found none other than Robbin Roger and Smiley Figgenbottom sitting around the fire like a couple of country squires!"

"What?" Caroline gasped in astonishment.

"Yes! It seems your brother took quite a liking to Smiley's stories of my past and soon learned all about old Robbin Roger. George sent his man to find Robbin in London and brought him out to Devon. I believe his intention was to humiliate me and perhaps even to see me back into the gaol if he could learn enough of my misdeeds from Roger."

She removed her glasses and placed them on the desk. "Upon my word! That's a fiendish plot." She added hopefully, "Did you learn anything damning about my brother?"

He grinned rakishly. "Oh, my darling, you don't know the half of it. But there is no time to explain. I must make myself presentable." He turned and started for the door. "Be a love and go to Germaine House immediately and announce my impending arrival."

"Now? Why so quickly?"

"I will explain everything later. I just don't want George to leave before I get there." Lucas stopped at the door, where an old man looking uncomfortable in his fine clothes waited for him. "Robbin, meet my wife. This is Mrs. Caroline Davin. Caro, this is the man who raised me, Robbin Roger Davin."

The old man lumbered forward, tugging self-consciously at the clothing George had apparently given him. He smiled and bowed obsequiously before Caroline, his faded blue eyes still watering from the cold.

" 'Tis an honor, ma'am."

Caroline swallowed hard before she managed to muster a pleasant smile. After all, this was the man who had beaten Lucas as a child. She could hardly bring herself to forgive him. Yet Lucas seemed to bear him no ill will.

"How good of you to visit Fallingate, Mr. Davin. I . . . I have heard so much about you."

"Come along, Robbin," Lucas called impatiently from the door. "We must make ourselves presentable. Monty be a good lad and see Mrs. Davin to the carriage outside will you? Whatever you do, Caro, do not let your brothe leave Germaine House. Tell him to come to Fallingate late this afternoon. Entice him in whatever manner you se fi but make sure he comes here before he returns to Know ton Park."

"Of course, darling."

When Monty and Robbin began to chat, Caroline slipped around the desk and hurried to the door. Lucas put aside his urgency long enough to tuck a hand beneath her hairline and press a kiss to her forehead.

"Ah, I missed you," he whispered. "Even a day was too long. When did you insinuate yourself into my soul?"

"When you were not looking," she whispered.

"Did you think I had gone for good?" He stared down at her with his uniquely intense eyes.

"No."

He shook his head wonderingly. "Madam, you have more faith in me than I do."

"Sir, is that not what marriage is all about?"

His eyes glinted with surprise, then approval. He smoothed a thumb over her right cheek. "What a remarkable woman you are, Mrs. Davin."

Thirty-one

Lucas and Robbin stood at the front door of Germaine House, waiting for it to open.

"Are yer sure yer want to go forward with this, boy?" Roger said in a raspy voice. He clenched and unclenched his fists at his side.

"I have no choice, Robbin," Lucas said, wishing to God his heart would stop hammering in his chest.

The door creaked open slowly, the motion clearly stating that whatever business they had with the countess could bloody well wait until the butler saw fit to address it.

The butler, once he appeared, looked as if he'd just eaten a lemon. His perpetually arched brows were wings of gray that shot up as if they'd been combed and starched. He glared at Lucas and Robbin, then blinked incredulously, as if he couldn't figure out why a horse thief was dressed like a gentleman.

"Yes?" was all he said.

"I am here to see Lady Germaine," Lucas said. "Show

me to her at once." He spoke so imperiously that Robbin looked up at him in awe.

"There's a good lad! Give him what for!"

"My name is Mr. Lucas Davin," he continued, ignoring Robbin's praise. "She will be expecting me."

The butler sniffed and narrowed his eyes, as if he'd just detected a foul odor. "One moment, sir. Please come into the drawing room. I will see if her ladyship is prepared to receive you."

He turned and walked stiffly through an octagonal marble entrance hall. A footman closed the door behind them. Robbin began to breathe raggedly and tears filled his eyes as he gazed around. Lucas gave him a supportive hand.

"Come along, old man, we can get through this together," he whispered.

The butler left them in a high-ceilinged drawing room richly appointed in the finest chinoiserie style. Floor-to-ceiling damask curtains smelled of musty history. Chinese silk shimmered on every wall. On a pale green wall hung paintings of Restoration ladies with white wigs and King Charles spaniels, and dark paintings of grandfathers and grandfathers' fathers. Lucas took in every detail with bittersweet recognition. Some of the decor was old, and some new. All of it composed the essence of agreeable elegance. Lucas feasted his eyes for what seemed an eternity, but at last the butler returned, his haughty airs slightly diminished.

"Her ladyship will see you now."

"Thank you, Harwood." Lucas nodded with a superior smile.

The butler blinked in surprise. How would a horse thief know his name? he doubtless wondered.

Lucas stifled a smirk and waited patiently to be led to the countess. Harwood gathered up his dignity and proceeded down the corridor.

Lucas and Robbin followed in silence, taking in the
sight of each familiar room they passed. The saw another
parlor, a billiard room, a library, and state rooms, one after
the other, each one more gilded and lush than its prede-
cessor. Lucas's heart rose higher in his throat with each
passing chamber. The feeling he'd had when he'd first
glimpsed Germaine House—that peculiar sense of longing
and familiarity—nearly choked him now.

"Ma'am," the butler said, turning at last into the room
at the end of the corridor, "Mr. Lucas Davin."

When Lucas and Robbin reached the double doorway,
they stopped short, both of them at once riveted and re-
pelled by the sight of the countess.

She sat regally on a brocade sofa against the far wall
next to Caroline. The women were dwarfed by their surroundings. The walls of the room were covered in red silk.
Against this vibrant backdrop hung a series of enormous
Italian paintings executed in a style that emphasized shadows and light. The room was littered with portraits, small
and large, each in an ornate gilt frame. The rounded ceiling
was splashed with a heavenly blue fresco; angels and cher-
ubs and souls loomed over them in frozen poses of weight-
less sanctity. Lucas took it all in and felt his stomach pitch
and churn. He remembered the last time he was in this
room. He remembered it all.

"What do you want of me, Mr. Davin?" Lady Germaine
said with obvious disdain. "I received you only out of respect for your wife. I trust this audience will be brief."

Lucas came forward, dragging Robbin with him, and the
butler reluctantly departed, leaving them to their privacy.

"Thank you, Lady Germaine," Lucas said. "May we
sit?"

She motioned to two gilded chairs placed across from
her on the Turkish carpet. Lucas took his time sitting, waiting until Robbin had settled uncomfortably in the seat nex

to him before speaking. And then he waited yet another moment while he locked gazes with Caroline. The look in her pale blue eyes was timorous, but a tiny, proud smile quirked at the corners of her mouth. He felt an overwhelming wave of courage and cleared his throat to begin.

"Lady Germaine, I would like to introduce you to the man who raised me, Robbin Roger Davin."

Her frigid eyes darted to the crumpled figure next to Lucas. His clothes were clean and befitting a gentleman, but he nonetheless bore the air of a servant. She assessed that much in a glance. Her steady gaze returned to Lucas.

"You may remember Mr. Davin," Lucas said evenly. "He used to serve you as a groom here at Germaine House."

Lady Germaine's eyes flickered with the first inkling of suspicion. What was he about? she would be wondering now. Lucas had planned his revelation carefully. He had waited a long time for this moment. A lifetime, in fact. He would not rush it.

"Back then he was simply called Roger. He did not earn the nickname Robbin until he started robbing to make his way in the world, after he escaped from your stables."

"Escaped?" Lady Germaine said archly. "You make it sound as if I were a gaoler, Mr. Davin. I assure you if this man left my services, it was not because he was being mistreated. If you have come here to threaten me with trumped-up charges of mistreatment of my dependents, your gambit will get you nowhere."

Lucas flushed with anger, but he willed himself not to lose his temper. "Roger did not leave your services because he was mistreated. He left because he feared for his life."

"This is absurd," the countess muttered to Caroline.

"Tell her ladyship your story, Robbin. Tell it to her just as you told me this morning."

Robbin cleared his throat, looking suddenly older than his sixty hard years. "Yer see, your ladyship, I had been a groom here at the estate since I was fifteen, that I was. When the fourth earl died, your son Basil, God rest his soul, I was forty-five. In spite of me age, I was taken like a schoolboy with his lordship's wife, Lady Elizabeth."

At this the countess gave a tsk-tsk.

"Not that I had any hopes of her returnin' me fond regards, ma'am. Oh, no! But I took especial care of her horse. And she spoke kindly to me now and then, unlike yerself. When her husband, the earl, died and yer turned out the Lady Elizabeth and the little Lord Tom-Tom, I offered her me services."

The countess's haughty expression dissolved into glinting melancholy. "You remember little Thomas."

"Aye, ma'am. Yer turned them out with money, but Lady Elizabeth, she had nowhere to go. Never fit in with the *ton,* did she? Didn't quite have all her wits about her, I see that now."

"And she never would," Lady Germaine said sadly.

"Aye, ma'am, she was too kind. Fragile as a bird. I told her I would take her to London in a fancy carriage, but Lady Elizabeth, she fell to weepin'. She refused to visit any of the people she had visited on the Strand when his lordship was alive. Without her noble friends and no family, she had nowhere to go. I put her up in an inn, but she had a melancholy fit. Couldn't even take care of wee Tom-Tom. She died two weeks later—of heartbreak, I always thought. That left only me to take care of the wee lad. dared not go back to your estate after helpin' her ladyship So I raised Tom-Tom meself. I raised Tom-Tom and that' the end of the story."

Lady Germaine's frown had grown deeper. Her perfec powdered face looked like a death mask. Her hard eye roved from Roger to Lucas, then recognition struck. Sh stared hard into Lucas's eyes, then recoiled with horror. "Oh, good God! It is you. You are Thomas!"

"Yes," Lucas said gravely. "I am Thomas."

Caroline pressed a hand to her chest. "Lucas! It is you?"

"Yes, my love." He smiled fondly at her, then returned his hard gaze to his grandmother.

"Thomas," the countess repeated.

Cold swept over Lucas and made him shiver. Hearing her call him by that name brought back an ocean of hurt feelings. But they were distant and manageable memories. He was no longer the boy she'd thrown out so long ago.

"I am Basil and Elizabeth's son. And I would have been the fifth Earl of Germaine if not for your cruel deeds, Grandmama."

She winced at the moniker. Then an amazing whirlwind of emotions swept over her face as she stared at Lucas— shock, wonder, horror, regret, love, and finally cynicism.

"I had to find a way to keep Tom-Tom fed in London, that I did," Roger continued, oblivious to the others. He rubbed his hands together as if he were just now working out the details. "After the money ran out, I took to thievin'. I couldn't take a real position, see, because I had to hide the boy. So I became a famous cutpurse, that I did, and when the boy here was old enough, I taught him me trade, as it were."

Robbin bobbed his head proudly and looked around for approval.

"Why?" Caroline whispered, stunned by these revelations. "Robbin, why didn't you return to Germaine House and try to help Lucas claim his inheritance after his mother's death?"

"Aw," he scoffed, waving the notion aside, "everyone knew Lady Germaine thought the boy was a bastard. She'd never recognize him."

"But *you* did not think he was a by-blow," Caroline

persisted. "You trusted Lady Elizabeth's virtue. Why did you not appeal to the king for justice for Thomas—rather, Lucas?"

Robbin snorted. "Yer think I could have got me little toe into Whitehall to see the king? Besides, I could not tell anyone who Lucas really was. Could I?" This last question he boldly aimed at his former mistress.

She cast her eyes down. "No, you could not."

"Yer see," Robbin explained to the others, "her ladyship's second son, Thornton, he wanted to be the Earl of Germaine. I got word that he planned to kill Lucas if he ever returned to claim his title. So I made Lucas forget who he was." He sighed remorsefully. "Sorry, lad, but I had to do it. For yer own good."

Lucas explained to Caroline, "I now know why I have so many scars. Robbin wanted me to forget who I was. He beat me whenever I mentioned Germaine House, or whenever I called myself Thomas. He wanted to convince me I was a nobody so I would never remember my real name and seek my fortune. He was afraid that if I did seek out my inheritance, I would be killed. Every time I remembered my legacy, I got a beating with a whip on my back. And since I was stubborn and did not want to forget, I was whipped plenty. I wanted to remember Father and Mother, and so I clung to the memories as long as I could. I even clung to the memory of Grandmama, though I knew she hated me. But finally, I forgot it all. I suppose I couldn't take the beatings anymore. In the end, all that I had left was sorrow for any orphan I ever met, and a hatred for the wealthy."

"I did not hate you," the countess responded, tears filling her eyes. "I simply had the family name and reputation to consider."

"And why was I such a blight upon the family name?" Lucas shot back.

"I did not think you were truly Basil's son. You must understand that. When I found out you were, I exhausted myself looking for you. But my efforts were for naught. Mr. Davin was doing his best to protect you from what he perceived as danger. He hid you very well. You see, your uncle Thornton died two years after becoming the fifth earl. He left no heirs. I discovered then that he had misrepresented your paternity. You were Basil's son, and I wanted to bring you home then, but it was too late. I could not find you."

"That means Lucas is the sixth earl!" Caroline choked out in amazement.

The countess's features hardened. "He would have been under ordinary circumstances."

"But now that I am a thief, you do not want me to sully the title. I know you so well Grandmama. You would rather give the title back to the crown than have me besmirch the family escutcheon, is that not so, your ladyship?"

She raised her head imperiously, but did not answer. She was uncertain of what to do, Lucas realized. He'd never seen his grandmother uncertain before.

"What did you so hate about my mother?" he demanded, rising to his feet. "Why did you find her so unacceptable that you would throw her out even though she bore the title of countess?"

"She was a lightskirt," the dowager countess shot back, rising with the help of her cane. "Your father was not the first man she had known. She was a baker's daughter and unfit to hold a title. She was not Quality, young man. She did not have breeding, and because of her, neither do you. When I was looking for you, I had hoped to erase her influence on you. But I see now that that opportunity is lost. You have taken after your mother and not your father.

That makes you wholly unsuitable to claim the title of earl."

"I have taken after no one!" Lucas roared. "I have done what it took to survive a horrendous betrayal by the family who should have protected me. How can you think that my father's blood, and his breeding, do not flow through my veins? You may have cast me out, but I could not rid myself of the Germaine legacy. I remember this place, damn you. I remember hunting with father and being presented before the king." He began to pace.

"When I first came to Cragmere but a month ago, the night you mistook me for the man who stole your horse, I wanted this place more than anything I had ever wanted before, though I did not know why. Though Robbin had done a good of job beating the memories out of my head, somehow it was still familiar. And when Caroline began to teach me to ride, I knew the lessons before she ever spoke them. The skills I had gained as a boy came back quickly. But again I did not know why, nor did I remember my past, until the painting fell and struck a blow to my head. Then the memories returned. And once I remembered, I could not help but act as the lord I used to be. A child does not forget his beginnings, no matter how much he may want to."

Lucas shook his head and paused, pressing his hand to his forehead, where the memories danced and taunted him. Then he grew calm and looked at his grandmother with wry bitterness. "You cast out my mother simply because she was an embarrassment to you. Because she did not know how to be witty and charming in London with the *ton*."

"No," the countess replied, and sank wearily back onto the sofa. "It was because her parents were not properly married. She was illegitimate, and she came from a long line of illegitimacy. Her only claim to nobility was a distant one. Her father was said to have come from the Hamilton line."

"Hamilton?" Caroline said, sitting up at attention.

"Yes. More than two centuries ago Viscount Hamilton had a bastard son by his paramour, Lady Rachel Harding. The child did not fare well after the death of his parents. He was raised by his maternal grandfather, but the grandfather lost his fortune. The child, penniless and illegitimate, made a poor match. His scions eventually fell into the merchant class and the line has been riddled with bastardy ever since. I did not consider that an appropriate heritage for a countess."

"And you still do not," Lucas said bitterly.

She gave him a defiant glare. "No, I do not. Basil married Elizabeth with no thought to the family line, or to his responsibilities. She was unhappy as a countess. It was not fair to her, either."

"Your concern for her was overwhelmingly touching, I am sure." Lucas sneered.

"But once they were married," Caroline argued, "and once a child was born of the union, how could you persist in your rejection of Elizabeth?"

"She hated Basil's duty to the family. She was sentimental. A romantic. She married him for love, but quickly realized that an earl must first be married to his title and family. She wanted him to throw his responsibilities away for her. I had to take a stand. I had to remind him that as an earl he could not choose love over duty."

The countess looked up at Lucas and smiled sadly. "You judge my actions harshly. But you do not understand the real responsibilities of an earldom. If you did, you would understand why I did what I did."

"How could I know of the responsibilities?" he snapped in return. "I was denied them by you, madam."

"Do not speak insolently to me, Thomas."

"I am not Thomas. I am Lucas. And I will be called by no other name."

Her wrinkled upper lip curled in a mean smile. "You are stubborn, I see. Just like your father. Well, Lucas, what is it you are after? Is it money you want?"

He shook his head with disgust. "No. I would not have your money. All I want is to live with my wife in peace. I want you to withdraw your accusations against me. I did not steal that horse, though I admit one of my cohorts did. You have gotten your bloody horse back. Just drop the charges. I swear I will never cross your threshold again if you just give me that. I will not humiliate my wife by remaining her husband if you are intent on ruining my reputation."

"Lucas!" Caroline cried out, jumping to her feet. "I will not put you aside simply to save myself embarrassment."

"Not embarrassment, my love. Ruination. You are sentimental and romantic just like my mother was. She married for love and it destroyed her. I will not allow this union to destroy you. If my reputation cannot be restored, I will leave you, Caro. Just as we had planned all along."

"No!" She hurried to his side, panic lighting through her like a flash of gunpowder. "I thought you loved me."

He beheld her with his wildly intelligent black eyes, and a dimple deepened in his left cheek. "Love does strange things, Caro. True love cannot be seen until it is far away. With some distance, I see now what is best for you."

"I think, sir, you are misguided."

"My grandmother is right on one matter. Love is not enough to compensate for the loss of one's reputation."

"Love from a man like you is worth the world," Caroline argued as tears gathered in her eyes. Lord, was he going to leave her after all? "Besides, you are not a thief. You are an earl, for heaven's sake!"

"Not quite," Lady Germaine retorted. "I have not recognized him as my heir. And considering his history as a thief, I doubt his claims would ever be recognized without my endorsing them."

"I do not care about your bloody title, or your damned money. All I want is to be married to my wife in a way that will not hurt her reputation."

A frown of wonder gathered on the countess's smooth brow and she drew her head back for a better look at him over her nose. "Are you serious?"

"Quite."

She grimaced, then an odd gleam shone in her eyes. "Then I must reluctantly reconsider my position. I will consider your request and answer you by messenger to-morrow."

Thirty-two

After their momentous interview with Lady Germaine, Lucas left Caroline to deal with George and Prudence. She had a terrible time convincing her brother and sister-in-law to return with her to Fallingate. Sensing that somehow Lucas Davin had won some sort of concession from the countess, they were reluctant to oblige Caroline. In the end, she won them over with the promise of an astonishing revelation. That much she knew she could deliver. She had no idea what else Lucas had in store for them.

When they arrived, Caroline left them with the butler and rushed up the grand staircase two steps at a time, hurrying down the hall to the library. She threw open the door and rushed in, stopping abruptly when she found Lucas at the far end of the room. He stood before the blazing fire with his hands behind his back. He was staring up at the portrait of Barrett Hamilton.

Caroline's heart rose to her throat and she blinked back tears of exhilaration. "My lord!"

She said no more. What else was there to say? How

could one sum up this incredible turn of events? It was nothing short of destiny working in their midst.

When he did not turn, she said, "Lucas?"

He turned slowly, revealing a dazzling and triumphant smile. "When you called me lord, it did not at first register. I thought you might be talking to someone else. To him, perhaps?"

He pointed to the painting, and she saw Lucas's remarkable resemblance to his distant ancestor. Why hadn't she noticed before? She supposed she had, but Lucas's likeness to Barrett Hamilton had seemed a mere coincidence before. Now, in hindsight, it seemed providential. She pointed at the painting. "If he were alive today, I would kiss him."

Lucas's eyes danced and he gave her a sensual, wry half smile. "That would be a chaste great-, great-, great-granddaughterly kiss, I hope."

"It would be a kiss of gratitude." She came forward, closing the distance. "Barrett Hamilton brought you to me. I am sure of it."

Lucas's brows curled on his forehead. He eyed her as if she were an irresistible confection. When she stopped inches from him, he reached out and coiled around his finger a ringlet that had fallen from her cap. "Are you becoming superstitious again?"

"Yes." She took his hand and kissed the back of it, pressing it to her cheek. "How else could any of this have happened? How could you possibly have been imprisoned in the only gaol anywhere near your family estate? How could you have stumbled into this scheme of mine?"

When he merely looked at her with doubt, she wrapped her arms around his waist, inhaling the musky, masculine scent of him. "If you had not come to your birthright exactly in the moment you did, you would never have had the opportunity even to remember your heritage! If anything had gone differently, you would be back in London by now and would never know of your past. It had to be the work of the ghost, Lucas."

He answered her with a kiss. He took her lips possessively, and with finality. She kissed him in return as if her life depended on it. He aroused her, soothed her, and contented her all at once. He pulled away at last and caressed her with his triumphant gaze.

"Caro, we did it. We pulled it all off."

"Are you sure we can take the credit?" She turned and together they gazed at the painting. "I sense he is no longer here, Lucas. I sense that Barrett is at peace at last. His spirit has left this house. I read in his diary that his curse would remain until something good was done in his name. Now that you have discovered your rightful place as the heir to the Germaine name, Barrett's ghost can finally leave this place. A descendant of his is finally happy."

"But I have not found my rightful place," Lucas reminded her, turning and taking her hands in his. His touch was a magic balm on her skin. "My grandmother has not recognized me yet."

"She will, Lucas, I just know it. She is not as cruel as she wants people to believe. On the outside she's starched to the seams, but inside she's as soft as figgy pudding."

He chuckled and smiled sardonically. "You are too good-hearted by half. Do not ever change, Caro. Promise me."

"I promise." She felt another kiss coming and tilted her head back. This one was short and oh-so-sweet. She looked up adoringly. "How did you ever forgive me for forcing you to undergo an exorcism?"

He threw back his head with a bark of laughter. "How could I not forgive you? No one has ever loved me enough to try to drive the devil out of me."

"I would feel completely foolish about it now," she said, meticulously straightening his cravat, "if I did not think that somehow the ghost had something to do with all these incredible events. Yesterday I was convinced there was no such thing as a ghost. Now I do wonder."

"Caro, there is no ghost, and I can prove it."

She pouted. "I do not want you to prove it."

"I must. Only then will we truly be at peace. And that is what I must talk about with George."

"He is waiting in the drawing room with Prudence."

"I have invited Dr. Cavendish and Mrs. Plumshaw to join us there. Shall we finish our business with George once and for all?" he said, offering her arm.

Caroline nodded and took it, preparing herself for the last of Lucas's secrets.

Lucas waited until Caroline had poured tea for everyone before speaking. He watched Theodore position himself next to Amanda on the couch and smiled to himself. Love was certainly in bloom at Fallingate, no matter how cold it was outside. The wind howled grievously, announcing the approach of a storm. A light rain pelted the windows, but soon the pitter-pat of drops turned into a drumming sound.

"Get on with it, will you?" George said irritably. "I did not come for a cozy afternoon chat. The weather is turning, and I should like to return to Germaine House before the rain falls in earnest. The roads are already a ruin. What is it you want to talk about, Davin?"

After pouring tea, Caroline sat next to Lucas. George stood by the fire, holding his saucer in one hand and his teacup in the other. Prudence, perched on a settee, was uncharacteristically subdued, Lucas thought, until he realized why. She was practically salivating over the scones on the serving table.

"Would you care for a bit to eat, Mrs. Wainwright?" Lucas politely inquired.

Prudence fluttered her drooping eyelids in a disdainful look. "I suppose I can force myself to indulge. I always teach my girls to accept hospitality graciously, even under the most hostile of circumstances."

George gave her an unusually harsh glare. "Really, Mrs. Wainwright, how can you eat at a moment like this?"

Caroline nevertheless offered the scones, then returned to her seat. Lucas cleared his throat and began the final act of their curious drama.

"I have asked you all here to tell you what I only recently told my wife. I have at last learned my true identity."

"Your identity? I did not know that was in question," George said, then added with an uncharitable sneer, "But I suppose a man in your position must always question his paternity."

"What have you learned, Lucas?" Theodore asked with great interest. He and Amanda hung on Lucas's every word.

"It seems my desire to help orphans was deeply rooted in my past. I myself was an orphan. I was raised by a former groom of the Germaine estate. He saved my life after the death of my mother."

Amanda clenched her fists in her lap. "Your mother? Was she a servant for the Countess of Germaine?"

Lucas exchanged a smile with Caroline. "No, Amanda. My mother *was* the Countess of Germaine."

Prudence took in a sharp breath and inhaled a piece of scone. It caught in her throat and she immediately turned red and coughed, spewing bits of dough over her expensive Grecian gown. When she could finally breathe again, she sputtered, "L-Lady Germaine? You mean Lydia?"

"No, Lydia's daughter-in-law, Elizabeth," Lucas said

coolly. "The wife of the fourth Earl of Germaine. She died shortly after my father. The dowager countess is my grandmother."

"Well, well, well!" Theodore said in his booming voice, laughing and smiling with glee. "Do I know how to pick them? I tell you, lad, I knew the moment I saw you that you would amount to something. You had aristocracy written all over your face!"

Lucas smiled at him, pleased to see the doctor so delighted. Theodore cared more about Lucas's disposition in Society than Lucas himself ever would. He wouldn't care a whit were it not for Caroline's future.

"I believe," Lucas continued, "that this revelation should end your concern, Mr. Wainwright, as to the propriety of our marriage. Your sister has married into the nobility. And we were married by her twenty-fifth birthday. That means that Fallingate will remain in her possession."

"Oh, dear! Oh, dear!" Prudence gasped, her hands fluttering against her bosom. "An earl! I can scarcely wait to tell the girls!"

"Mrs. Wainwright," George snapped, "do be still."

"But, Mr. Wainwright, think what this will mean for the girls. Why, they have connections with blue blood! Just think what people will say in Madame LaRoche's salon."

"They will say very little, Mrs. Wainwright, if the girls have a pittance of a dowry. Without Fallingate—"

"But, Mr. Wainwright, you have the income from the mill."

"That is precisely the problem," Lucas said, interrupting.

George whirled on him with a vicious glare. "What do you know about my mill?"

"Quite a bit, I am afraid," Lucas said with a benign smile. "I grew suspicious about your intentions and circumstances, Mr. Wainwright, when I observed how perplexed my presence made you, even before you knew anything about me. I spoke with Caroline's land agent, Mr. Dorris, at the miners' picnic. He mentioned in passing that one of his relatives had lost his job at your mill because production was down."

Lucas could feel the growing interest of the women as he spoke. Caroline, in particular, looked from him to George and back again.

"It occurred to me that if your business was doing poorly," Lucas elaborated, "you had a powerful motivation to get Fallingate into your own possession."

"You are a presumptuous puppy, sir," George snapped.

Lucas smiled. "Yes, when necessary. I stopped by Knowlton Park on my way to London yesterday and did some investigating. I found out that your cotton mill is nearly bankrupt."

"What?" Prudence gasped out, putting aside her plate of scones. "George? Tell him he is wrong."

George turned red. He sucked in his handsome cheeks and raised a brow in outrage. "No one at Knowlton Park would have told you any such thing."

"No one had to. I read your papers in the drawer of your office on the third floor."

"That's absurd. I lock my office, and I'm quite sure our servants would never have opened it for you."

"You forget that your esteemed guest Smiley Figgen-bottom, whom you chose to treat like a king in the hopes that he might give you incriminating evidence about me, is one of the best housebreakers in all of Seven Dials. He opened your office for me after the others had gone to bed."

"How dare you!"

"Fortunately for you, I convinced Smiley that he ha more to gain by continuing to sponge off your hospitalit than by stealing your valuables outright. But if I were yo

I'd return to Knowlton Park posthaste and see that he hasn't absconded with your jewels."

"George! You said that disgusting little man was going to the gaol."

"Shut up, Prudence!"

"Once in your office, George—may I call you that?—I saw from your ledgers all the evidence of financial reversals that I needed to conclude that you would do anything to get your hands on Fallingate."

"How dare you pry into my affairs!"

"You see, Caro, without the income from Fallingate's mines, your brother will be utterly penniless."

Caroline stared blankly at Lucas, trying to register this shocking intelligence. Then she turned her bewildered gaze to her brother. "George, I could have helped. I would gladly have let you share my income. Why did you not tell me?"

"Because he is not nearly as generous as you, Caro," Lucas replied as he began to pace. "Your brother wanted all the income from the mines, not merely a portion of it. He had no intention of sharing it with you."

"Is this true, George?" Theodore said, frowning with disapproval. "If so, your father must be rolling over in his grave."

"Yes, it is true," George shouted. A lock of his impeccably combed hair fell in disarray over his sweating forehead. "This house should have been mine. I was the son. I was the firstborn. It was only our sentimental mother who thought a daughter should inherit."

"But you inherited the mansion on the Strand and Knowlton Park," Caroline argued, her astonishment and feelings of hurt giving way to outrage. "You inherited all father's money. It should have been enough."

"It would have been," Lucas observed, "if George had any business sense at all. But he made a mess of his investments and did not treat his employees decently. As a result, his business failed and he needed Fallingate so badly that he was willing to haunt the premises to make sure he got it in the end."

No one responded at first. George's complexion turned from red to a greenish white.

"You see," Lucas continued, "George was so intent on claiming Fallingate that he painstakingly fed the rumors flying around London that the estate was haunted."

"How dare you make such an accusation against my husband!" Prudence cried out.

"Easily," Lucas replied. He went to the pull and rang for the butler, an act that had been planned in advance. Henry entered with a cloth bag and handed it to Lucas without a word.

"Thank you, Henry." Lucas reached into the bag and pulled out a mask, a wig, and a sheet. The women gasped. "Do not be frightened. I have not murdered anyone. Caro, you remember this face?"

He held up the mask and Caroline let out a gasp of wonder. "Good Lord, it is the ghost of Barrett Hamilton!"

"Is that what you saw outside your window?" Amanda asked.

"Yes," Caroline replied breathlessly. "And that is what we saw the night of the exorcism."

"I found these peculiar items in George's office," Lucas explained, letting them drop back into the bag. "I realized after hearing everyone's anecdotes that every time a suitor saw the ghost of Lord Hamilton, it was either before, during, or after a visit from George. Since George transported them all from London, he had plenty of time to plant the notion of a haunted house on the trip out here. And then he made an appearance as the ghost himself. When I came George was unaware of my presence, at least until Feather sent a messenger 'round to Knowlton Park. Feathers, I be lieve, on occasion donned the costume when George was otherwise engaged. Am I right?"

George looked up at him with burning hatred. "Yes."

"Why would Feathers help perpetrate such a dreadful deception?" Amanda asked.

"He always favored George," Theodore speculated. "I've warned Caroline about that before."

"Butlers are generally a little old-fashioned," Lucas added. "He might not have thought it proper for a woman to inherit so great an estate. It would not surprise me in the least if he thought restoring Fallingate to the male heir was putting things in their proper order."

"That's precisely what he thought," George said darkly. "And he was right. Only he appreciated the injustice of what our father had done, giving the mines to a girl! Not to mention the fact that he thought Lucas Davin was unworthy of Caroline."

"Was it Feathers who appeared outside the window during the exorcism?" Caroline asked her brother.

He nodded. "Yes. I was there as well."

"You were the one who punched me in the garden," Lucas said.

"Yes. I had grown concerned that you might have suspected my plot after I lost my temper during our first interview. I was so furious that you had slipped past me unnoticed into this household that I suggested that your life was in danger. It was indiscreet of me. I wanted to dispel any suspicion, and so I had Feathers appear in the window, with the intention of walking into the room myself moments later. That, I thought, would prove I wasn't involved in any ghostly appearances."

George wiped the sweat from his brow. "But you'd gathered unexpectedly in the state room with doors that readily opened to the terrace. How was I to know that Davin would give chase in a damned downpour? In order to rescue Feathers and retrieve the costume from him, I had to flee back outside through a side door before I'd even made my entrance. I had no idea you were conducting an exorcism, of all things. It was ironically appropriate, don't you think? After I took the costume from Feathers and hid it in the bushes, I encountered Davin and planted a facer before he could recognize me."

"And you left poor Feathers there to die," Caroline said reproachfully.

"I did not know he was ill, I tell you! When I left him he was heading back to the west wing. Is he still . . . ?"

"He's still alive," Caroline whispered, "by some miracle. But it won't be long. Why did you embark on this hoax? You loved me once, George. I know you did."

George sank down in a chair and ran both hands through his now disheveled hair. She had never seen him so unkempt.

"Davin is right," George admitted in despair. "I did it to keep suitors away from you. I didn't want to hurt you, Caro. I just wanted to make things right for Prudence and the girls. I didn't know how else to secure their future."

His long limbs looked suddenly gangly, and Caroline remembered how awkward he'd been as a boy. Though exceedingly handsome, George had never had a lick o sense. And so while life should have been handed to hin on a platter, instead he'd always struggled to impress peo ple. It must have cost him a great deal—much more tha he could ever afford. He'd apparently been living far be yond his means in an effort to please the grasping wido of Colonel Hallwell. Knowing that took away some of tl sting of the betrayal from Caroline.

"How could you, George? Did you know what pair felt when you chased my suitors away?"

"I was not thinking of you, Caro," he groaned, a looked up at her with a combination of regret and ang

"You started it. You pretended to be the ghost when you very nearly married the son of that earl. The boy returned to London terrified and the rumors began to fly. A few years later, when I learned the stipulations of Father's will, I saw an opportunity to make sure you did not inherit. I merely took advantage of the humbug you yourself began."

"Oh, George." Caroline sighed sorrowfully.

He sank back in his chair, his handsome features awash in defeat and guilt.

"Why did I see the ghost, then?" Caroline asked him. "You did not mean to frighten *me* away, did you?"

He frowned. "Of course not. Once I finally learned of Davin's presence here, I tried to frighten him off, but he didn't even seem to notice."

"That's because he wasn't expecting a ghost," Theodore piped in.

"I thought perhaps if I frightened you, Caro, you would tell Davin about it and he in turn would become superstitious. Not to mention the fact that I was angry with you. I wanted to scare my little Mouse."

"Don't ever call me that again," she said coldly.

"Very well," he said stiffly, and rose. "And you won't have to ask me to leave. I will not stand by and have you pity and mock me. And no matter what you say, Davin, you'll always be a damned horse thief in my eyes."

"Mr. Wainwright!" Prudence said, heaving herself to her feet. "He is an earl. You cannot speak to him in that manner."

"Shut up, Prudence, and get in the bloody carriage." George pivoted and stomped from the room.

Prudence Wainwright, looking wholly meek and humiliated for the first time since Caroline had known her, slunk out after her husband, as much as a box of a woman could slink. Caroline followed them to the door and watched as they fought their way to the carriage through the now blistering downpour. She turned back to face her friends, utterly speechless.

Lucas, however, still had more to say. He held open his hands in submission to their authority. "I have yet to explain my association with Smiley Figgenbottom. He was the one who stole my grandmother's horse. We had come out from London to plan our robberies of the Germaine and Fallingate estates. I had planned to put an end to the robbery when I was in London, but with Smiley living like a lord at Knowlton Park, there's no danger of that coming to pass. The gang won't come out without Smiley. If the truth be known, Caro, I was indeed the leader of a ring of thieves. You must know that."

"We do," Caroline said simply.

"You're not angry that I had planned to rob you?"

"Robbers rob."

"Then you forgive me?"

"Nothing to it, my boy," Theodore said, cheerfully waving him off. "We knew what you were when we dragged out of that gaol."

"No, we did not know what he was," Amanda corrected him with joyful smile. "But we do now."

As if to confirm that statement, Henry entered with a letter on a silver plate. "Mrs. Davin," he said, "Lady Germaine's footman just brought this around."

"Thank you, Henry." Caroline took the letter and opened it, reading quickly. Her face lit with joy as her eyes scanned the words. "It's from your grandmother. She says that even an old woman can learn from her mistakes. She's had a change of heart. She's willing to recognize you you will come to see her tomorrow."

She clutched the letter to her heart, then rushed into his arms. "Oh, my lord, I am so happy for you."

"My lady," he whispered, "none of this would have happened but for your love."

Theodore and Amanda took turns hugging them and the doctor joyfully shouted at Henry to bring champagne, enough for the entire household.

"We have good news to share as well," Amanda said, reaching out for Theodore. "We are going to married."

"Oh, Amanda!" Caroline cried out, hugging her and crying with joy. "I have never heard such monstrous good news! I am so happy for you."

"Not as happy as I am, my dear, I can assure you," Theodore said, kissing Amanda's cheek.

Lucas shook Theodore's hand and kissed Amanda. "I scarcely know what to say. I can't come up with any more miraculous developments. Oh"—he chuckled ruefully—"there is one last matter regarding George."

Lucas reached into his pocket. "It seems George was very thorough in his scheme. In his office I found a receipt for the purchase of Lord Hamilton's diary. Apparently, he bought it and placed it in the attic, hoping you would think exactly what you did—that it had been placed their by the builder of Fallingate."

Theodore took the receipt and eyed it with amazement. "The boy had far more imagination than I would have given him credit for. He must have known Caro couldn't resist a book if her life depended upon it. And with her romantic notions, he doubtless hoped she would start imagining the ghost herself. And you did!"

"Yes," Caroline said, shaking her head with wonder. "I am amazed how fully I believed the ruse. Near the end, I was absolutely convinced there was a ghost here at Fallingate."

"You are too sentimental, Caro," Amanda said with smiling reproach.

"I like her just the way she is," Lucas countered.

Caroline heaved a sigh. "I thought I knew Barrett and Rachel intimately. I am a little sad to think it was all in my imagination. I was convinced they were the ones who brought Lucas and me together."

"What?" Theodore said indignantly, pulling out a cheroot. "*I* brought you together. Give credit where credit is due, my girl."

"No, Teddy," Lucas said, coming to Caroline's side. He pulled her close and slipped his arms around her waist. "Fate brought us together. Nothing less than fate itself."

He leaned his head down and kissed her softly, reverently. It was a kiss fit for a countess, for that is what she was now. While they indulged in their sweet passion, the doctor and the former governess slipped out the door, leaving them to their solitude. Caroline stroked Lucas's cheeks and when he pulled away, she gave him another quick peck on the lips. "I cannot seem to ever get enough of you, Lucas."

"You do not have to, my love. Now that all our troubles are resolved, you will not be able to get rid of me. I never much liked the idea of India. Ghastly weather there, I'm told. Much too hot."

She nodded toward the window, where a gloomy mist swallowed the last rays of light, turning dusk into darkness. "You think this weather is preferable? Rain day in and day out?"

"Yes," he murmured, nibbling her lips as he began to unbutton the front of her gown. "Because it rains on you. I love you, Caro. I think I've loved you from the start. All I ever wanted was to be worthy of you. And now I am."

"You always were," she said, laughing as tears formed in her eyes. "I do not care if you are a lord or a thief. You are mine. And I love you."

He kissed her eyes, then whispered in her ear, "I love you. Forever."

He slipped his hand inside her open gown and cupped a hand around a tingling breast. She exhaled and groaned at the same time, but there was one more question she had to ask.

She gripped his hand, stilling his gentle caresses, and looked into his eyes. "Why did you call me Rachel?"

He blinked and frowned. "I called you Rachel?"

"Yes. When we made love. You don't remember?"

"When we were . . . intimate?"

"Yes."

"No. No, my love, I'm sure I didn't."

"You did, Lucas. I swear."

He shrugged and gave her a lopsided grin. "Went off my head?"

She smiled and hugged him close. Looking over his shoulder at the window, she thought she saw two shadows watching over them.

"I do have the most impossible imagination," she said, and pulled away, smiling at him.

"Can you imagine making love to your husband?" he asked seductively, resuming his caresses.

"Oh yes, my lord. My fair lord," she added with a twinkle in her eye, giving him a kiss he would always remember.

Epilogue

They stood at the window in rain that had poured down on them for more than two centuries and felt nothing but the warmth of love that glowed inside he house. Now that there was happiness in what was once blighted place of betrayal and heartbreak, they were beond the discomforts and sorrows of the world. Their enturies-old search for peace had ended at last with the nion of these two lovers.

"They are so in love," she said in a voice that harmozed with the wind.

"Just as we were," he answered in a low moan that ended with the breeze. He reached for her hand. After ars of searching the moors for her, always seeing her appear around a corner or fade into the sunset, he could ch her at last, thanks to Lucas and Caroline. He could l Rachel, and now that he held her in his grasp, he uld never let her go.

Dost thou think it was terrible of us to take over their ies?" she asked, looking up at him with a glint of mis-f in her eyes.

He gazed on his beloved with timeless passion. "Nay, my love."

She laughed, and it sounded like rustling leaves. "He called her Rachel."

He smiled. "And so she was. For one night."

"And he was Barrett," she added, remembering the pleasure of their last earthly night of love. "For one unforgettable night."

"It was not too much to ask, methinks. Not when the joining hath healed the wounds, the blood of my curse."

She nodded and sighed with a sense of peace she hadn't known in centuries.

"It is time to go," he whispered on the wind. "Art thou prepared?"

"Aye. I have waited years for this moment. It is a happy place now."

As Lucas and Caroline fell in a passionate heap on the sofa, Barrett and Rachel turned and disappeared in the mists where they had once made love on the hill.

Forever sighed the wind.